ALLFROST ENDGAME

ALLFROST ENDGAME

BOOK 3 OF THE PHANTOM FROST SERIES

Alfred Wurr

A Wurreal Games Book

For Chloe and Jaydin.

Contents

ALLFROST
ENDGAME

Chapter 1

Atomic Clock

Dixon held his palm a foot from the pulsating white globe hovering above the snow-covered dais. Turning from the orb, he came toward me, retracing his steps over slushy snow, his movements stiff. In the late-morning light, the lines on his face were deeper than I remembered, but he seemed much stronger now. Much better than when he had arrived atop Caelumtor—the tallest of the New Olympus archipelago's mountains—the night before.

"You okay there, Harland?"

He jabbed a thumb by his shoulder. "How many of these Allfrost nodes are there?"

Not for the first time, I suppressed a grin at his ill-fitting T-shirt, jeans, and sandals. In all my time at the Institute, I had never seen Dixon wear anything other than a suit.

"What?" He frowned, sweeping a hand across his bare white scalp. "You don't like the new hairdo?"

"Nah." I lifted my cap a moment, exposing the smooth and icy roundness of my own head. "It looks good on you."

"Right," he said with a snort. "All part of the desert spa package."

I smiled inwardly. *There's the Dixon I know.* "Yeah, the Eurus are nice that way."

His gaze hardened. "I hope to show the commie bastards my gratitude someday."

My head bobbed. "You know it."

He waved a hand. "All that aside, what's funny?"

"Nothing," I replied. "It's just, I'm still getting used to seeing you in civvies."

He glanced down at himself and cocked an eye at me. "It's better than my birthday suit."

I held up my hands, a vision of Dixon's gangly body, bruised and burned, ejected from a human-sized steel canister in a puff of fog, playing in my mind. "Tell me about it."

"Well? How many nodes?"

I thought a moment. "I'm not sure."

Smaragnisos might be mine, but my memories of the island were incomplete, especially from before my incarceration at the Bodhi Institute.

His eyebrows rose. "That wasn't in the vials?"

"It might be," I said, "but I haven't taken them all yet."

"Why not?"

"I've been busy." *Saving you.* I shrugged. "And they mess me up."

He grimaced. "How many vials do you have left?"

"A dozen or so."

He motioned to my hat. "Take them."

"I plan to." I looked toward the trail leading deeper into the jungle, and a gust of wind, smelling of flowers and damp earth, warmed my face. "After we talk with Hue."

"See that you do," he said. "We need you whole and well."

I rolled my eyes. "Thanks for your concern. Anyway, I'm pretty sure the Smaragnisos chamber has only a dozen nodes or so. It's mainly here to give me a place to live when visiting New Olympus. The more influential chambers—"

"Not just for this island," he said, cutting me off. "For the whole machine. If the Group's going to help fix it, we need to know what we're dealing with."

I stroked my chin. "Hue said there are about a thousand per Allfrost chamber. I'm pretty sure that's just an average, though."

"And how many chambers are there?"

"Several hundred," I replied. "Gun to my head, I'd say six hundred worldwide."

He whistled. "That's about sixty thousand nodes. That's a lot of ground to cover. How did you manage it?"

"It wasn't hard," I said. "Not with all the other Sentinels to help. That was half a millennium ago, though. Since then, it's just been me."

He looked thoughtful. "And you don't know what happened to them?"

"Not really," I replied. "Like I said before, they vanished, looking for my people."

He blew out a breath. "I'm surprised you didn't throw in the towel years ago."

"It's what I swore to do." *The Allfrost is all. Preserve the Allfrost.*

He nodded. "We're a lot alike."

I scrunched an eye. "How's that?"

"We're protectors," he said, spreading his hands. "You of the Allfrost. Me of the Bodhi Institute."

"Yeah, I suppose so." I snorted. "I'm surprised you'd say so, though."

"Why's that?"

"I don't know." I thought back to my time at the Bodhi Group's Institute of Research and Development. "I guess because you've never seen me as a human being."

"Why would I?" He looked me up and down. "You're a snowman, for Pete's sake."

I looked down at my body for a moment. "I'm a lot more than that." Sure, three stacked spheres of snow and ice formed my basic structure, but they shifted and moved with all the suppleness of human skin, and my hands and long, muscular arms—also ice and snow—were nearly human in form. Turning up an icy palm, I conjured a frost ball and dismissed it. "You ever see one of those snow sculptures do that?"

"That only proves my point."

"Oh yeah? Check this out." I shifted my bottommost sphere and grew taller as it split into two snowy legs. Just as I'd done a few days earlier in an abandoned movie theatre on the planet Zarechus. "Human enough for you?"

His eyes widened. "Huh. Not bad. I didn't know you could do that."

"Me neither." I shifted back to normal. "Not until recently anyway. That's the great thing about amnesia. The journey of self-discovery."

"It's a neat trick," he said, "but to answer your question, no. However you look or act, you're still not human. No more than getting on all fours and barking makes me a dog."

My jaw tightened. "I suppose that made it easier to keep me prisoner."

It had been less than two weeks since I'd escaped Dixon and the Institute on a mission to thwart a disaster I couldn't quite remember, and I hadn't forgiven him for his part in my imprisonment.

He's paid a price for it, though. In a strange twist of fate, the security director's attempts to reacquire me had led to his own capture and torture by the Eurus, a faction of enemy gods operating out of the Soviet Union. *Karma's a bitch.*

Even stranger, I'd ended up rescuing him. Dixon, my former jailer. Transporting a metal cylinder containing him, not the Sentinel I'd expected, from the Gobi Desert across thousands of miles to the safety of New Olympus.

"At first it did, but it got harder." He paused a moment. "If it matters, I like you, Winterboy."

"Shivurr," I said. *Still with the code name?*

"You might be a snowman," he continued, "but you're no snowflake. A bit too much into those arcade games, but you've got grit. I respect that. I have for a long time now."

"Even though I'm not human?"

He scoffed. "What's so great about humans? I know a lot of them. Trust me, half are commie assholes, and, with rare exceptions, the rest are nothing special. And even if you had been human, I wouldn't have let you go. Not back then."

"And now?"

"Now I'm glad Green helped you escape."

My eyes darted to the bruises on his arms and legs, inflicted during his time as a Eurus captive. "Despite what happened to you?"

His nostrils flared. "At least now we know what the Russkies and Eurus bastards plan to do. Maybe that makes it worth it."

He had a point. If what Dixon had learned was true, the Soviets, infiltrated by the Eurus, planned to launch a first-strike nuclear attack on the West. He wasn't sure how, but he believed they intended to use the Allfrost to set off US nukes while still in their silos, then launch their own nukes to finish things off.

I gave him a sour look. "You guys should have listened to me."

"Obviously," Dixon said, "but it might have helped if you had spoken English or something other than that gobbledygook you call a language. Now I hear you speak German. Like a lot of us at the Institute. Come to think of it, why did you take so long to try Latin back then?"

I paused before replying, contemplating the question. "I don't think I could speak any of them then." Flashes of the time ran through my mind. "Before I approached the Group, I tried removing my memories." I tapped a finger against my hat's visor. "And it didn't go so well."

His grey eyes narrowed. "What are you talking about? The Group did that."

"The Group did most of it, yeah." *Way more.* "But I had tried doing it myself, not long before I showed up at the Nevada chamber. When that failed, I asked the Group to help, thinking they'd do a better job."

"Hold on. Are you saying you operated on yourself, before the Institute?"

"Uh-huh," I said. "Not for the first time, either." I chuckled ruefully. "Even when I've had help doing it, there have usually been complications."

"I know," he said. "Memory loss."

"Sometimes skills too." I looked down at my snowy self. "Unlike you, I think with my whole body, so when I get injured, I sometimes forget how to do things. Like how to speak English."

"Right," he said. "The eggheads mentioned skill loss in their reports, but I didn't make the language connection. And this is permanent?"

"It depends." I considered the question for a moment. "If it's just simple trauma, my body recovers, in time. But if I lose mass, memories and skills—depending on the location—don't always return. Unless I can recover the lost material somehow. Like with the Bodhi Group vials."

He blinked. "That's a crazy risk to take, then."

"I know, right?" I sighed. "Since it went so poorly, I decided never to try it again after the first time."

He arched an eyebrow. "Yet you did."

"Yup," I said. "A day or two before I showed up at the Nevada chamber. Whatever I wanted to forget must have been important enough for me to risk it again, especially without help." *I wish I could remember what it was now, though.* I waved a hand. "Anyway, because of that, my linguistic skills were a bit compromised when I approached the Group. For some reason, languages are often the first to go when I'm injured. Beats me why."

His lips pursed. "But you spoke Latin, eventually. About a month after coming to the Institute."

I bobbed my head. "Sure, after I'd had more time to recover. I guess my mind worked around the damage somehow. Maybe my German would have returned eventually too. If the Group hadn't made things worse. Not that it would have mattered. Even when I had learned English again, no one wanted to listen." *That would have meant losing their chance to study me.*

Dixon's face flushed. "I'm sure they had their reasons. Regardless, our priority now is figuring out how to stop this thing."

"If there's still time," I growled, knowing that, even with the Bodhi Group's help, it might already be too late to reverse the Allfrost's corruption before Baduriel and the Eurus enacted their plan. "You guys gave them ten years to do whatever they wanted. Who knows how far along they are now?"

"Well," he said, clearing his throat, "even if you had been free, securing this machine would have been tough to do solo."

I glared. "Which is why I went to the Group in the first place."

"Take it easy," he said, making a downward motion with both hands. "You'll have our help now. Whatever this computer program says needs doing, we'll help do it, if we can. At least, if I've got anything to say about it."

"Allfrost Controller," I said. "His name is Hue."

Dixon made a face. "Odd name for a ghostly blob of light."

"That's what he calls himself," I said. "I think because he changes colour all the time."

"Whatever he's called," Dixon said, "I hope he's got good news. If I can't convince the Group there's a way to stop this, odds are the powers that be will order a first strike of our own before our weapons can be used against us."

"Are you serious?" I sputtered. "That won't stop the Soviets from counterattacking."

His shoulders rose. "Maybe not, but we're not going down without a fight."

I scowled. "It'll be an apocalypse." A cleansing fire, like the demon Baduriel had promised. "You know that, right?"

He clapped me on the shoulder. "Then we'd better move."

Bird calls and the drone of insects rose above the wind as we re-entered the forest and made our way down the trail toward the Smaragnisos Allfrost chamber. I shuddered as the warmth of the jungle washed over me and drew the zipper of my winter jacket higher. Looking down, I sent the Underfrost to my feet, smiling as mud and leaves froze and crackled beneath me with each step.

Nice. My control and skill with the Underfrost had grown substantially in recent days. Studying the sun peeking through the canopy of leaves, I considered the warmth around me. Provided I was hydrated and rested, I no longer felt much discomfort in the too-warm weather. *The vials are working.*

Several turns of the trail later, the jungle foliage fell away, and a sheer wall of rock covered in green vegetation came into view. Beckoning for Dixon to follow, I proceeded down the path, which dropped away sharply to an opening near the wall's middle. Once beneath the overhang of rock sheltering the cave entrance, I danced light from my glowing hand across the floor and sides of the ancient lava tube, which was sealed completely by ice.

"Well," Dixon said, "that's a problem."

"Not for me." Glancing his way, I pressed a palm to the ice and leaned in. After a moment's hesitation, my hand sank into the wall up to my wrist.

"Neat trick. How are you doing that?"

"Trade secret." Seeing his glare, I smirked. "Just kidding. The ice is like a doorway to the Underfrost."

While I could sidestep into the Underfrost without ice or snow, its presence made crossing over—in either direction—and staying there a lot easier.

Dixon's throat rumbled. "That's not going to help me get through." He sighed. "I guess you'll have to go on without me."

I waggled a hand. "Not necessarily. We'll have to move fast, though. So you don't freeze during the trip."

"What trip?"

"Through the Underfrost," I said. "I can pull you over with me, and we can stroll through the ice together."

His eyes flared. "Isn't that risky?"

I pulled off my winter coat and handed it to him. "Just stay next to me."

He wasn't wrong. Travelling through the Underfrost had risks for both of us. For me, the danger of succumbing to its lure, for Dixon the cold. Yet I'd brought my friends and a stolen car across its threshold for a short time, only a few days earlier, and everyone had come out of it fine.

"Are you sure about this?" he said, pulling on the jacket.

As long as he stayed close, I could keep him submerged in the Underfrost and shield him from its energies. But without me, he'd be fully exposed to its chilling effects. He might pop back into the normal world fast enough to emerge unharmed, but doing so within solid ice . . . I didn't want to think about that.

"Pretty sure," I said, trying to sound confident while recalling the depth of the ice in my mind. "How long can you hold your breath?"

He narrowed an eye. "Why?"

"You're going to need to hold it." I knew from my time at the Bodhi Institute that Dixon was a jogger and hoped that meant his lung capacity was better than average. In the middle of a wall of ice, there would be no air for him to breathe. While, for reasons I still didn't remember, lack of oxygen had never been a problem for me when likewise submerged, Dixon wasn't a creature of the Underfrost.

He swallowed. "A couple of minutes, if I'm not exerting myself."

"What about while jogging?"

"Not sure," he said. "Half that, maybe."

"That'll do," I said, travelling the tunnel's ice section in my head. I extended an arm toward him. "Give me your hand."

Muttering to himself, he slapped his palm into mine. "This Hue better be worth the trip."

"Get ready," I said, pulling him into a walk. "Here we go."

I pushed into the ice, taking Dixon into the Underfrost with me, and led him toward the Allfrost chamber. Depending on its density and temperature, solid matter—even when in the Underfrost—could be slow and difficult, if not altogether impossible, to move through. At least not without going far deeper into the Underfrost than was safe. Yet in ice and snow, we moved as if through water.

As we jogged, my mind wandered back to a week or so ago, when I'd travelled the same tunnel and found the Allfrost Controller, Hue, on the far side. After renewing my acquaintance with him, I had ended up leaving by Allfrost transporter, flung through the Underfrost to the Institute, to rescue my Californian friends from Dixon and the Bodhi Group. Which I'd succeeded in doing, escaping past Baduriel and a gang of his fire elementals while the Institute burned.

And here I am coming back with Dixon. Feeling a persistent tug on my arm, I turned to regard him, still moving. His eyes were wide and his cheeks bulged as he gestured toward his mouth. *Oh, crap.*

Chapter 2

Prime Mover

I broke into a run, tugging Dixon with me as he struggled not to breathe. *Hold on.* His face continued to redden and his chest twitched and cheeks ballooned. *Almost there.* Finally, the ice gave way, and I raised us from the Underfrost. Beside me, Dixon doubled over and sucked in huge gulps of air.

Grabbing his elbow, I put a hand to his frost-covered back. "Are you okay?"

He coughed a moment, stood taller, and inhaled again, steadying his breathing. "I need a minute." He studied the glowing walls of the lava tube a moment before glancing back at the ice. "You sure that's only four hundred feet?"

My shoulders lifted. "Pretty sure."

He shook his head. "I must be out of shape, then."

I chuckled. "Come on. The way is easier from here."

After we walked a few minutes more, the rocky tunnel opened out into the Allfrost chamber proper. The light blue glow of its icy walls revealed an egg-shaped cavern, three hundred or more feet across at its widest point, and a ceiling that hung a hundred feet overhead. Across the space, a ball of roiling frost energy crackled above an Allfrost power node's rune-covered dais.

"It's like Alpha site," Dixon said, using the Bodhi Group's name for the Allfrost chamber in Nevada. He pointed at a wall. "Same symbols, too."

"Oh yeah." I could read most of them now, even obscured as they were by ice. "They're mostly instructions and warnings."

"Figures." He looked around. "What's causing the walls to glow?"

I shrugged. "Crystals behind the ice." I cupped my hands to the sides of my mouth. "Are you here, Hue?"

Hue's holographic humanoid form materialized atop the dais and drifted down to us. "Greetings, Sentinel Shivurr."

A tholos transporter—a circle of pillars, supporting a conical roof—stood nearby beneath which a sphere of snow ten feet in diameter oscillated between floor and ceiling. Tholoi were capable of launching Sentinels like myself, encased in huge balls of snow, through the Underfrost to distant locations, so they were standard issue for Allfrost chambers. Through scientific principles even I didn't understand, travelling this way was orders of magnitude faster than doing so through normal space.

"Hey, Hue." I looked over my shoulder at Dixon, whose mouth hung open. "This is Harland."

Dixon raised a hand in greeting. "Holy hell."

Hue glowed red. "Of course. Bodhi Institute Security Director Harland Dixon. I am aware, Sentinel Shivurr." Which made sense, since I'd told Hue all about Dixon just days ago. "How came the director to be in your company?"

"That's an interesting story." I brought Hue up to speed on the broad strokes of my adventures since I had last seen him.

"I am relieved you are well," Hue said, his red fading to mauve. "Now that you have returned, are you at last ready to resume the Allfrost's restoration?"

I nodded. "That's sort of why we're here. We think the Allfrost is being corrupted."

Hue turned a golden yellow and his glow intensified. "To what end?"

I scowled. "Nuclear Armageddon."

"Before you get into all that," Dixon said, "is there somewhere to sit around here?"

"Uh, not sure." Since Dixon wasn't a complainer, I kept forgetting he was still recovering from his rough treatment at the hands of the Eurus. Copious amounts of the gods' soda pop, Ambrola, had helped him to recover faster than usual, but oxygen deprivation on our way here had probably taken a toll. "How about it, Hue?"

The hologram extended a limb, and the ice and snow covering a section of nearby floor sank like water into sand, revealing a stone floor inscribed with ornate designs. Seconds later, a plush sofa materialized atop the cleared space.

"What the hell?" Dixon reached out a hand to touch one of the sofa's armrests. "How's that possible?"

Hue coloured purple. "The Allfrost's architects included furniture in most chambers in deference to their warm-blooded avatars."

Dixon plopped onto the sofa. "Yeah, but where did it come from?"

I looked at Hue. "An interdimensional null space, right?"

It was only a guess. The inner crown of my hat served as a portal to one. In so doing, it gave me a place to store things—whatever could fit through the opening. At the moment, it held dozens of cans of soda pop, bottles of water, and the last of the vials I'd rescued from the Institute.

"The Underfrost," Hue replied. "An interdimensional null space would require a prohibitively large portal through which objects would need to pass."

"Oh, right," I said, snapping my fingers. Since the Underfrost overlapped normal space, putting an object into it didn't require changing its location, at least not in normal space. It simply made it immaterial, so it didn't take up any space in the regular world. Which was great, since when you wanted it, it reappeared wherever you'd left it. Unless, of course, the object was moved by some force. "I get it. That's pretty slick."

Dixon leaned back in his seat and slapped the armrest. "It's cold but comfy." He waved toward me with an upturned hand. "Proceed."

"Right," I said, looking at Hue. "Where was I?"

"Nuclear Armageddon, Sentinel."

"Right." I recapped what I'd remembered of the coming cataclysm, adding what Dixon had told me since I'd rescued him from the Eurus's clutches. While Dixon had been the one being questioned, the Eurus interrogators had let slip a few details of their plan, which had been enough for him to fill in the gaps.

"I see," Hue replied after I'd finished. "To restate, you believe the Eurus have been modifying the Allfrost in some way that will enable them to set off nuclear missiles while they are still in their silos."

"You got it." Olivia had recently speculated the Faction were interested in Allfrost chambers because they sought to capture Allfrost Sentinels. As a New Olympian demigod married to Wilhelm—aka Boreas, the ancient Greeks' God of the North Wind—she was likely to be right. However, given what I now knew, it seemed more likely to do with the Eurus's nuclear ambitions. "It explains why they've been looking for chambers and leaving monsters behind, right?"

Hue's ghostly head inclined. "Sabotage by hostile entities would explain much. The rate of the Allfrost's decline has in recent years been higher than even global warming and a lack of maintenance can readily explain. Yet setting off nuclear missiles is not part of the Allfrost's design."

Dixon shot me a look. "How does it work? You said it cools the planet, but not how."

I thought a moment, and to my delight, the answer came easily. "By raising or lowering the Underfrost in the right places at the right times. If done right, it can alter climatic patterns."

"Wait." Dixon's lips pursed. "Lowering the Underfrost. It warms things too?"

I shrugged. "Sure. Each node in the machine is capable of doing either."

He looked thoughtful. "How warm can one of those nodes make things? Warm enough to set off a nuke?"

I scratched my head. "I don't know. Would an atomic bomb be set off by heat?"

"Beats me," he said. "Enough heat could disable one, I bet. Maybe fry some critical components."

"Right." I ran through the implications. "Come to think of it, enough cold could do the job too. If the nodes' safeguards were removed, they could be used to generate enough snow, cold, and ice to trap the missiles in their silos, or to freeze out the crews manning them." I began to pace. "The nodes would have to be in close proximity to a given silo, but someone with access could program them to reposition themselves and probably figure out a way to remove the safeguards too."

Dixon's eyes narrowed. "And these Eurus have that?"

"I'm not sure." I pivoted back to Hue. "Would I know how, Hue? Normally, I mean."

"I do not believe so, Sentinel," he replied. "While you would have had sufficient clearance and general programming knowledge, what you have proposed would require fundamental changes to the Allfrost's basic systems. Not even Allfrost Controllers, such as I, who are experts in its operation, systems, and maintenance, would be capable of such substantial reconfigurations or design modifications to the machine itself."

"Really?" I asked, surprised.

He inclined his head. "Doing so is beyond the scope of our duties. Simply put, we are not inventors."

Dixon grunted. "Knowing how to drive a car doesn't mean you can build one."

"Okay," I said. "Then who?"

Hue paused a moment before continuing, "Only someone with deep knowledge of the machine's design, I should think. This is expertise the Eurus gods are unlikely to possess."

"Then who might have it?" I asked.

Hue's colour drifted to blue. "Only one of the Allfrost's original architects."

"You mean Boreas?" I used Wilhelm's older god name, figuring Hue would be more familiar with it.

Hue's body shifted to green. "Correct."

"Who else?" He had said architects. *Plural.* I thought of my encounter with fire elementals at the Allfrost chamber near Lunar Crater and when escaping the Bodhi Institute, and a suspicion that had been growing in my mind for days crystallized. "Baduriel?"

"Affirmative," Hue replied.

Dixon made a choking sound. "You mean the horned guy that attacked the Institute?"

"Yeah." I turned up my palms. "He must have been there to modify the Allfrost node."

As surprised as I was, it made sense. From what Dixon had told me, after invading the Institute, Baduriel had blazed a trail straight down to its depths, where an Allfrost node had been placed for study. Giving pursuit, Dixon had found the demon and his fire elemental minions gathered about the node with its control orb raised.

Dixon's nostrils flared. "How does a pyromaniac end up building a machine designed to cool the planet?"

"We were friends," I said as broken cognitive connections rejoined in my body. "The three of us. Boreas, Baduriel, and me."

Hue glowed lime green. "That is my understanding."

Of course. The feeling that I knew Baduriel's face when I saw him at Castle Abadom made sense now. I wasn't just recognizing him from the attack on the Bodhi Institute. I was remembering him from long before.

Dixon's face writhed. "You were friends with a fire demon?"

Hue darkened, becoming dull gray like a storm cloud. "This was before Baduriel's fall from grace."

Triggered by Hue's words, memories came back in a rush. "Baduriel was once a god. Like Boreas or Hanale."

"Technically, he remains so," Hue replied. "Only his avatar and status have changed. When the divine punish their own, they condemn them to servitude until they redeem themselves."

"Right." I stared through Hue, remembering. "That's what happened to Baduriel. He did something to mortals, and it led to war. Lots of people died."

Dixon leaned in. "What did he do to people?"

"I don't remember exactly." I rubbed my temples as if to summon the memory. "Experimentation, I think."

That the gods would have had a problem with that back then surprised me. That long ago, even the New Olympians had not been particularly concerned about how the divine treated mortals.

In fact, Baduriel had been one of the few that treated humanity well at the time. *So why would the other gods have condemned him for it?* I wondered. Pushing the thought aside, I turned back to Dixon. "Until then, he really seemed like a good guy. Definitely not someone that would harm people. Yet whatever he did must have been pretty awful since he was declared anathema for it and sent to serve in Hades."

The Anathema were often pressed into service, be it toiling in harsh environments, fighting in wars, or punishing mortals. Anything that was unpleasant but needed doing.

Dixon's brow creased. "Doing what?"

"Providing for the energy needs of Zarechus," Hue said, referring to the planet to which Scott, Caleb, and I had found ourselves transported days earlier. His translucent head tilted as if he were reading from a book. "Fire demons are masters of energy production through fire—be it exothermic reaction, chemical fire, combustion, nuclear fusion or fission."

I snapped my fingers. "He creates those fire elementals to help him in his work." Seeing Dixon's expression, I added, "They're sort of like robots."

He scoffed. "And here I thought demons spent all their time castigating mortals for their sins."

"Not at all," Hue said. "The Bureau of Divine Retribution has penal colonies on Hades, and fire demons sometimes work there on secondment, but it is demons of other forms and expertise that typically serve as the Bureau's agents on Earth."

Dixon's eyebrows bunched. "Are you putting me on? Demons actually punish people and condemn them to Hades?"

"That was once the case," Hue said. "However, according to the latest information available, factionalism over the past few millennia has led to a decline in the administration of earthly retribution. Indeed, many other divine services and processes have suffered similar deterioration."

"Anyway." I waved a hand dismissively. "The point is, what Hue's suggesting makes sense. Baduriel must be modifying the Allfrost. Its global distribution and access to the Underfrost's energy gives him a way to act against the silos all at once across a wide area. That's got to be why we've been seeing him at chambers and nodes."

"That tracks," Dixon said, "except how is he finding these Allfrost nodes when they're normally hidden in the Underfrost?"

I thought a moment before replying, "I don't know, but he's definitely got a way. Before escaping the Gobi Desert encampment, I overheard someone say that finding the nodes was hard, but they were close to done."

Hue cleared his virtual throat. "If even a single node were located, someone with Baduriel's knowledge could access it to locate still others."

My eyes lit. "All of them, from any one node?"

Hue's colour shifted to red. "Only those closest to a given node, but using that technique, one could traverse the network and gradually locate them all, and if he changes a sufficient number, he may be able to remotely distribute updates to others."

"Damn it." I resisted the urge to glare at Dixon. So much time had been lost fighting the Eurus because of the Group. *Whatever*, I thought, thrusting aside my regrets about approaching them. "But to target the missile silos, they need to know where to find them, don't they? And those locations are secret, right?"

A puff of fog came from Dixon's mouth. "Between satellites, spies, and traitors, chances are the Soviets know where most of them are by now. Maybe even all of them. And missile silos are not easy to move."

I growled. "Then they could be almost ready to act."

"Except they seem to need you," Dixon said, blowing into his cupped hands. "You and any traces of you they can get their mitts on."

"Sure," I said, recalling what Dixon had told me the previous night, following his rescue. Apparently, the Eurus were nearly as interested in finding samples of my essence as in finding me. "They must be after what I know about the Allfrost."

"I don't think it's that," he replied. "I mean, they're after what you know, but I don't think it's your knowledge of the Allfrost. Hue just said, except for this Boreas guy, this fire demon, Baduriel, knows more about the machine than you, so they've got all the Allfrost expertise they need. No, my best guess is they're trying to find something, and only you know, or knew, where it can be found."

"Okay," I said. "That doesn't really help us, though, since I don't know what that could be."

"Sentinel," Hue began, "I may know."

I extended a hand toward the hologram. "Shoot, Hue."

His translucent body shimmered and changed to purple. "I believe they seek the location of the Allfrost's prime chamber. Invoking nodes, corrupted or not, across the entire machine at once can only be done from there, and foreseeing this danger, years ago, with my assistance, you moved the chamber to a secret location and hid it in the Underfrost. After which I purged its new emplacement from my records, leaving you as the sole holder of that information."

Triggered by his words, fragmentary memories rose to mind. "I remember. Sort of." I rubbed my temples, trying to summon the prime chamber's location. "But not where it is now."

"Then all is well, Sentinel," Hue said. "I should add that even if the Eurus or Baduriel were able to find the prime chamber, they would have to raise it from the Underfrost, and they would need to bypass security protocols even so. Something I believe they would find most difficult."

My forehead scrunched. "But, if Baduriel built it, he'd still have access, wouldn't he?"

"Not in this case," Hue said. "Prior to leaving Allfrost Prime, you locked out all control functions, setting an access key—tied to specific particles of your essence—which includes song and dance performance aspects known only to yourself. Moreover, after Baduriel's fall from grace, his access to the Allfrost was re-voked. Using his expertise, he has evidently been able to over-come individual nodes, but he will have a harder time with the changes we made to secure Allfrost Prime. Perhaps he may fig-ure out a way past our safeguards eventually, but if he makes any mistakes, Prime will go into defensive mode, submerge into the Underfrost, and move itself again. The only surety he has of success would be for you to grant him access."

"What about another Sentinel?" I asked. "I mean, I know they're gone, but for argument's sake."

"I think not," Hue said. "Another Sentinel might aid Baduriel's attempt to circumvent security, but only you possess the means to unlock Prime in the proper manner."

I shook my head. "Except I don't. Not anymore."

"Don't be so sure," Dixon said. "This has got to be why the Eurus are after the vials." According to Dixon, the Eurus had offered him his freedom in return for his help acquiring the bottles, knowing they held my memories. "They're after the location and the key. And since you still don't remember them, they must be in the vials. There's nowhere else they could be."

I considered his words. "Yeah, you're right. Either the ones I have or those still in the Bodhi Group's hands."

Dixon's eyes flicked to my cap. "Which means, it's time you drink the vials you've already got."

Chapter 3

Probing Question

I nodded, knowing he was right. "Before I do, Hue, are you able to check the nodes and see what Baduriel's been doing to them? Whatever he's done, we need a way to reverse it. And if we can't, it would at least be good to know how many he's altered and how far he has to go. That should give us an idea of how much time we have to stop him."

"Of course." Hue gestured toward the orb floating nearby. "I will consult with other Controllers as well. As I will need to travel the network, I may be away awhile."

"You'll actually be gone, physically?"

"Yes," he said. "Certain functions require physical presence, as a security measure. Remote access, while convenient, also permits easier subversion of the Allfrost's functions. It is this measure which has no doubt required Baduriel to physically visit nodes and chambers, slowing his progress. Fortunately, I can transmit myself as a particle stream between nodes via the Underfrost."

"Why not send a duplicate copy of yourself?" Dixon asked.

"His code is embodied in his hardware," I said. "Just like you and me."

He lifted an eyebrow. "So?"

I spread my hands. "He can't make a copy of himself any more than you or I can."

"That is correct," Hue said. "My holographic matrix is stored and operates across a discrete network of cooperative microscopic crystals that are not readily replicated."

"How long will you need?" I asked.

"I am unsure," Hue replied. "Perhaps a few days, depending on what I learn from the other Controllers."

"Okay," I said, thinking of the vials I was planning to take. "Give it twenty-four hours at most, then return here and let me know what you've learned. While you're gone, I'll take the rest of the vials and wait here for your return."

"Very well," Hue said, heading for the dais. "Until then, Sentinel."

"Bye, Hue."

The hologram shifted into a cloud and streamed into the energy sphere floating above the Allfrost dais.

When all of him had vanished, I turned to Dixon. "You might as well head back to the domus. I'll meet you there after Hue gives me his report."

Dixon stood and, shivering, rubbed his palms together. "Works for me. How are you going to get back without the boat? Swim?"

"Nah, the Allfrost transporter." Gesturing to the tholos, I explained how it worked and snapped my fingers. "I'll be back like that." I nudged his arm. "Come on. I'll walk you back to the beach."

"No need," Dixon said, teeth chattering. "I'm a big boy. I can find my own way."

I smirked. "Not past the ice."

"Oh yeah," he said. "Good point."

Besides, Dixon didn't have an identity ring, and without one, New Olympus's security defenses might regard him as a threat. Heck, despite Smaragnisos being my domain, I'd even tangled with a troll out in the jungle only days ago, and there might be other dangers on the island that I'd still forgotten. Either way, it seemed prudent to escort him.

Traversing the lava tube's ice section went far smoother this time around, probably because Dixon now knew how long he'd have to hold his breath, and we soon found ourselves back in the jungle. The day had warmed even further and, after the relative silence of the Allfrost chamber, the air seemed to roar with buzzes, birdsong, and breeze.

As we strolled the trail that would take us back to the beach where we'd arrived on the island, I started to worry. If Allfrost Prime's location and access key weren't already in a vial in my hat, the vial I most needed must still be in the Bodhi Group's hands. Possibly at one of the facilities that had dragged their feet returning their vials to the Institute. If Dixon had revealed their top-secret locations during questioning, the Eurus—bound to realize the labs were softer targets than the Institute—might already be on their way to them.

Sure, he'd told me he had resisted telling the Eurus anything, but doubts still nagged at me. Just days ago, in the Schmidts' Las Vegas basement, Wilhelm had slapped a hand to the head of a captured Eurus operative and tried to read the guy's thoughts. If the Eurus had pulled the answers they wanted from Dixon's mind, would he even be aware of what had happened?

"So," I said. "When the Eurus had you, what did they do exactly?"

He shot me a look. "What do you think?"

"I'm just wondering, did anyone try to read your mind?"

He scowled. "Like with a lie detector?"

"No. The gods have telepathic abilities." I tented my fingertips against my forehead. "Did anyone touch your head like this, or did you ever feel any . . . I don't know . . . presence in your mind while you were there?"

"Maybe." Dixon swallowed and stared into the distance. "I was pretty muddled for a lot of it. Now that you mention it, they might have. I figured they'd given me drugs of some kind, to soften me up or make me more susceptible to their demands." He frowned. "They can really do that? Probe someone's mind."

"Yeah," I said, "though it can be resisted. I think. Do you remember resisting?"

He shrugged. "Their questions, sure. I've been trained to do so." He sighed. "Not against mind reading, of course, but if they'd gotten what they wanted, I suppose they'd have stopped the questioning."

"Maybe." He'd been held by the Eurus, but a demon had conducted most of the interrogation. "I wouldn't put it past the Anathema to keep at it for kicks, though. Many of them are like that." The conversation I'd overheard in the Gobi Desert encampment minutes before rescuing Dixon sprang to mind. One of the speakers had stated the person they were questioning must be kept sane and able to function because his task would require finesse. I hadn't been sure what to make of it at the time, but I thought I did now. "Since they wanted your help to get the last vials of my essence from the Bodhi Group, they probably didn't want to push you too hard." When Wilhelm had telepathically probed the Eurus operative's mind, he'd been worried the guy would end up a vegetable. "If they did, you'd be a lot worse off."

He gave me a flat look. "They used more than harsh language."

"Sorry," I said, giving him a glum look. "I know they did."

"Forget about it." His jaw scissored a moment. "Now that you mention it, toward the end, there was a voice that seemed to cut through all the noise, even my own breathing and . . . all that. Promising—since I refused to tell them our facilities' locations—that I could stop the pain by agreeing to get the vials for them." He glanced my way. "You think maybe they were trying to brainwash me to do their bidding?"

"Yeah," I said, "I do."

"Bastards." His hands balled into fists. "We've got to stop them, Winterboy. Whatever it takes."

"Agreed," I said. "Whatever it takes."

Dixon scratched his chin. "These gods declared anathema, what's to keep them from refusing to serve?"

"Oh, anyone can refuse," I said. "But being allowed to serve is considered a mercy. You get a shorter sentence and something to do. The alternative is spending the entire duration trapped in an Animavas."

Dixon's eyes narrowed. "What's an Animavas?"

"A special container," I said. "One designed to trap and hold their essence. Which is why it's also called a soul trap. Among other things."

He puffed out a breath. "These so-called gods don't mess around."

"Nope," I said. "They don't." Memories of the Eurus rose in my mind, and I frowned. "It's hard to believe the Eurus Faction is working with the Anathema, though. Wilhelm and crew might see them as renegades, but the Eurus consider themselves defenders of the legitimate order. Working with the Anathema violates everything they claim to uphold, but I guess they've justified it to themselves, somehow."

Shrugging off my parka, he handed it to me. "Or, like on our side, not everyone on theirs knows what's going on."

"There's a thought," I agreed, slipping the warm coat back on.

We walked in silence thereafter, both of us no doubt thinking of what had happened and what was to come, until the jungle at last gave way to a white sand beach. Off to our left, my buddy, Scott Green, and the Schmidt's dog, Bear, a big black-and-white Alaskan shepherd, waited in the shade of a Banyan tree, watching the Pacific Ocean's azure waters batter the shore.

Spotting us, the tall and thin, early-thirties computer programmer clambered to his feet and pushed black-rimmed eyeglasses higher up his long, slightly sunburned nose. He smoothed his short brown hair, still mussed from sleep, before touching his stomach. Though the god Aceso had healed the bullet holes in his abdomen, he still seemed to experience pain now and again.

I decided not to mention it, though, and after I brought Scott and the dog up to speed, my three companions paddled off in an outrigger canoe toward the Schmidts' cottage, leaving me alone on the sandy shore. I watched them go awhile, enjoying the sunny sky, gentle breeze, and rhythmic crashing of waves, then re-entered the jungle, and returned to the Allfrost chamber.

Let's do this. I made my way over to the sofa, still sitting in the only snow-free area of the floor. Taking a seat, I removed my hat and rooted around inside. I pushed aside Ambrolas and other sodas, sticking my arm in up to my shoulder, and something hard floated away as my fingertips brushed it. With a thought, my arm stretched and thinned, growing longer.

I had no idea how large the null space might be, and I pushed aside a budding worry that the items within it might drift permanently out of reach. So far, objects placed inside had stuck around the opening—perhaps part of Wilhelm's design for it—and I had to hope they would continue to do so.

I pulled my hand free and, touching the Underfrost, raised ice from the floor, sculpting the top flat to form a rudimentary table. Satisfied, I pulled vials from my cap, careful to avoid the bad one, which I'd wrapped in cloth to distinguish it from the others. Instead of my essence, that vial held an Alterclavis.

When I had taken the device out in the past, it had swapped places with its twin thousands of miles away. The first time, it had taken Scott and me along for the ride. The second time, I'd used it to repeat the trip, intending to rescue an Allfrost Sentinel, and I'd come back with Dixon instead. As useful as the last time had been, I had no desire to repeat the journey now. Especially knowing that a Eurus named Atriel, and his compatriots, would be waiting for me when I did.

When vials covered the makeshift table's surface, I laid the last few on the sofa next to me. I took one in hand, pulled the stopper, and downed the contents. Before it could affect me, I repeated the process until a half dozen bottles later, my head clouded and a wave of nausea came over me. Gripping another, I struggled with the stopper and drank again.

Two containers later, the room spun as I grabbed for another, determined to finish what I'd started. The bottle wasn't where my eyes told me it should be, though. Attempting to compensate, I swept my hand to the side and sent the vial spinning. I lunged for it as it fell and caught it an inch above the stone floor but, unbalanced, tumbled off the sofa in the process. Wrestling myself to my back, I laid my head against the sofa cushion and reached for the stopper, but endless cold welled out from my middle and dreams took me.

I woke face down, groggy and bleary-eyed, blinking at the brightness of the chambver. Coughing, I drew my arms to my chest, plowing furrows in the snow beneath me, and pushed, raising my torso from the floor.

"Sorry to wake you, Sentinel," said a voice.

"Huh?"

Chapter 4

Paralyzing Fear

My limbs felt stiff, and my back creaked as I turned toward the speaker. "Ugh." Sitting up, I propped myself against the sofa and held out a hand to block the glare of Hue's face. "You're back already?"

"Already?" He turned orange. "It has been many hours since we last spoke."

"Really?" Spotting a discarded bottle, I picked it up. "Those vials really did a number on me." Standing, I counted the still-full vials, four in total, before gathering them up and returning them to the safety of my hat. "Is there somewhere I can put these empties, Hue?" If I put them back in my cap, I knew it would be a chore when I later tried to find the unused ones. "Is there a recycling bin around here?" A cylindrical stone container appeared about ten feet from my position. "Nice."

"Would you like my report, Sentinel?" Hue asked as I scooped empty vials from the floor.

"Absolutely." A stab of pain shot through my head, and I winced, dropping a vial. "Ouch."

Hue floated closer, glowing pink. "Are you unwell?"

Closing my eyes, I rubbed my fingertips against my temples. "It's just the reintegration process. I took too many at once."

"Does it always cause you pain?" he asked, his voice soft.

"Not always," I said. "It's been different every time."

"I am sorry you are suffering," Hue said. "Has it been worth it? Have you recovered the location of Allfrost Prime?"

"I'm not sure." Sitting on the sofa, I propped an elbow on the armrest, rested my chin upon my upturned palm, and tried to recall the prime chamber's location. After several moments, I shook my head. "Nope."

"Regrettable," Hue said. "What of the authentication key?"

My lip curled. "Not that either." Which meant it lay either in one of the four vials in my hat or in one of the samples the Bodhi Group still possessed. From what Dixon had said, the Group still had a dozen or so. If true, the odds were three to one the Group's vials contained Allfrost Prime's location and key. On the plus side, with Dixon's help, getting them should be a piece of cake, if we got to them before the Eurus did. "What did you find out, Hue?"

A semi-translucent three-dimensional globe of Earth, ten feet in diameter, flickered into view a few feet above the floor. As I identified Europe, Asia, and Africa, glowing dots of light, some red, some green, appeared across the continents.

Allfrost nodes, I thought.

"As you can see," Hue said as the globe rotated, "approximately twelve percent of the nodes in the Northern Hemisphere have been compromised."

I shrugged. "That doesn't sound so bad."

"Not on a global scale, Sentinel." Hue waved a hand, and the huge ball revolved on its axis until North America faced us. "However, they comprise the majority of nodes located in the continental United States. If, as you surmise, the Eurus's goal is to impact the entire US nuclear arsenal, this number should be adequate to their needs."

I chewed my bottom lip. "I was afraid of that." I studied the globe, finding red dots across Russia and Europe, though not as many as over North America. "Why are those nodes red too?"

"They are also compromised," Hue said.

My eyes widened. "That's weird, isn't it?"

"How so, Sentinel?"

"What's the point of changing them?" I asked. "It's not like he's going to disable nuclear silos there, right?"

"He must need them for some other purpose," Hue said. "Perhaps to draw power from them. However, I cannot be certain without further analysis."

I thumped the side of my fist against the sofa's armrest. "Either way, it seems Baduriel's finished with his Allfrost changes and stopping him now all comes down to the vials. At least until we can reverse what he's done to the nodes."

"Correct, Sentinel." Hue floated closer. "Are you ready to resume the Allfrost's restoration, then?"

"Sure, but—" I blinked as something occurred to me. "Is Baduriel the reason the Allfrost has been in decline?"

"Not exclusively," Hue replied, "but his actions are likely a factor, given the nodes are no longer operating according to their original design."

"Don't worry, Hue. With Dixon's support, maybe the Bodhi Group will finally help."

Hue coloured red. "An organization with their resources would be of tremendous assistance, but are you sure a second attempt is wise?"

I snorted. "No, but it's a risk I've got to take, and I'll be on . . ." I trailed off, feeling cold. Colder than usual, I mean. My elbows crackled as I struggled to move them. "Something's wrong."

"What ails you, Sentinel?"

"I don't know." I walked toward the dais. "My limbs are stiffening."

"Perhaps I can help." Hue floated nearer. "I do not know if you recall, but I possess some diagnostic and first-aid capability. Sentinels are often exposed to hazards that require it." He reached out a spectral hand that flared bright white. "The vials you have taken seem to have created an imbalance in your system. I am afraid you must leave the chamber immediately until the symptoms subside. The jungle's warmer air, coupled with your constant movement, should ameliorate the effects. Keep moving until they subside or you may find yourself unable to move and vanish into the Underfrost, permanently."

"H-okay." I walked for the exit, each step an effort. "Can't stop. Won't stop."

Hue floated beside me, still talking. "I recommend you minimize contact with the Underfrost and avoid consuming any more of your essence until well after these effects subside. Doing either will only exacerbate your symptoms."

"Yeah." My eyes scraped in their sockets as I tried to roll them. "I figured that out for myself." When we reached the ice blocking the lava tube exit, I swore. Without sinking into the Underfrost, there was no way past it. "How do I get through, Hue?"

"Fear not," he replied as the ice faded from view. "I have dismissed it to the Underfrost for now, and there it will remain until your return."

I tried to nod, but my neck would no longer move. "Thanks," I managed, barely able to move my jaw. "I'll be back as soon as I can."

Plodding forward, each step an effort, I ascended. Halfway up the lava tube, the air warmed slightly, and my pace improved. By the time I emerged into the jungle, my limbs had softened enough that I no longer feared turning into an ice sculpture. I still felt colder and stiffer than normal, though, so I made my way back to the beach and strode the shoreline, enjoying the salt air and wet sand, which squished with each step taken but, surprisingly, failed to adhere to my bare icy feet.

When a rise of rough volcanic rock dotted with plant life blocked my way, I looked inland at a wall of green. *I might as well explore a bit*, I thought, pushing my way into the foliage.

As I ducked beneath branches and sidestepped tree trunks, my body continued to warm, and I considered my next steps. Undoing Baduriel's Allfrost modifications was an obvious long-term goal, but obtaining the last vials from the Institute took precedence.

Whether they contained Prime's location and access key or not, I needed them to be whole again. I definitely couldn't risk them falling into the Eurus's hands, which meant it was time to get back and talk with Dixon about returning to the Institute.

Once I had my essence back, Dixon could see about securing the Group's aid while I sought Wilhelm's advice on how best to proceed. If nothing else, the latter's expertise as a co-architect of the Allfrost would be invaluable in its repair.

Stepping out onto a damp reddish-orange path, I made my way to the Allfrost node clearing I'd shown to Dixon, crossed to the jungle on the far side, and broke into a trot toward the Allfrost chamber, feeling almost normal. As I rounded a bend in the trail, a screech drew my gaze to the canopy of tropical leaves above, which blocked all but brief patches of the blue-and-white sky. A moment later, even they were blotted out by a shadow that swept in from the side. Leaves rustled and branches bent, pushed aside by powerful gusts of air, and I reeled back several steps as the talons and curved beak of an eagle—any of the appendages large enough to engulf my head—descended toward me.

A griffin, I realized as the beast landed on the muddy trail, a dozen feet ahead.

Eagle eyes fixed me with a stare. "Sentinel Shivurr?" a feminine voice said, though the creature's beak did not move.

"Uh, yeah." My eyes flicked to the griffin's lion hindquarters, and I gripped the Underfrost. "That's me."

The griffin's long, tawny tail, tufted at its end, twitched. "I bring tidings from Leonidas." Again, the words seemed to manifest in my mind rather than be heard.

"You're a herald," I said as old memories surged. The New Olympians—Wilhelm especially—were geneticists extraordinaire, often modifying existing species or making entirely new ones, upon which they later based their avatars. Sometimes to improve them, sometimes out of curiosity. Griffins were an old design, out of fashion, but their ability to fly made them great messengers.

The griffin bowed her head. "My name is Paratus."

"Nice to meet you," I said. "I'm Shivurr."

"I am aware," Paratus replied. "Leonidas asks that you return to Caelumburg immediately."

I drew forward a step, thinking of the small town nestled atop Caelumtor where my friends awaited my return. "Has something happened? Are my friends okay?"

"I know not," Paratus said, ruffling her feathers. She drew her wings to her body and knelt low. "The meeting regards the Eurus threat, and I am to fly you back."

My eyes lit. "Really?" Their light skeletons and broad, powerful wings might allow griffins to fly, but carrying all but the lightest passengers in Earth's gravity was a no-go. "I'm pretty heavy."

"Indeed." She sat on her haunches and tapped the black leather harness strapped to her body. "However, I am equipped with an antigravity device."

I thought a moment. "Thanks, but no need. I've got a faster way." *One that doesn't involve flying.* Visions of plopping into the ocean from a thousand feet up swam through my head. Besides, if all went well, I'd make it back to Caelumburg even before Paratus could reach the mountaintop where the town resided. "Please tell him I'll be there as soon as I can."

"Very well," Paratus said, extending her wings. "If you insist."

"Thanks," I said, watching the griffin take to the air.

When she could no longer be seen, I rushed along the path, down the lava tube—which was still clear of ice—and entered the Allfrost chamber.

"Greetings, Sentinel Shivurr," Hue said, floating over to me as I entered. "Are you well again?"

I flexed my arms and wiggled my body. "All good, Hue." I motioned to the giant snowball oscillating within the tholos's ring of columns. "Is it safe for me to use the transporter?"

Hue's light shifted, becoming chartreuse. "Where do you intend to go, Sentinel?"

"Caelumburg," I said, walking toward the transporter's departure pad.

"I believe that should be fine," Hue replied, floating alongside me. "Especially as the distance is not far, making your time in the Underfrost brief. At worst, you may feel yourself regressing. If that happens, I suggest sunning yourself until things settle down again."

With Hue's reassurances, I jumped onto the Allfrost transporter's departure platform, a stone circle with a raised border. I crossed to the pedestal at the far side, rested my palms on the edges of the basin sitting atop it and envisioned my desired destination. An instant later, a viewscreen shimmered into view, just beyond the platform's edge, and a stone-paved road lined with thick forest appeared upon its surface. With a thought directed at Hue, the camera panned up, displaying the stone monolith of Septimius's Arch.

Rather than going directly into Caelumburg, I had chosen a spot just outside its boundaries as my landing zone. I knew from a recent visit that a security field of some kind enclosed it. Passing through the field in normal space without going through an arch would bring guardians down upon an intruder. I wasn't sure if entering town while immersed in the Underfrost would do the same, but I figured arriving outside and walking in to be the more prudent option.

I dropped a handful of snow into the basin before me, signalling my desire to initiate transport, and a giant snowball rose from the stone beneath my feet. When it had engulfed me, the snowball sank back into the stone, taking me with it. Intangible in the Underfrost, it rolled forward before being launched up and through the tholos's ceiling, accelerating toward its destination.

Chapter 5

Conclave

Moments later, I rose from a mound of shattered snow, surrounded by trees and underbrush. Already melting in the warmth of mid-morning, the snowball sank into the forest floor, and I turned in a circle to get my bearings. I spotted a wall of grey stone sitting atop a nearby rise and made my way toward it. Hopping over a stream flowing lengthwise along the ridge, I climbed the bank and stumbled my way out onto a stone-paved road with Septimius's Arch on my right.

As I entered the arch's middle passageway, its namesake golem assembled from a rocky pile with a clatter.

"*Subsistite*," Septimius said, barring my way. "*Quis vos estis?*"

"Allfrost Sentinel Shivurr," I said, holding up my ring. "I believe I'm authorized to enter."

I held my breath as the guardian golem regarded me with his glowing green eyes before stepping to the side. "You are to proceed directly to the conclave, Sentinel Shivurr."

"Where is that?" I asked.

The golem paused before answering. "A guide will meet you in town."

"Cool," I said, striding past him.

Trusting that the guide Septimius had spoken of would find me, I walked the town to clear my head, smelling flowers and woodsmoke and keeping to the sunny sides of the streets. After the ride through the Underfrost, as Hue had surmised, my limbs felt stiffer again, and I didn't want to freeze solid. Glancing at a nearby sculpture, I smirked. *Caelumburg's got enough statues already.*

It had been night during my recent visits, and the town looked more cheerful now with its buildings' colourful painted facades shining in the morning's sunlight. Orienting myself and finding my way through it was also easier now, but I felt fairly sure that had more to do with the latest vials I'd taken than the increased illumination.

With each corner turned, I realized the vials had restored my knowledge of the town nearly completely, in the form of memories of long-ago visits. I smiled, recognizing the black pyramid of the Miraculeum, where the gods made their avatars and other wondrous things. The square where Olivia, Caleb, and I had discovered the aftermath of a battle between escaped Anathema gods and New Olympian guardians. And of course, the road that led to Aceso's domus, where I'd reunited with Scott.

Most residents I passed looked human, but the odd ookmir and android wandered about as well. I was pretty sure none of the human-looking folks were gods, and I guessed they must instead be their trusted agents. Like Maya, the woman who had helped me get into Aceso's bedroom the other day. That or those who at some point had washed ashore on New Olympus's islands.

While every effort was made to keep outsiders from finding the archipelago in the first place, people sometimes slipped through the net of illusions by accident or their own curious intentions. The majority that did had their memories altered before being repatriated to their home countries. However, in rare cases, some ended up staying permanently. Whatever it took to keep the islands from becoming known to the larger world.

I nodded to myself, pleased by the ease of my recollections.

Wait until I tell Wilhelm. The thought brought memories of my New Olympian friends to the fore, and I understood the near-immediate connection I'd had with them during our reunions. They were all there to varying degrees: Wilhelm, Olivia, Hanale, Leonidas, and Cleo. Of course, in those recollections, they'd often gone by other, more godly names. Boreas, Orithyia, and more. *I'm healing.*

The demon, Baduriel, flashed in my mind abruptly. While I remembered our friendship had existed, I still couldn't recall much else about it. Thinking of the demon brought to mind a vision of slaughtered men and ookmir strewn about a rocky plain. I struggled to recall more about the experience but gave up after a moment. Perhaps my mind wasn't ready to deal with the negativity of that fragment of experience, or the missing details weren't in the vials I'd so far taken.

Even if they were, it could take months, maybe longer, to integrate and review the centuries my already-recovered memories spanned. To make them my own again. Right now, many of the older events flitting through my mind felt more like stories I'd been told of things that had happened to someone else. Either way, I'd have to take the last four vials soon. *Maybe tonight at the domus.*

"Shivurr! Oh my God." Lilith, a short, pale and pretty girl of sixteen, dressed in a T-shirt, shorts, and running shoes, came closer, twirling a long shaft of hardwood. Bear padded along at her side. "There you are. We were getting worried."

"Hey, Lil." Stooping, I patted the dog's thick fur as he sniffed me in return. "Where are the others?"

She pushed a lock of long dark hair behind one of her ears. "They went back to the house. To shower after class." She gripped my shoulder for a moment and laughed. "Scott and Caleb were so tired."

I arched an eyebrow. "Class?"

"Martial arts class." Her nose stud glittered as she raised her chin. "Leonidas is teaching us all how to fight." She swept the staff through the air, feigning an attack. "You know, quarterstaff, swords and archery."

"Cool," I said. "How'd that get started?"

Shrugging, she rolled one of her earrings between her fingers. "Scott and Caleb asked him. So they could learn how to use the sword and shield they found in that castle."

"Oh yeah," I said, recalling Abadom Castle, where Scott had practised sword fighting with Virgil and Caleb had set a chair alight with a blast of energy from the shield. "That's a great idea."

Her blue eyes gleamed. "Not that he's let them use either yet. They have to use wooden ones."

My head bobbed. "And you and Alan decided to join them?"

Her gaze hardened. "Yeah . . . we need to be able to protect ourselves. I mean, we'll never be as good as Leonidas, but it can't hurt, right?"

"Totally," I replied.

"Anyway," she said, brushing hair from her eyes, "Hanale sent Bear and me to find you. They're having a meeting or something."

Turning, the dog looked back over his shoulder and yapped.

"Come on." Putting a hand on my shoulder, she turned about. "Bear wants us to follow him."

"Sure," I said, falling into step beside her. "Any sign of Wilhelm or Olivia yet?"

She shook her head. "Not yet."

She led me to the far side of the fountain, up a broad set of stairs, and into an open-air patio canopied by a monolith of stone. On the far side of its flagstone tile floor, a group of people sat on plush lounges. Beyond them, light and airy music came from somewhere within a green garden dotted with a rainbow of colourful blooms.

"*Aloha*," Hanale said as Lilith and I approached. The god stood on bare feet between two divans, thick tattooed arms crossed over his belly. Six feet tall and brown-skinned, he appeared about forty years old, though I knew him to be far older. He wore black shorts that reached his knees and a garish Hawaiian shirt, predominantly red in colour and patterned with flowers and palm trees. "Good of you to join us, Haukea Kane."

I smiled at the Hawaiian nickname, meaning "snow-white man." "Howzit, Hanale?"

"Well enough," Hanale replied, brushing a lock of long black hair from his eyes. "Where have you been? Brother Scott returned with the one called Dixon some time ago."

"Uh, I guess I slept in," I said, rubbing my neck. That was, if lying passed out in the Smaragnisos Allfrost chamber after taking too many vials of my essence qualified as sleeping.

My eyes drifted to Cleo and Leonidas, who sat nearby, leaning against each other on one of the divans. Fit, strong, and attractive, the two looked every bit the demigods that they were, and they returned my gaze with grim expressions. The former wore white robes and sandals, highlighting her light brown skin and jet-black hair. The latter, surprisingly, wore a dark business suit and tie that clashed with his long dark hair and beard. As with Hanale, despite looking to be in their thirties, both, I knew, were far older.

"What's up?" I asked, looking at Hanale. "I hear you wanted to see me."

His eyes flicked to Lilith. "*Mahalo*, Keiki."

"Thank you, dear," Cleo added. "You may go now."

"Uh." Lilith looked around. "Okay."

"Thanks, Lil." I gave her a wink. "I'll see you back at the domus."

Her lips writhed a moment. "Okay. Bye." She patted Bear's head. "Come on, boy."

After the pair had left us, Hanale turned his gaze back to me and gestured to an empty sofa. "Have a seat, brother."

"Sure." I fell back onto the sofa, reshaping my lower half to a more humanoid configuration to better fit the seat, and traded looks with the gathered gods. "What's going on? You guys look worried."

Chapter 6

Taken

Leaning forward, Leonidas stood. "Before you get into that, I will take my leave as well and begin preparations. It may take some time to get everything ready."

"Good idea, brother," Hanale said.

Leonidas gave my shoulder a gentle nudge with the back of one of his hands as he passed me. "See you soon, Shivurr."

I cocked an eye. "Uh, sure. Of course."

As Leonidas walked away, Hanale extended a hand toward Cleo. "Go ahead, sis."

She cleared her throat. "What do you remember about the Eurus, Shivurr?"

I thought a moment, reviewing what I'd learned in recent days and what I'd recovered by drinking vials of my stolen essence, before replying, "They're rogue gods, operating from behind the Iron Curtain. They want to restore the old world order, in which human beings worship them."

"Correct," Cleo said, sounding pleased. "And for years now, they have been using their powers and influence over Eastern bloc governments in an attempt to achieve that goal. Alas, it is against this which we have and must always struggle."

"I couldn't agree more," I said, thinking of the networks of fanatical human operatives the Eurus had bought with the promise of godly favour and offers of ascension to demigod status. "It's my struggle too."

Zealots, I thought with a scowl.

It was through these worshippers as much as Baduriel's actions that the Eurus were able to threaten the Allfrost and the

West's nuclear arsenal. I got the desire for immortality and god-like powers, but killing people to get them was inexcusable. These bastards had to be taken down.

The corners of her mouth quirked. "I know, and I'm glad to hear you say so, since we could use your help."

"Sure." My eyes ticked to Hanale and back to Cleo. "With what?"

Cleo smoothed her robes. "There's something odd going on in Berlin. People have been going missing for a few months now." She glanced at Hanale. "We think as many as several dozen."

I leaned forward. "You've got people in Berlin?"

"Of course." She stood and paced. "Conducting counterintelligence against the Stasi, KGB, and Eurus. As I am sure you realize, it is important to keep an eye on their activities against Western governments."

My head bobbed. "Are these agents of yours . . . are they like you guys? Gods, I mean, or demigods, at least."

"A few," Cleo replied. "However, most are mortals in our employ." She sighed. "In any case, the point is people are vanishing, and we need to find out why and put a stop to it."

"Okay," I said, mulling it over. "What do you think happened to them?"

"At first," Cleo said, "we thought the Stasi were behind it."

My brow wrinkled. "Who are the Stasi?"

She scowled. "The East German secret police. Their government's eyes, ears, and fists. They call themselves the Shield and Sword of the Party."

"Not the people?" I asked.

"Hardly," she replied. "They have been known, on occasion, to kidnap East German defectors and return them to East Germany by force. However, after looking into it, all the disappeared were West Germans." She shrugged. "It may still be the Stasi's doing—for reasons unknown—but recent developments have cast doubt on that."

I scratched one of my temples. "The Eurus, then?"

She made a face. "Perhaps. At least in part."

"Okay," I said, "but how can I help?"

She uncrossed and recrossed her legs. "By assisting with our investigation."

"Me?" I scoffed. "Why? I'm not Sherlock Holmes."

Hanale slapped a hand on my shoulder and sat next to me. "Maybe not, brother, but you may see something others don't." He looked at Cleo. "Tell him."

Cleo shifted in her seat. "There was an incident at one of our safe houses, an apartment in West Berlin, which we believe is related, and there were signs of Underfrost use."

My eyes widened. "Are you sure?"

"Of course," she said. "We have camera footage . . . and there are other indications." She smirked. "Snowfall, intense cold and spontaneous frost formation, indoors no less. As if you'd been there, using the Underfrost."

My jaw dropped. "Really?" I studied her face. "Do you think it's another Sentinel?"

"Perhaps," she replied, "or at least another of your people." She glanced at Hanale. "Maybe a frost adept of some other kind. Either way, you are the best equipped to investigate and, if it comes to a fight, the least likely to suffer harm at a frost wielder's hands."

"Couldn't it be a Eurus god?" I asked.

She looked doubtful. "That is most unlikely."

I raised a brow. "Why not? Aren't there those among you capable of using the Underfrost? Wilhelm—Boreas, I mean—can, can't he?"

"True," Cleo said, trading looks with Hanale. "Boreas is the most adept of us in cryogenic manipulation, but it is a rare ability among us."

"Which is why we are hoping you can assist us," Hanale said. "Your frost proficiencies may permit you to see something we missed."

Cleo inclined her head. "Even if you are only able to confirm that the Underfrost was used, it will be worthwhile. However, if there is a frost wielder at work, we are hoping you may be able to track him when another attack occurs. You are able to see the Underfrost, after all. By following the disturbances made by the frost wielder, or wielders, you may be able to find the missing."

I shook my head. "Trails don't last long in the Underfrost."

"We know," Cleo said. "For that reason we want you on site to tour the city, looking for signs of cryogenic field disruption. Failing that, you will at least be close by the next time there is an incident. We have all our agents on high alert. They will send word to you the moment they observe anything untoward." She stared. "Will you do that for us?"

"Of course." If another Sentinel was in Berlin, I had to find him. For his own sake, but also for what he might be able to tell me. *He might even be able to help with fixing the Allfrost.* "Whatever I can do."

"Good man," she said. "We felt confident you would feel that way. Accordingly, Leonidas has already begun making arrangements for our operatives to take you to Berlin and assist with your investigation. At their observed frequency, it may be a few days before another incident, but we have accommodations in the city where you can stay and rest when you are not investigating."

"Days?" I held up my hands. "I can't stay there for days." I told them about Baduriel's and the Eurus's Allfrost ambitions. "Dixon says more vials are en route to the Institute. I need to get to them before the Eurus do."

"Understood," Cleo said. "However, by your own admission, the vials are not all there yet, and it will take time for the Eurus to infiltrate the Institute to get at them, even if they were."

I growled. "Unless they just launch an assault and take them by force."

"Doubtful," she said, waving away a fly. "The Eurus prefer subterfuge when feasible, and after your last visit, the Institute's defensive readiness will be at its highest levels. Mounting a force of sufficient strength to guarantee success—outside their domain, with our own people countering their actions— will take time. In any case, you should wait for Boreas to return and join you in your quest. He is still away on Zarechus but will return within three or four days. Which gives you plenty of time to investigate in Berlin."

"I don't know," I said, wincing. I thought it over a moment before my eyes lit. "How about Dixon and I go get the vials first, then I go to Berlin?"

Hanale grunted, and his eyebrows bunched. "Going alone is too dangerous, brother. The Eurus may be waiting for you, and neither this Dixon nor the Bodhi Group can be trusted." He wagged a finger at me. "The last time you went to the Group alone, it did not go so well."

I snorted. "Yeah, I remember. One of you guys could come with me, though."

Cleo and Hanale shared a brief look.

"I am afraid that is not possible," Hanale said. "Cleo, Leonidas, and I must remain here, watching over New Olympus. We are already too few for the task."

"Why not go to Berlin for now, Shivurr?" Cleo asked. "Coming back by transporter takes only an instant. You can drink the vials you already have—once you are ready—just as easily while you are there. If they have the secrets needed, the urgency will be less. If not, you can decide what to do then."

Hanale nodded. "The use of the Underfrost in Berlin may suggest that a Borealan, even an Allfrost Sentinel, is working for the Eurus. If so, finding him may be as important as getting the Group's vials."

I scowled. "Why would a Borealan be helping the Eurus?" Borealan was the name my people had given themselves, while Allfrost Sentinels were Borealans who had sworn to protect the Allfrost. "And why would they need him?"

As Borealans were direct beneficiaries of the Allfrost's cooling power, it seemed unlikely any of them would be involved in something that hurt the Allfrost. Least of all Sentinels who had sworn an oath to watch over and defend it. Not to mention, to the best of my knowledge, no Borealan other than me had been seen in a long, long time.

Cleo shrugged. "The only way to know is to find him. Perhaps another of your kind will allow the Eurus to access any of your essence they recover and find Allfrost Prime without you. If that is true, removing him from the equation˙ may be crucial to foiling their plans."

"Yeah, good point." Thinking again of Wilhelm and my recent Zarechan adventures, I asked, "Did Wilhelm find out anything about the Nameless?"

"The what?" Cleo asked, cocking an eye.

"Monsters," I said, grabbing at my chest. "They look like people. Dead people. With vines and leaves and stuff growing out of them." I wiggled my body. "And they move all twitchy."

"Ah, yes," she said, looking at Hanale. "Boreas has not had time to fully investigate that particular mystery." Her gaze drifted to the side, and her eyes swivelled as if reading something upon the air. "He did share his initial findings with us, however."

"And?" I prompted.

Her lip curled. "They appear to be infected with a plant-fungus hybrid. One that feeds off electromagnetism. It may be why they are attracted to the Abadom area. It is too early to say, but they may go dormant, into a form of hibernation, when their energy levels run down. The electrical storm caused by the power obelisks likely awakened them, or at least attracted them to the area when you were there." Her lips pursed. "If Boreas had not activated the obelisk power grid, it is possible you would not have encountered them."

"Just bad timing, eh?" I said with a shake of my head. "How does something like these things even happen? It doesn't seem natural."

"I agree," she said. "As does Boreas. He believes these particular creatures may have been engineered."

"Really?" My jaw dropped. "You mean someone actually made them?"

"Quite possibly," she replied.

"That's crazy." I stroked my chin. "Why, though?"

"A good question." She shrugged. "Perhaps Boreas will be able to tell us more when he returns."

Hanale nudged me. "Giving you time to go to Berlin."

"True," I said with a sigh. "All right. I'll go to Berlin. It's kind of a big, crowded city, though, isn't it?"

"Very much so," Cleo replied.

"Won't that be a problem for me?" I looked down at myself. "I'm not exactly covert."

She looked me up and down. "No, you are not. However, you have learned to shapeshift again, have you not?"

I waggled my head. "Sort of, yeah. It's how I managed to rescue Dixon." I reminded her how the ability had allowed me to don coveralls and infiltrate the Eurus's Gobi Desert camp. "It was dark, though, and no one got close enough to get a good look." I grimaced. "I'm just not that good at it."

She smiled. "Fear not. I am sure you will get better with practice."

I held up my hands. "Not in time. Not enough to fool anyone in daylight. Especially not close up. It takes a lot of concentration too, and I won't be able to do much else while I'm maintaining it."

"No matter." She studied her fingertips. "We believe we have a solution to that. One that will allow you to keep with ease whatever form you choose to take. You will still need to be discreet, avoiding close contact with mortals, but it should be enough to allow you to move about without drawing undue attention. Leonidas is making the arrangements, and he will show you more when he is ready."

I frowned. I couldn't help but wonder what possible solution there could be, but I knew my god friends were resourceful. "Will you keep an eye on the kids while I'm gone?"

"We will," she replied. "As will Bear."

"Oh yeah." Knowing the dog would be with them was comforting. I still didn't remember the full story behind the pooch, but he had stood with me against monsters many times his size in Death Valley, and he'd led Lilith and Alan here to the safety of New Olympus when they'd been set upon by Eurus agents days ago.

A vision of the dog's eyes glowing with fire flitted through my mind. *Is Bear a god?* It was a crazy thought. Yet at his core, Wilhelm—and many other gods—existed fundamentally as a ghostly essence. One that could inhabit physical bodies called avatars. While humanoid forms seemed most common, there were avatars of other types, as well. Given all that, the Alaskan shepherd might be an avatar occupied by a god.

Like Caelus, I thought. Just the other day, the escaped prisoner, Caelus—a god himself—had been recaptured wearing a stolen troll avatar. One he'd still been wearing when I'd questioned him about an intruder to Caelumtor named Atriel.

It made perfect sense, yet something didn't quite fit. While far smarter than the average canine, the dog still behaved like one, embodying the best aspects of his species, loyalty foremost among them. The gods, by contrast, were humanlike in their wants, needs, and desires. No, whatever else Bear was, at his core he was a dog, heart and soul, I felt sure.

"All right," I said. "I'll do it. When do we leave?"

"As soon as your disguise"—Hanale's eyes seemed to twinkle—"and your companions are ready."

"Oh, man." Still seeing the flames in Bear's eyes, I sat up straight. *I almost forgot.* "I've got to get back to the domus."

Cleo arched an eyebrow. "Is something amiss?"

"Nah," I said, getting to my feet. "I just forgot to do something for Caleb. Are we done, then?"

She regarded Hanale a moment before nodding to me. "When all is ready, someone will fetch you."

Chapter 7

Party of Two

Dodging the occasional passerby, I raced through the streets of Caelumburg and soon entered the front yard of the Schmidts' domus. I paused by the house's columned portico, taken aback by the daylight colours of the garden's flowers and greenery.

Nice. I turned in a circle, my gaze falling upon the capsule that had held Dixon resting against some shrubs—where Scott and I had laid it a few days ago. *We've really got to get rid of that.* I padded up the front stairs. *First things first, though.*

Banging through the domus's front entrance, I made my way to the atrium and looked around.

"Oh, hey," I said, spotting one of the Schmidts' silver-and-onyx androids standing by a wall. I strode over and whispered near its ear before sending it on its way. Smiling, I smacked my palms together and went to look for Scott, and my three teenage friends, Caleb, Lilith, and Alan.

I found them in the dining room sitting at the far end of the room's long table upon which open books, loose papers, pencils, and dice mingled with soda cans, Slurpee cups, and discarded pizza boxes.

As I entered, Bear gave a short bark, and I stooped as he came running over to me, tail wagging.

"See?" Lilith said, glancing at her boyfriend, Alan. "I told you he'd be here soon." She looked my way. "They wanted to go looking for you, but I told them you were in a private meeting."

Alan, a handsome, lithe, and muscled teen, raised a hand in greeting. "Hey, Shivurr."

"Glad you're here, dude," Caleb said. The teen, much shorter than his buddy Alan, blue-eyed, with longish face and hair, pulled out the chair next to himself. "Have a seat."

"Thanks," I said, rubbing the dog's head. Sitting, I looked my friends over. Each wore new-looking T-shirts, shorts, and sandals, provided to them by the Schmidts' house androids. "Where did you get the books?"

"The library, I guess." Alan jabbed a thumb toward the android. "He got them for us."

"What kept you?" Scott asked. "I was getting worried."

"We all were," Alan added, using his fingers to comb shaggy, sun-bleached brown hair from his bronzed face.

Snorting, I told them about passing out in the Smaragnisos Allfrost chamber. "I'm fine now, though."

"That's crazy, man," Scott replied. "What was the meeting with Hanale about?"

"Uh." I grabbed a cold slice of pizza from one of the grease-soaked boxes. "I might be taking another trip . . . to Berlin."

Scott's eyes widened. "Why there?"

Having just taken a bite of pizza, I held up a finger and chewed.

"Take your time," he said with a grin.

Swallowing, I put the slice down. "There's trouble there. Cleo thinks the Eurus might be involved." I filled them in on the broad strokes of what I'd been told but downplayed the risks. Since the gods had asked Lilith to leave before starting the meeting, I wasn't sure how much I should share, so I kept most of the details—like the possibility of one of my kind being there—to myself for now. "Anyway, they think I can help."

"Berlin?" Alan regarded Lilith. "That Greta chick is from Berlin."

"If she wasn't lying," Lilith said with a sneer.

My eyes widened. "The one that tried to kidnap you guys?"

Both teens nodded, looking worried.

I sighed. "They're not back yet, eh?" By they, I meant Alan's brother and his girlfriend, Lucy. The young couple, escorted by Olivia, were currently on the run from a red-headed woman named Greta and two headbanger thugs. Given what Alan and Lilith had witnessed before fleeing the same attackers, I felt sure the would-be kidnappers were Eurus. No doubt hoping to grab my friends and use them to find me.

Alan hung his head. "Nope."

"What's taking them so long, Shivurr?" Lilith asked.

"I wish I knew." Using a spatial transposer, the three should have been able to return to Caelumburg in moments. That they weren't yet here meant they hadn't been able to get to one or had been caught. *Or worse.* "I'm sure Wilhelm will be able to contact Olivia when he gets back."

The morning after rescuing Dixon, I'd tried several times to call Olivia on the Walkman she'd given me—which she had modified to allow us to speak to each other—but gotten no answer. I had to hope Wilhelm would have more luck.

Lilith grimaced. "What's keeping him?"

I shrugged. "Baduriel must be hard to find." Knowing Wilhelm's capabilities—which I grasped better now that I'd swallowed the latest batch of vials—I could almost pity those who felt the god's wrath. "Anyway, Olivia will keep them safe." As a demigod, she was better equipped than most to do so. "Who knows? They may even beat him back here."

"I hope you're right." Alan's hazel eyes met mine. "School starts soon, and my parents are going to freak if we're not home by then."

"Worrying isn't going to help, guys," Scott said, rubbing his upper arm and wincing.

"Something wrong?" I asked.

"My arm's sore," he said, continuing to massage his bicep. "Leonidas smacked me pretty hard during training."

"Oh yeah," I said. "Lilith said you're training to be warriors."

Scott gave me a lopsided grin. "Leonidas doesn't think so. Apparently, we're all soft and out of shape."

"He might be right." Caleb raised his elbow and winced. "I can barely lift my arms."

"Not me." Alan puffed out his chest. "I totally could have gone longer."

Caleb grinned. "Sure, dude."

"All right, enough chitchat." Scott scooped a twenty-sided die from the table. "Time to play. Are you in, Shivurr?"

"Nah," I said, standing. "I want to talk to Dixon. Have you guys seen him?"

Scott glanced toward the courtyard door. "Last I saw him he was in Wilhelm's office."

"Thanks. I'll be back in a bit." Crossing the courtyard garden, I entered Wilhelm's office and spotted Dixon sitting in a plush chair next to a bookshelf, with an open book in his hands. The Bodhi Group security director, despite the warmth, had swapped the T-shirt and shorts he'd worn when I'd last seen him for a dark business suit, gold wristwatch, and dress shoes. As he had had nothing on him when he'd arrived at the domus, I felt sure the clothing and watch had been provided by one of the Schmidts' household androids. "What are you reading?"

"*Art of War*," he said, holding up the book. "What kept you? I figured you'd be back yesterday."

"Worried about me?" I asked, coming closer.

He gave a wry smile. "Yeah, actually. Without you, these people might never let me go, and the Hawaiian fella doesn't seem all that friendly."

"I'm not surprised." Forming legs, I took a seat in a chair opposite Dixon. "Hanale's not a fan of the Group, and he knows what you guys did to me."

He held up his hands. "Mea culpa. Do you want another apology or my help stopping this thing?"

"An apology's not going to change the past."

"Agreed," he said, nodding. "All I can do is try to make amends, but to do that, I need to get back and report to the Group, so how's about asking your buddies here to make that happen so we can start working on a solution?"

I shook my head. "Not until Wilhelm returns."

Even if Dixon was truly on my side, it didn't mean the Bodhi Group would feel the same way, even after he reported to them what he'd learned about the Soviet–Eurus plan. Nor could I be sure the Group would act in ways I would like.

I scowled. *Nope.* I'd given them the benefit of the doubt ten years ago, and they'd made me regret it. I wasn't going to take any chances now. *Fool me once.*

Dixon fixed me with a stare. "The sooner I get back to the Institute, the sooner I can get the rest of the vials for you."

"I know." I'd taken the Institute's entire supply on my last visit, but some vials had been absent at the time, undergoing study at other Bodhi Group facilities. After my escape from his custody, Dixon had sent out a recall order, and, since then, those remaining vials had been making their way back to the Institute. "You think they're all there by now?"

He checked his wristwatch. "Most of them should be by now. The rest won't be far behind."

"Are they secure?" Seeing his brow crease, I added, "The labs that have the other vials, I mean."

"They're not the Institute," he replied, "but they've got agents on duty. Not to mention they're top-secret labs, so the Eurus won't know where to find them."

"I hope so." I made a face. "If they do know and they send Baduriel to fetch the vials, I don't think human agents, even well-armed ones, will be able to stop him. I mean, you couldn't keep him out of the Institute, even with army soldiers on your side."

Dixon gave me the stink eye. "We were taken by surprise, and he didn't get the vials, did he?" He looked down. "Come to think of it, he didn't even try. Not that it would have mattered." He jabbed a finger at me. "You were already driving away with them in Kellerman's car by the time he got inside."

"Kellerman?"

"The guy whose car you stole."

"Oh." I shifted in my chair. "Right. I remember him. Tell him I'm sorry, all right? When you get back to the Institute, I mean. For now, try to be patient, okay? It shouldn't be much longer."

He snapped his book shut and tossed it onto a small table next to his chair. "So, your big plan is to sit around here doing nothing, waiting for your alien friends to return?"

"No, not nothing." Taking a seat across from him, I told him about Berlin. "Maybe what's going on is related to the Eurus's plans for the Allfrost."

He grunted. "Summer snowfall does seem like a hell of a coincidence."

"Exactly," I replied, "and I can't pass up a chance to find one of my people."

His eyes narrowed. "Why not?"

"Because they're all missing," I said, "and he might need my help."

He rubbed his bare scalp. "Unless he's working with the Eurus, willingly."

"Maybe," I said, recalling my earlier reasoning, "but it's hard to believe a Borealan would harm the Allfrost, let alone a Sentinel. If he's helping them, the Eurus must have him fooled somehow, but if I can find him, I can tell him what's really been going on."

He leaned forward. "I get you want to help this guy, if he actually exists, but going behind the Iron Curtain is risky."

"I'm only going to West Berlin."

He wagged his head. "Check a map. They might call it West Berlin, but the entire city is in the heart of East Germany, and these Eurus bastards must have far-reaching influence in the Eastern Bloc. Those were Soviet soldiers at the Gobi Desert camp. Which means you're going right into the lion's den. What if you're captured?"

I gave him a lopsided grin. "I ran the same risk when I rescued you. Besides, you said it yourself. I can't sit around doing nothing, waiting for the enemy to make their move." I sat back, working things through in my mind. "If they've got a Borealan on their side already, Prime's location and access key might be all they need now. But if I can get him away from them, they'll be back to square one."

"Fine," Dixon said after a long moment. "You can't go there alone, though. I'll tag along and watch your back."

"No need," I said, holding up a hand. "Someone's supposed to be coming with me, to show me around and stuff."

"Either way, you can't have too much support, especially not in a place like Berlin." He leaned even closer. "I've got field experience, Winterboy. Plus, I can make a few calls and get us some support from the Bodhi Group. Maybe even from the CIA or our British friends."

I bit my cheek. "I don't know."

"What don't you know?" he asked. "At least one of your friends' safe houses has already been compromised. One of the Group's or CIA's might be a better choice. Not to mention, I'm no slouch in a fight."

"Yeah, I suppose." Leaning back, I regarded him closely. "It's only been a few days since the Gobi Desert, though. Are you sure you're ready?"

"I'm fine." Dixon lifted an open can of Ambrola from the table next to him. "These have me feeling much better already."

"That's good," I said, "but how do I know you won't run off and tell the Group about this place?"

His eyes flashed. "That's what you're worried about? I've no idea where we are, other than an island somewhere in the Pacific Ocean, but if it makes you feel better, you have my word I'll stand by you and help you as best I can. This mission is top priority, and I want some payback against these Eurus bastards, if I can get it. Besides, the more I can tell the Group when I finally do give my report, the better." He expelled a breath. "Like I said before, once all this reaches the president, we could be at DEFCON 1 before you know it. A hair's breadth from launching a first strike of our own while we still can."

I nodded. What he said made a lot of sense, and now that I thought about it, I didn't want to leave Dixon behind with Scott and the kids anyway. The security director was a man of action, and he might get up to something in my absence. Like trying to escape from New Olympus. But if he came with me, I could keep an eye on him. *And what better way for Dixon to start making amends?*

"All right," I said, warming to the idea. "You can come." As he'd suggested, his intelligence agency connections and position in the Bodhi Group might prove useful. As would the man himself. Being the patriot I knew him to be, one who'd just endured torture at the Eurus's hands, I knew he'd risked everything in service of his cause before. With the existence of his country and people at stake, I probably couldn't find a more zealous ally. "That is, if our hosts don't object."

"If they do, convince them otherwise," Dixon said. "If they want your help badly enough, and I think they do, they'll agree."

I folded my arms. "I don't give ultimatums to my friends." Though, in truth, I doubted they'd mind if Dixon joined me.

He spread his hands. "You do if it's important enough—if it's the right thing to do."

Before I could reply, Lilith burst into the room, entering from the courtyard. She held the Walkman I'd loaned her in one hand and wore the headphones over her ears.

"What is it, Lil?" I asked.

"There you are." Coming closer, she slipped the head-phones from her head, letting them hang about her neck. "Olivia called."

I popped up from my chair. "She did?"

"Uh-huh." The teen held up the Walkman. "My character's paralyzed, so I started listening to music, and I could hear her voice."

"On a cassette player." Dixon snorted. "I think you're imagining things, girl."

"Olivia modified it," I said, "so we could keep in touch. She likes to tinker."

Dixon rolled his eyes. "Of course she does."

I turned back to Lilith. "What did she say?" If Olivia would soon return with Brad and Lucy, all my plans might change.

She shrugged. "Just that they're all right and going to be a while longer."

Damn, I thought. *So much for that.*

Dixon pursed his lips. "Where are they?"

"Not sure," she replied. "They're trying to get to Canada. There's supposed to be a transporter there. Anyway, she wants you to call her on this tomorrow."

My face fell. "That's it?"

"Uh-huh." She handed me the cassette player. "She faded out after that. The batteries died, I guess."

"Yeah," I said, pocketing the device. "They tend to do that, especially when making a call."

"Do you have spares?" she asked.

"Nope," I said, "but maybe one of the androids can get me some." I glanced at the door through which she'd come. "Are the guys still playing D&D?"

She nodded. "Are you coming?"

"You go ahead," I said. "I've got to check on something first."

I left Dixon to his book and made my way to the kitchen, where an automaton stood huddled over a counter. It looked my way as I came closer but kept pushing small wax pillars into the top of a large white cake. Placing a final candle, it stepped back, allowing me an unobstructed view of its work.

At the centre of the icing, "Happy Birthday, Slim" had been written in red in precise, flowing script, and sixteen unlit candles, each equidistant from its neighbours, circled the cake's outer edge. *Perfect.*

In the excitement of recent days, I had almost forgotten making a promise to get Caleb a cake for his birthday. Technically, the day had already passed, but I figured better late than never. He and I had been through a lot lately, and I knew he'd been unable to celebrate with his family because of it.

I grimaced. Then again, he didn't seem to think his parents would be missing him, so maybe it was better that he celebrated here with his closest friends.

Well, Alan and Lilith at least. I frowned, thinking of Lucy and Brad, who were still in danger. *Please keep them safe, Olivia.*

I slapped the android gently on the back. "Thanks . . . uh, do you have a name?"

"I am designated Andy Four."

I bobbed my head. "I'm Shivurr."

"I am aware, sir."

"Of course," I said, glancing at my identity ring. "I appreciate your help."

"Is there anything else you require?"

"Uh, yeah." I pulled out the Walkman and removed a battery. "Can you get me more of these?"

"Certainly." The robot took the dead battery from me. "How many would you like?"

"How about a dozen?"

"Very good," Andy Four replied. "I will bring them to you shortly. Will you wait here?"

I shook my head. "I'll be in the dining room for the next while. If you don't find me there, leave them on the side table in my bedroom, okay?"

"As you command," he replied, walking away.

"Thanks." I snatched a box of matches from the counter and lit the candles. Waving away their acrid smoke, I shuddered as the candles became a ring of mini fire elementals on an icy plain in my mind's eye.

A moment later, they were flaming wax once more.

Easy, Shivurr. I tossed the match into a nearby sink. *Get a grip.* Shying from the heat, I gently raised the cake from the counter and, shielding the blaze with a hand, headed for the dining room. I pushed my worries aside and, thinking of the coming party, smiled. *He probably thinks I forgot.*

Chapter 8

Time to Motor

Caleb swallowed a mouthful of birthday cake. "If you're going to Berlin, I want to come. You might need my help, dude."

"Yeah." Alan's jaw tightened. "No way I'm missing out again. Besides, I've always wanted to see the Berlin Wall."

"Me too," Lilith said, stroking Bear's head, which lay across her lap.

Scott exhaled noisily. "Yeah, count me in. You might need a computer guy, and I can try out my German."

"Sorry, guys." I looked at Dixon, who had joined the party a few minutes earlier. "This is going to be too dangerous."

Lilith put a hand on my shoulder. "Don't you want the company?"

"Sure I do," I said, "but I'll feel better knowing you're all safe. It's bad enough Brad and Lucy are still being chased by the Eurus. I can't put you guys back in danger too."

"Come on, Shivurr." Caleb waved a hand at the cake. "I'm sixteen now. I'm practically an adult."

"Yeah," Alan said. "We're not kids anymore."

"Forget it," Dixon said. "Winterboy's right. This isn't a high school field trip."

"So," Alan said. "In Vietnam, they—"

"I know all about Vietnam," Dixon said, cutting him off. "All the more reason for you to stay here. I've seen enough . . ." He trailed off. "You're not going."

"Whatever, agent man," Alan said, nostrils flaring. "What's the Bodhi Group anyway? I've never heard of you guys. At least, not until you kidnapped us."

"That's by design, kid," Dixon growled. "Unlike the FBI or CIA, we don't draw attention to ourselves. To most people, if they've heard of us at all, we're a boring multinational doing research and development. Top-secret work, yes, but since our successes and actions never reach the press, we're not that interesting."

"Really?" I asked, surprised. "How do you manage that?"

He smiled. "Anything we do that might draw scrutiny, we do under different names and government departments."

"And what if I tell someone the truth?" Alan asked. "Like a reporter?"

"I wouldn't recommend it," Dixon replied, his face expressionless. "You'd sound like another nut making up stories about Area 51. Though, technically, we're Area 52."

"You're one of the men in black." Caleb shoved Alan's shoulder. "I told you they exist."

"You seem like a good kid," Dixon said, as if Caleb hadn't spoken. "Why would you want to betray your country?"

"Anyway, guys," I said, drawing everyone's attention, "I know you want to help, and I appreciate it, but I need you to stay here and wait for Olivia."

Caleb looked at his friends and back to me. "Okay, dude. Whatever you say. But be careful, okay?"

"Count on it, Slim."

"What about me?" Scott asked. "I'm an adult." He grinned. "Sort of."

I snickered. "I was hoping you'd stay too and watch . . . keep everyone company." I tapped a D&D manual, hoping Scott wasn't too eager to leave the safety of Caelumburg again so soon. Not after being shot in Las Vegas and our subsequent adventures on Antara and Zarechus. "Besides, I can't take away their Dungeon Master halfway through a campaign."

"Good point." He sighed theatrically. "When you put it that way, I suppose I'll have to stay."

"Thanks." I took a deep breath. Smelling Scott's coffee and the remains of white icing and chocolate cake on my plate, I considered taking another bite. "That's settled, then."

I'd have liked to have my friends with me, of course, but Dixon, and whoever Hanale and Cleo were teaming me up with, would have to do for company. Besides, if all went well, I'd be back in a day or two. Hopefully to find Wilhelm, Olivia, Lucy, and Brad waiting for me as well.

A shadow darkened the open courtyard door, and I turned.

"What is this?" Leonidas asked, entering the room. He'd traded his business suit for long shorts, a white tank top, and a flowery Hawaiian shirt. "Cake?" His jaw pulsed. "This is not suitable nourishment for young warriors in training."

Alan scoffed. "It's just cake."

"Is that so?" Leonidas pulled the cake plate closer.

"Yeah," Caleb said, "and I'm not a warrior, dude."

"Really?" Leonidas cocked an eye. "Did you four not ask me to train you? Surely you have not so soon changed your minds." He motioned to me. "Or do you wish always to depend on others to protect you?"

Scott and the teens shook their heads and studied the table.

"Go easy, Leonidas," I said, slapping Caleb's shoulder. "It's his sixteenth birthday. It's kind of a big deal." *Killjoy.*

Leonidas's smile was diabolical. "Very well. Enjoy your repast, children." He lifted an already-cut wedge of cake from the plate and took a bite. Still chewing, he continued, "Tomorrow, we will begin your training with a run around the Circus Caelumtor." He swallowed. "Perhaps retching upon the stones of the roadway will amend your thinking."

"Sure thing, dude," Caleb said, grabbing another piece of cake.

"What are you doing, Caleb?" Lilith asked. "Didn't you hear him?"

"That's a tomorrow-me problem," Caleb said indifferently.

I looked at Leonidas. "Anyway, what brings you by?" *Aside from killing the mood.*

"I've come for you," he replied. "It is time to prepare you for your trip."

"Already?" I asked, glancing at Dixon.

Nodding, Leonidas gestured to the doorway. "Once you are

prepared, you and your team will depart directly."

Dixon stood. "Then I'd better come with you."

Leonidas's brow wrinkled. "Oh?"

"Uh, yeah," I said, enumerating Dixon's background. "He's perfect for this mission."

After a long pause, Leonidas sniffed. "Very well. Shall we depart, then?"

"Cool," I said with a smile, glad he saw it my way. "Yeah, I suppose so." *The sooner we go, the sooner we'll be back.*

After saying goodbye and reassuring my friends I'd be back in no time, I followed Leonidas from the room, with Dixon in tow.

"Being kind of hypocritical back there, weren't you?" Dixon asked as we walked, looking at Leonidas. "Giving the kids a hard time about the cake, yet eating some yourself?"

Yeah, I thought. I'd been wondering the same thing.

Leonidas shrugged. "Unlike the younglings, it will do me no harm."

Dixon snorted. "Does that matter?"

"It does," the god replied. "They must become aware of their bodies and the impact their actions have upon them. Through that awareness they will learn to control their desires. Only by doing so can they achieve their full potential. That is, if they are to improve and become the warriors I know they can be. Hopefully it is not too late for them to learn. Better to have started when they were still pups." He glanced at Dixon. "You are a manner of warrior yourself, and despite your years, you are still fit. Unlike so many mortals past their prime. That tells me you also know the importance of discipline and self-restraint."

"Sure," Dixon said. "They could definitely use some of that. The stoner kid especially."

"His name's Caleb," I said.

"Right," he agreed, "that one."

"He's not a stoner," I added. He'd shown a lot of potential since I had met him a few weeks before. *Well, not just that,* I thought, remembering the weed Olivia had confiscated from the teen.

"If you say so, pal." Dixon turned his gaze back to Leonidas. "Anyway, I preach the same discipline to my men. Which is why eating the cake yourself seemed hypocritical is all."

There's the pot calling the kettle black, I thought. The security director often spoke of his love of freedom, yet he'd helped keep me incarcerated at the Institute for years. Still, he had a point about the cake.

"That, too, was a lesson for them," Leonidas replied.

"How so?" I asked.

He shot me a look. "By teaching them that achieving their goals may require them to deny themselves what others do not."

"Ah," I said. "Like not eating cake even when others do."

"Precisely." Leonidas's teeth shone. "Besides, truth be told, the cake looked delicious, and I was famished."

I chuckled and turned my gaze to the street ahead. "Where are we going?"

"The Miraculeum," he replied, pointing a finger.

In the distance a black pyramid jutted above its neighbours. One housing technology capable of manufacturing the gods' avatars, and pretty much whatever else they might want or need. *A building of miracles.*

"Oh, shoot." I patted my jacket. "I still need batteries for my Walkman."

"Ah, yes." Leonidas dug into the pockets of his shorts. "Andy Four told me of your request." He handed me two packages of batteries. "I believe these will serve you well."

"Thanks." Slowing my pace, I dropped the boxes into the null space inside my cap. "So, who else is coming?"

"Maya Day will accompany you," he said. "I understand you met her recently."

"Yeah," I said, thinking of the fair-skinned, fair-haired young woman with an Irish accent. *Huh, her last name's Day.* I hadn't caught her surname at the time, and we hadn't interacted long, but she'd seemed nice. "We met at Aceso's place. Why her?"

Leonidas motioned us down a side street with a hand. "It was she that first notified us of the trouble in Berlin, and she knows much of the city and our operations there. You could not have a better guide."

"How are we getting there?" I asked.

"Spatial transposition," Leonidas replied. "Rather than a lengthy flight, you will arrive at your destination in seconds."

I nodded, looking at Dixon. "Cool. We'll get back just as easy too." Turning back to Leonidas, I asked, "Is it only Harland, Maya, and me, then?"

Leonidas gave me a devilish grin. "There is another."

"Can I get a gun?" Dixon asked before I could respond.

"Why would you need one?" Leonidas asked, sounding puzzled.

Dixon shrugged. "Can't be too careful, if people are being snatched off the streets."

Leonidas stroked his beard a moment before replying, "I think not. Your purpose on this mission is solely to provide advice and, through your connections, support. Shivurr and Maya will see to defense, should it be necessary."

"Excuse me?" Dixon's nostrils flared. "Security's what I do." He grabbed Leonidas's shoulder as the god walked away. "I'm talking to you."

Leonidas stopped but didn't turn. "Remove your hand," he said, his voice low and dangerous.

Face reddening, Dixon did so. "You got a problem with me, Chief?"

"I do not trust you." Leonidas moved away again. "I know what you and your Group have done."

"It's okay," I said, pulling up by Leonidas's shoulder. "Harland's on our side now."

The New Olympian demigod scowled. "Perhaps. Time will tell." He looked back at Dixon, who had fallen a few steps behind. "Shivurrous may have forgiven you your crimes against him, but we, his friends, cannot so easily do the same. Not before much atonement on your part, at least."

The god's words stirred recollections of good times and bad Leonidas and I had had during our long friendship, locking more of my recovered self back into place. *And I'd forgotten him.* Too caught up in my own feelings, I'd so far not really considered what my absence and memory loss had done to those who cared for me.

"Fair enough," Dixon said, holding up his hands. "Forget I asked."

Leonidas stopped and whirled on him. "And should you betray him in Berlin . . . by the lost moons of Zarechus, I will make your Bodhi Institute shake for it."

Dixon's eyes narrowed and his jaw pulsed. "It's been shaken before, Chief, and it's still standing."

"Okay." Stepping between them, I looked at Leonidas. "Harland's given me his word he'll help. That's good enough for me."

He regarded me a moment before his throat rumbled briefly. "Very well."

"Cool." I let out a breath, relieved. The New Olympians had grown more enlightened over time, but they weren't saints, and when angered they could forget how fragile mortals could be. Even if Dixon wasn't exactly a friend, I didn't want him dead before we'd even started. "Now that that's out of the way, time to motor."

Our conversation ended, we hiked in silence until Leonidas led us past a row of statue-fronted columns and down a ramp into the Miraculeum. The cool interior, lit by glowing strips of ceiling stone, smelled oddly of incense, greenery, and moist earth. Descending through a labyrinth of hallways and stairs, we passed through an open doorway into a high-ceilinged rectangular hall.

"So, why are we here?" I asked Leonidas, though I had an idea.

He waggled his bushy eyebrows. "We're going to see what we can do about your look."

"Right," I said. "Hanale and Cleo mentioned a disguise."

"This way." He walked us over to two mannequins clothed in dark fabrics standing against the far wall, next to a clothing-laden table. "We believe we have a solution to make you far less conspicuous during your time in Berlin."

Snorting, Dixon looked me up and down. "It'll take more than a new set of clothes to do that."

"Oh, I disagree." Leonidas smacked my shoulder and gave me a wink. "I believe you will find that clothes maketh the snowman."

Chapter 9

Bespoke Suit

I ran a hand over the dark fabric worn by one of the figures. Textured like burlap, the material deformed and stretched like rubber. It was one piece, with full-length sleeves and legs, reminding me of the coveralls I'd worn to infiltrate the Eurus's Gobi Desert camp, where I'd rescued Dixon.

"I get it." Still fingering the cloth, I looked over my shoulder at Dixon. "This'll help me keep a more humanoid shape."

Leonidas pulled the garment from the mannequin. "It will do better than that." He held it out to me. "Try it on." The god slapped one of his muscled thighs. "You'll need to alter yourself to form legs, of course."

"Just a sec." I took off my winter jacket and draped it over the now-naked mannequin's shoulders. Taking the unzipped coveralls from Leonidas, I shifted the snow of my bottommost sphere. When I stood upon two well-defined humanoid legs, I bent a knee and shoved a foot down a pant leg, snugging my foot into the stockinged end. Stepping into the other leg, I shimmied it higher and twisted my torso, fumbling for one of the arms. "Where is it?"

"Allow me." Leonidas stepped closer and, grabbing my hand, guided it into the sleeve. "There we go."

"Cool beans." The material stretched as needed in whichever direction I tried to move it, making getting into the one-piece garment easy. *It's more like a jumpsuit than coveralls*, I thought, drawing the zipper up to my neck. Already the change in my body's layout had grown uncomfortable, and I longed to relax back to my default form. I extended my arms and glanced down at myself. "It fits."

"Almost." Moving to stand in front of me, Leonidas brought one of his hands to his neck and pressed his middle and index fingertips together. "There's a button in the collar. When you are satisfied with your current shape, give it a squeeze."

"Okay." I fumbled at the neck of the outfit. The action required enough coordination that my humanoid shape slipped a bit, but I restored it with a scowl. At last, my fingers closed on a lump beneath the fabric at the neckline. "Got it."

"Press it once to activate," he said.

"Okay." I squeezed my fingertips. "Done."

His brows rose. "Do you feel the change?"

"No, not—" I broke off, feeling the fabric tighten about me, becoming stiffer and more supportive. *Whoa.*

Before I'd clicked the lump, the fabric had hung loosely, giving way with every movement of my limbs and torso. Now, the fabric still stretched with my motion, but only so far. Consciously, I let my altered form relax a bit. Flexing slightly, I felt the suit resist, tightening about my legs and abdomen, urging me insistently back toward the human shape I'd worn when clicking the collar. With its pressure, the suit provided me immediate feedback and support whenever and wherever my shape might start to slip. I took a few steps, noting that at the same time the fabric still allowed my arms and legs to move freely at my joints.

"How does it feel?" Leonidas asked.

"Amazing," I said. "It really makes holding this shape a lot easier. I barely need to concentrate now."

"Excellent," Leonidas said. "That was my intent."

"How does it work?" I asked.

"That's a long conversation," he said. "Suffice to say, it is made of a smart fabric."

"Which means?" Dixon asked.

Leonidas smiled. "The material morphs, within limits, to fit the wearer. Once locked in, it will automatically resist any change of overall shape while still allowing for the natural movement of your limbs and torso. What's more, it will remember the last locked-in shape. In which case, activating the collar will cause the suit to gradually revert to the previously chosen target state."

"Oh, I get it." I caressed the material. I'd still have to form rudimentary legs to get into the suit, but, once reactivated, the suit would guide me from there, without need of a mirror to check my appearance or any trial and error. "How do I get it off, though?"

Leonidas touched his neck. "Squeeze the collar again, and it will relax itself."

"Awesome," I said, doing as he suggested.

"I am glad you like it," he said. "Through its feedback, keeping an altered shape may eventually become second nature."

I smirked, resuming humanoid form before clicking the button again. "All it's missing is air conditioning."

"Alas, there was insufficient time," Leonidas replied without a trace of a smile. He grabbed a pile of folded cloth from a table by the mannequins. "Perhaps when you return, we can add that."

"Uh . . ." My eyes darted left and right. "I was kidding."

"I was not." Leonidas handed me a pair of black pants. "Wear these over the suit. It will give your outfit a more natural appearance."

"Are these adaptive too?" I asked, slipping them on.

"To some degree, yes," Leonidas replied. "Though they are configured to maintain a looser fit. We want them to look like pants rather than tights." He placed loafers at my feet. "You should wear these as well. Walking about in stockinged feet would also spoil the look we are trying to achieve, and they will protect your feet and help them keep their shape."

"Nice." Elongating my foot with a thought, I pulled on the left shoe. I did the same with the other shoe, stood taller, and looked down at myself. "How do I look?"

"Acceptable." Leonidas pointed down and twirled his finger. "Spin around."

"Okay." I turned a full rotation. "What do you think?"

"Hmm," Leonidas murmured. "You have no buttocks. It is too flat."

I twisted my neck, trying to look over my shoulder. "Really?"

"Here." He waved a hand, and a mirror image of myself

appeared in the air a few feet to my front. "Regard me." Standing next to the mirror image of me, he turned away and tapped his backside. "It should resemble this."

"Are you sure?" I asked. "Isn't that kind of . . . muscled?"

"Nonsense," he said. "This is how a properly maintained gluteus maximus should appear. You've been too long among sedentary mortal scientists. Now relax the suit and try again."

"Okay," I said, snapping my collar and shifting form. "How's this?"

He smacked his lips. "Still too flat. Keep trying. You can do better."

I sighed. "All right."

After a half hour's effort, Leonidas nodded. "I believe that should suffice, but there is still room for improvement."

My shoulders slumped. "Seriously?"

"His butt's fine," Dixon said. "It's his height that's the problem. A seven-foot giant is going to draw nearly as much attention as his usual form."

"Oh, yeah." Slimming my body while maintaining my usual density meant spreading myself over a longer length. I focused a moment, packing myself more tightly, and I felt myself grow shorter. "How's that?"

"That'll do," Dixon replied. Shaking his head, he patted his stomach. "I wish I could do that. It'd save me a lot of time at the gym."

Leonidas stroked his beard, regarding me. "You will still not pass as a human being, of course. A human avatar would be required for that, and we've no time to develop an organic vessel that can survive you . . . and you it."

"What do you mean?" I asked. "You really think I could occupy an avatar?"

"Realistically, no." He grimaced. "The crystalline cells of which you are made must sheath themselves in snow and ice, keeping themselves cool enough to remain above the Underfrost. Yet doing so while integrated with an avatar necrotizes the host's organic cells." He looked thoughtful. "No, even with the enhancements of an avatar, the human body is an unsuitable host. Perhaps in time a way can be found, but, as I said, doing so would take far longer than we have."

Dixon grunted. "You seem to know a lot about it."

"It is a problem we have tried to solve before," Leonidas said, wrinkling his nose. "With poor or short-lived results."

I rubbed my chest. "Who made this suit?"

"I did," Leonidas said. "Though in truth, the Miraculeum does the actual manufacturing. I merely express what I desire. Still, communicating one's desires properly is its own sort of challenge."

Dixon scoffed. "The building?"

Leonidas's chin dipped. "It is both a structure and a machine. Built by Boreas, Hephaestus, and several others, ages ago. It is capable of creation itself, using the raw materials with which we supply it."

Dixon whistled. "That's amazing. And you understand how all this works?"

Leonidas's brow furrowed. "Only a handful of us, such as Boreas, still fully grasp the building's underlying technology."

"How's that possible?" I asked, finding it hard to believe the gods had allowed such expertise to be lost.

"There is no need, really," Leonidas said. "When you have machines to produce most anything you can imagine or desire, what does it matter if you understand how the technology works?"

Dixon scoffed. "You're saying any idiot can make it work?"

"Correct." Leonidas gave the security director a sidelong look. "With training, I daresay even one such as you."

Dixon snorted and cast a glance my way. "I walked into that one." He turned back to Leonidas. "And when your machines fail, who fixes them?"

Leonidas shrugged. "They fix themselves."

"Kind of boring, isn't it?" Dixon asked. "Having everything done for you."

"It can be," Leonidas replied. "That is why the true divine take avatars to mingle among and watch over mortals. It gives them a way to feel again and find meaning."

Everyone needs a purpose, I thought.

"Them?" Dixon frowned. "Aren't you one of them, Chief?"

"He's a demigod," I said, the memory coming easily now.

Dixon looked Leonidas up and down. "You're part human, then?"

"To some degree," Leonidas said. "At least until I fully shed this mortal coil. When that day comes, I shall be truly divine, free to occupy whatever avatar I might choose."

"Sounds creepy." Dixon shuddered. "Tossing your body aside like old snakeskin."

Leonidas's beard wagged. "Not at all. I am merely transferring my consciousness and memories to a crystalline essence." He looked at me. "Ascending to a higher form of life, like Shivurr here."

I snapped my fingers, remembering. "Your minds and memories are copied over to crystals."

Leonidas inclined his head. "Transferred and enhanced. In this alternate form, we gain great power and eternal life."

I looked at Dixon. "It's kind of like a computer hard drive."

"Sounds to me like you're kidding yourself." Still looking at Leonidas, Dixon swirled his index finger by his temple. "A copy of your mind isn't the original you."

"In this case, it is," Leonidas said. "The transition is gradual, occurring throughout our lived lives. In this way, continuity is maintained." He waved a hand at Dixon. "The cells of the normal human body die and replace themselves regularly. In several years, the bulk of your body is completely replaced with new cells. Does that mean you have died? No, the individual remains."

Dixon looked skeptical. "How long does this process take?"

"It depends on the individual," Leonidas said. "Hundreds of years at least. In some cases, thousands."

"Huh." Dixon glanced at me. "Like the Ship of Theseus."

"Correct." Looking startled, Leonidas regarded him with pursed lips. "You know your Plutarch. Planks of a ship or parts of a body, the concept is the same." He peeled a dark coat from the other mannequin and held it out to me. "Try this on."

Taking it from him, I pointed to the dummy where I'd hung my winter coat. "I've already got a jacket."

He shook his head. "It will draw attention in the midst of summer in Berlin. Bad enough you will be wearing a coat at all, you will want something that appears lighter weight."

"But I like it." I fingered a burn in the jacket's outer shell. "It keeps me cool."

"As will this," he replied. "The suit you wear and this coat include special insulating properties. They will be as effective in keeping you cool, I assure you."

I studied him with a narrowed eye. "You think?"

"I know." He lifted my jacket from its perch and studied the front a moment before rotating it a hundred and eighty degrees. Dark burn marks covered its back, earned during the course of my recent adventures in Nevada. "Besides, this one has seen better days."

"Yeah," I said. "We've been through a lot together."

"Very well." He gave the jacket a sniff. "As you have become attached to it, I will have it restored for you. It will be as good as new when you return from Berlin."

My eyes lit. "You can do that?"

"Of course." He gestured to the dark coat in my hands. "Now try it on."

"All right." To my surprise, despite being thinner than the winter jacket, it seemed to insulate me just as well. Like the shapesuit before I'd activated its function, the coat's fabric seemed to stretch and adapt to fit me. I buttoned my coat and examined myself in the mirror. "Not bad."

"Check your pockets," he said.

"Cool," I said, withdrawing black gloves.

"Put them on. They will disguise your hands."

"Okay." Regarding my claw-like fingertips, I dulled them with a moment's concentration before pulling on my new hand-wear. "Pretty slick."

"Now to complete your disguise." He passed me a dark bundle of fabric. "Try this on."

I stretched it wide. "What is it?"

"A cowl." Leonidas touched his nose. "To shroud and shape your head and face."

"That's a great idea." I wedged my cap beneath my armpit and pulled the bag over my face. "Uh, how am I supposed to see through the cloth?"

"Here," Leonidas said with a chuckle. I felt hands on my face, and the fabric slid across my nose until openings in the mask centred over my eyes. "How is that?"

"Better. Thanks." Looking toward the mirror, I studied the mask, which hung loosely about my head. "How do I activate it?"

"It works similar to the suit," Leonidas said. "Except I have set this one to a preprogrammed configuration to guide you in shaping your face properly."

I expelled a breath. "That's a relief." Reshaping the large parts of my body was one thing. Facial features were another. I felt the sides of my head. In order to approximate human ears, I'd formed ridges around the auditory canals there, but they lacked the intricate folds and curves of the human outer ear. "It won't hurt, will it?"

He tossed his shoulders. "You will experience no more discomfort than you do when reshaping any other part of your body." He fumbled at my neck. "Simply squeeze the button in the collar here and adjust your face to match the pressure of its contractions. Once the mask reaches the programmed shape, it will hold the position more rigidly, as the suit does with your body."

"Okay," I said, doing as he asked.

As expected, the fabric tightened, gripping my face with varying degrees of force, like a thousand fingers working putty. Closing my eyes, I mentally shifted my face and scalp, contracting myself wherever the fabric felt tight, relaxing it where the cloth felt loose. Abruptly, the entire hood stiffened and the squeeze of its touch evened out. I looked into the mirror and gasped. My head and face had taken on a distinctly human outline. I smiled and felt the hood yield to accommodate the expression, but only so far.

"Cool." I ran my fingers over my cheeks. "I don't even have to concentrate anymore." I donned my cap, adjusted the brim, and looked at my companions. "How do I look?"

"Splendid," Leonidas said. "However, you may wish to turn off your hat's glow."

"Oh, right." With a thought, the hat's blue light faded, returning to its original black. "Better?"

"Much," Leonidas said, smacking his palms together. "I believe that will do it." He cast a look toward the door and his eyes narrowed. "Hmm . . . your travelling companions should be here by now. Wait here a moment. I will see what is keeping them." He stirred the air with a hand. "Keep experimenting. I should not be long."

"Sure thing." I tilted my cap to a more jaunty angle and studied myself in the mirror. Relaxing the suit, I reshaped my body and continued to sculpt myself into a tall, thin, and dark approximation of a human being. In every aspect the opposite of my usual form. *But still cool.*

"Hey," I said, turning to Dixon several minutes later. Taking off my cap, I deactivated the hood's grip on my features, pulled it off, and let my head and face flow back to their original states. "I'm sorry about Leonidas giving you a hard time earlier."

He waved a hand dismissively. "Don't worry about it."

"We're on the same side now at least," I said, wondering, not for the first time, why Dixon and the Group had betrayed me all those years ago. Had it merely been fear of the unfamiliar or something deeper?

"Better late than never," he replied, giving me an appraising look. "If it hadn't been for—"

"Oh my goodness," said a voice from the door, cutting Dixon off.

Chapter 10

Bird or Devil

A blond, fair-skinned woman of about thirty years, wearing a checked tweed blazer, an ivory-and-navy striped T-shirt, and jeans, regarded me from the doorway. "Is it yourself, Mr. Shivurr?" She came closer, teeth shining, eyeing me up and down with bright green eyes. "Lovely to see you again."

"Hi, Maya." I beamed, recognizing her immediately. "It's good to see you again too."

She clapped me on the shoulder and glanced to the side. "Who's your man?"

"Harland Dixon," he said, shaking her hand. "Good to meet you, Day."

"And you, Mr. Dixon." Her ponytail swung as she looked back to me. "Your disguise will do nicely."

"What do you think, Harland?" I asked, shooting him a look.

The corners of his mouth twitched. "I think the Shadow knows."

By the Shadow, he meant the crime-fighting main character of an old radio show, which he'd played for me at the Institute. Able to read minds and turn invisible, the Shadow was super cool, and I grinned at the comparison.

Maya laughed. "Oh, you're right. Those old radio plays are grand." She squeezed my arm. "Did you ever find your burglar?"

"Uh, yeah," I said, recalling when we'd first met a few days earlier. "I did, actually." I coughed, embarrassed. "Turns out it was just Wilhelm."

Her eyebrows rose. "Really? As in Boreas Wilhelm?"

"Uh-huh," I said. "His body, at least."

She covered her long nose and open mouth with her hands. "Oh, I see. That must have been somewhat awkward."

Flashes of the planets Antara and Zarechus flitted through my mind. "It got pretty weird all right."

Behind her, Leonidas appeared in the doorway. A black bird with dark and shiny feathers sat upon his raised forearm.

A raven, I realized as the animal's head turned to regard me.

"What's with the bird?" Dixon asked.

Leonidas raised his arm higher. "This is your final teammate."

Wondering how a raven could be of help on our mission, I moved closer. "He's a beauty."

The raven preened. "Thank you, Sentinel."

I retreated a step. "It can talk?"

"Of course I can." The bird glanced at Leonidas. "Has he not been told?"

Leonidas glared back. "Not yet, Caelus." He looked at me. "I was about to do so."

"Caelus?" I'd spoken to a Caelus a few nights earlier. "The troll?" That one—a recaptured member of a group of escaped Anathema gods—had been an ookmir, not a raven. Then realization clicked. "You're in a new avatar."

"Oh, very nice," Caelus croaked. "I spent only a few days in that ookmir body." His head wagged. "Caelus the Troll, indeed."

"He has promised to be of help to you," Leonidas said. "To make amends for his recent actions."

Just like Dixon, I thought.

"With the promise of clemency," Caelus added.

"I figured," I said with a nod. It made sense that Caelus would want to make a deal. He and his fellow escapees had caused a lot of havoc before they had all been recaptured—Caelus among the last. In the end, the fugitives had only added to their sentences. "As a raven, though?"

Leonidas pursed his lips. "An ookmir would be far too conspicuous for this mission, not to mention harder for you and Maya to control." He sneered at the bird on his arm. "Though perhaps a snake would have been more appropriate for this one."

"Droll, Leonidas," Caelus said, ruffling his feathers. "Very droll."

I looked at Leonidas. "Yeah, but why Caelus?"

Leonidas shrugged. "He knows both the Eurus and Berlin. He resided there before his fall from grace, charged with keeping an eye on the Eurus activities after the termination of World War Two. His knowledge will be somewhat dated, of course. It has been almost twenty years since he was stripped of his avatar and tossed in a jar. However, if nothing else, he will be able to perform aerial reconnaissance."

"Really, Leonidas," Caelus said. "Must you persist in discussing me as if I am not here?"

"What's to stop him from escaping?" I asked. Bringing a paroled Anathema along seemed risky. "He could just fly away."

Caelus croaked. "I have given my word not to do so, Sentinel."

"And this." Leonidas swept his fingers across the bird's throat, revealing a dark collar, barely discernible against his black neck feathers. "This collar will, among other things, inhibit his powers and prevent him from quitting his avatar."

I glanced at Dixon and Maya before turning back to Leonidas. "What powers?"

Leonidas counted on his fingers. "Telepathy, telekinesis, energy discharge."

My lips wrinkled. "Is that all?"

He nodded. "Of equal importance, the device has the advantage of making Caelus's divinity harder to detect. That may be critical, given there may be Eurus gods present in Berlin. On both sides of the wall."

"Wait." I held up a hand. Half-remembered facts bobbed at the edges of my mind. "You guys can sense each other?"

"Yes," he said, "when in close proximity, without special measures taken to shroud ourselves. In part, that is why we are sending this team. The Eurus will not detect you the way they would a god or even a demigod, and Maya and Dixon are mere ... that is, they have no divinity to detect." Clearing his throat, Leonidas handed a bracelet to Maya. "Put this on your wrist. When wearing it, you will be able to see and speak with Caelus across great distances. In fact, when you wish, you will be able to see and hear what he does via its telepathic interface."

"I've used similar devices before," Maya replied.

"Good." Leonidas held up one of his index fingers. "If he ventures beyond the reach of the bracelet, his avatar will take over and fly itself back into range. The necklace has been specially modified to remove his control of the avatar under such conditions. You can also issue a recall command via the bracelet when necessary."

I frowned. "Won't that be a problem if they get too far apart?"

He seesawed his head, side to side. "Keep him within fifty kilometres or so and there will not be a problem. The intent is to allow him room to scout but not flee entirely."

"I get it," I said. "It's like a virtual leash."

The raven croaked again. "You shall have no need for it, I assure you, Sentinel."

"I hope not," I said, reminded of the bird I'd seen at Dublin Gulch, and the one Alan had told me they'd seen in California. "Have you ever been a turkey vulture?"

Caelus cocked his head. "No, I cannot say I have."

"Right." It couldn't have been Caelus, of course. He'd been imprisoned here in Caelumburg until a few days ago. *Maybe another god, though?*

"Such a bird would not be suitable," Leonidas said. "Not being native to Berlin."

"No, I wasn't suggesting that." I told them about my and my friends' encounters with the red-headed vultures. "Could it have been a god in an avatar, spying on us, do you think?"

Leonidas narrowed an eye before wagging his head. "There seems little doubt it was a Eurus spy, but almost certainly it was just an enhanced member of the species. A true divine would not have fled nor been dissuaded by a few bullets."

"Yeah," I replied, "I suppose you're right. Anyway, this raven body is a beautiful upgrade." I resisted the urge to stroke the bird's back, reminding myself it was Caelus inside. "What happened to the ookmir avatar?"

"Take him, please." Leonidas handed Caelus to Maya before returning his attention to me. "Seeing as it was a stolen and valuable piece of hardware, it has been returned to stasis until it is needed."

"Sentinel," Caelus clambered up Maya's arm, extended his wings, and ruffled his feathers as he settled atop her shoulder. "I understand you did not find the Allfrost Sentinel for which you went searching."

"No." I jabbed a thumb at Dixon. "I found him instead."

"Pity." He looked thoughtful a moment. "It is possible you missed the Sentinel, though, no?"

"Maybe." The only prisoner the Russian grease monkey, Yuri, had seemed to know of had been Dixon, and I felt pretty sure the mechanic had been too frightened of me to have lied. "But I doubt it." I shrugged. "Maybe there's one in Berlin, though."

"Fear not," Caelus said, shifting back and forth on his perch. "If not a Sentinel, perhaps we may find Atriel in Berlin, and you can question him further regarding the subject."

Atriel. I suppressed a shudder, recalling the nightmarish creature who had confronted me in the tunnels beneath Caelumburg. The last I had heard, Atriel had been in the Gobi Desert, and that was only a few days ago. *Berlin is a long way from there.* Then again, with spatial transpositions and jet airplanes, he'd had enough time to get pretty much anywhere by now.

"Did he say he was going there?" I asked, knowing the two had joined forces for a time before Atriel's escape from New Olympus and Caelus's recapture.

"No," Caelus said, "but he is one of the Eurus, and Berlin was rife with their kind when last I was free." He cast a glance toward Leonidas. "And I understand that that has not changed."

"Even if he is," I said, "I don't think I'd recognize him." I searched my memories, but I saw only the monstrosity of muscle, tendons, and bone from the tunnels below. "Not in whatever body he's in now."

"Strange," Caelus replied. "The way he spoke of you, it seemed like you had at least met each other before."

My eyelids fluttered. "Yeah?" Abruptly, the apparition in my mind's eye shifted, becoming a person—a regular-looking human being of average height with short blond hair and a medium build. My jaw dropped as I recognized the man as Atriel in his usual avatar. *I do know him.*

"I'm here for you," Atriel had said in the tortured, almost incoherent voice of an avatar that had not been designed to speak.

He wasn't threatening me. He had attacked me, yes—shocking me with lightning—but only after I had lashed out at him first. Feeling faint, I staggered over to the table and braced myself against its surface. *He came to rescue me.* A sharp pain shot through my head, and I rubbed my temples. *He's a Eurus, though.*

Leonidas touched my arm. "Are you unwell?"

Swallowing, I shook my head. "Give me a second." *Why would a Eurus think he needed to rescue me from my New Olympian friends?* Could I be one of the Eurus? *No way.* I'd gone to the Bodhi Group for help stopping the Eurus's plans. I scowled, trying to recall more, but failed. I felt another stab of pain behind my eyes. "Maybe it's the suit."

He tapped his fingers against his neck. "Then deactivate it for now. You will not need to hide your true self until Berlin."

"Right," I said, doing as he suggested. With the suit flicked off, I reverted to my normal shape and groaned. "Oh, that's good. Much better."

"Speaking of Berlin," Dixon said, "when do we leave?"

"Whenever you are ready," Leonidas replied.

Maya held up a hand. "I need to eat first."

"Can we grab a bite in Berlin?" I asked.

"My fridge and cupboards are empty." She checked her watch. "I'd suggest a restaurant, but the sun won't be up there for a few hours."

"Eat at the hotel," Leonidas said. "If the kitchen staff are not yet awake, I am sure a staff member will order you something from a meal box, if you request it."

Oh yeah, I thought, recalling the stainless-steel containers. Through them, using spatial transposition, food and other goods not found on New Olympus could be requested from anywhere in the world.

Just days ago at Aceso's Caelumburg domus, I'd enjoyed pizza, sent hot and fresh from Manhattan, and half-frozen drinks. The former had arrived within thirty minutes of placing a written request inside one of the point-to-point transporter boxes.

The stainless-steel containers had seemed magical at the time, but old memories I'd recovered since then had made their workings simple and clear, at least at a high level. Wherever a corresponding box had been established, trusted personnel waited, ready to visit nearby stores or restaurants, buy the desired items, and send them back via the transporter box.

The time it took varied based on the request, but the network and personnel were efficient and well situated in urban centres, so you'd get most things fast and, for high-demand, non-perishable items, some stock was often kept close at hand.

"That will work," she said. "That is, if these gentlemen don't mind watching me eat."

"I could do with a meal, myself," Dixon said with a smile.

"Excellent." Leonidas looked at Maya. "Be sure to guard what I've given you well."

"Of course," she replied. "I just hope they're not needed."

They? As far as I knew, he'd only given her the bracelet. Unless he'd given her something else earlier. Whatever he meant, I let it pass.

"As do I." Leonidas clapped his hands together and waved at the exit. "In that case, I will leave it to Maya to see you to the transporter. Good hunting and *viel Glück.*"

While Maya led us through the streets of Caelumburg, I thought of Berlin, recalling more of the city as shattered memories, directed by my reminiscences, reconnected. Unfortunately, most were from before the city had endured two world wars, and I knew it had changed much since then. Chances were I'd be as lost in the city as any newcomer, but I pushed the thought aside. With Dixon, Maya, and Caelus to guide me, I'd be fine.

The real challenge would be finding out why people were going missing. Normally, I wouldn't even know where to start, but maybe following this hypothetical Sentinel's trail through the Underfrost would steer us in the right direction. If not, I'd seek out a Eurus or two and see about persuading them to fill in the gaps. If Caelus was right and Berlin was truly swimming with them, finding one should be a breeze.

"Here we are," Maya said, taking us up wide steps, past a line of stone columns, and into one of Caelumburg's many temple-like Greco-Roman buildings. Shafts of sunlight entering from openings in the soaring ceiling lit the interior, revealing dozens of marble buildings arranged in neat rows.

"Is this a crypt?" Dixon asked as we strode among the tiny structures. "These things look like mausoleums."

Maya wagged her head. "Each building in this hall is a transporter tied to different parts of the planet, allowing near-instantaneous travel between destinations." She drew to a stop by a building near the hall's middle. "This one is ours."

"Hold on." Dixon grasped my upper arm, stopping me from entering. "Are you okay with this? Having your atoms scrambled and beamed across the world like in some sci-fi TV show?"

"It's fine," I replied. "I've done it before."

"What if something goes wrong?" he asked. "When I die, I'd like there to be something left to bury."

"No one's dying," I said, surprised. Whatever his faults, Dixon had never seemed afraid of anything. *I guess everyone's got their phobias*, I thought, hoping this wasn't going to be a problem. "The gods have been doing this a long time."

He blew out a breath. "Is it even me that'll arrive on the other side?" He glanced from Maya to me. "After our atoms are scrambled, will it be any of us?"

Maya's brow furrowed. "Of course it will. We're travelling by spatial transposition, not getting beamed up by Scotty."

His lip curled. "What's the difference?"

"The difference"—she held up her index fingers and crossed them over each other—"is spatial transposition temporarily changes the relative location of regions of space. Which means, when activated, we don't actually go anywhere. The space in which we're standing does, and by exiting the relocated volume of space before it reverts to normal, we will remain in Berlin. Understood?"

Dixon fluttered his eyelids. "Uh, yeah. Sort of. Except it sounds like nonsense. Space doesn't move."

"Usually not of its own accord," Caelus said from the woman's shoulder. "Yet even the shape of space-time may be sculpted by the hands of we divine. Location is relative, after all. In any case, I believe the point Ms. Day is making is, you're not disassembled or altered by the process in any way."

"Why the building, then?" he asked.

Maya swung the door to the tiny structure inward. "They are what powers the transposition. Not to mention they keep occupants within the area of effect, deal with changes in air pressure and temperature, and ensure a sterile transfer."

"Fine," Dixon said with a scowl. "Let's get this over with, then."

"Grand," Maya replied, stepping through the door. "I would hate to have to leave you behind now." She motioned to a wooden bench, the stainless-steel room's sole piece of furniture. "Have a seat, if you like. The room may shake as the transposition locks in." She closed the door when we were all inside. "It doesn't happen often, especially for earth-to-earth transports— there are fewer variables to consider—but you never know."

Sitting, Dixon gave her a questioning look. "Earth-to-earth?"

She nodded. "Caelumtor is a gateway to many places, including other worlds."

Dixon snorted and glanced my way but said nothing.

"Is everyone ready?" Maya asked, still standing.

"Wait a sec." Shifting my body and face, I thumbed the switches on my new suit and hood and looked at her. "I'm ready."

She dipped her chin. "Here we go."

Chapter 11

Terrible Things

A moment later, the walls glowed faintly. They cycled through the same colour sequence I'd seen in the tunnels beneath Aceso's domus when Scott, Caleb, and I had fled from Atriel to the planet known as Antara, before ending up on another world known as Zarechus. Abruptly, the light faded, and she pulled open the door. "That's it. Welcome to Berlin."

Opening the door, I stuck my head across its threshold. An apartment decorated with floral pattern wallpaper, furnished with plush chairs and a long sofa, had replaced the Caelumburg hall. A wooden desk and straight-backed chair sat in a corner by the windows. Through the latter's gauzy curtains, street lights cast pools of illumination onto an otherwise dark street.

As I took it all in, the raven, Caelus, leaped from Maya's arm. With a few flaps of his wings, he landed atop the seat back of one of the chairs. Waving Dixon and me past, Maya closed the door to the transporter room, waited a moment, and opened it again. The door swung inward to reveal a wallpapered room with framed paintings adorning the walls, chests of drawers, a wooden desk, and a bed.

"See?" Maya looked at Dixon. "The room has now reverted."

"You're a magician." Dixon strode over to the window, pushed the curtains aside, and looked out. "That's really Berlin out there? It's hard to tell in the dark."

"You'll get a good look yet." She checked her wristwatch. "Sunrise is not far off now."

Wandering across the living area, I peered through a doorway into another bedroom. Like the rest of the apartment, the room seemed comfy, but I saw no sign of personal items or decorations.

"Is this your place?" I asked.

She shook her head. "No one lives here. This is a shared access point."

"It looks like a hotel suite," Dixon said.

"That's what it is," Maya replied. "The gods of New Olympus own the entire hotel. It's one of their many corporate holdings."

I nodded to myself. The gods—immortal, smart, and innately powerful—had had millennia to invest and acquire financial power and wealth. It made sense that, while doing so, they had established corporations through which they could accomplish much while staying largely anonymous.

"Smart." Dixon bobbed his head. "A hotel makes it easier to explain different people coming and going."

"Absolutely," she said. "And it is also a convenient place to stay upon arrival in the city."

He stroked his chin stubble. "How do you keep the cleaning staff from taking unplanned trips to Caelumtor?"

She flashed her identity ring. "They'd need one of these, along with sufficient authorization."

I felt my own ring through the gloves I wore. Silver with a golden centre stone encompassed by alternating black and silver circles and dotted with gems of blue, red, and green. It had been given to me by Olivia about a week earlier. Without the authority it granted, I probably wouldn't have made it to Zarechus nor been able to order Abadom's keeper program to sic its golems on Baduriel during the transporter room fight.

"Still," he said. "Your staff must wonder about people constantly coming and going from this room in particular."

Maya waved a hand dismissively. "Most of the staff know its true nature. Some even know about the gods themselves, and they're all loyal and sworn to secrecy." She took a few steps and opened a door, beyond which a hallway could be seen. "Come on. Let's get a bite to eat. I'm famished."

We followed her along a carpeted hallway lined with land-scape paintings and down a flight of stairs. Entering the hotel's marble-floored lobby, she took us past the front desk to a room filled with tables and chairs.

"Wait here." Maya set Caelus down atop the back of a chair and hung her purse next to him. "I'll go see about the food. Do either of you want anything?"

"Coffee," Dixon replied, "and toast, if you've got any."

"A soft drink for me," I said.

Nodding, she left.

"I've been thinking," Dixon said after we'd sat waiting a while. "Caelumtor."

"Yeah?" I prompted.

"Caelum," he said. "That's Latin for heaven, if memory serves, but what's the *-tor* part signify?"

"Gate," I said, remembering. "Tor is the German word for gate. Together, they mean Heaven's Gate." *Or maybe sky gate*, I supposed.

Caelus squawked. "It is known as a portmanteau."

Dixon shot the bird a look. "I know what a portmanteau is, bird. Thanks."

"Boreas," I said, remembering. "I mean, Wilhelm, has an affinity for them. The gods do that a lot. Knowing so many languages, they tend to mingle their words."

"They're not deities, Winterboy," he said, rolling his eyes. "They're aliens. Strange and powerful but alien life. Like you."

"I'm not an alien," I said, shaking my head. "I'm from here. From Earth." Wilhelm had told me as much back in Nevada, but I now knew it like I knew my own name. "I remember that now." *And I've been here longer than humanity.*

Dixon shrugged. "You're alien to me."

"Ditto," I said with a grin.

"Here we are," Maya said, entering from the lobby. A middle-aged man wearing a suit and tie—short light brown hair and trim moustache carefully combed—followed her, carrying a serving tray filled with drinks. "Right over here."

"*Guten Morgen*," the man said. "*Mein—*"

"English, please, Tyndareus." Maya gestured to Dixon. "I don't believe Herr Dixon speaks German."

Dixon held out one of his hands and teetered it side to side. "It's been a while, but I can get by."

"Very good, Herr Dixon," Tyndareus said, handing Dixon a mug of steaming dark liquid.

"Perfect," the security director replied, blowing on the coffee before taking a sip. "Just what the doctor ordered."

Looking at Maya, Tyndareus said, "For whom are the soft drinks?"

Maya jabbed a finger at me. "Those are for Herr . . ."

"Kuhlmann," I said, recalling a German surname I'd used long ago. "Shivurr Kuhlmann."

"Of course," Tyndareus replied, putting an ice-filled glass and two bottles—one with a white label, the other black—down on the table before me. "Will you gentlemen be staying with us here at the hotel?"

"That remains to be seen," Maya said before either Dixon or I could reply. "It is likely, but we will let you know."

With a nod, Tyndareus finished emptying the tray and left us, wishing us a good meal.

As Maya and Dixon dug into their meals, I took a bottle of the strange soda pop in each hand. White letters on the black bottle read Nacht Cola. *Night Cola*, I translated, presuming the name came from it being a dark drink. I checked the other label—black letters on a white background—and snorted.

Nicht Cola. "What's 'Not Cola'?"

Maya smiled. "It's a clear soda. Like Sprite or 7-Up."

I studied the bottle. "I've never heard of it."

"It's a new brand." Maya pointed to the black label on the Nacht Cola. "They both are."

"Are they any good?" I asked.

Her shoulders twitched. "I haven't tried them, but they're quite popular. There are signs all over town." She raised a hand and swept it left-to-right. "Nacht Cola. *Für eine gute Nacht in der Stadt.*"

Dixon snickered. "Night Cola. For a good night in the city, right?"

"Yes," Maya said. "Loaded with caffeine, no doubt."

"I'll be the judge of that." I lifted my mask and took a gulp of each. Nacht Cola had a slight cherry taste and reminded me of other dark colas I'd drunk in the past. Nicht Cola, as expected, was colourless and sweet with a hint of lemon-lime flavour to it. Smacking my lips, I poured the Nacht Cola into my glass. While I preferred Ambrola and the soft drink brands I'd grown used to at the Institute, these weren't half bad. Yet there was some peculiar flavour in the mix I couldn't quite place.

"So, what's the plan?" Dixon asked when most of the food and drink was gone.

"I've arranged for a car," Maya replied. "It'll take us to the latest attack site, and we'll look around."

He looked thoughtful. "I should make some calls first and reach out to my contacts."

"That's a good idea," Maya said. "We'll drop you off at my apartment on the way, and you can make your calls from there. As it happens, I'd planned to drop you there first anyway."

Dixon smirked. "We're in Berlin only a few hours, and you're already trying to take me home. I'm a bit old for you, aren't I?"

Maya's face reddened. "I'm older than I look, but don't get your hopes up." She wagged a finger at him. "I've heard about you, Mr. Dixon."

"I told you, my friends call me Dixon," he said, taking a bite of his jam-smeared toast. "No mister required."

"Much of it not good," she said. "What you did to dear Shivurr, for one. Simply put, I've been told not to reveal any more of our operations here than necessary."

Dixon stopped chewing. "You don't trust me?" he asked around a mouthful of food. Chewing a few more times, he swallowed and wiped his mouth. "Why not? I already gave Winterboy my word I'd help and that I'd keep your secrets."

She tossed her shoulders. "I'm sure I don't need to tell a former CIA agent the importance of a need-to-know approach to information sharing."

His jaw muscles bunched. "Then why risk bringing me here? Isn't this hotel a secret too?"

"There wasn't much choice," she said. "While we could have rendered you unconscious for the trip, doing so would hardly motivate you to help our cause."

"Why would that matter?" Dixon asked. "Given how powerful your alien friends are, why not try to force me to help anyway?"

"The gods of New Olympus do not operate that way," she said. "Not anymore."

Which is why they're at odds with the Eurus, I thought. "Is your apartment close?" I asked, trying to change the subject.

She nodded. "In Charlottenburg."

I made a face. "We've got to leave Berlin?"

Her chin wagged. "Charlottenburg is one of the city's districts." She swirled a finger by one of her shoulders. "We're in Kreuzberg right now."

The concierge, Tyndareus, appeared in the lobby doorway. "Your car has arrived, Frau Day."

"Wonderful," Maya said, glancing at Dixon and me. "Shall we?"

Dixon smacked my shoulder. "You ready?"

"No time like the present," I said, getting to my feet. *Ugh.* I braced myself against the table and winced.

Maya put a hand on my shoulder. "What's wrong?"

"Nothing." I took a deep breath and straightened my shoulders. "I'm all right. I guess this altered shape is getting to me."

"Do you need to rest?" she asked, taking Caelus on an arm. "Perhaps reverting to normal for a while will help."

"Nah, I'm okay," I replied as the feeling diminished. "Anyway, I've got to get used to it, right?"

"Very well," she said, looking uncertain. "This way."

The lobby floor shone with morning's early light as we left the dining room, and I squinted. With a wave to the woman behind the front desk, Maya strode across the marble, pushed open glass double doors and led us out to the street.

Outside, a black sedan with tinted windows waited at the curb, and the four of us piled into the spacious back seat. Making quick introductions, Maya gave the dark-haired, olive-skinned driver, Antiphates, our destination in German, and the car took off, merging into the light flow of early-morning traffic with ease.

We drove down austere streets lined with apartment blocks and trees. Still feeling a bit off, I lowered my window a crack, letting in warm morning air, which reeked of soot and railway ties, and wrinkled my nose. "What's that stench?"

"Trabants," Dixon said. "Terrible things. Eco-crimes on wheels."

"Aren't those from East Berlin?" I asked, struggling to recall the TV show or movie where I'd once seen them.

"Uh-huh." Maya pointed. "However, East Berlin is right over there, and the wall only stops people from crossing."

"Pollution knows no borders," I said with a scowl, watching the blur of graffiti-covered concrete racing by. *So, that's the Berlin Wall.* "Damn, it's ugly. Why did they build it?"

Dixon sneered. "To stop their citizens from leaving."

I rolled my eyes. "I know that, but why do they want to leave? How bad could it be over there?"

"Why do you think?" he snarled. "People want to be free."

"In part." Maya waggled her head. "Though it was more than that at the time."

"How so?" I asked.

She spread her hands. "After World War Two, poverty was rampant in East Germany."

"Thank the Reds for that," Dixon said, interrupting her.

She inclined her head. "And the Nazis before that."

Both influenced by the Eurus, I thought.

She looked out the window. "Naturally, many people chose to leave, seeking better lives in the West. Eventually, when East Germany had already lost many of their best and brightest, the government moved to prevent further emigration. In 1961, they began constructing that monstrosity."

"It was just barbwire at first," Dixon said, "but they kept adding to it, and the entire stretch of it is a kill box these days."

"Brutal," I said, regarding the drab beige buildings, fifteen or more floors high, looming beyond the curtain. For twenty-two years now, West Berlin had been entirely walled off. A prison, like I'd seen in movies, with guards patrolling its borders, ready to murder any who dared to cross its edges without permission. *An entire nation of prisoners*. The driver turned down a side street, and the wall retreated. "You think they'll ever take it down?"

"Fat chance," Dixon said. "That thing's here to stay."

After another fifteen minutes navigating a warren of streets, we left Dixon at Maya's place and drove on to the New Olympian safe house that had been the site of the most recent Underfrost-related attack. The driver dropped us off in front of a five-storey apartment building, which stood jammed against its neighbours with no space between. Cars of numerous varieties lined both sides of the narrow street, parked beneath the shade of Linden trees, forcing the driver to double-park while we exited.

"Caelus," Maya said, lifting her bird-laden forearm high, "please keep watch for trouble."

"As you wish," he said, taking flight and vanishing into the canopy of overhanging trees.

"Hmm." Turning, I leaned back and looked up the side of the building. "It looks pretty normal to me."

Except for that, I thought, spotting a pile of snow resting against the building's foundation. About to mention it to Maya, I held off, figuring she probably already knew about it.

"That's no surprise," Maya said, drawing my gaze. "Nothing happened out here." With a look up and down the sidewalk, she stepped toward the building's glass doors. "Come on. I'll show you." Producing a key ring from her purse, she unlocked the door and let us into the building. "The room where the main attack occurred is a bit of a mess."

"Do the New Olympians own this building too?" I asked, keeping my voice low as she ushered me into a small elevator. "It's not a hotel, is it?"

"No." She leaned toward the elevator's control panel, fumbling a key into a slot above the buttons, and the lift rose. "It's just an apartment building." As the elevator creaked and groaned, she continued, "We're headed to the top floor. We rent out other floors to the general public to keep things looking normal."

My eyelids fluttered. "Don't the neighbours wonder about different people coming and going?"

"There's less turnover here than the hotel," she replied. "And those stationed here portray themselves as extroverts with frequent guests."

"And that works?" I asked.

"So far," she said. "If anyone suspects anything, at worst they might think it an MI6 or CIA safe house of some kind. Certainly, they would never suspect gods to be behind it."

Unless the Eurus were the ones doing the looking, I thought.

Exiting the elevator, we strode down a carpeted hallway, stopping at a numbered door. Maya pressed her ear to the wood for a moment, fiddled with her key ring, and reached for the lock.

"I hope I can help," I said with a sigh, feeling suddenly doubtful.

"Well," she said, turning the key in the lock, "I'll be surprised if you can't."

My chin dipped. "Why?"

She swung the door inward. "Take a look."

I stuck my head inside, feeling frosty air on my face. At the sight of the interior, my eyes darted to the ceiling and my mouth gaped beneath my mask. "What the hell?"

"Yeah," she said, "it's been doing that since the incident."

Chapter 12

Sid Frigid

Snow descended slowly from the ceiling, and a thick layer of it covered the broken and scattered furniture littering the floor. Off to the side, a blond man with a trim beard shovelled snow toward the far end of the room, where just beyond him, through an open doorway, steam rose from a porcelain tub. I blinked several times. Cleo had mentioned snowfall, but I hadn't expected it to still be falling.

Maya's head crowded in next to mine. "It won't warm up, either, not even with the windows open."

The man with the shovel turned at her words. "Good morning, Frau Day."

"Good morning, Heinrich." She mimed shovelling. "You can keep at it. Don't mind us."

Nodding, he turned back to his work.

Maya nudged my back, urging me inside. "We're melting the snow to keep the room from filling up with it."

"Would it do that?" I asked.

"We're not sure," she said. "Either way, we didn't want to take the risk or have it melt and damage the floor or apartments below."

"Oh, yeah." Looking around, I pointed to a camera high on a wall. "Was that on during the attack?"

"It was indeed. Come on, I'll show you." She led me to a desk on the far side of the living room and lifted the corner of a tarp laid over it. "Give me a hand with this."

"Sure." I came closer, kicking something with my shoe. Stooping, I pulled a bottle from the snow and upended the empty container before reading its label. "Nacht Cola."

"Ah, yes," she said. "Our friend Heinrich likes his soda pop."

"He's a man of taste." I dropped the bottle into a nearby trash can and grabbed the edge of the tarp. "Ready?"

"If you are," she replied with a smile.

Carefully, Maya and I hoisted the sheet. Spilling the accumulated snow onto the floor, we cast the tarp aside and turned back to an array of still-lit TV screens. I scanned their black-and-white displays, noting they covered the building's entrances, hallways, and the interior of the elevator by which we'd ascended.

"Quite the setup," I said.

"We like to keep an eye on things," she replied. "This being a safe house. Which is a good thing or we'd not have captured footage of the attack." She tapped her fingers in the air, and the video on one of the screens changed and began to play at high speed. "Almost there."

"How are you doing that?" I waggled my fingers. "Invisible keyboard?"

"Cognitive display." Tapping her temple, she gestured at the air in front of herself. "It exists only in my mind, but I can interact with it as if it were real. The divine prefer such things to physical mechanisms. It eliminates the possibility of their technology being compromised by mortals. At least mortals without authorization."

"Cool." It sounded different than how Hue, the Allfrost Controller, used telepathic means to know my wishes without the need for words. Maya's actions reminded me more of Scott's when he had—at my request—locked me into a containment field a few nights past. He too had seemed to be interacting with some unseen, intangible device. I still couldn't remember ever using such a thing myself, but I figured chances were good I'd remember having done so, eventually.

At last, Maya tapped the glass of the TV screen she'd been studying. "This is where it gets interesting."

The footage showed four people crowding into the elevator. They were an odd bunch. The tallest wore ripped jeans and a sleeveless T-shirt. A punk rocker, judging by his shaved head, piercings, and the hair gelled into a fan of spikes atop his scalp. The guy to his right—with his short hair, slacks, button-up dress shirt, and cardigan sweater—looked to be the punk's polar opposite. Yet despite their differences, both men jerked and slouched, apparently ready to fall. As if fearing as much, their other two companions—a woman in a loose blouse and long skirt and a man wearing a striped tracksuit and sneakers—each had a firm grip on the unsteady men's arms.

Are they drunk?

The woman touched a button on the elevator's control panel, and her hand seemed to sparkle.

I leaned closer. "What was that?"

"Electricity," Maya replied.

My eyes widened. "Is she a god?"

"Demigod." The playback stopped abruptly. "The woman and the man in the tracksuit are our people."

I tapped the centre of the screen. "And the drunks?"

"We're not sure," she began, "but they're more than drunk."

"How so?"

Maya motioned to another screen. "Take a look here."

The screen's display changed slightly, showing the interior of the apartment in which we now stood, snow-free and undisturbed, and a man watching the same TVs Maya and I now studied.

"That's Heinrich," she said, jabbing a thumb over her shoulder toward the fellow currently shovelling snow into the bathtub.

I leaned my elbows on the desk and examined the display. Standing, on-screen Heinrich strode over to the hallway door and opened it, and the seemingly intoxicated men from the elevator twitched their way into the room, urged inside by the New Olympian agents.

I pointed a finger. "Can you freeze it there?"

"Of course." The display stopped moving with a flick of her hand. "How's that?"

"Back it up a few seconds." Leaning in, I studied the screen. "Now step it forward, slowly. Frame by frame, if you can."

"All right," Maya said. "What do you see?"

"I'm not sure." I gawked as the punk's blank face looked into the camera. "Holy . . ." I pressed my index finger against the TV screen, where tendrils rose above the collar of the guy's Clash T-shirt. "Check out the vines."

Maya blew out a breath. "That's new."

Just like the Nameless. Except those monsters had been engulfed by vegetation, with wriggling masses of it erupting even from their eyes. By contrast, the vines peeking from the punk's collar were easy to miss. *They kind of walk the same, though.*

"I saw something like them on Zarechus," I said, describing the Nameless in detail.

She gave me a sidelong look. "And they called lightning down from the sky?"

"It sure looked like it." I stared into space, revisiting the memory. "I mean, yeah, it was during a thunderstorm, but one of them touched a guy and he went all twitchy and fell. Like he'd stuck his finger into an electrical socket."

Her forehead scrunched. "That is interesting." She gestured to the screen. "Especially given what happens next." The playback resumed. "Watch this."

On screen, the shorter detainee, Cardigan Guy, grasped the demigod woman's neck as if trying to strangle her. She scowled and, gripping the guy's arm with both hands, pivoted on a foot and tossed him over her hip. As he hit the ground, she stepped back, raised her hands, and shot lightning from her fingertips into the guy's body. Apparently unfazed, the downed man climbed to his feet.

I shot Maya a look. "What the heck?"

"I know, right? Now, watch the punk."

Behind the fighting pair, the punk's head snapped to the side, and before the tracksuit-wearing agent could grab him, he twisted away, snarling. Seconds later, ice formed on the walls and floor, and snow burst from thin air. The punk—now covered in a layer of ice—became translucent before vanishing entirely. Looking left and right, the agent swiped at the air where the punk had been, and the indoor snowfall grew stronger, becoming a blizzard of driving snow that blinded the camera entirely.

I stood taller, expelling a breath. "What happened after that?"

"We're unsure," Maya replied. "The apartment was much colder than it is now, and the agents chose to flee. It was that or freeze to death. By the time they'd called for backup and went back in, both captives were gone."

"No surprise," I said, "if they can turn invisible." My eyes flicked to the other TV screen, still paused on the group ascending via the elevator. "Why did they have the men in custody anyway?"

She swept snow from her hair. "They were being snatched by men in suits—East Germans, we think, judging by the style of their clothing and hair—and our people managed to foil the attempt. With all the other mysterious abductions occurring lately, they brought the men here for their own safety and to question them. Given what happened, they were right to do so."

"What are they, do you think?" I had thought them some form of Nameless, but the punk's use of the Underfrost had raised doubts in my mind.

She exhaled sharply. "A god wearing an avatar, I'd have said, except . . . I've never seen any humanoid avatars with vines growing out of them. I think your Nameless are more likely."

"Yeah," I said, "they move a bit like them too, but nowhere near as twitchy." I looked around. "Even so, what would they be doing here on Earth? Zarechus is a long way off. Yet if they're not the Nameless, what else could they be?"

She shrugged. "A new type of avatar, perhaps." She caught gently falling snow on the palm of her hand. "Yet they also appear to have command of the Underfrost. That's not a typical ability for the gods."

"Right," I said, remembering what Cleo and Hanale had told me. Of the divine, few but Boreas, who was away on Zarechus, had cryogenic abilities. Recalling the punk's vicious expression before he'd vanished reminded me of a famous punk rock musician I'd once seen on the news. "So how does this Sid Frigid dude have the abilities of one of my people?"

"I wish I knew," Maya replied.

"Me too." I pointed at the TVs. "Can you show them entering the apartment again, slowly?"

"Absolutely," she said, waving a hand.

The footage reversed quickly before creeping forward, and I scrutinized Sid Frigid, looking for any clue to explain the mystery of his existence. Just before Sid shrieked, his lips moved, as if he were speaking.

I jabbed a finger at his mouth. "What's he saying?"

"I don't know," she replied.

"The Allfrost is all," said a voice from behind us, drawing my attention to Heinrich, who stood by the bathroom door, leaning on his shovel.

"Preserve the Allfrost," I said, the remainder of the motto springing automatically to mind.

Heinrich's eyes widened. "That is correct."

"You know it?" Maya asked.

"It's one of our mottoes," I said, glancing her way. "Allfrost Sentinels, I mean. We'd use it as a greeting and farewell among ourselves. With differing rejoinders. Hail the Allfrost. Defend the Allfrost. That sort of thing."

"Hmm." She bit her lip. "He's acting a lot like a Sentinel, but he can't be. I mean, he looks human except for the vines." Her jaw dropped. "Unless it's an avatar, occupied by a Borealan."

"No chance," I said, remembering Leonidas's words in the Miraculeum. "There's no avatar capable of containing someone like me."

"Perhaps the Eurus have figured out a way," Maya replied. "Anything is possible."

"Maybe." I turned away from the screens and examined the apartment. "I wonder what set Sid off."

"What do you mean?" she asked.

I shrugged. "I don't know. He was just standing around." I pointed at the windows. "Then he looked over . . ." I trailed off, looked into the Underfrost and gasped.

An Allfrost node—invisible and intangible in the warm world—sat over by the window with its far side extending a foot beyond the building's outer wall.

And it's activated, I thought, noting the glowing runes upon its dais and the control orb hovering above. *That explains the snowfall.* I smirked, recalling the trouble I'd had finding an All-frost node in Death Valley after battling monsters at Dublin Gulch. *I should have just looked in the Underfrost.* Amnesic and overheated and worn out from battle, I'd simply not thought to do so. Then again, in the desert—which had still been warm despite night having fallen—that long-inactive node would have been harder to see than this active one. *Even if I had thought to look for it that way.*

Maya touched my arm. "What is it?"

"An Allfrost node." I reached out and willed it closer. Shuddering, it slid over the floor, pushing through the room's furniture with only a moment's hesitation. The vials of myself I'd been consuming were making interacting with the Allfrost second nature again, which gave me an idea. "Give me a second."

Rather than bring it over into the physical world—there not being a large enough unobstructed space—I vanished into the Underfrost and boarded the Allfrost node's glowing symbol-covered dais. Unlike the node I'd brought back to life in Death Valley, this already-active node required no special steps or crystals to restore it.

I touched a hand to the ball of roiling frost, which hovered at hip level above the platform, and visualized my desire; a moment later, the snow stopped falling. Stepping off the dais's edge, I bent over and gave it a push—using both my mind and body. It sailed through the apartment's outer wall like a curling rock, maintained its horizontal position for a moment, and began to slowly sink.

Cool. I smacked my hands together and resurfaced back to the normal world. "That ought to do it."

"You stopped the snow," Maya said with a smile. "Well done."

"Thank you." Heinrich flexed his fingers. "The snow had almost beaten me."

"You're welcome," I said. "It should start to warm up in here now too." *Unfortunately.*

"Then I had better call for assistance," Heinrich said, slipping past Maya and me. "Before the melting accelerates."

"Oh, right," I said, wincing. "I didn't think of that. Do you want me to change it back?"

"No." Maya held up her hands. "Don't do that. Now that the snow has stopped, I'm sure Heinrich and a few others can clear this up quickly enough."

"Okay, sure." I drew on the Underfrost, generating a chill. "Then I'll keep it cold in here until we leave."

"Thanks." Maya rubbed her arms. "What would an Allfrost node be doing all the way up here?"

"They're all over," I replied. "Though normally at ground level. Beats me how that one ended up here." I thought a moment. "Maybe during this building's construction."

Heinrich hung up the phone. "Help is on the way." Sighing, he grabbed his shovel and began working again.

"Do you have an extra shovel?" I glanced at Maya. "We can spare a few minutes, right?"

She nodded. "As you wish."

As it happened, Heinrich did have another scoop, and Maya and I took turns helping him load the tub—where the snow melted rapidly, for some reason—until the telephone rang.

"I'll get it." Maya passed me the shovel, ran over to the desk, and snatched up the telephone receiver. After a brief conversation in German, she hung up the phone and looked at me. "We've got to go."

"What's up?" I asked.

"That was Tyndareus," she said. "There was an incident at the hotel."

"What sort of incident?"

"I'll tell you in the car." She waved to Heinrich. "Sorry, Heinrich. Help should not be far off now."

Chapter 13

Stranger Danger

My shoulder pressed against Maya's as the driver steered the black sedan through the streets. Traffic had increased since our arrival at the snowed-in apartment, and the going was slow.

"What happened?" I asked.

"Our agents were attacked," she replied.

My eyes lit. "By whom? The Eurus?"

She fired a glance my way. "Maybe. They were parking by the hotel. Men jumped them. That's all I know."

"Are they okay?"

"We'll soon find out."

"Wait." A chill washed through me. "We forgot Caelus."

"No, we didn't." Maya tapped the bracelet Leonidas had given her. "He's gone ahead to scout."

"Oh, right." I slumped back in my seat. In the excitement, I'd forgotten the link Maya shared with the raven. "Good."

We turned onto a broad street, joining a long line of cars edging their way forward. Across a grassy and treed centre median, traffic moving the opposite direction also seemed to crawl. As I watched pedestrians stride wide sidewalks, past shops, department stores, and restaurants, an idea came to mind, and I shifted my attention to the Underfrost, looking for Allfrost nodes like the one I'd found in the safe house apartment. None were in sight, but the desire to find them activated something in my mind. Abruptly, I knew there were nodes out there among the buildings. Not only that they existed, but their distance and direction. Some sat close, but most were far off, and they were distributed haphazardly.

"Holy crap," I said, looking at Maya. "I can sense Allfrost nodes." I waved a hand at my window. "All around us."

"That's amazing," Maya replied after I'd described the sensation as best I could. "It sounds similar to how animals sense Earth's magnetic field."

"I suppose," I said. "If Earth had thousands of poles." Sitting back, I closed my eyes and concentrated specifically on the nearest node to me, and details on its activation state and overall health manifested in my mind. "This is awesome. There must be an Allfrost chamber around here." Switching to a more macroscopic view, I tried to gauge their overall number and distribution. After ten minutes of visualization, I frowned and threw up my hands. "I don't get it."

"Something wrong?" Maya asked.

"Yeah," I said. "There should be more nodes. If there's a chamber here, I mean."

She looked thoughtful. "The entire city was heavily bombed in World War Two. Could that have affected them?"

"I . . . don't know." I wagged a finger at her. "That's a good thought. Things in the Underfrost are largely immune to what goes on in the regular world, but, yeah, explosions with all their heat—"

"Here's the hotel," Maya said, cutting me off. "Let us out in front, Antiphates."

"Of course," the driver replied, pulling into the space in front of the hotel reserved for loading and unloading passengers. "I will wait here for you."

Hopping out, Maya and I made our way into the lobby, where the impeccably besuited and proper Tyndareus awaited us. "*Guten Tag*, Frau Day." He looked my way. "Herr Kuhlmann."

"*Guten Tag*," Maya replied, scanning the lobby. "Where are the men, Tyndareus? Are they okay?"

He nodded. "They are uninjured."

"What happened?" I asked.

"Please, have a seat." He motioned toward sofas set around a low-slung coffee table. As we took our seats, he continued,

"They were returning with another catatonic person when they were set upon by men with guns, who demanded they relinquish the detainee. More East Germans, they believe, based on their clothing and manner."

"East Germans?" I glanced at Maya. "Just like the men who tried to grab Sid Frigid and the other guy."

Tyndareus's eyes narrowed. "Who is Sid Frigid?"

"That's kind of a long story," I said, standing. "May I speak to them?"

Tyndareus cleared his throat. "I am afraid that will not be possible at present, Herr Kuhlmann. The men have returned to the field. In search of their attackers, I believe, or perhaps they are hoping to find more of the befuddled."

"Ah, hell." I glanced at Maya. "I wanted to ask if they'd seen any signs of the Underfrost being used."

Despite Sid's similarities to the other catatonics, as far as I knew, the punk was the only one to have manifested frost abilities, and I wanted to know if there were more out there like him. I wasn't sure what it would tell me, but unique or not, Sid's ability to manipulate the Underfrost and access Allfrost nodes like a Sentinel couldn't be a coincidence. Not when the Eurus were looking for me, the last Sentinel known to exist.

Maya placed a hand on my forearm. "Are you okay, Shivurr?"

"We've got to find Sid Frigid," I said, explaining my reasoning.

"I agree," Maya replied. "How do you suggest we go about doing so?"

"Hmm . . ." I murmured, thinking. "Maybe the Allfrost can help." I pointed a finger toward the ceiling. "Is there a way to see a room on the top floor? I'd like to get a look at the city."

"Of course." Tyndareus stood. "I will fetch you a key. One moment."

A short time later, I ascended to the hotel's top floor, leaving Maya behind to further question Tyndareus and other hotel staff about recent events. Wandering the hallway, checking door numbers, I found the room matching the key in my hand, let myself in, and strode over to the windows. Spreading the drapes wide, I looked out upon the white, red, and grey buildings of West Berlin. Most were similar in height to the six-storey hotel in which I now stood, but the odd tower rose twice as high. Broadleaf trees and grassy boulevards filled the gaps between edifices and, unlike those I'd seen beyond the Berlin Wall, the facades of these structures were soot-free and more varied in design. Before I could take it all in, a raven alighted on the wide ledge beyond the glass, dropping from above with a fluttering of wings, and came toward me.

I opened the window, letting in a blast of warm air, car horns, and the rumblings of vehicles. "Hey, what's up?"

"Good day, Sentinel," Caelus replied. "Ms. Day suggested I join you. May I be of service?"

"I don't think so." I leaned my elbows on the windowsill and held my chin in my palms. "I'm trying to find Allfrost nodes, but you won't be able to see them."

The bird's head tilted. "For what reason?"

"To find their Allfrost chamber." I'd done it before. Routinely. The nodes I'd sensed on the drive over had stirred memories that told me that much, even if the specifics of how were still lost. "It should be wherever they're most concentrated, I think."

He raked his beak through the feathers of one of his wings and regarded me. "Why do you seek it?"

"I need to find someone," I said.

"Ah, yes," Caelus replied. "The one you call Sid. Ms. Day has shared her knowledge of this creature with me, requesting I keep watch for him. How does finding an Allfrost chamber assist with the search?"

I shrugged. "I don't know. I think maybe he's trying to get to it, based on how he reacted to the Allfrost node at the apartment. And the thing he said." *The Allfrost is all. Preserve the Allfrost.* "It's like he thinks he's an Allfrost Sentinel. If that's true, he might be trying find the chamber."

"Perhaps," the bird said, "but he might simply be attracted to the nodes themselves, would you not agree?"

"Sure," I said, "but either way, the chamber's the best place to start. The nodes should be most concentrated around it, and if the chamber is still operational, I may be able to use its Oculi to search for him."

"That is a fine idea, Sentinel." Turning about, he stepped to the side and looked out over the city. "Proceed."

"I'm glad you approve," I said, returning my gaze to the skyline to look for nodes. "Shoot. The buildings are in the way." Unfortunately, being able to see into the Underfrost didn't allow me to see through intervening obstacles. "I need a bird's-eye view."

Caelus extended his wings. "Alas, this avatar is incapable of carrying a load such as you."

I snorted. "No kidding."

"What about a helicopter?" He thrust his chin toward an airplane climbing above the treeline some miles away. "Chances are good Ms. Day or the one called Dixon can arrange one to fly you over the city."

"No, that's okay." I focused on the Underfrost and studied the skyline, discerning faint halos of light, varying in intensity, above distant trees and buildings. Cocking an eye, I accessed my ability to detect the health, direction, and distance of Allfrost nodes, and as I overlaid what it told me with what I could see, a three-dimensional model of their layout formed in my mind. "I think I can work around it."

"Excellent, Sentinel."

Beyond their unusually low numbers, the nodes within range of my senses were scattered inefficiently, and many were either dormant or inoperable.

"Maya was right," I said. "Bombings must have damaged this area's nodes."

"Unsurprising," Caelus replied. "The entire city was effectively levelled by such aerial attacks only forty years ago."

I thumped my fist against the windowsill. "Even hidden in the Underfrost, nodes would have been scattered by all that." I shook my head. "The Allfrost chamber was probably destroyed." Even if it was still around, finding the chamber with the nodes in their chaotic distribution was going to be a long shot. "Oh well. We'll just have to drive from node to node and hope we stumble across Sid or the chamber. Maybe we'll get lucky."

A knock drew my gaze to the door. "Who's that?"

"That is Ms. Day," Caelus said, spreading his wings. "And my cue to take my leave. Fare thee well, Sentinel."

"It's me, Shivurr," Maya called as the raven took flight, her voice muffled by the hotel room door. "Open up."

"Hey." Crossing the room, I pulled the door wide. "What's up?"

Her lip curled. "Dixon's gone. I sent Antiphates to pick him up at my apartment, but he wasn't there. There was only a note to say he's chasing down a lead."

I sighed. "I'm not surprised." Stepping into the hallway, I closed the door behind myself. "He's not someone who would sit around waiting for long." I snorted. "Now that I think about it, I bet he wanted to be left at your place so he could operate more freely."

Maya bit her lip. "You don't suppose he's going to tell the Group what he knows, do you?"

I thought a moment. "No. He promised he wouldn't."

"And you think his word is good?"

I shrugged. "Telling the Group now only increases the chance of nuclear war. At least without more information. He knows that."

"I hope you're right," she replied. "Shall we go looking for him?"

"Nah," I said. "He knows where to find us. He'll show up or call when he's done doing whatever he's doing. Hopefully with more intel on the abductions."

"Speaking of intel." Maya pulled a thick folder from beneath her arm. "I've been reviewing profiles on the missing, trying to find a pattern to the abductions."

I shot her a look. "And?"

She whacked the folder with her free hand. "As best I can tell, they're random people, and none are East German defectors, as we had at first theorized." She made a face. "They skew a bit young, but that's about it."

I thought of Wilhelm's avatar wandering Aceso's domus. "Could they be . . . I don't know . . . dispossessed avatars?"

"No way," she said. "Not after seeing these files. The abducted are normal citizens, with families and friends. Avatars have no history beyond those established by the gods who possess them. Not to mention the gods prefer avatars of the finest physical condition. Most wouldn't be caught dead in an avatar with a potbelly or balding head."

"True," I said. While it wasn't unheard of for one to choose a less-than-perfect form, it was the exception, not the rule. "And they don't normally have vegetation growing out of them either." Crossing my arms, I stroked my chin between thumb and forefinger. "Are the kidnappers doing that to these people, do you think? Changing them into these catatonic . . . changelings, I mean?"

She grumbled. "It would make sense, except they're abducting people who are already affected. And what would they have to gain by changing people into these things? What would anyone?"

"Good question." I pictured Sid Frigid and Cardigan Guy on the Charlottenburg apartment's CCTV footage, and my jaw dropped. "Maybe to turn them into avatars."

The thought was disturbing, and I felt sure my New Olympian friends like Wilhelm, Olivia, and Hanale would never do such a thing. That was a given, yet would even the Eurus be willing to take over real sentient people, subsuming their wills? *Yeah, they would.* Thinking of what I knew of the Soviet Union within which the Eurus operated, it seemed all too plausible. Its authoritarian regime had already suppressed, if not completely eliminated, individual freedom, imprisoning and disappearing those who challenged the status quo. Taking over people's bodies seemed the logical next step.

"I don't think that's possible," she replied. "At least, it's not supposed to be."

I glanced her way. "Like Sid Frigid channelling the Underfrost isn't?"

Maya grimaced. "Even so, it would make no sense."

"Why?"

She threw up her hands. "The gods have no need to take mortals for avatars. Not when they can make their own."

"Sure." I wagged a finger. "The New Olympians can. They've got the Miraculeum, but what about the Eurus?"

"They can as well," Maya replied. "They possess the same knowledge and technologies—their own Miraculea."

"Oh yeah." A swell of memories told me it was true, and I hung my head. Miraculeum referred to the type of building. The one on Caelumtor might be rare, but it wasn't unique. "In that case, I don't know. Maybe they're changing people into monsters to cause trouble in West Berlin." I thumped the door frame. "We need more information. We've got to find Sid. He's our best chance to learn more."

"Agreed," she said, "but how do you propose we do that?"

"By visiting Allfrost nodes," I said, explaining my reasoning. "It may take a while, but it's worth a shot."

"Very well," Maya said, sounding unsure. "Let's do it."

For the next few hours, with Caelus providing air support and guided by my inner sense, we drove the streets of West Berlin, searching for Allfrost nodes. Daytime traffic was heavy and the going slow, though, and by noon, we had managed to visit only a half dozen locations and found no signs of the Allfrost chamber or the changeling, Sid Frigid.

How hard can finding a frost-wielding changeling with a Mohawk be? I wondered, feeling increasingly frustrated. It should have been easy. Then again, according to Cleo and Hanale, there were divine in the city, on both sides of the wall. Gods with seemingly supernatural powers who lived here, and presumably the world over, with mortals entirely unaware of their presence. It seemed incredible. Had there never been a single exhibition of the gods' powers or technology that would have drawn the attention of the media? No epic battles? Especially given the divine's ongoing factional conflicts. There must have been . . . so why didn't everyone know or at least suspect they existed?

A memory locked into place, answering the question for me. When something that would reveal their existence occurred, the gods and governments covered it up, of course. Like they were trying to do with the abductions now. It probably wasn't all that hard to do either in a modern world, which had come to dismiss the ancient gods of Greece, Rome, and other cultures as mere myths. Only extensive photographs, video, and eyewitness testimony would be likely to convince the majority of the world otherwise. Extraordinary claims required extraordinary proof. Without that, those claiming to have witnessed seemingly supernatural events were easily dismissed as quacks, nutcases, and conspiracy theorists. And to aid the process, the gods could always employ a little telepathic suggestion to adjust people's recollections when necessary.

I snickered to myself. *These are not the gods you're looking for.*

Maya nudged my arm. "I need a break. How about we grab some lunch back at the hotel?"

I frowned a moment before expelling a breath. "Okay." I extended my awareness of Allfrost nodes in the direction of the hotel. "We can check out a couple more nodes on the drive back. They're on the way . . . more or less."

Twenty minutes later, buildings became familiar again, and as we neared the hotel, a surge of cryogenic energy flared in the distance.

"Stop the car." Turning in my seat, I peered at the wall of a nearby building, my attention focused on the Underfrost, and confirmed the source to be an Allfrost node, perhaps a bit more than a mile away.

"What is it?" Maya asked.

"Sid, I think." I pointed in the node's direction. "That way."

Under my direction, Antiphates executed a four-point turn and took us toward the still-surging Allfrost node.

"I'm sending Caelus ahead," Maya said after I had told her what I'd just experienced. "If it's Sid, he can track him. As long as he doesn't vanish again."

Several turns later, my seat belt pressed hard against my body, and the car pulled over to the side of the street.

"What's going on?" I asked, tapping the driver's shoulder. "Why have you stopped?"

Antiphates glanced over his shoulder at me and pointed at the windshield. "Checkpoint Charlie."

Chapter 14

Border Control

A few hundred feet ahead, uniformed men stood next to a small building in the middle of the street, and nearby, a white sign with black lettering declared in four different languages, "You are leaving the American sector." Which meant that the Allfrost node I'd felt surge—and presumably Sid Frigid himself—was located across the border, on the other side of the Berlin Wall's death strip.

"Ah, hell." Thumping the passenger seat headrest, I slumped back in my seat and watched a car drive up to the checkpoint. "Can we cross anyway?"

"Not without a visa," Maya replied, "and those take a few days to get. Besides, you don't want East German border guards getting a good look at you, do you? They would want to see beneath the mask."

"Crap." For a moment, I considered making a run for it, crossing the no-man's land between West and East, but I quickly decided against it. I'd be an easy target for the guard towers, and if I attacked them first or even in retaliation, I'd create headlines and possibly an international incident. *Letting the Eurus know where to find me.* And even if I did make it to the far side, the Stasi would pursue me, and I'd have a hard time losing them in daylight. Ducking into the Underfrost was an option, but chances were good I'd have to stay there longer than I dared. *Unless I want to stay there permanently.*

"How about Caelus?" I might not be able to cross over without incident, but the bird sure could. "Can he confirm it's Sid, at least?"

Maya nodded. "He's almost there."

While Caelus went for Sid, the driver, Antiphates, turned the car around and found a parking spot on the other side of the street.

A few minutes later, Maya spoke. "Caelus says there's no sign of Sid, but there's snow on the ground."

"Is it still snowing?" I asked. *That'll give the Stasi something to think about.*

After a moment, she shook her head. "He says it had already stopped when he got there. There's a layer on the ground, but it's melting fast."

"Huh," I said. "Sid's getting better with the nodes."

Her eyes lit. "You think?"

"Yeah, I do." I sighed. "You might as well call Caelus back." I sat back in my seat, deflated. "Let's get lunch."

"Don't worry, Shivurr." Maya rubbed my shoulder. "We're not beaten yet. You can take us back to the hotel, Antiphates."

Turning my gaze to the window, I sat upright, catching sight of a familiar face among the throng of pedestrians. *Well, look at that.*

"Wait." I jabbed a finger. "There's Dixon."

The security director turned as we pulled up next to him, and his expression showed no hint of surprise at our arrival.

Lowering my window, I winced as a blast of warm air hit me in the face, harsh even through my mask. "Get in front."

With a glance left and right, he hopped in beside the driver and slammed the door. "How did you find me?" He looked at us over the seat backs. "The bird?"

"Just lucky," I said, filling him in on our pursuit of Sid Frigid. "What are you doing here?"

He smirked. "Same as you. Investigating."

"Any luck?" Maya asked.

He nodded and looked at her. "The Company's onto the abductions. They figure it's some kind of Stasi operation, running a catch-and-release program for West German citizens."

By Company, I knew from our past conversations, he meant the CIA. "Why would the Stasi be abducting West Berliners?"

"My guess?" He swirled a finger by his temple. "Brainwashing them with socialist ideas, then releasing them back to the West. As Stasi sleeper agents, they can be called upon to act when needed. In the meantime, they've got another West German voter converted to their cause, acting as an agent of influence, one that can be used to spread misinformation."

"I don't know," Maya said. "Why civilians? Wouldn't it be better to target people working for the government or military installations? The Stasi's done so in the past. Like with the Romeos."

He gave her a flat look. "Only government and defense employees going missing for a few days? Too obvious."

"What are Romeos?" I asked.

"Spies," Maya said. "Stasi agents trained in the art of seduction."

Dixon sneered. "They target lonely West German women—those with access to secrets—and seduce them, hoping to convince them to betray their country. At least they did; I'm not sure if the program is still active or not, now that awareness of it has grown."

I frowned, disturbed by the notion. "And that worked?"

He nodded. "People do crazy things for love."

"They're pretty slick," Maya said. "They research their targets well, learning their likes and dislikes even before initiating contact."

Dixon looked at Maya. "I'm surprised you know so much about them."

She shrugged. "You know who I work for. There is little they do not know."

"Hang on." I waved my hands. "Don't the women realize they're being used when these creeps ask them to pass them secrets?"

"By that time," Maya said, "the poor girl's already fallen for the Romeo. And when he says he'll be jailed or worse if he can't pass his superiors something—"

"They're threatening my family," Dixon said, cutting her off. "Please, you must help me. The information I want is meaningless. How can it possibly do harm?"

She pointed a finger at Dixon. "Precisely. You would have made a good Romeo in your younger days."

"Thanks." Dixon grabbed his chest. "And ouch."

The security director seemed appalled by the Romeos, but I wasn't sure there was anything he'd stop at to protect his own country. He'd expressed regret over my treatment, but he'd still participated in it. Given that, were his past overtures of friendship another form of seduction?

Nah, I thought after a moment. The Bodhi Group was already getting what they wanted from me, no false friendships required. Whatever Dixon had done, he'd been upfront about it. It was in the past, and he was on my side now . . . probably.

I thought of Baduriel, my friend turned enemy. *I guess every relationship is a gamble, though.* The dice may come up snake eyes now and again, but you've got to keep rolling anyway or end up alone. *And what's the point of living like that?*

Dixon's face reddened as our eyes met. "What?"

"Nothing." I shuddered. "I was just thinking about how awful that is. If they'd do that, what's a little brainwashing?"

For a dictatorial regime, programming citizens would make perfect sense. To hell with free will, differing viewpoints, and working towards consensus.

"In a group, dominance is freedom," Baduriel had once said, long ago, before his fall from grace. The memory was foggy, lacking context. "Without it, one must make concessions to the desires of others, and even the most acquiescent have their demands. Usually to be seen as something other than the pathetic wretches they truly are." He smirked. "The short wish to be seen as taller. The ugly to be regarded as beautiful. The stupid to be thought smart."

"It's monstrous," Maya said. "If it's true."

Dixon scowled. "Of course it's true. Some abductees have already been returned, after being gone only a day or two. Most don't have a clue what happened to them." He snorted. "Though a few figure they were abducted by aliens. I suppose those ones have it right."

"Just some?" I asked.

"A lot are still missing," he said. "I figure the brainwashing takes longer for some, or it doesn't work on everyone."

Maya sighed. "It likely doesn't end well for the latter."

Looking her way, I grimaced. "You think they're killing those who can't be brainwashed?"

"Maybe," she said, "or sending them to a Siberian gulag. They certainly can't let them return home and report what happened to them."

"That tracks." Dixon shot me a look. "It's mostly the first to go missing that haven't come back. My guess is those folks are dead, victims of the indoctrination process when the Stasi and Eurus were still figuring things out. Nowadays, they've probably gotten it all refined. Either way, I know firsthand what these Eurus bastards are capable of." He tapped his temple. "How they get in your head. If they're working with the Stasi, this brainwashing theory could be all too real." He looked thoughtful. "That could also explain why the abductions haven't drawn the attention of the general public. They could be simply enthralling people. Making it look like they're going with their kidnappers of their own accord."

"You might be right," I said.

Still, I wasn't sure if the gods' telepathic abilities could truly alter people's personalities and beliefs. My recovered memories told me the divine had certainly influenced people in the past but, as far as I knew, such interventions didn't persist. A god might exert his will upon a mortal for a time, but people tended to revert to themselves and their original modes of thought, eventually. If what Dixon suggested was true, they would have had to find a way to make the brainwashing permanent, or at least a lot longer-lasting than normal, to be worth the trouble.

Dixon thrust his chin toward me. "You don't look convinced. What are you thinking?"

"Just that there may be more to it." Trading looks with Maya, I told Dixon of our theories on the quasi-Nameless changelings we'd seen in the Charlottenburg safe house footage. "The stuff growing inside them could be a way to control people."

Blinking, he bobbed his head. "Maybe. Then again, you've only got the footage of two of them to go by. There's nothing to say all the abductees are like them." He scoffed. "Catatonics stumbling around West Berlin are hardly useful covert agents, and it doesn't explain those who have resurfaced none the worse for wear. Either way, whatever they're doing to these people isn't good."

I glanced over my shoulder at Checkpoint Charlie. "How do you suppose they're getting them across the border? Without anyone noticing, I mean."

Dixon smiled. "Someone's noticed." He held up a hand before I could reply. "I know what you mean, though. The CIA boys wondered the same thing, and they've got a lead on that. There's a building near here where they've observed lots of weird comings and goings. They figure it's being used as an underground railroad."

"Weird how?" I asked.

Leather rustled as he shifted in his seat. "People going in and not coming out for days. Some apparently drunk with blank expressions on their faces, sometimes escorted by sober-looking men in unfashionable suits."

"Huh," I said. "You figure the drunks are the catatonics?"

"Yep," he replied. "Under some sort of influence to make them easier to handle. And those walking in under their own power must be the Stasi agents kidnapping them. My guess is they've dug a tunnel across the border. They picked a great spot, too. Right next to the wall. If I were digging a passageway to the far side, that's the street where I'd do it."

My eyes bulged. "You've been there?"

He nodded. "I just came from there. I wanted to scout the exterior to get the lay of the land."

"Has the CIA sent anyone inside to take a look?" Maya asked.

"Just into the hallway," he replied. "Not the apartments. The case officer doesn't want to risk tipping off the Stasi until they know more."

"Good." Maya looked thoughtful. "If the Eurus are involved, the situation is more than the CIA can handle. And if only the Stasi are behind it, they would just find another way to move their victims across. Maybe use border checkpoints where the East German border guards have been ordered to let them through. If they haven't already been doing so."

Still fixated on the mysterious building, I was only half listening. "If there's a tunnel, Sid might be using it to cross the border." As I uttered the words, it occurred to me he might instead just ghost over to the Underfrost to cross unseen. Yet anyone staying too long in the Underfrost risked being lost in it forever. *Unless it doesn't work that way for him.* "We've got to get in there and check it out."

"That works for me." Dixon held out a piece of paper. "Here's the address."

"That's close," Maya said, giving the paper a cursory glance before handing it to the driver. "Antiphates, please take us to this address."

"Cool." I sat back in my seat, and as the car picked up speed, I pulled lightly on the Underfrost, cooling the interior. Outside, a group of kids with wild hair and a blaring boom box crossed the street in front of us. I grinned, realizing that despite my disguise, in this neighbourhood of punks, new wavers, and other oddly dressed folks, I fit right in. "Nice job, Harland. Finding this place, I mean."

"Thanks," he replied. "Let's hope there's more than just squatters living there."

Chapter 15

Unit Six

A short while and a few turns later, the Berlin Wall drew in close on our right, and we followed its length awhile. Curving at a broad intersection, the twelve-foot-high concrete barrier continued down the middle of a side street, leaving only a sliver of roadway and a wide sidewalk on this side.

"There it is," Dixon said, pointing at a four-storey modern neoclassical building standing at the narrow street's corner. It was an impressive, brooding structure, covered in a layer of grime, with castle-like cornices protruding beyond the roof's edge. "Eighty-seven Sebastian Street. Pull over here. I'd rather our CIA friends don't see us watching the place. It'll only confuse them."

With a nod, Antiphates did as Dixon asked, and we sat studying the building's many doors and windows.

"Do people live there?" I asked.

"Uh-huh," Dixon said. "According to the agency, it's owned by an international conglomerate, and they rent the place out."

"Probably the Eurus," Maya said.

"Could be," he replied. "Anyway, there are several different tenants, so we should be able to enter without being challenged. The main entrance is the tall arch directly opposite the wall. The smaller doors around the perimeter provide direct access to the basement apartments."

I pursed my lips. "You really think there's a tunnel in there?"

"Why not?" He aimed a finger at the windshield. "Apparently, a couple guys dug one just up the street, back in '67. The only difference I can see is those boys dug their tunnel from this side over to the east, trying to help family members escape to freedom. If the Stasi are behind this, it may have been the other way around."

"It may," Maya said, grimacing, "and instead of freedom, this one is being used to lead people to captivity or worse."

He growled. "It led to worse in '67 as well. The tunnellers were betrayed by a family friend and gunned down the moment they reached the far side. One died, and the other was tossed in prison after a show trial."

"That's horrible." I sighed. "We should check out the basement suites first, then. If there's a tunnel, it's got to be in one of them."

Dixon made a face. "The thing is . . . those who have vanished have only been seen using the main entrance. Not one has been observed going into the cellar suites. It makes no sense, but the agency's surveillance suggests they're going up to a second-floor unit. That's its balcony on the far side of the main entrance—probably a nice view of the death strip from there."

I squinted. "There can't be a tunnel from that floor."

"Obviously." He tossed his shoulders. "Who knows, maybe they cut a hole in the floor to gain access to the basement. It would help throw off suspicion."

"Yeah," I said, "or maybe there is no tunnel."

"What do you mean?" Dixon asked.

I stroked my chin. "Maybe they're not taking people to East Berlin. Maybe they're brainwashing or doing whatever they're doing to them right here."

"You might be right," he said. "There's only one way to find out."

"Which suite?" Maya asked.

"Unit Six," Dixon replied. "After entering, it should be the first door up the stairs to the right."

"All right," I said. "We should wait until dark to go in. If things go pear-shaped, I'd like to have the cover of darkness. In case we need to fight . . . or run away."

"In that case," Maya said, "let's head back to the hotel. We can grab that bite to eat and rest until dark. And while we're gone, Caelus will keep watch in case Sid shows up here."

We returned to the hotel and had lunch together, after which Maya secured rooms for us to rest until nightfall. Still adjusted to New Olympus time, my friends were pretty tired. To my surprise, I wasn't feeling too great either, and I was happy at the prospect of a few hours to relax. I'd been keeping my altered shape for hours, and even the sodas I had drunk at lunch weren't quite enough to fend off a budding headache. Probably because I'd mainly consumed Nicht Colas, which, judging from their name, must have lacked caffeine.

Once inside my room, I stripped off my disguise and morphed back to normal. The unused room had warmed in the summer heat, and I drew upon the Underfrost to cool it, and the walls soon filmed with hints of frost.

"Oh yeah. That feels awesome."

I thought about drinking a Nacht Cola or even an Ambrola as a pick-me-up, but with evening still hours away, I decided sleeping to gather my strength was a better idea. Lying back on the bed, I closed my eyes and fell asleep.

A knock on my door woke me sometime later, and I hopped from bed and checked the peephole. Recognizing the distorted image of the hotel's concierge, Tyndareus, I pulled the door inward.

"Hey." I blinked, realizing my headache was gone.

"Good afternoon, Herr Kuhlmann." He held out a shiny ballpoint pen and a folded rectangle of paper. "Here is the pen and map of Berlin you requested."

"Wicked," I said, taking them from him. "You're the best. Thanks."

"You are most welcome." He turned and walked away. "Do let me know if you need anything else."

"Thanks. I will." Closing the door, I looked down at myself, realizing I'd forgotten to restore my disguise before speaking with Tyndareus. *Huh, he didn't even react.*

I walked back to the bed, straightened the comforter, unfolded the map, and spread it out. After studying it a moment,

I marked out the Allfrost nodes I'd visited earlier in the day, based on the street names I could recall. With that done, I marked out the approximate location of the hotel, Maya's apartment, the Charlottenburg apartment where I'd found the first Allfrost node, Checkpoint Charlie, and the mysterious Sebastian Street building. Using those known spots as waypoints, I spent the next while familiarizing myself with the city's layout, working my way outward to its edges, where West Berlin ended and East Germany began.

Now, where's that Checkpoint Charlie node? It had to be Sid Frigid that had activated it, and if he wasn't at the Sebastian Street apartment, that node would be the next logical place to look for him.

Using the checkpoint's position as a starting point, I drew a line north. I stopped when I'd covered the distance I'd sensed the node to be when we had sat parked by Checkpoint Charlie and drew a line around the words Deutscher Dom.

A cathedral? I nodded to myself. *Great.*

If there actually was a tunnel beneath the Sebastian Street building, I intended to use it to get to the other side and look for Sid, and I'd begin my search there, at Deutscher Dom. Satisfied, I grabbed the map, lay back and continued to study it, memorizing street names and nearby landmarks until the telephone rang. Hopping from bed, I crossed the room and picked up the receiver. "Hello?"

"Good evening, Herr Kuhlmann," Tyndareus said. "Frau Day requests you join her and Herr Dixon in the restaurant."

"I'll be right down." I hung up the phone, resumed my altered form, and dressed. Folding up the street map, I tucked it into a coat pocket, pulled my hat over my cowl, and went down for supper. *Time for some sodas.*

I found Dixon, Maya, and Antiphates sitting at a table in the far back of the restaurant, away from prying eyes. Giving the waiter our orders, we sat and laughed and talked for a few more hours about trivial things, requesting more food and drink periodically. Each of us seemed content to push business aside and enjoy the moment of calm. As my restored memories told me, sometimes life was enjoying the small moments between crises.

As dinner wound down and the light beyond the lobby doors dimmed, I looked at Dixon. "Hey, how did you get around town today?"

"The subway," he replied.

"Without cash?" I asked, knowing the security director had arrived on Caelumtor naked.

He shrugged. "The Group spotted me some."

My eyes darted to the bulge I'd noticed beneath his jacket. "What else did they spot you?"

Dixon tugged at his blazer. "Just a little protection."

I gave him a steely look. "Try not to use it, okay? We don't need the police chasing us."

He looked offended. "I'm a professional, Winterboy."

A professional pain in my butt. I looked at Maya. "How's Caelus doing?"

"He's bored," she said. "No one matching Sid's description has come or gone." She stared a moment, the way I'd seen her do when communing with the raven before. "Only two men and one woman have entered so far. Each came on their own, stumbling along as if inebriated. None have yet left."

"Huh." Ducking my head, I raised my form-shaping cowl above my mouth and took a sip of Nacht Cola from my glass, enjoying the sweet cherry taste and soothing coolness before swallowing and smacking my lips. "Maybe they really were drunk."

"A bit early for that," Dixon replied. "Something's going on in there for sure."

"Yeah," I said, swirling an ice cube around my mouth, "but they came alone. They obviously weren't being kidnapped."

He looked thoughtful. "Maybe they're Stasi agents. If not, I don't know what to make of it."

"Well," I said with a sigh, "there's no use speculating, I suppose. We'll just have to get in there and find out what's going on ourselves." I finished off the last of my drink and tapped another ice cube into my mouth. "This Nacht Cola is growing on me. Hey, are there T-shirts for this stuff? I'd like to bring some back for Caleb and the gang."

"I don't see why not," Maya replied. "I'll ask Tyndareus to look into it."

"T-shirts?" Dixon scoffed. "Are we on an op or vacation?"

"Why not both?" After my amnesia, having mementos of things I'd done had grown in its importance to me. If I ever lost my memories again, at least it would provide me clues into who I'd been. "It'd be nice to have a few souvenirs."

Maya checked her watch. "Well, it should be dark enough now." She pushed back from the table and stood. "Shall we?"

Piling back into Antiphates's car, we drove east awhile, wending our way through the streets. The air had cooled somewhat, and the business types and regular folks were mostly gone, replaced by greater numbers of the more wildly dressed. Some sported shaved heads, tattoos, piercings, torn jeans, and khaki army jackets; others looked more like Sid Frigid with flamboyantly styled hair of varying hues, black leather studded with spikes, and combat boots. Eventually, even these passersby dwindled in number as we reached the wall dividing the city and turned left to follow its graffiti-covered length toward the Sebastian Street building.

Looking out the front passenger window, Dixon sneered. "Look at that crap."

"What?" I asked.

"That." He pointed out the window at a wall covered in spray paint. "The graffiti. Reminds me of a truck stop toilet."

"Yeah, it's ugly all right." I studied the messages, scarcely visible in the street light. "I guess it's a form of protest or something."

"Please." He snorted. "Who are they preaching to? The East German Party isn't seeing this shit. Not on this side."

I shrugged. "I suppose, but what do you want to do? Post guards to stop people?"

He smirked. "Nah, but it does make me wonder if a little brainwashing is all bad. We'd want to instill a different set of values than the Stasi, of course."

"You're kidding, right?" I asked, hoping he wasn't serious. I shot Maya a look. "Mr. Freedom wants to brainwash people."

He held up a hand. "Not for regular citizens, of course, but it could be used for criminals. The real incorrigible assholes, at least. It'd free up some room in prisons."

I thought of the creeps I'd encountered in recent weeks. The thugs that had tried to rob my friends at Lunar Crater. The casino security guards that had shaken down Alan and Caleb. *Those guys sure could use an attitude adjustment.* "Yeah, but who decides what's criminal?"

"The same people that do already," he said. "Society, lawmakers, judges."

"It still seems wrong somehow." However they were controlling people, brainwashing or whatever, it wouldn't stop at criminals. Eventually it would widen. For all the right reasons, attempts to end wrongthink would occur before long. *Wouldn't I want to use it too?* To drop the need to disguise myself by forcing people to see me not as a snowman but as a human being? Even if I didn't have the right? "It's too open to abuse. In the end, it'd turn into a horror show."

His shoulders rose. "In the Stasi's hands, sure. Like any tool, it's how and why it's used that matters."

"It seems like more of a weapon to me." I thought about the Eurus's nuclear plans. "One too dangerous to be in anyone's hands."

"To be continued, Winterboy." Dixon nudged Antiphates's arm. "Let me out here."

I glanced at Maya as Dixon climbed out the passenger door. "Where are you going, Harland?"

Closing the door, he thrust his head through its open window. "To keep watch while you and Day go inside."

My brow knit. "You don't want to come in?"

He shook his head. "Someone's got to run interference with the Company's agents. You don't want them coming in after you, do you?" His eyes shifted to Maya. "If you need me, send the bird." He patted the windowsill. "Good luck."

"You too," Maya said. "Take us to the corner, Antiphates."

A short while later, we exited the car and, with the Berlin Wall at our backs, approached the building's entrance.

"Let's check the apartment upstairs first," I said in a low voice, sidestepping a discarded Nacht soda bottle and a loose sheet of newspaper. As Dixon had implied, since everyone had supposedly been using the main entrance, it made sense to go there before checking the basement. Seeing her nod, I led the way to tall doors nested within a towering sand-coloured arch and opened them. *Here goes.*

Chapter 16

Unlawful Entry

The entryway smelled of old lumber and dust, and globes of electric light revealed a short flight of stairs bordered by brass railings, leading to a landing surfaced with black and white tiles. Seeing no one, we made our way quietly down a hallway of well-worn brown carpet to a staircase. Ascending the steps, which creaked beneath our feet, we stopped at a door atop the first landing.

I touched Maya's arm and put my mouth near her ear. "Let's knock. If someone answers, I'll act like I'm catatonic, and you say you found me in the street. Ask to use their telephone to call for an ambulance. Hopefully that'll get us inside."

"Okay," she said, rapping on the wood. "Why not?" After several seconds with no answer, she knocked again, more loudly this time. "Hello?"

I leaned toward the door and listened but heard no sound from within. "I guess no one's home." Gripping the doorknob, I gave it a twist and, to my surprise, it turned. *Nice.* I gave Maya a thumbs-up and pulled the door wide, revealing a dark foyer with several closed doors. Flourishing a hand, I said in a low voice, "Ladies first."

Nodding, Maya pulled a tiny flashlight from her purse, snapped it on, and crept into the apartment with me on her heels. She stopped just inside and held a finger to her lips. "Still quiet," she said after a moment in a soft voice.

"Good." I pulled off my gloves and stuffed them in my pockets. Lighting one of my palms, I danced the beam over the doors to my left. "I'll check these two, if you want to check the others."

"Sure," she whispered, creeping over the old hardwood to the lobby's far end. "Be sure to check the walls and floors for hidden passages."

The first door on the left led to a small bedroom with a carefully made single bed, lit by dim light entering from a window on the far side. After checking the walls and floor, I did the same to the adjacent laundry room before exiting into a second hallway beyond. Glancing out a window to my left onto the building's inner yard, I crossed to another door and, entering a bedroom larger than the first, searched it and its en suite bathroom but found nothing of note.

As I stepped from the main bedroom back into the hallway, footsteps and light came from glass double doors to my left. Before I could move, they swung inward, and Maya shone the beam of her hand torch at my chest.

"There's nothing over here," she said.

"What room is that?"

"Kitchen." She looked back over her shoulder. "There's a living room, dining room, and another bedroom that way." She jabbed her chin at the door from which I'd emerged. "Anything?"

"Nope." I clenched my fingers, dousing the light shining from my palm, and joined her in the kitchen. Glancing around, I put my gloves back on and pointed at the fridge. "Did you check in there?"

She nodded. "It's filled with Nacht Cola. No food, though."

"Cool." Tugging open the fridge door, I saw she was right. "Whoa."

She chuckled. "Someone loves soda pop as much as you do."

"Challenge accepted," I said with a smile. Grabbing a bottle, I looked around. "Do you see an opener?"

"Over there." Maya aimed her flashlight at the counter. "Is this really the time, though?"

"Sure." Snatching up the bottle opener, I popped the cap. "It's nighttime. What better time for a Nacht Cola?"

Her teeth shone. "You should be their mascot, Mr. Shivurr."

"Oh yeah?" I raised the bottle as if for a toast. "Night Cola. For a good night in the city."

"Well done," she said, giving me a golf clap before looking around meaningfully. "Let's hope a good night includes finding out what's been going on here."

"Right." I took a sip and wandered toward glass double doors through which another room could be seen. "Back to business."

"That's the living room," Maya said as I opened the doors and passed through them.

Light streaming through diaphanous curtains, covering floor-to-ceiling windows at the far side of the space, revealed a sofa and easy chair centred about a wooden coffee table. Entering, I crossed over to the windows. Close up, they revealed themselves to be French doors leading to a tiny balcony. A balcony that, as Dixon had suggested, provided a perfect view of the Berlin Wall.

Two walls, actually, I thought, able to see the death strip in its entirety for the first time since arriving in the city. The twelve-foot-high concrete barrier on this side and another concrete wall on the far side. In between, floodlights atop guard towers swept over the hundred-foot-wide no-man's land. At ground level, cars and men with machine guns and dogs patrolled the streetlamp-lit asphalt road, which ran parallel to the walls.

I scowled beneath my mask. "They'll really shoot anyone trying to cross?"

"Most definitely." Maya took a seat on the dusty dark green sofa and looked around the unoccupied apartment. "They've done it before. It's diabolical, but that's the DDR."

"DDR?"

"The Deutsche Demokratische Republik," she replied. "The German Democratic Republic."

I snorted. "Democratic." My own recovered memories of the USSR rose to mind, and I better understood Dixon's feelings toward its regimes. Regimes that thought nothing of murdering people to control them and keep them from leaving. "It's like a sick joke."

Something about the scene resonated, triggering memories of a Eurus god's words. *Zelus.*

"We are not villains," Zelus had said, wearing his usual avatar: a fit and tall Caucasian male dressed in a military uniform, with greying hair, still thick, and a bushy moustache beneath a pointy nose. We'd been standing in a large hall somewhere. Other Eurus, their faces blurs in my mind's eye, stood nearby, watching. "We are this planet's saviours. From nuclear annihilation and capitalist greed. You have seen the projections. Surely you are concerned."

"You know I am," I replied. "But I don't like how you treat people. Like they're your subjects."

"Even among gods," he said, "we are all subjects. Subjects of our feelings for, and the expectations and demands of, those around us. Total freedom cannot exist in a group."

"Even so," I said, "you've no right. People aren't your pets and playthings."

He snarled. "Yet they must be controlled. For their own and this planet's good. With their mortal imperative to reproduce, their numbers increase each day, as does the West's growth and consumption."

My brow creased. "Wilhelm says mortals deserve the chance to find their own way."

"Boreas is a fool," Zelus said. "He watches passively, acting only to oppose us and to avert the most extreme mortal-caused disasters. Like a dog's master, letting his hound run free of fence or leash. It seems like kindness until the beast runs in front of a speeding car and it is too late for the master to save it. The mortal dogs are on the freeway now, and it is rush hour. Already their wars and atomic weapons tests have reduced the Allfrost's capacity to stave off a global warming of their own making. These dangers can only be stopped by collective action. Long-term thinking beyond their brief lifespans. Therefore, it is up to us to think and act for them."

"You underestimate them," I said. "They're not all like that, and they've got a lot of potential. Look at what they've accomplished lately."

His eyebrows rose. "Like what?"

I pointed a finger skyward. "They've landed on the moon."

"All the more reason," Zelus replied, waving a hand. "They are no more ready for the stars than for nuclear weapons. No, we must turn back the clock to simpler times, before they destroy themselves and all life on this planet."

"Are you okay?" Maya asked, touching my arm.

The memory, almost a vision, subsided.

"Yeah, I'm fine." I wasn't, though. Zelus's remembered words troubled me, but that we'd had the discussion at all concerned and puzzled me far more. The Eurus were the enemy, so why had I been talking to one of them? *Some sort of peace talks?* I tried to recall more context but failed. My own words meant it had to have been sometime after the first moon landing in 1969. Yet it also had to have been before I'd gone to the Bodhi Group and ended up a prisoner. I struggled to recall the faces of those who had stood nearby at the meeting but continued to see only blurs. "I was just thinking about the wall."

Maya took a step. "Shall we check the basement suites?"

"Not yet." I turned away from the window. "I'd like to look around up here a bit more."

"Why bother?" Her eyes roved over the area. "There's obviously no one here, and no sign of anything unusual. I checked everywhere. No trap doors, no secret passages."

"Yeah," I said, "but maybe we should look again, just to be sure. You heard Dixon. No one's been seen going into the basement. They came up here." I glanced at the windows. "And that's a long way to dig . . ." I trailed off, an idea coming to mind.

Maya eyed me. "What are you thinking?"

I studied the old peeling wallpaper. "Did any of the rooms look like they could double as a transporter? The study, maybe?"

"Oh, that's an interesting idea." Smiling, she stood. "Let's—"

A creak of wood interrupted her, and we stared at each other a moment, wide-eyed.

Putting the empty bottle of Nacht Cola on the coffee table, I grabbed Maya's arm and pulled her toward the kitchen. We crossed the living room on tiptoe, stepping lightly, and hid behind the door leading to the front hall.

A moment later, visible through a crack between door and frame, a man stumbled inside. Not bothering to turn on the lights, the twitching figure lurched into a clumsy one-eighty and shut the doors behind himself. Pivoting again, he lifted his nose a moment, and I held my breath as he looked our way and seemed to sniff the air. Moving like a marionette, he turned and fumbled his hands against a door to his immediate right. Several bumps later, the door swung inward, offering glimpses of coats and hangers before it shut again.

I tugged at Maya's elbow. "Did you see how he moved?"

"I sure did," she whispered. "That's got to be another abductee."

"Let's grab him," I said, taking a step.

Entering the front hallway, I moved slowly, wary of the hardwood. Crossing the long rug that ran the length of the front hall's floor, I entered a cloakroom and strode past a wall of coats, making for the door on the far side. Banging through it, I spotted the intruder as he whirled to face me.

He raised half-closed hands, and I rushed him. Ducking beneath his arms, I brought my shoulder up into his waist, grabbed him by the legs, and heaved him into the air. Weaving one of my hands between his legs, I gripped the back of his knee and swept it to the side while bending at the waist. His body thumped to the hardwood and the walls shook and plaster fell from the ceiling. Before he could move, I rolled across his body, grasped one of his arms with one of mine and wrapped my other arm about his neck.

"Stop fight—" A blast of light, bright as a flashbulb, flared, and electricity coursed through my body, and I cried out in pain. Spots danced in the air before me and my body ached, but I tightened my grip and drew on the Underfrost, cooling the air around me. When the light and electricity faded, I swept the guy's arm between my thighs and clenched them together. With my left arm now free, I punched him twice in the face.

"Please," he shouted in German, his breath fogging the air. "Stop hitting me."

"Then stop struggling," I said in the same language, holding my fist high.

"Do as he says," Maya said in English, kneeling by my side, holding a gun in one hand and flashlight in the other. "*Bitte.*"

At last, the man went limp.

"What do you want from me?" he asked, stuttering from the cold.

"Keep him covered," I said, firing a look at Maya before releasing my captive and clambering to my feet.

As I straightened my coat, I assessed the room, furnished with an easy chair, side table, and floor lamp but little else. Spotting my hat by the chair, I scooped it from the floor, set it on my head, and studied the man. Dressed in brown corduroy pants, golf shirt, and sneakers, he looked about thirty years old.

"Who are you?" Maya asked.

"My name is Günther." He spoke in English this time, with only a faint German accent. Sitting upright, he propped himself against the wall, and looked around. "Günther Muller. Where am I?"

"Nice try," I said, blinking to clear my vision. "What are you doing here?"

His forehead wrinkled. "I do not understand. Is this a kidnapping? If you want money, I can pay you."

Maya brought the gun closer. "Are you ascending?"

"What do you mean?" he asked. "Please, may I stand?" I extended a hand and helped him to his feet. Dusting himself off, he looked out the window. *"Die Mauer?"* He shot me a look. "Why have you brought me here?"

"You came here on your own," Maya said. "You don't remember?"

"No," he replied. "Please tell me what is going on."

"Okay," I said, narrowing my eyes. "What's the last thing you do remember?"

He turned up his palms. "Relaxing." He glanced at the window. "At my home."

"Where's home?" I asked.

"Spandau," he said.

"Ballet?" By which I meant a popular new wave band.

"Berlin," Maya responded before Günther could reply. "Spandau is another neighbourhood. On the city's western edge."

"Oh." *Maybe I believe you, Günther.* I stuck out a hand. "Can I see your wallet?" Nodding, he dug into his back pocket, pulled out his billfold, and handed it to me. "His ID matches." I folded the leather and held it out to him. "How is it you speak English?"

He shrugged, taking back his wallet. "I learned it in school. It is not uncommon."

I pointed at his stomach. "Do you mind lifting your shirt?"

He took a step back. "Why?"

"Just do it, please," I said. "I need to check something. You want to get out of here, don't you?"

"Very well." He raised his shirt with both hands, exposing his stomach and lower chest.

I waved a hand at Maya. "Can I get some light?"

"Of course." She pulled her hand torch from her pocket and handed it to me.

Switching it on, I shone it at Günther's abdomen, illuminating a spiderweb of dark lines decorating his pale skin like a bad tattoo job.

"By the Allfrost," I murmured, resisting the urge to step back. I pointed at one of the lines, and it seemed to pulse and twist ever so slightly. The writhing lines didn't break the skin, but they had the look of an earlier stage of the vines protruding from the necks of Sid Frigid and Cardigan Guy on the security camera footage. *Disgusting.*

As before, I thought of the Nameless abominations I'd encountered on Zarechus. Could the lines on Günther's belly and chest be the early stages of whatever had happened to those people? Whatever the case, this was far more than brainwashing, and if Günther was any example, those affected weren't even aware of what was happening to them.

"Are you quite satisfied?" Günther said, lowering his shirt. Sounding annoyed rather than horrified, he had evidently not seen the lines marring his skin. "May I go now?"

Before I could answer, footsteps thundered behind us, growing louder by the moment.

"Someone's coming," I said, locking eyes with Maya. "Get ready."

Nodding, she pulled her weapon free of its holster, and a few moments later, the footsteps stopped. "Maybe it's another tenant," she said.

"Wait here." I handed her the flashlight and headed for the front hall. "I'll take a look."

As I stepped into the cloakroom, a crack reverberated from the hallway, followed by a bang. Sweeping frost from thin air, I waited until the door leading to the foyer opened. As it swung inward, I slipped into the Underfrost, vanishing from sight. A dark figure entered the room a second later.

Stepping past him, I spun about, popped from the Underfrost, and held my handful of frost to his face. Holding it like an ether-soaked rag, I wrapped my other arm around his waist and sent cryogenic energy into the dude's warm body.

Electricity coursed through me, as it had when I'd tackled the first intruder, Günther. Snarling, I turned away from the accompanying flashes of light and held on until his struggles ceased.

"Everything okay?" Maya called from the other room.

"Yeah, I got him." Laying him on the floor, I gripped his wrists and dragged him into the bedroom.

"What did you do to him?" Günther asked, wide-eyed.

I studied the newcomer's khaki army jacket and shaved head before stooping to check his pulse. "He's alive."

"Do you need a hand?" Maya asked.

"No, thanks," I said over my shoulder. "Just keep an eye on Günther." I checked the skinhead's pockets and found only a half-empty pack of cigarettes, a box of matches, and a black-handled switchblade. Lifting his shirt, I recoiled. As with Günther, dark, creepy lines spiderwebbed across this guy's belly and seemed to wriggle beneath the light cast from Maya's flashlight. "Ugh, I think I might hurl."

"*Mein Gott*," Günther said. "Are those tattoos?"

A floorboard creaked in the cloakroom, and I straightened, whirling in place, and reached for frost.

"Easy!" Dixon stood in the doorway with his hands—one of which held a pistol—raised. "It's me."

"What's going on?" I lowered my arm and dismissed the frost I'd summoned. "Trouble?"

Dixon glanced at the raven perched on his shoulder. "The bird thought you might need help."

"What about those CIA agents?"

"Gone," he said. "After wrestling a catatonic into their car." His eyes roved between Günther and the skinhead on the floor. "What do we have here?"

"Check this out." I lifted the bald guy's shirt.

"Is that what you saw on the punk?" Dixon asked.

I nodded. "Not as far along, but yeah, I think so."

He grunted. "Any signs of frost ability?"

"No," I said, "but they both gave me a nasty shock." I trembled for emphasis.

His eyes widened. "Lightning?"

"It looked that way," I replied.

Dixon's brow furrowed. "This isn't brainwashing, is it?"

"I doubt it." I thought a moment. "At least, not just that. I think they're—"

"Sentinel," Caelus said. "Perhaps you should discuss this in private."

"Right," I said, glancing at our captives. "We should get Günther home . . . or maybe to a hospital. He doesn't seem to know what he's doing here."

"And you believe him?" Dixon asked, sounding skeptical.

"Yeah, I do." He might just be a great liar, but his answers to my questions had seemed to be honest ones. He truly hadn't seemed to know what he was doing here. His loss of memory, electrified skin, and spastic movement upon entering the apartment had to have something to do with the vines growing beneath his skin. "And I think whatever's infecting him brought him here."

"But why here?" Maya asked.

Günther's eyebrows bunched. "What do you mean infected? I am not sick." He touched his chest. "Am I?"

"I'm sorry, Günther." Maya holstered her weapon. "We think you may have been infected with a parasite."

"No." He put a hand over his heart. "How could that be? With what?"

She placed a hand on his shoulder. "We don't know, but try not to panic. Come on. Let's get you some help."

"Are you letting me go?" he asked.

"If that's what you want," she replied evenly, "but I suggest you let us take you to a hospital."

"Very well," Günther said, walking with her. "That may be best. I could swear that raven spoke."

"Raven?" Maya patted his arm. "What raven is that?"

He sighed. "You do not see it? I am very confused."

"Try not to fret," she said. "We will get you fixed up right as rain." Guiding him through the doorway, she stopped and looked back. "I'll have Antiphates take him to a hospital and be right back."

"Fatty," Günther said, sounding confused. "This is how you refer to your auntie?"

"Pardon," Maya said, closing the cloakroom door.

Dixon looked about. "Not much furniture. What do you think? Is there a trapdoor to the basement?"

I shook my head. "Maya already looked."

Squatting, Dixon tilted the skinhead's face toward himself. "Then why did they come in here?"

Crouching next to them, I studied the piercings on the guy's face. "I think this room might be a transporter, but I'm not sure how to activate it."

Abruptly, the punk's eyes popped open, and his body coursed with electric light.

"What the hell?" Dixon fell back on his hands as the room shuddered.

"It's activating," I said, looking around as the walls wavered, the windows dimmed, and the room went black.

Chapter 17

Outside the Box

A faint light returned a moment later, but the room's walls did not. Corrugated steel, painted orange, replaced them, standing somewhat closer than the apartment's walls had. The window had vanished too, replaced by a circular opening a foot in diameter through which light and air entered. Beyond it, the floodlights of the Berlin Wall's kill zone had been replaced by a glass fixture lighting a white stone wall, and beneath our feet, the bedroom's hardwood had changed to polished steel.

"We just transported," I said. *But to where?*

Dixon walked over to a rectangular outline in the steel wall, where the door leading to the cloakroom had stood back in the Kreuzberg apartment. With the raven, Caelus, perched on his shoulder, he fiddled with the latch and the door shifted a few inches.

My forehead creased. "Are you sure that's a good idea?"

"We can't stand around here forever," he replied, tugging the door sideways, revealing a grand hall.

"Whoa, nice." I sidled up next to him to get a better look.

Unlit chandeliers hung from a ceiling painted to resemble a cloudy sky, framed by ornately patterned gold. Fifteen-foot arches on the left led to massive windows. To the right stood arched doorways of reflective glass, and between each arch, candle-shaped electric lights added to the illumination.

My eyes dipped to a short set of steel stairs, the paint worn away by countless footsteps, which descended to the hall's checkerboard marble floor.

"Look out," Caelus squawked.

Something pushed me between the shoulders, snapping my head back, and I tumbled down the steps, landing hard on the marble. Still sprawled on the floor, I groaned, "What the hell?"

"Ouch." Dixon lay on his back beside me, his body coiled, rubbing his knee. "That smarts."

"Behind you," Caelus shouted, his wings flapping overhead.

Footsteps clanged on the metal stairs behind me, and I pushed my chest from the floor. As I turned to look, a blur of motion rocked my head back. Blinking away stars, I raised my arms defensively, catching sight of the recently unconscious skinhead's face, his eyes blank and passionless as he rained blows down upon my upraised limbs.

Cocking a leg back, I lashed out and landed a foot near the guy's midsection. The blow lacked finesse but succeeded in knocking him back, and he crashed down against the metal stairs and lay there as if all life had left him.

I rose to my feet and, hands haloed in frost even through my gloves, moved toward him.

"Is he dead?" Dixon asked, climbing to his feet.

"I'm not sure." Stooping, I grabbed the punk's wrist and checked for a pulse. "No, he's still alive." I slapped the guy's cheek. "He's just unconscious again, I guess."

"What did you do to him?" Dixon asked.

"Nothing," I said. "I just kicked him and he fell down and stayed there."

I took a few steps back, taking in the metal container, which sat atop a base of metal bars.

"It looks like a shipping container," Dixon said from beside me. "It must have taken some doing to get it in here."

"Yeah." A flicker of motion drew my attention to the container's interior where the room's furniture could no longer be seen. *The transposition must have reverted.* I gestured to the collapsed punk. "Come on. Help me get him back inside."

I gripped the guy by his armpits and Dixon grabbed his legs, and together we half carried, half dragged the inert body up the steel stairs and deposited him on the container floor.

"How do we get back?" Dixon asked. "Can you activate this thing?"

The raven, Caelus, hopped atop the prone man and regarded me. "I suspect it was this creature, Sentinel."

"Yeah." I nudged the guy with a shoe. "You're probably right. I sure didn't do it. At least, I don't think I did."

"Great." Dixon looked toward the exit. "So, we're stuck here. Wherever here is."

Caelus jumped from the man's chest. "No more than fifty kilometres from Ms. Day, I should think. Were it farther, the collar I wear would have taken over this avatar and be flying it back toward her." The bird looked side to side. "Besides, this transporter looks quite slipshod, suitable for only a short-range transposition. My guess is it is a temporary erection."

Dixon snorted. "Aren't they all?"

"All right," I replied, heading for the exit. "Let's find out where we are."

"Really? Not even a snicker?" Dixon harrumphed. "The boys at the Institute would've loved that one. Jimenez and Springer especially."

"Ah, yes," Caelus said. "Very droll, Dixon. My apologies. I was a bit distracted by our change of venue."

"Too late, bird."

Out in the hallway, the nearest floor-to-ceiling window looked out upon broad walkways of packed sand, which gave way to a manicured lawn bordered by an outer ring of trees. The darkness beneath those trees made it impossible to see how far the park extended, but I had a feeling it went on for some time.

"Well, that doesn't help much," Dixon muttered in a low voice.

"Open the window, Sentinel," Caelus said from his perch on Dixon's arm. "I will reconnoitre the area."

"Good idea," Dixon said, sounding impressed.

I pulled on the latch, and the bottom half of the window swung open like a door. "Just be sure to come back."

"I have no choice, Sentinel," Caelus replied. "The woman, Maya, still holds the other end of my leash."

"Are you in contact with her?" I asked.

The bird's beak bobbed. "I am."

"Good," I said, relieved. "Is she okay?"

"She is." The raven's feathers ruffled. "Though she's quite eager to know where we are."

"You'd better get going, then." I pointed at the shipping container. "Harland and I will wait in there."

Dixon's eyebrows bunched. "Why's that?"

"In case someone activates the other end again," I said. "If they do, we'll be taken back where we came from."

Dixon gestured toward Caelus. "What about the bird?"

"We'll leave the door open," I said before turning to Caelus. "If we're not here when you return, find your way back to the hotel in Berlin. Okay?"

"Very well," Caelus said. "Then I will leave you."

The raven hopped from Dixon's arm, spread his wings and took to the air.

"All right. Let's get inside." Turning, Dixon strode toward the transporter, put a foot on the first of the steel steps, and looked around the hall. "What do you suppose this building is?"

"Some sort of palace," I answered. "Judging by the fancy decor."

"It's pretty impressive." Dixon climbed the stairs and stepped inside the container with me on his tail. "These Eurus know how to live."

"Yeah," I said, remembering, "they do like nice things."

"Look at this dumb-ass." Stooping by the unconscious skinhead, Dixon rubbed the man's shaved head. "He looks barely twenty. He's got his whole life in front of him, and he does this to himself."

"You mean the vines?"

He shook his head. "The tattoos and piercings. Like his body's a piece of garbage. His parents must be so proud."

"It's a free country."

"No, it isn't," he said. "Not anymore."

"Sure—" I broke off, getting his drift. "You think we're in East Germany now?" Seeing his nod, I said, "Huh. How about that? We made it across the wall after all. Anyway, maybe it isn't a free country, but it should be."

"Of course it should." He scowled. "So what?"

I waved a hand at the skinhead. "So, he's free to dress however he wants. It's called freedom of expression."

"Uh-huh, and I'm free to judge him for it. It's called freedom of thought."

I made a face. "Yeah, I suppose so."

Dixon lifted the man's shirt. "Jesus." He extended a finger toward the spiderweb of dark lines on the guy's abdomen, which writhed and throbbed abruptly. Falling back onto his hands, he crab-walked toward me before regaining his feet. "They fucking move. What the hell are they?"

"I'm not sure," I said. "Günther had them too. Some type of plant, maybe." I tapped my index finger against my temple. "One that's able to control him somehow."

"What makes you think that?" he asked.

I described the Nameless I'd seen in the town of Abadom and my growing theory about the changelings. "The Nameless's vines were a lot more noticeable, but my guess is something similar is growing inside of this dude. Something in its early stages."

"Christ." He rubbed his stomach with one of his hands. "They're infecting people with a parasite so they can control them."

I frowned. "I think so. That's got to be the source of the electricity too." I pictured a man spasming beneath a Nameless's touch, visible through the doors of the Abadom theatre where my companions and I had taken shelter. "The Nameless on Zarechus were like that too." Lightning striking an obelisk flashed in my mind. "They seemed attracted to electricity, or they attract it. I'm not sure which. I don't know. Maybe they can even command it."

"Interesting," Dixon said. "But why is this guy unconscious?"

I thought a moment. "Maybe the parasite's drained after shocking me." Remembering how Günther had behaved normally after tussling with me at the apartment, I added, "And the host is too weak to resume control. At least, that's my guess."

While being like the Nameless might explain Günther, the unconscious skinhead, and most of the other abductees I knew of, they didn't explain Sid Frigid. If he too was infected with a plant-based parasite, why did he have apparent command of the Underfrost and what was his connection to the Allfrost machine?

"These Eurus are hard-core bastards," Dixon snarled. "Brainwashing was bad enough, but this is goddamn biological warfare."

I nodded. "It sure explains all the disappeared."

He crossed his arms and leaned against the wall. "How are they doing it, do you think? Infecting people, I mean."

"That's the million-dollar question. If we figure that out, maybe we can put a stop to it." I looked down at the skinhead. "Though I suppose that won't help this poor dude."

Sliding down the wall, Dixon rubbed his injured knee. "Well, when we get back to New Olympus, maybe your alien friends can shed some light on things. If they're the gods you think they are, they should be able to produce a cure for it."

Dropping down next to him, I leaned my head back. "I sure hope so."

"Hey," he said. "Is this the thing you came to the Group about? I mean, it's not nukes or global warming, but is it related?"

"I don't think so." I scanned my memory. "This feels new."

A sound of flapping came from the door, and Caelus flew inside, landing next to the unconscious man.

"Well?" Dixon asked. "What did you see?"

"We are in Potsdam," Caelus said. "A small city at the south-western edge of Berlin."

"Told you, Winterboy," Dixon said. "Welcome to the DDR."

I smirked, glad for the confirmation. "How far did we travel, Caelus?"

"Roughly thirty kilometres," the bird replied. "Perhaps a bit more."

My throat rumbled. "That's a long way to walk through hostile territory."

Dixon scowled. "The hard part will be getting back across the wall."

I looked at Caelus. "Any chance Maya can pick us up?"

"I will ask." After a moment, Caelus's beak moved side to side. "She cannot cross the border without a visa, and obtaining one requires at least a few days." He paused again. "She is returning to the hotel to seek help, however. In the meantime, she suggests you take the opportunity to explore the palace."

"Ah." I nudged Dixon. "So this is a palace."

Caelus's head dipped. "Das Neue Palais."

The New Palace, I thought, translating the name automatically. *Never heard of it.* "How do you know that?"

The bird's wings twitched. "I recognized it, of course. From a previous life."

"Great," I said. "What can you tell us about it?"

"Nothing likely to help in your search." The raven hopped onto the skinhead's chest. "Only that it is a large rococo palace, built in the seventeen hundreds for King Friedrich the Second. You may know him as Frederick the Great. Oh, and I attended a party here once, long ago. I should have recognized the hall outside, but it has been a few hundred years since I last saw it, after all."

"Don't sweat it." I clambered to my feet. "No one's memory is perfect. Least of all mine. Anyway, let's do it." If the palace was a Eurus base, the opportunity was too good to pass up. "Carefully."

The bird wagged his head. "As I will not be helpful searching the interior in my current body, Ms. Day suggests I search the grounds for a car, in case you need to travel."

"All right." *Good thinking, Maya.* "We'll leave the window open and see you back here in ten minutes."

With an explosion of feathers, Caelus flew out the container's door, and Dixon and I followed.

"Odd, isn't it?" Dixon said, surveying the hall.

"What's that?"

"No guards," he replied.

"Yeah," I said, smelling old wood and a faint hint of mustiness upon the air. "I guess they don't need them. The only ones using the transporter are the changelings and their kidnappers." The thought triggered a sudden realization, and I snapped my fingers. "That must be it."

He gave me a sidelong look. "What must be what?"

"Why the transporter activated." I pointed at the container door. "It must have been the infected guy. I bet it reacts to anyone with those vines inside them."

"That's possible." He squinted. "Except why can't we get back? He's still in there."

I shrugged. "Maybe it's one way or won't work unless the parasite, or whatever it is, is conscious." I gasped. "The parasite might even be the one issuing the command."

"Hmm ..." He regarded the skinhead through the container's open door. "I hope you're right. If you are, we might be able to convince it to take us back."

"We can sure try," I replied, not sure the thing inside of them could be reasoned with, but I kept my doubts to myself. "That is, when we get back from searching."

"Right," Dixon said, looking around. "Let's split up. It'll be faster that way."

"Sure." I examined the area. From what I could see of it, the entire hall was roughly seventy-five feet long. At about fifteen feet wide, most of its width was filled by the transporter container, but a narrow passageway ran between it and the windows. I pointed at the gap. "How about you go that way while I check this side?"

Dixon pulled his gun. "That works."

"See you back here in ten." I trod toward the doors at the hall's far end. Each opened onto the same richly decorated anteroom with an unlit fireplace and gold-painted chairs with round backs lining the walls. I spotted a door to the right and another on the far side but decided against going deeper, preferring to stay nearer to the shipping container for now. Moving to the next door, I found a suite of rooms filled with beds, sofas, fireplaces, hardwood floors, and elaborately patterned area rugs.

Fancy digs. I pulled off a glove, lit my palm, and cast the beam over the carvings and paintings decorating the walls and ceiling. *I wonder who lives here now.* This now being East German territory, it must technically belong to the state, but I had to wonder if a Eurus god had used his influence to squat here unmolested.

A click and rattle came from an unexplored door a moment before it opened, and I froze, stifling a gasp. *Shit.*

"There you are," Dixon said, stepping into the room. "I figured I'd run into you this way." He closed the door behind himself and turned back to me. "Did you find anything?"

"Just all this beautiful stuff."

Looking around, he curled his lip. "It's a bit much, don't you think?"

I shrugged. "I like it."

"Figures," he said with a smirk. "There's no accounting for taste."

"You've got that right." I thrust my chin toward the door. "Did you find anything that way?"

"Yeah," he replied. "No people, but I did find something curious." He jabbed a thumb by his shoulder. "Come on. I'll show you."

Passing through several rooms, we entered another vast hall, dimly illuminated by light entering through windowed arches along the far wall. In contrast to the room where we had arrived, this one seemed designed to conjure up images of a seaside grotto. In service of which, the walls had been painstakingly covered in seashells and semi-precious stones. While above, a fresco of clouds and angels loomed over a checkerboard of floor tiles. The latter were arrayed in distorted patterns, giving the illusion of a surface viewed through shallow water.

"Whoa," I whispered. "This is amazing."

"Uh-huh," he said, "but that's not what I wanted to show you." Our shoes clomped against the marble floor as he led me over to a stack of crates sitting at the room's centre. He tapped a rectangle of paper pasted to the side of a crate. "Check it out."

"Okay." I shone the light of my palm over a shipping label and frowned. "Nacht Cola." I fired a glance at Dixon. "So?"

He waved at another box. "This one's Nicht Cola."

"Cool." I smiled. "There's almost a week's supply of it." I looked around the beautiful room. *Pretty nice storage room.* "What's it doing here, though?"

"Exactly," Dixon said.

My brow furrowed. "Maybe it's considered contraband here, and they're hiding it from the Stasi."

"I highly doubt it." He tapped the shipping label with his finger. "Check out the sender's address. That's in East Berlin, which means this stuff came straight from the factory."

My jaw dropped. "This stuff is *made* in East Germany?"

"That's what it looks like." He pulled out a pen and pad of paper and scribbled on it. "When we get back, I'll ask the Group to look into it."

"Where did you get the paper and pen?"

"The hotel," he replied absently. "Something's not right here. These drinks, their marketing, it's too slick for the DDR."

Spotting a crowbar resting atop the crate, I grabbed it. "Let's pry it open and take a look." Tucking the tool beneath an arm, I doused my palm's light, dug my glove from a pocket and re-donned it. "Maybe it isn't what it says it is."

"Good call," he said, stepping back to give me room. "Never assume."

"Exactly." I wedged the crowbar into the wood, and a wrenching sound filled the cavernous hall as I pulled on it. "Yikes, that's loud."

"Might as well keep going," Dixon whispered. "If there's anyone around, they'll have heard it already. You're almost there."

Shoving the tip deeper, I levered it again, generating another screech, but I kept sidestepping and repeating the motion until the lid came free.

"That did it." Dixon stepped closer and raised the wood high. "Give me some light."

"Sure." I aimed my glowing palm at the box's interior, revealing dark bottles nestled in orange plastic crates, and lifted a Nacht Cola partway from its place. "Okay, that's really odd,

East Germany making soda pop. Do they even do that? Isn't that Western decadence?"

"Oh, they make it," he replied. "Just not well, usually." He pretended to gag. "I tried their Cola knock-off once."

"And?"

He stuck out his tongue. "Tasted like motor—"

Footsteps came from the door through which we'd entered the room, and the beam of a flashlight danced in the shadows beyond.

"*Hallo?*" called a voice in German. "*Ist jemand da?*"

Chapter 18

Host of Problems

Entering the grotto, the newcomer, wearing a light blue button-up shirt and pants, raised his flashlight and panned it about the room.

Crap. Grasping the shipping crate lid, I lifted it, blocking the light before it could reveal us, and motioned to Dixon to get down.

"What are you doing?" the guard said in German, and his shoes tapped closer. "Show yourself."

"Ah, good," I replied, also using German. "You are here." I doused the light emanating from my palm. "Can you help me?"

To my relief, his footsteps continued to grow louder. Whatever else happened, I didn't want him to run and raise the alarm. Readying myself, I waited until his shoe taps came more from my right than my front.

Now. I slipped into the Underfrost and let the wood fall, wincing as light glared in my eyes. Averting my gaze, I looked for Dixon, catching sight of him an instant before he crouch-walked out of sight behind the crate.

"Where are you?" The guard's head turned left and right, and he rushed toward me, holding a gun and flashlight. "Come out."

Sidestepping, I reached for his gun with intangible hands, popped from the Underfrost, and yanked the weapon from his grip before he could move. He reared back and raised his flashlight, but before he could bring it down, Dixon rose up behind him, wrapped an arm about the guy's neck, and yanked him off his feet.

"Easy," I said in English as the man gagged. "Don't kill him."

"Stay quiet and stop fighting," Dixon said in German, his lips close to the man's ear, "and you'll live through this." Nodding, the man ceased his struggles. "Smart man." Dixon released his grip and stood. "Stay down."

I picked up the guard's fallen flashlight and shone it at his chest. "Do you speak English?"

He looked to be somewhere in his thirties, pale and kind of pudgy, with thinning light brown hair cut short.

The guy nodded. "You are American?" he asked in English.

"What makes you think that?" I asked.

He sneered at Dixon. "That one's German is . . . not good."

"Whatever, dough boy," Dixon retorted.

Holding the guard's gun so he could see it, I asked, "What is this place?"

His brow furrowed. "You do not know where you are? How is this possible?"

I frowned behind my cowl. "Come on. You know what I mean. What's going on here? Why are you changing—"

A bang came from the ceiling above and, wincing, I shot Dixon a look. "Keep an eye on him, would you?" I said, handing him the guard's gun. "I'll be right back."

"Will do," he said. "While you're gone, Fritz here can impress me with his English."

"My name is Rolf," the guard said. "Not Fritz."

Voices drifted down to me as I ascended the stairs, and I followed their murmurings to a second-floor anteroom where light came from an open door to my right. Giving my vision a moment to adjust to the glare, I crossed to the door on tiptoe, edged an eye past the door frame, and looked in on another massive hall. Of similar size to the grotto-style room below, this one had marble with gold filigree, huge paintings bordered in gold, and a ceiling that looked like an inverted bathtub.

Shit. I ducked back out of sight. Across the space, visible beyond the backs of two uniformed men, a giant of a man with scarlet skin sat upon a large chair. *Baduriel?*

Sidestepping into the Underfrost, I looked again and shook my head. It wasn't him. This guy had the demonic horns and smouldering gaze, but he was portlier, his nose bulbous and his eyes beady. I stepped into the room, still hidden in the Underfrost, and spotted several more men, dressed like Stasi secret police standing at the room's periphery, watching the conversation.

The demon's horns blazed to life without warning.

"Lord Oborateles, I understand my words are upsetting," said a thin man, speaking English with a German accent. Grey-haired and clean-shaven, he wore a grey uniform with epaulettes and flat-topped hat that came to a peak in front, with a black band and visor. "Yet I must urge you to contain yourself. This palace is a historical treasure. If it were to burn, the Party would insist on knowing how and why. Even my superior's authority is not absolute, and it is likely our plot would be uncovered. Moscow and the Eurus leadership would learn of it soon after, and they would, I am told, consider what we are doing to be a betrayal."

Oborateles's eyes narrowed. "Discovery would be bad for all of us, Colonel Stein." The flames emanating from the demon's horns guttered and died, and he wagged a finger. "And your rank within the Stasi will not protect you or your comrades. You are Eurus first and foremost, after all. Whereas my brethren and I, already Anathema, have much to gain and comparatively little to lose. Detection may mean a return to service and suffering, but our lives are long and redemption will come eventually. However, for you and your fellows, ascension and your dreams of a unified socialist Germany will never come."

Stein stiffened. "Of course, my lord comrade. I mean only to advise you to the best of my ability."

"With risk of discovery in mind . . ." Oborateles looked around. "You are quite sure these men can be trusted?"

The colonel inclined his head. "Like me, they have tired of empty promises, and they have pledged loyalty to me and Generaloberst Krebs."

"And how is the colonel general?" Oborateles waved a hand dismissively. "Never mind. Continue with your report, Colonel Stein. I must return to the Gobi Desert soon, before I am missed."

"As I was saying," Stein said, "our agents have now collected most of those infected with the original formulation."

"How many more?" Oborateles asked.

Colonel Stein stood taller. "More, my lord?"

The demon nodded. "How many of those infected with the early formula remain to be captured?"

"We cannot be certain," Stein said. "By our best estimates, fewer than thirty."

Oborateles thumped the armrest of his chair. "Why so many?"

Colonel Stein took a step back. "Those remaining drank the alpha formulation. Unlike the beta group, they are not easily controlled. They must be located and physically apprehended."

"Alpha formulation." The demon scowled. "I had thought we had solved these problems after Abadom. We were to have moved out of the experimental phase before conducting Earth trials."

Abadom? I suppressed a gasp. *These guys created the Nameless.*

"As did we, my lord," Stein replied. "Fortunately, while they draw more attention, those infected with the alpha organism tend to remain in their homes, perhaps to be near an electrical source. Like the early subjects tested at Abadom, they stay largely dormant and out of sight until there is sufficient electrical activity to draw them out. Fear not."

"And what of the gamma formula?" Oborateles asked. "Have those infected with it shown any signs of these . . . growths?"

"None above the skin," the colonel replied. "And it has been weeks. Short of a reasonably thorough medical examination, the infection will go unnoticed. This new species is less aggressive with greater capabilities and knows how to keep itself hidden. Until the right time, even the host will remain unaware of its presence. Aside, perhaps, from occasional periods of lost time when the organism or one of your kind takes over. We have added other safeguards as well."

"Such as?"

"Until the organism fully matures, it will need fresh infusions of our soda pop to survive, and it will compel the host to consume more on a regular basis. If any new problems arise, cutting off supply of the problematic soda pop formulation will cause the symbiont to die."

Oborateles smiled. "And customer loyalty is assured. Well done. Then it is ready for mass distribution, yes?"

"It is, my lord," Stein replied, "and distribution has begun. Your comrade Azrileus has been indispensable in this regard. Without her genius, we would not have known where to begin." He looked around the room. "As soon as the last of alphas and betas have been dealt with, we will shut down operations here and focus solely on production again. For now, we are operating on a twenty-four-hour schedule to make up for the unanticipated distractions."

The demon stroked his chin. "And have those sodas tainted with the alpha and beta formulations been removed from shelves?"

The colonel coughed. "Not all, I am afraid. Many crates of Nacht and Nicht Cola were already purchased from stores, and in most cases there is no way to know by whom. However, by now, most have likely been consumed, and those infected will have manifested their symptoms. Thus, we can conclude the worst is over." He shrugged. "We will continue to monitor for further incidents, but soon enough discovery will no longer matter."

Oh, boy. I put a hand to my mouth, thinking of the Nacht Cola I'd drunk before leaving the hotel, and those still in my hat. Come to think of it, I'd felt ill after drinking them. At the time, I'd thought it was my altered shape and the constrictions of my suit. Was it my body reacting to that garbage?

"Very well," Oborateles said. "Have the last of those affected been cured and sent home?"

Stein nodded. "Those of consequence, yes. The others have, or will, receive the new formula and be added to our workforce."

Oborateles cocked an eye. "Are you sure that is wise? The greater the number of missing, the greater the chance our adversaries become aware of what we are doing."

The Stasi colonel waved a hand. "These are degenerates. Worthless punk rocker types, drug addicts, and other such filth. None are likely to be missed."

"I see," the demon replied. "And why do you need them?"

The colonel stiffened. "We are sending them abroad to assist at our other factories, where labour is not as easy to come by. The changelings are good only as labourers, performing menial tasks, loading trucks and so forth, but that is primarily what we need at present."

"Naturally." The demon tapped the armrest of his chair. "And how goes the work getting a symbiont to integrate with the Allfrost Sentinel's essence?"

There is another Sentinel. They had to have come by an Allfrost Sentinel's essence from somewhere. *Unless it's mine.*

"I am pleased to report success," Colonel Stein replied. "However, the temperatures involved have been problematic. The mycelial symbiont is able to protect the host's body against hypothermia, but only for a time. Consequently, the essence must be extracted before the symbiont is overwhelmed or the host and symbiont will die. As we speak, Azrileus works to increase that duration, but even now it should suffice for Lord Baduriel's purpose. Controlling it is the larger problem."

Oborateles's brow knit. "How so?"

Stein's shoulders rose. "It tends to escape our custody and wander off. Yet, it always returns before the symbiont fully succumbs to hypothermia."

The demon grunted. "How odd."

"It is puzzling," Stein replied. "However, as a hybrid of multiple organisms, its erratic behaviour is no doubt a consequence of the interplay of the different wills of its constituent life forms. Fortunately, it has not drawn attention to itself." He frowned. "Aside from the occasional precipitous drops in temperature and spontaneous snowfalls across Berlin."

That must be how they've tracked it, I thought.

"Still," Oborateles said, "we cannot have the creature wandering away when we need it. Can you not contain it?"

"Not thus far," Stein replied. "It is able to dematerialize itself and pass even through solid walls."

Oborateles scratched his nose. "Where does it go when it wanders?"

"All over the city." The colonel waved at the tall arched

windows to either side of Oborateles. "On both sides of the wall. We are not sure why, but perhaps some fragments of the source Allfrost Sentinel compel its actions. Nonetheless, our engineers are exploring ways to keep it confined in the future."

"Very well." Oborateles looked around. "I will pass your report along. Carry on the good work, Stein, and you will soon receive your reward."

Speaking an unfamiliar word—in another language, I presumed—the demon grew insubstantial, and his chair flickered and juddered as if shaken by invisible hands. A moment later, it sat empty and moved no more.

Stooping over the throne, Colonel Stein snatched something shiny from the seat and, giving it a cursory glance, pocketed it.

An Alterclavis? Unlike the transporter my companions and I had used to get to Berlin, an Alterclavis was more precise in what it transported, representing an advanced leap in the technology. One that had surprised even Wilhelm when I'd told him about them. I'd only become aware of their existence myself after one had twice sent me to the Gobi Desert. The first time, I'd swapped positions with Atriel, who had apparently possessed his own Alterclavis, paired to mine. For that reason, I'd since been careful to keep the device in the null space inside my cap, where it couldn't activate. By the looks of it, Colonel Stein shared one with Oborateles, which meant the Eurus had produced more than one.

Stein motioned to his guards and came toward me. "Come."

Uh-oh.

Chapter 19

Caffeine Trip

I backpedalled, spun on a heel, and exited the room. Passing through the antechamber, I slipped into the stairwell and resurfaced from the Underfrost, fighting my way out of its embrace. *I almost pushed it too far that time.* Shaking off the effects, I tiptoed down the steps with the Stasi's footsteps echoing behind me. At the bottom, I turned right into the apartments Dixon and I had already explored, shut the door behind myself, and braced a foot against its bottom rail. As the footsteps grew louder, I pressed my cheek to the wood and exhaled as they passed me by.

I counted to ten before cracking the door a sliver and finding the stairwell empty. Pulling the portal wide, I dashed across to the first-floor antechamber and stuck my head inside. To the left, visible through tall windows, the colonel and his guards got into two large black sedans, and when they had driven from view, I returned to the grotto but found no one inside.

Where did they go? I checked behind the soda crates but found no sign of Dixon or the security guard who had surprised us. Returning to the hall where we'd first arrived, I sighed, spotting Dixon with a raven perched on his shoulder. He sat upon the shipping crate stairs with his gun trained on the Stasi guard, Rolf.

"There you are," Dixon said. "Everything go okay?"

I nodded. "Yeah, but why didn't you wait?"

"Ten minutes was up," he replied, glancing at Caelus. "I figured one of us should get back here to meet the bird. Besides, it seemed safer to wait here. So, what was that noise?"

"A lucky break," I said, telling them what I'd heard, unworried by the Stasi guard's presence. The way I saw it, as a Stasi agent stationed here, he must already know as much as I had managed to learn.

Dixon blinked. "That explains the crates of soda pop. They must keep a supply here for the infected passing through. Like this Sid Frigid character you've been chasing."

"It looks that way," I said.

He growled. "Then we need to get back and let the Bodhi Group know. This needs to be contained before it spirals out of control."

I regarded the shipping container. "We'll have to make it work before we can do that."

"That might be a problem." Dixon looked over his shoulder, where the skinhead changeling still lay unmoving. "No one has come through yet." He looked at Caelus, perched on his shoulder. "What's the word from Day?"

Caelus stopped combing his beak through his wing feathers. "Ms. Day has returned to the Sebastian Street apartment, in hopes of finding a means to activate the transporter."

Dixon frowned. "I thought she was at the hotel, arranging for our extraction."

The raven wagged his head. "Tyndareus has taken command of that initiative."

"Okay," Dixon said. "How long until we've got a way out of here, then?"

The bird paused for several seconds. "By Ms. Day's current estimate, several hours, perhaps longer."

Dixon swore. "Rolf here says he's guarding the palace alone, but someone's bound to arrive to relieve him in the morning."

"It doesn't matter," I replied. "I'm not going back yet."

He shot me a look. "What are you talking about?"

"I've got to check out this factory first," I replied, recalling the conversation I'd just overheard. "I think Sid might be there."

He frowned. "The frost punk's not the priority anymore. We know what they're doing now."

"Yeah, but Oborateles said they need Sid for their plans. That's reason enough to get him away from them. He's their backup plan, in case they can't get me."

Dixon paused a long moment before replying. "Okay, that's sound reasoning." He tapped the pocket of his jacket. "I've got the address right here. Caelus tells me it's in an industrial area of Berlin."

My eyes flicked to the raven. "How far?"

"Perhaps a half-hour drive or so," Caelus replied.

"Perfect," I said. "Then we need a car and a map."

"I've got that covered." Dixon wagged his gun at the security guard and held up a pair of keys. "Fritz here has a car, and he can show us the way."

The Stasi guard scowled. "As I said before, American, my name is Rolf, not Fritz."

"Quiet, Fritz." Dixon looked at me. "The only problem is how we get back to West Berlin after we're done at the factory."

I shrugged. "One thing at a time. Besides, Tyndareus is working on it. If we're lucky, he'll have a way out for us by then."

"He'd better," Dixon said, "or we'll have to come back here, and one of us will have to drink some of that tainted pop to try to activate this transporter again."

My eyes widened. "Good idea!" Sweeping off my cap, I dug inside it. "Where's that bottle?"

He held up his hands. "Easy, Winterboy. That was a joke. You can't drink that garbage."

"I already did," I said.

"Oh, yeah." Dixon sat taller. "I forgot. Are you feeling all right?"

"Sure," I said, continuing to dig in my hat. "I'm fine. I mean, I felt ill for a while, but I think my body neutralized whatever was in it. This stuff isn't meant for someone like me."

He chuckled. "Right. The eggheads said your gut's better than a garbage disposal."

"Pretty much." My body might look all snow and ice, but other elements were mixed in there, which needed to be replenished now and again, and my system wasn't picky about the source of those nutrients. "Found it." I pulled a bottle of Nacht Cola from my hat. "Anyway, I've had a half dozen of these already, and I feel great."

"Sentinel," Caelus said, "are you saying drinking that soft drink will permit you to activate the transporter?"

I nodded. "That's my guess. Not the drink itself, but whatever is inside of it."

"He means the parasite." Dixon shuddered. "You're still taking a helluva of risk, Winterboy. You want vines growing out of you?"

"Nah," I said. "It won't get that far." *I think.* I studied the bottle a moment. "Anyone got an opener?"

Dixon held up a hand. "Don't take it now. Save it until we need it. You said it yourself, Tyndareus might have another exit for us by then."

"Yeah," I said, realizing he was right. "That makes sense." Securing the bottle, I returned my hat to my head. "Caelus, let Maya know what we're going to do, okay?"

"She is aware," the raven replied.

I looked around. "Let's get out of here, then."

"Sentinel," Caelus said. "Maya asks for you to wait."

My brow creased beneath my mask. "For what?"

"For her arrival," he replied. "She is preparing to activate the transporter on her end."

"What?" I frowned. "How?"

The bird's feathers fluttered. "She has been listening to you, through me. She is aware of your speculations regarding Nacht Cola, and she has chosen to consume some to test your theory."

"She can't do that," Dixon said. "She's human. She'll be infected for sure."

"Too late, I'm afraid." The bird's tail twitched. "It is a risk she has already taken."

A flutter of light came from the cargo container. Visible through its open door, the prone form of the skinhead—overlaid with a ghostly image of Maya, standing above him—grew insubstantial. Milliseconds later, the woman's spectre solidified, leaving no sign of the unconscious man.

Maya smiled. "It worked."

I held my head in my hands. "What did you do?" The empty soda bottle she carried—no doubt grabbed from the same soda-filled fridge from which I'd grabbed mine—already told me the answer. "You're infected now."

Dropping the bottle, she descended the metal stairs. "I couldn't let you go running across East Berlin without me. I'm your escort, and I have sworn to watch over you."

"Oh man." The ruined, twitching bodies of the Nameless flashed through my mind's eye. "What if it kills you or . . ." I clawed at my chest. "What if you start growing vines out of your skin?"

She grimaced, putting a hand on my arm. "Try not to worry. I heard you talking." She jabbed a finger at the Stasi, Rolf. "If the Stasi and Anathema have been curing the infected, I'm sure the New Olympians can do the same for me."

Dixon exhaled audibly. "I suppose it's done now."

Taking off my cap, I scratched my head. "Maybe you should go back now. We don't know how long symptoms take to manifest. You can head back to Caelumburg and—"

She held up a hand. "I did not just drink that bottle to turn around and go back. Investigating this factory is important, and I'm coming with you. You're sweet to worry about me, but whatever is going to happen is going to take more than a few hours. Now stop arguing, okay? The sooner we do this, the sooner we can all go back. Together."

"Aren't you scared of what might happen to you?" I asked.

She nodded. "Terrified. Now please stop talking about it, all right?"

Standing, Dixon clapped a hand to her shoulder. "Your sense of duty is impressive, girl. I figured your generation were all a bunch of hippies."

Maya smirked. "What's wrong with hippies? They're just as interested in doing right as your generation."

He shrugged. "Maybe. The problem is they're so often wrong about what's right."

"Come on," I said before Maya could reply. "We'd better move."

We made our way back through the apartments to the palace's front entrance, where Stein and his men had taken off in the sedans. While Maya found a bathroom, I grabbed a few more bottles of Nacht Cola from the grotto hall, in case we needed them for study or something. Five minutes later, we exited the building and, led by Rolf, crossed a floodlit courtyard, our shoes crunching gravel with each step.

As we passed through the courtyard gate, I turned and saw the palace's red-and-white facade for the first time. Backpedalling slowly, I gawked a moment at the smoke-blackened statues standing along the roofline and the domed cylinder projecting above it, topped by three figures holding up a fanciful crown.

Amazing. I took a moment to absorb the view and, with a soft whistle, turned to follow my companions.

Rolf's tiny two-door car sat alone, a hundred feet from the palace gate, next to another old building, smaller than the one we'd just left, with dual curving staircases. To the right, a long curving colonnade connected it with an identical structure standing a few hundred feet away. To my relief, no other people were visible in the vicinity. Aside from it being late, I figured this was most likely because the palace and its adjacent structures were situated in a large park and thus isolated from the rest of town.

A good spot for secret dealings, I thought. *Away from prying eyes.*

"A goddamn Trabant," Dixon muttered, urging Rolf forward. "This'll be cozy."

"I'll drive." Maya tugged open the driver's-side door and, pulling the seat forward, extended an arm to Rolf. "Hop in."

"I've got shotgun," I said, walking to the car's far side.

"Caelus," Maya said, "keep watch from above, please. Let me know if you spot the police or other dangers."

"As you wish," he said, leaping into the air. With a few flaps of his wings, he vanished into darkness.

"Slide over, Ralph," Dixon said before climbing into the back seat beside our prisoner.

"That is not my name," the Stasi replied.

Dixon snorted. "You're a hard man to please, Ralph."

Settling into the front passenger seat, I pulled the door shut as Maya did the same. A moment later, the engine groaned and belched exhaust, and the car accelerated.

Chapter 20

Industrial Espionage

Through the tiny Trabant's side windows, the dark and sooty facades of buildings that had survived the last world war still bore signs of damage, including bullet holes, presumably fired from machine guns. I shook my head, marvelling that somehow, despite it being nearly four decades since their making, the holes had never been repaired.

The old buildings were eventually replaced by newer structures, which, while not soot-stained, were colourless, featureless concrete monoliths. In some ways, they were even sadder to look upon, and they looked so similar to each other, I had to wonder how residents ever managed to find their way back home. More than that, I couldn't imagine why such beautiful old buildings had been left rotting nearby and these functional but sullen and soulless structures erected instead.

"Why are they all the same?" I asked, pointing to one.

"They are *Plattenbauten*," Rolf said from the back seat.

I turned to face him. "They're prefabricated?"

He nodded. "From large concrete slabs."

"They're drab," Maya said, "but cheap and easy to build."

Dixon's lip curled. "The wonders of communism."

"You Westerners . . ." Rolf muttered.

"Yeah?" Dixon prompted.

Rolf sneered. "You believe yourselves so superior. Yet despite your riches, perhaps because of them, you allow people to sleep and starve in the street." He glanced out the window. "Here, everyone has a job and a home."

Dixon chuckled without humour. "Yeah, right. A shitty job and a shitty hovel for everyone. It's fair, I give you that. You've all got a place to live but little reason to keep living. And it's not quite the same for everyone, is it? You Stasi, members of your Party, you all live better than the common man, don't you? Better food, better jobs and opportunities, more freedom to travel."

"That is untrue," Rolf sputtered.

"Yeah, you do," Dixon said. "Don't try to deny it. You've guaranteed everyone a life of subsistence and denied them the option of ever achieving more—except by backstabbing and spying on their neighbours—and you pat yourselves on the back for it."

"To ensure order," Rolf said with a scowl. "To protect the people against subversive forces and keep the streets safe for decent folk. Far better that than your country's organized crime, drug addiction, riots, and murders."

"Safety at any price," Dixon spat. "Take my freedom, just keep me safe. People like you make me sick."

Rolf made no reply, and I didn't know what to say. I valued freedom highly, probably more than most, having had it taken from me by the Bodhi Group. Yet the problems Rolf had mentioned were real. Nightly news programs, movies, and TV shows were filled with muggings and murder. Often occurring in broad daylight, while passersby looked on. Total freedom meant anarchy. For people to live together peacefully, there had to be a balance between the two.

Yet controlling people's lives, what they said, where they went, and what they thought seemed worse than anarchy. If you need to build a wall to keep people from leaving, and you're terrorizing and executing people for speaking their minds, you've crossed over from merely being wrong to being full-on evil.

A few blocks later, the prefabricated buildings fell away and were replaced by the smokestacks, factories, and warehouses of an industrial district.

"Not much farther now," Maya said.

Dixon nudged my arm. "Why do you suppose the Eurus have been doing it? Creating the changelings, I mean. It's got to be more than just controlling people."

"Beats me." I looked at Rolf. "Do you know?"

The Stasi guard bit his lip. "Whatever is going on specifically is, as you Americans say, above my pay grade. I was told only that secrecy is crucial, and I have been ordered not to ask further questions."

I made a face. "And that satisfies you? People are being kidnapped and experimented on. Your superiors are meeting with demons, and that's all fine with you?"

Rolf coughed nervously. "I have been assured that what is being done will lead to a world united in peace. One in which the earth's resources are not wasted as they are under capitalism. Yes, there will be some suffering—some deaths, even—before that can occur, but isn't such a world worth the deaths of the few if it means a better life for our children, and our children's children?"

Dixon snorted. "What a load of horseshit. You must know more than that."

"He might be telling the truth," I said. "I mean, think about it. If the situation were reversed, would you tell your subordinates everything?"

Dixon scoffed. "The situation would never be reversed."

"Wouldn't it?" I met his eyes. "You were okay with what the . . . what happened to me."

"That was different." Dixon studied his gun. "There were extenuating circumstances."

My brow furrowed. "Huh? Like what?"

"Never mind," Dixon said. "We're not discussing this in front of this guy."

"Fine," I said, turning forward in my seat. "For now."

"There it is," Maya said several blocks of uncomfortable silence later, pointing to a hulking box-shaped building three storeys high that loomed in the distance. It was surrounded by a wall the height of two men, the top of the stone boundary bristling with barbwire. As the car slowed, a truck exited through a wide gate near the barrier's middle, and a guard manning the entrance moved wooden barricades back into place.

"It's still operating," she said, swinging the Trabant to the side of the road and cutting the engine.

I nodded. "Stein said they're working overtime to keep up with demand."

"What now?" she asked.

I thought a moment. "Can you ask Caelus to take a look inside? See if he can spot Sid or anywhere he might be?"

"Of course," she replied.

"Anyone got a match?" Dixon asked.

"I like your thinking," I said, "but first we've got to find Sid. If he's here. After that, get out the marshmallows."

A short while later, the raven alighted on the sill of the open driver's-side window and looked into the car. "The factory is still operating. They are loading trucks in the back."

"Any sign of Sid?" I asked.

"I did not see him," Caelus replied. "However, armed soldiers are guarding a nearby building, and I saw people in lab coats inside, through an open skylight."

"Nice," Dixon said. "Sounds like a good place to start searching."

"Getting inside is going to be a problem," Maya said. "I don't think we'll be able to bluff our way past the guard. Not dressed as we are." She leaned toward the windshield and looked up. "If not for the barbwire, I'd suggest going over the wall."

"Then we'll have to fight our way in." Dixon raised his gun. "If we move fast enough, they won't know what hit them."

Maya's lips thinned. "That's far too reckless. There could be a small army inside one of the buildings. Even if there isn't, if anyone gets to a phone, we'll have every cop in the city down on us."

"Yeah, true," I said distractedly as a truck emerged from the factory complex gate and came toward us. Crates of soda could be seen peeking above the short wooden fence enclosing the truck's uncovered bed. "I've got a better idea." I pointed at the windshield. "Follow that truck."

Maya smiled and started the car. "Okay." The car lurched into motion and swung a hundred and eighty degrees. "We're hijacking the truck, I take it."

"Yep," I said.

"Nice thought," Dixon said as, a few hundred feet ahead, the truck turned right. "That could work."

Shifting forward in my seat, I pressed a hand to the dash. A moment later, I ping-ponged between Maya's shoulder and the passenger door as the car's little engine whined.

"Easy, Day," Dixon said.

"Sorry," Maya replied. "I'm trying to get a feel for the car's capabilities." She glanced my way. "What's the plan when we catch them?"

"Just get me close," I said as traffic lights a block ahead changed to yellow and the truck's tail lights brightened. "Quickly. Pull up behind it before the light goes green again."

"All right." Closing the distance, she stopped the Trabant a few feet from the idling truck's back side.

"Here goes," I said, shoving my door open and spilling out onto the pavement. As I slammed the door, the light changed, and the truck rumbled and shook into motion.

Damn it. I sprinted for it, inhaling noxious diesel fumes. Reaching high, I grabbed onto the wooden guardrails enclosing the truck bed and lifted myself from the ground. I hung there a moment, windmilling my legs through the air until my feet hit something with a metallic clang. Pushing against whatever it was, I hoisted myself up and hugged the guardrail's top slat. *Made it.*

Orange crates of Nicht Cola, stacked higher than the guardrails, filled the cargo area, leaving no room for me. Having no other choice, I leaned back to check the truck's undercarriage and began sidestepping my way toward the cab.

When I reached it, the whirring of a Trabant's high-pitched engine grew closer, coming from the far side of the truck. Figuring it must be Maya offering a distraction, I leaned right, thumbed the truck's passenger-door handle, and pulled it open.

"*Was?*" a voice shouted from within.

The truck's brakes squealed, and the door ripped outward, taking me with it.

"Shit!" Off balance, I flailed, grabbing the door's top with my free hand. Instead of falling, I swung out over the rushing roadway, mashing my nose into the inner glass of the passenger-side window. The truck halted, and I unlocked my aching fingers and turned toward the truck cab.

"*Wer sind Sie?*" asked a clean-shaven man in his thirties with a bulbous nose and short-brimmed cap, regarding me from the driver's seat with bulging eyes.

Before I could answer, the door behind the driver opened and Dixon's head popped into view. "Don't move, Fritz," he said, holding a gun to the driver's head. "*Aussteigen.*"

With the driver covered, I looked around for signs of trouble and blew out a breath, relieved. Save for the sound of running engines, the streets of the industrial area were quiet and empty of life.

We'd better hurry, though, I thought. A police car might turn onto the street at any moment. Seeing a truck askew in the street, they'd no doubt stop to question us. If that happened, things would go south fast.

Rounding the truck cab, I followed Dixon as he hustled the driver over to the Trabant, where Maya waited, holding a gun on Rolf, who still sat in the car's back seat.

She motioned to the truck driver. "What do we do with him?"

I jabbed a thumb at the truck. "Get him and Rolf to help us unload the cargo."

"Good thinking," Dixon said. "The guard at the factory gate would certainly wonder why it's returning fully loaded." He glanced about. "Not here, though. A bunch of crates in the street will draw attention we don't need."

Maya nodded. "Caelus says there's a good spot to unload it nearby."

"Great," Dixon said. "Lead the way. I'll follow in the truck."

We drove to a dark warehouse a few streets over and, with the aid of our two prisoners, unloaded the cargo and piled it against a wall. When the last crate was dropped, we gagged and bound Rolf and the truck driver with strips of cloth torn from their shirts before stuffing them into the Trabant's back seat.

"I'll hide in the truck bed," I said to Dixon, smacking my palms together. "The guards might get curious if you've got a passenger with you."

"Works for me." He tossed his suit jacket into the truck cab and turned back to me. "Be ready to move. Things could go pear-shaped fast."

I chuckled. "Not as long as I'm wearing this suit." I looked at Maya. "You'll keep watch through Caelus?"

"Of course," she replied. "I'll be right outside the gates in case there's trouble."

"Perfect." I leaped up to the truck bed. "Let's go."

As I lay down by the cab, Caelus alighted on the wooden guardrail, and the vehicle shuddered and rolled forward.

Here goes.

"The entrance approaches," Caelus said a short while later. "Good luck, Sentinel. I will be watching."

As the raven took flight, I pulled an old tarp—which I'd found when unloading soda pop crates—up to my neck and held it by its edge, ready to duck beneath it.

Soon after, the truck slowed, turned, and stopped. I strained to listen, but over the engine's rumble, only the occasional word of German could be heard. After a brief pause, the truck rocked back into motion, and I expelled the breath I'd been holding, smiling as the red brick walls of a three-storey building slid past. *We're in.*

Tossing the tarp aside, I rolled to my stomach, pushed myself to my knees, and grabbed the wooden guardrail to steady myself as the truck shifted beneath me. Moments later, visible above the railing, a loading dock, crowded with people, swung into view. I scurried to the truck's tail, staying low, and leaped to the ground before taking cover behind a stack of crates. There, hidden from casual view, I scanned the area.

What do we have here? To the right of the loading dock, a few hundred feet away, two men holding assault rifles stood guarding the entrance to a building. *That must be the one Caelus meant.*

While Dixon backed the truck into position, I dashed closer to the men, using crates, stacks of empty pallets, and trash bins to mask my approach. When only open space separated me from them, the rumble of a truck's engine died, drawing my gaze. Over by the loading dock, men and women moved toward Dixon's truck, holding full crates of soda pop. Beyond them, another truck on the far side of Dixon's roared to life. A moment later, it crept from its stall, and a forklift emerged from within the factory's gaping cargo doors, holding a pallet of orange plastic crates on its tines.

Satisfied the workers were no immediate threat, I turned back to the guards and considered my next move.

Sidestep into the Underfrost? I shook my head. *Not yet.* I still wanted to keep that option as a last resort. Besides, I couldn't open the door that way, and forcing my way through solid matter, even while Frost Walking, was tough. Sure, moving at high speed made it easier, but I wasn't sure I'd have enough of a running start from where I stood. *I need a distraction.* After a moment's thought, I conjured a frost ball and sent it arcing over the heads of the soldiers. It struck a stack of empty soda crates, sending them tumbling to the ground.

"*Scheisse*," one of the guards shouted. "*Was ist das?*"

Shrugging, the other guard raised his rifle and motioned to his partner to follow.

Now. With their backs to me, I stole from cover, heading for the door they'd been guarding. When I was halfway there, the head of a guard snapped my way, and his brow creased an instant before his eyes widened and his gun rose. *Damn.*

I charged him, sweeping frost from the air as I moved and sending it flying.

A froth of white punched the guy's chest an instant later, and he screamed and clasped his hands to the impact point, but it was too late. The projectile's shock wave of energy, travelling through the Underfrost, had already done its job, supercooling everything in its path faster than any normal cold ever could. In this case, heart, lungs, and other soft tissues. Shivering uncontrollably, he collapsed without having fired a shot.

A few steps away, the other guard turned his gaze from the fallen crates, his expression a clone of the first guard's confusion. I redirected toward him, still moving full-tilt, and crashed a frost-charged fist into the dude's jaw, rolling his eyes up in their sockets.

Easy now, I thought, grabbing the stunned guard's arm before he could fall.

I dragged him a few feet and laid him down next to his partner as footsteps approached.

"Need help?" Dixon skulked closer, his gun drawn but aimed at the ground.

My gaze went to the workers loading the cargo truck. "Shouldn't you be watching them?"

"Don't worry about them." He swirled a finger by his temple. "They're seeing nothing but crates and cargo trucks. More changelings, I guess. Whatever's inside them makes them great workers."

"Yeah," I growled. "Perfect slaves." I pointed to the guards. "Keep an eye on them, would you?"

"You bet." He holstered his gun and, stooping, reached for one of the guards' assault rifles. "That's what I'm here for."

"Thanks." I tried the door the two men had been guarding. To my relief, it opened, revealing an empty interior. Light came from the frosted glass of a door directly across the room. "Let's bring them in here."

Behind me, Dixon had gathered up the guards' weapons. He'd slung one across his shoulder and had the other trained on the two downed men. "*Aufstehen.*" The men staggered to their feet—rubbing their injuries—and we urged them into the anteroom. With terse commands uttered in German, Dixon sat them against a wall in the empty room and looked at me. "Go ahead. I've got these boys covered."

"Thanks." Gripping the knob of the frosted-glass door, I hesitated and looked back to Dixon. "What were the extenuating circumstances?"

His face scrunched. "What?"

"For what the Bodhi Group did," I said, keeping my voice low, "when I came to you guys for help. You said there were extenuating circumstances for what you did."

He arched an eyebrow. "You want to talk about this now?"

"Yeah." About to enter the lion's den, I didn't want to keep wondering any longer.

He sighed. "You'd been seen talking to the wrong people before you showed up in Nevada. We figured the Soviets cooked you up in some secret Siberian lab."

I scowled and looked down. Fuzzy memories of meetings with Zelus and other Eurus within the Soviet hierarchy, discussing the Allfrost's decline, came to mind. "That was before I knew the Eurus were involved with Baduriel. I was trying to get their help too. The Allfrost covers the entire world, you know, not only the States."

He shrugged, still keeping his borrowed rifle on the seated guards. "Either way, we couldn't trust you. The higher-ups decided to study you instead."

My eyes lit. "Is that why you'd always go on about commies and socialism? Because you figured I was a Soviet agent?"

"Yeah." A few breaths passed. "What I said about the Russkies was all true, but I was also feeling you out. I suppose I was trying to rationalize what we were doing to you. If you'd confirmed you were a bad guy . . . well, you know."

"And?"

"You're no commie." He smirked and looked my way. "You're no Republican either. I'm not sure what you are."

"How about reasonable?"

He chuckled and his eyes flicked to my shoulder. "Are you going? We don't have all day."

With a nod, I turned and opened the door.

Chapter 21

Vial Plans

The room beyond was huge. Lost in shadows, its ceiling lay two or three storeys above, held up by sharp-edged, unadorned pillars with peeling white paint. The distant walls alternated between murky windows and brick. At floor level, corralled within a barbwire-topped chain-link fence, shadowy silhouettes wandered between pools of incandescent light cast from hanging lamps.

I held my breath and stepped inside, letting the people behind the fence see me. To my relief, they kept milling about, as if I wasn't even there. *More changelings*, I thought, exhaling.

Taking a left, I skirted along the fence and made my way to the holding pen's far side, where an open area filled with desks, tables, and office chairs awaited me. Seeing no one, I stepped inside and, moving among the desks, leafed through papers and opened drawers. My eyes strayed to the holding pen, where a nearby changeling shambled across a shaft of light before drifting out of view.

Where are the secrets? I thought, turning my attention to the wall opposite, along which several doors could be seen. By the light coming from small rectangles of clear glass inset into their top halves, some were currently occupied, but others were unlit.

As I pondered my next step, a shadow fell across one of the lit windows and vanished. Muffled, unintelligible conversation followed. Feeling exposed, I crossed to the nearest door, its window dark, and slipped through. Inside, jars, bottles, beakers, and flasks sat on long counters and shelves, declaring the space to be a chemistry lab.

A mad scientist's lair if ever I saw one, I thought, guessing this must be where new drinks were formulated, including those changing people into catatonics.

I walked the room, scanning diagrams and charts taped to the walls and incomprehensible figures and formulas on a dusty green chalkboard. Moving past them, I stopped in front of an illustration of the human nervous system. A red circle had been drawn at the top of the figure's spinal column. Lines marked in several colours ran from that point throughout the body. Each line was labelled, but whoever had done it had crappy penmanship. The only word I could make out was *Myzel*.

"Mycelium?" The translation for the German word popped into my mind, along with a vision of the tubular roots of mushrooms, and I shuddered. *Is that what's inside those people?*

A muted shout snapped my gaze to the chalkboard. I froze but heard nothing further, and I skulked over to the door and peered out its small window. The wall trembled faintly, and a few heartbeats later, a woman appeared, entering into view from the left. She wore slacks the colour of dried blood and a baggy yellow sweater, and her wrinkles and short grey hair gave her the appearance of someone on the far side of sixty.

"I believe we have it now," the woman said in German, dancing through the desks toward the chain-link fence. She spun on a heel, and I withdrew deeper into the darkness of the chemistry lab. "The symbiont grants even this body a new vitality."

A thin man in a white lab coat drifted into view. "I am glad you are pleased, mistress. We have made significant progress during your absence, and I am happy to say the frost host's viability has increased substantially as well."

She beamed. "Wonderful, Horst. Show me."

The couple turned and walked away, and when their steps were scarcely audible, I inched the door open and chased silently after them.

I had almost caught up to them near the far side of the warehouse when they turned right and moved out of view. Wary of a trap, I ghosted into the Underfrost and strode forward, entering an open section of floor space wedged between the chain-link holding area and what I presumed to be the warehouse's brick outer wall.

The grey-haired woman and thin man stood with their backs to me, surrounded by an array of light stands, regarding a man who lay on a gurney at the room's centre. Unable to see the guy clearly, I drew closer and gasped at his Mohawk hairdo, ripped jeans, and Clash T-shirt.

It's Sid. The frost punk lay unmoving with his eyes closed. Wires, running to nearby monitors and other devices, were connected to his temples, chest and other body parts. Although he was unconscious and breathing evenly, leather strips had been strapped across his chest and lashed about his wrists.

The man in the lab coat, Horst, pushed aside a wheeled metal table set next to the bed, its top covered with glittering surgical utensils and other tools, and touched the bound man's arm.

"How long?" the woman asked.

"More than a day," Horst replied, taking Sid's wrist. "Longer than the survival times of previous hosts, and the host still lives." He studied his watch before lowering the punk's arm. "We theorize that the symbiont does not intervene until absolutely necessary, at which point it returns here to permit extraction of the frost essence."

"Excellent," the woman said. "That exceeds even the viability of the Eurus hybrid."

He nodded. "I am glad you are pleased, mistress."

She placed a hand on the bound man's arm. "Is the essence within the host now?"

"Not at present," he replied.

The woman looked around. "What of the containment measures?"

Horst adjusted his thick-framed eyeglasses. "In place but untested. With your permission, I will prepare to test them now. I believe we have given the symbiont sufficient time to recover and fix the frost damage to the host."

She waved a hand. "By all means. Proceed."

"Very good." Horst took a step and paused. "Mistress Azrileus?"

"Something on your mind, Horst?"

"I understand infecting mortals with the regular symbiont," he said, smoothing his thinning hair. "As resources for your people alone, they are well worth the effort. Not to mention the influence so gained, but . . ."

Azrileus arched an eyebrow. "Yes?"

He cleared his throat. "I do not understand the need for a second frost host."

She frowned. "As I said, these fragments of the Sentinel's essence need to be integrated into a larger organism to be useful for our purposes."

"Of course, mistress," he agreed, "but Moscow has their own such creature, do they not?"

"Not quite the same," she replied.

"Regardless, why a second one?" Horst strode toward a stainless-steel cabinet and popped open the doors. Reaching in for a moment, he straightened and brandished a sealed vial and hypodermic needle. "It strikes me as redundant. Would our efforts not be better spent elsewhere?"

"Options," Azrileus replied. "If your Eurus comrades discover our true plan, we will have no choice but to locate the Allfrost's prime chamber on our own. Even if they should remain ignorant of our endgame, we cannot trust that they, too, will not renege on their promises. We are Anathema to them, after all."

Holy shit. I took a step closer. *She's a demon.*

"Besides," she continued, "they have a different sample. It is as likely our extract contains the key as the one they possess."

My mind raced. *Where did they get the samples?* The only ones unaccounted for were those recalled to the Institute following my escape. *Unless they really did find another Sentinel.*

"Though," she said, "it is most probable that neither we nor the Eurus have it."

"How so?" Horst tapped the hypodermic needle, which he'd filled from the vial with a dark liquid.

She caressed a hand across Sid's forehead. "Despite the damage done to him, only a small fraction of the Sentinel's entire essence had been taken from him. Unless the Group knew specifically where it was and had a reason to remove it, it would be mere chance if those had been the particles extracted from him. That is, those containing the memories we seek."

Not if I guided the removal, I thought.

"And," she continued, "of those many sample vials, we and the Eurus have obtained only two. Nearly all the remainder, I am told, have been recovered by the Sentinel himself."

"How do you know this?" Horst asked, sticking the needle into Sid's arm and injecting him.

"A Eurus mole," she replied. "Embedded at the Group's Nevada facility where the Sentinel was held."

My brow furrowed. *A mole at the Bodhi Institute?*

Getting an agent placed at the Bodhi Institute couldn't have been easy. I knew from Scott and Dixon that the Bodhi Group ran deep background checks on new hires. Aside from looking for gambling problems, drug use, and political red flags, new hires were subjected to physical exams. Even if an avatar could pass such an exam, the mole would have to work for the Group for at least a year, with a spotless record, before being considered for the Institute.

Horst placed the needle on a nearby cart. "Can his report be trusted?"

Her chin dipped. "Baduriel corroborates it."

Horst scowled. "Then the Sentinel has them all now."

Azrileus's head wagged. "Not the samples sent to other facilities. These have since been recalled to Nevada, but a vial remains at a facility in New York City, according to the mole. Evidently, that facility's director pleaded for additional time to complete some in-progress experimentation. As we speak, the Eurus are making plans to retrieve it."

"Excellent, mistress," he said with a smile. "What of the Allfrost Sentinel himself?"

"Still missing," she replied, "and confused. Despite the vials he recovered from the Institute." The faint hum of machinery and moans of the nearby changelings filled the pause before she spoke again. "He may not have consumed them yet, however, and Zelus believes there is still hope he will yet choose to return to fulfill his promise to the Eurus."

I fought to close my mouth. *What the hell does that mean?* Sure, I'd been talking to the Eurus. But like I had told Dixon not fifteen minutes ago, if I'd been seen among the Eurus, it was only because I'd sought their help with the Allfrost. *Same as I did with the Bodhi Group.*

I shook my head. *No, that's not right.* The Eurus *were* the danger to the Allfrost. With the help of Baduriel and the other Anathema, they had been altering it, preparing to use it to either disable US nuclear missiles or set them off in their silos. There was no way I'd have gone to them for help stopping their own plan.

I might have pled with them not to go through with it, though. I had friends among them whom I could have approached. Not many—the most zealous among them seemed like total A-holes—but some of the more moderate of their number were good folks. Factions come and go, but feelings between individuals often survive ideological rifts between larger groups. The wall kept people apart, but it didn't change how Germans felt about friends and family caught on the other side the day the DDR's ruling party had rolled barbwire down the streets of Berlin.

In the same way, when the gods had split into factions, my feelings for those among the Eurus I counted as friends hadn't simply vanished. So, when I'd realized what they were trying to do, it was quite plausible, even likely, I'd have tried diplomacy first.

By the Allfrost. That was why Atriel had come to rescue me. A vision of the Eurus god appeared in my mind. Not the nightmarish creature I'd faced in the tunnels beneath Caelumburg, but the avatar he'd worn when I'd last seen him years ago: a slightly built man in his forties with thick, curly brown hair and a salt-and-pepper beard. *We're friends.* I'd known Wilhelm and most of the other New Olympians far longer than Atriel, but it was true. *He must have thought I needed help getting back to the Eurus or something.*

Heat welled through my middle. Could I be one of the Eurus? One of the enemy. *No.* I couldn't believe it. Even if I'd made a deal of some kind with the Eurus, I would never have promised to do anything that would harm Wilhelm, Olivia, or any of the New Olympians. Yet, knowing they wouldn't approve, I might not have told them what I'd been doing with the Eurus either. They wouldn't have understood.

Horst smoothed his trim moustache. "Unless the Sentinel has learned of the Anathema's involvement. Given his history with Lord Baduriel, would he still help?"

She pursed her lips. "His cooperation will be convenient, but it is no longer essential. Not with our friend here at our disposal. First we will use him to find Shivurr, and if the Sentinel should prove recalcitrant, we will take what we need from him by force and implant it into this vessel. Once the essence has been integrated, this one will know the location and be ready to issue the necessary commands, as if he were the Sentinel himself."

He nodded. "And what if Shivurr cannot be found? If he has the memories we need—"

"Fear not." Azrileus touched a hand to the bound man's wrist. "Again our friend here may be our saviour. For we will use him to seek out the prime chamber ourselves, as the Eurus do now with their own creature. You must have realized by now that this one has the capacity to perceive the nodes of the Allfrost. That is why it wanders. It seeks them out."

"For what reason?" Horst asked.

She touched a finger to her bottom lip before responding. "Perhaps acting on some primal urge to fulfill the Sentinel's core mission or to find the Sentinel himself. Whatever the reason, we should be able to use that to our advantage. As for the small matter of the authentication key, Baduriel is working on alternatives, should all else fail."

Horst rubbed his moustache. "Still, there is much uncertainty. We do not really know if we can find this chamber or its key or if Moscow will live up to their end of the agreement, nor if Lord Baduriel can truly manage without the key."

"There is." Azrileus stroked the unconscious man's hair. "Yet we here have done all we can to prepare the way for my brethren and to set humanity on a course for a better world. A world in which no mortal stands above another. True equality, no crime, no decadence, no division."

"No freedom," Horst intoned, staring into the distance. "No discord. No pain. I look forward to that day, mistress."

I swirled a finger by one of my temples. *Okay, nut bag.*

He had said the words—which had the ring of an oft-spoken mantra—with religious fervour, as if describing a future utopia, but it sounded like a nightmare to me, and I was sure Dixon would feel the same.

No discord, no pain. Sure. No freedom? No, thank you.

They're zealots. The same sorts of assholes Olivia and Hanale had spoken about with disgust.

How Horst could think this way puzzled me, but more than that, I wondered how the Allfrost and the symbionts paved the way to achieve it. The Eurus's nuclear intentions might allow the Soviets to dominate the world, putting an end to liberty, but they would still face rebellions even then, and that meant discord and a whole lot of pain.

"Now," Azrileus said, "it is past time we tested this containment field."

"Of course." Horst strode toward a stainless-steel cabinet set against the red brick wall and popped open its broad double doors. Reaching in, he straightened and brandished a shiny metal urn. "The injection should have had adequate time to work by now."

Coming closer to him through the Underfrost, I gave the container a closer look. It reminded me of the jar Baduriel's men had used in the transportation chamber in Abadom Castle, trying to vacuum up Wilhelm in his spectral form.

An Animavas, I thought, remembering the name one of the thugs had used for it back then.

"Here we are." Horst uncapped the jar and slotted the container into a holder next to the gurney. A thin rubber hose ran from the stainless-steel enclosure along the bed's protective railing and behind the unconscious man's neck. "Initiating transfer now." He pressed a button on a panel next to the enclosure, and the hose fluoresced, sparkling with a rainbow of colour. "Transfer complete."

"And the containment field?" Azrileus asked.

"Ah, yes. Of course." He strode over to a pillar and flipped a switch on the metal box affixed to it. "Containment field enabled. Now we wait."

Before long, the subject twitched, his head rose from the bed, and his eyes fixed on Azrileus and Horst. A moment later, he looked in my direction.

Chapter 22

Self-Discovery

Sid continued to eyeball me, moaning and struggling against his bonds. Wondering if he could somehow see me, I looked down at myself to ensure I was still in the Underfrost. *Yep, still there.* I retreated a few steps, not sure what to make of it, before bumping into something, but when I turned to look there was nothing there.

Squinting, I extended a hand and felt a spongy resistance to the air. I pressed harder and the countering force increased accordingly. My mind flashed back to Caelus, inhabiting an ookmir body, trying and failing to punch through another invisible barrier. I wasn't sure if *that* one had extended into the Underfrost, but whatever containment fence Horst had raised sure seemed to do so.

Pivoting on a heel, I felt my way along the force field, finding no opening. *Come on.* I took a deep breath and let it out slowly. *Settle down, Shivurr.* There was no need to panic. Azrileus and Horst had no idea I stood nearby, and they couldn't see me. I just had to wait until they dropped the field. Except, returning from the Underfrost was already seeming less important than the rational part of my mind told me it should be. In fact, why did I want to leave anyway?

I looked back as Sid banged his heels against the gurney. His eyes were open, tracking my every move, and his neck and arm veins bulged as he struggled against his restraints.

"Come," Azrileus said. "Help me free the subject."

Uh-oh. As the couple rushed toward the gurney, I resumed my frantic search for an opening. Given the wild looks Sid had been giving me, I had no doubt that, once free, he'd be on me in moments. Visions of vines erupting from his skin to pierce and infect my body raced through my mind, and I started to hyperventilate. *Come on.*

"He is vanishing," Horst said from my rear.

"Give it room," Azrileus commanded.

I fired a glance over my shoulder toward the bed. Sid, now standing, came at me slack-jawed, with his arms extended. Unable to retreat, I tried to sidestep, realizing that the symbiont-infected man, infused with Allfrost Sentinel essence, was now in the Underfrost with me. Which meant we were as solid to each other as if we were both in the regular world.

Don't touch me, I thought, raising my arms defensively. Sweeping my limbs aside, Sid lunged and locked me in a bear hug, stinking of bad breath and body odour. I wrenched my elbows outward to break his hold, bunched his T-shirt in my hands, and tugged him sideways while sweeping my foot against his ankle. He stumbled but used his grip on the lapels of my coat to keep from falling.

As we wrestled, cabinets shook, IV stands fell, and wheeled carts rolled, disturbed by our passage through them, despite our near but not absolute regular-world intangibility. Finally, peddling my feet against the floor, I shoved him like a linebacker, and we stumbled toward the hallway until the containment field's spongy resistance enfolded us. Bracing myself, I pushed at Sid's chest, keeping him at bay as he leaned toward me.

His mouth gaped, and white vapour streamed from inside, engulfing my head. *Back off, dude.* I tilted my head away from him, but it was no good. My vision clouded and my cheeks tingled and warmed. I'd felt the same sensation before, and I knew abruptly that the crystal-filled vapour streaming from Sid was my own stolen essence.

Damn. Though I'd been pretty sure it would be mine—based on what Azrileus had said—and was happy to recover more of myself, I'd still been hoping the essence Sid possessed belonged to another Allfrost Sentinel. It would mean I wasn't the only one of my species left in the world. Shaking off the disappointment,

I parted my lips and drew in a sharp breath, sucking the sparkling fog into my mouth through my cowl. When the vapour petered out, Sid dropped through my hands and thumped against the floor, where he lay unmoving.

Ugh. I winced, feeling a sudden turmoil in my guts. There was something else in the cloud I'd just inhaled. Something foreign. *What the heck is that?* I could only guess a little something extra must have been added to the essence they'd pumped into Sid. Something necessary for the frost essence to integrate with the symbiont-human hybrid. Before I could get too worried about it, the sensation faded to nothing. *Whatever it was, it's gone now.*

Spotting Azrileus and Horst approach, I sidled to my left, hugging the containment field wall as they stood over Sid a moment. Their lips moved as they came closer, but their words were lost to a growing pounding in my head. Stooping, they lifted the unconscious man by his arms, dragged him over to the bed, and laid him upon it. When they finished reattaching wires to the punk's head and body, Azrileus wiped a thin layer of frost from the prisoner's face, leaving it wet and glistening in the artificial light.

"What has happened?" she asked as the pounding in my head faded. She wiped her hand on her pants. "Was it the containment field?"

"I do not know." Horst flipped switches on a large box with several dials and a green display that sat atop a nearby cart and grabbed the handle of a wand-like device wired to it. A metal protrusion on one end had the look of an antenna of some kind. Turning back to the bed, he adjusted the dials on the box and ran the wand over his patient. "It is not possible."

"What is it?" Azrileus asked.

"The frost essence." He gawked at her. "It has left him."

"How?"

Horst shrugged. "Perhaps the organism expelled it. I am unsure."

Azrileus looked around. "The containment field remains active. It cannot have gone far." She picked up the jar that had held my essence. "Bring the cart. We will scan for it systematically."

Uh-oh. If they had a device that could detect my disembodied essence, I was pretty sure it would have no problem at all finding me.

With a nod, Horst laid the device in his hand atop the box. Shaking his head at Sid, he followed Azrileus, pushing the cart holding the scanning device into the hall.

Huh, I thought, watching both of them pass beyond where I knew the containment fence to be without so much as a pause. Either the force field selectively ignored them or it worked only on life forms of frost like me. *Unless the field is only present in the Underfrost.* I suppressed a thrill of excitement. If so, stepping back into normal space might be all that was required to escape the area. The Underfrost felt good, though. Too good.

I smacked my cheeks. *Get it together, Shivurr.* It was time to get out of here, but with Azrileus and Horst watching, I'd have to take them down before they could raise an alarm, then make a run for it. My eyes narrowed. But before leaving, I'd have to ask Azrileus about the promise I'd supposedly made to the Eurus.

The thought released a cascade of recollections, and details of my conversation with Zelus, already half remembered in the Sebastian Street apartment, resolved in my mind.

In that memory, Zelus gave me a pitying look. "Do you not tire of Boreas's excuses, Sentinel Shivurr? The Allfrost declines, yet have he and his New Olympians raised a finger to help you restore it?"

"He will," I replied. "I told you. He's got his reasons, and he's been busy."

Zelus gave me a hard stare. "And you believe him?"

"Of course. He's my friend."

He gestured to a horned figure standing nearby, whom I now recognized. "You try, Baduriel."

Baduriel stepped forward. "We were friends once too, were we not, Shivurr?"

I scowled. "For my part."

"For mine as well." He clapped a hand on my shoulder. "Let us be again. I have paid for what I did, for more than a dozen mortal lifetimes, and I have repented. I ask for your forgiveness and your help in achieving redemption. Doing so means only good for you and yours. All we ask is for your help repairing and, when the time comes, activating the Allfrost."

I studied the floor. "You're not just talking about fixing it, though. You want to change it too."

"Merely enhancements necessary to our plan," Baduriel said. "The machine's core functionality will remain intact."

"So you can disable the nukes?"

Zelus shook his head. "So you can."

"Correct," Baduriel said. "It will take one such as you to set things in motion once I and my brethren have completed our work."

I stared him in the eyes. "And you'll disable all of them?"

He nodded. "Everywhere. Even those of our mortal allies."

"What say you, Sentinel?" Zelus asked, raising two fingers. "Twice already, we have averted nuclear disaster since mortals opened Pandora's atomic box. It is inevitable that someday we will fail, and this world you so love will end in fire. That is, unless you help us end the threat—permanently."

My brow creased. "I don't know." His words made sense, but Boreas would have called it undue interference in the destiny of mortals.

Baduriel threw up his hands. "If that is not sufficient, when I restore the Allfrost to its original design and functionality, I will add a few changes to allow you to search the Underfrost for your vanished people."

"Think about it," Zelus said. "You need not decide yet, as it will take time for some necessary groundwork to be completed."

I hesitated, unable to turn down saving the world lightly. Besides, the prospect of finding my people and, as one of its sworn Sentinels, restoring the Allfrost was beyond enticing. "Okay, I'll consider it."

"Excellent," Zelus said. "But do not tell Boreas or his compatriots of our intentions, or they will surely interfere."

Returning to the present, I clapped a hand to my mouth. I *had* been working with them and, knowing Boreas wouldn't like it, I hadn't told him or any of my New Olympian friends. I felt a flush of shame but, remembering my reasoning at the time, pushed it away. My intentions had been good after all. Nothing less than saving the world from an inevitable nuclear apocalypse and the Allfrost from collapse.

All good things.

Except, years later, I'd found out Zelus had been playing me. He had no intention of disabling *all* the world's nukes, just those in the US, so they could force the West to submit to Soviet rule. Sure, they might have to destroy a city or two before Western governments capitulated, but the Eurus figured it a small price to pay. When that happened, through the Soviets, the Eurus would rule the world.

I should have known.

Having learned the real plan, I'd known I had to stop it, but going to Boreas wasn't an option. Not until I'd fixed things. So I had pretended everything was fine and sought out the Group instead.

And my problems went from bad to worse.

Old angers surged, and the swirling fog of blues and whites engulfing me thickened. I'd been in the Underfrost too long, had sunk too deep, and I had to surface soon or lose myself in it. If it wasn't too late already. Rising anger fought with a sleepiness that urged me to stay, and I swam up from the Underfrost's depths and, after a long moment, popped back into the regular world.

Both Azrileus's and Horst's jaws dropped, and they stared wordlessly.

I raised a hand. "Uh, hi," I said in English.

Back in the regular world, a haze of red lay between us, a dozen feet from me. *So that's the containment field.* Turning, I saw it curved in a wide arc, forming a virtual cylinder that enclosed me, the nearby bed, and other equipment.

Azrileus's eyes narrowed. "Who are you?" she said, also in English.

I looked down at myself, belatedly remembering my disguise. "I'm Shivurr."

One of her eyebrows rose. "The Allfrost Sentinel?"

I nodded.

She pursed her lips. "You look nothing like him."

"Uh, yeah. I'm in disguise." I summoned a handful of frost and dismissed it. "It's me, though."

"I see." Her eyes flicked to the gurney where Sid lay. "Where did you—"

"Is Baduriel around?" I looked about as if he might appear at any moment, using the opportunity to study my surroundings. The red haze rose upward about fifteen feet to a metal ring, a few inches thick, hanging from wires attached to still higher support beams and ductwork. Between the two, the air looked clear, with no tinge of red.

Too high to jump, though.

"He is off planet at present," Azrileus said. "Have you recovered all your memories, then?"

"Almost." I jabbed a thumb over my shoulder at Sid. "Thanks to him."

"How did you get in here unseen?" She raised a hand before I could answer. "Never mind. The Underfrost, of course." She glanced at Horst and back to me. "Your arrival is most fortunate. What brings you to us?"

Knowing the promise I had made gave me an idea of how I might get free. "Uh, Baduriel sent me. He wanted me to check on your progress with the soda . . . uh, gamma formulation."

She wagged a finger at me. "You are lying."

"No, I'm not." I was, of course. Unfortunately, I'd always been a crappy liar. Taking a few steps closer to her, I pressed one of my palms to the scarlet field. It failed to yield, verifying it still worked even in the regular world. *At least on me.* I waved a hand at the barrier. "Do you mind?"

Her chin moved side to side. "I do not think that would be a good idea."

I tried to act nonchalant. "Why not?"

Her eyes narrowed. "You think me a fool?"

"Uh, no," I said over the faint honk of a distant car horn. "I don't really know you."

She waved a hand dismissively. "Baduriel tells me you were as confused as ever during your last encounter." She motioned to the chain-link fence where the infected milled about. "And whether you have recovered your memories since then or not, this facility is the last place he would have sent you." Her eyes darted to the containment field activation switch. "No, I am afraid you must remain here while I consult with Baduriel and my other colleagues."

So much for that idea. I ghosted slightly, pushing against the field, testing for weaknesses.

Watching me do so, Azrileus smirked. "I think you will find the Underfrost offers no means of escape either." Her eyes darted to the man on the bed behind me. "This force field was built specifically to contain those with your particular abilities. That you were not able to pass through it just now convinced me more than anything that you are who you say you are, despite your altered appearance. How did you manage to alter yourself so thoroughly, by the way?"

I slipped fully back into the regular world. "This isn't necessary." My gaze flicked left, right, and to the ceiling, looking for a way out. Extending myself through the Underfrost, I tugged on its energies, just beyond the wall, drawing snow from thin air. "Really."

Cocking an eye, Azrileus extended an arm and caught a few snowflakes in her open hand. "How quaint." Her palm flared reddish orange for an instant, and a puff of steam rose upward from her curled fingers. "Yet hardly a convincing reason to release you."

I snarled beneath my mask. After years imprisoned in the Bodhi Institute, being held against my will again further stirred an anger that hadn't settled since recalling Zelus's betrayal. "That was only a test." My arms rose and my hands swirled. A gelid gust of wind tore through the warehouse and the gently falling flakes became a vortex of ice and snow, driving nearly parallel to the floor in its fury. "You're going to want to let me out now."

"You forget, Sentinel." Azrileus thrust a finger at the chain-link area. "There are innocents about."

I shrugged. "They're already as good as dead." I didn't really mean it, though. In fact, I'd directed the worst of the tiny storm to where she and Horst stood, leaving the caged area largely untouched.

"This is pointless." Azrileus shielded her face with a forearm as the storm grew in fury. "Unlike you, we can simply vacate the area."

Bending over at the waist, she grabbed Horst's arm and together they escaped through a nearby door, slamming it shut behind themselves.

Left alone, I turned in a circle, until my eyes fell on Sid's bed. I glanced up and smiled at the hanging lamp swinging wildly above him. *It just might work.*

Climbing onto the bed, I stretched tall, one foot wedged between Sid's legs and the other perched precariously on the bed's edge. Extending my arms, I leaped up, grabbing the metal lampshade. Though it was hot, even through my gloves, I gritted my icy teeth, held on, and swayed forward and back with my legs. With each swing, I sailed in increasingly larger arcs. When my arms ached and ominous screeches of strained metal and wiring came from above, I released my hold and sailed through the air.

I thudded into the containment field's scarlet curtain, but instead of a smack in the face and chest, I felt myself slow to a gradual stop. Entirely unhurt, I hung there by my fingertips a moment until, with a grunt, I heaved my body higher while pushing against the force field with my shoes. Scrabbling up the barrier, I swung a leg atop the metal bar, straddled it a moment, and lowered myself to the far side.

A moment after my feet touched the floor, the door through which Azrileus had fled swung open. She emerged with hands awash in flame, squinting into the storm until her eyes landed on me.

Here we go.

Chapter 23

French Exit

Growling, Azrileus raised her hands, and arcs of fire shot from her outstretched fingers toward me, hissing and spitting as they cut through the blizzard.

Whoa. I sidestepped the spray, but even through my clothing a bonfire of heat warmed my left side. *Hot, hot, hot.* Clamping my palms together, I pushed a bubble of frost energy outward from my middle to shield myself. *Better.*

"I am afraid," Azrileus said, keeping up her assault, "our alliance must now come to an end."

Tendrils of flame licked past the translucent blue-white swirl protecting me. Snarling, I buffed the waning shield and my shoulders drooped beneath a wave of fatigue. I sagged like a punctured tire and sucked in gulps of air and my forehead dripped, but I held on until Azrileus finally dropped her hands.

Now. I ripped frost from thin air and hurled it at her, sending her into a crouch. Seeing her eyes dart left, I sent more frost sailing to her side an instant before she dodged in that direction, and she snarled as the ball frosted her shoulder white. Taking advantage of the opening, I rushed her, dropping my shield, and swung a clenched fist at her jaw. Before it could land, an invisible force gripped my chest, pushing me back.

What the hell? I slid across the floor, shoes squeaking, until the containment field caught me. *Telekinesis.* "Cheater."

The invisible grip on my chest relented as Azrileus climbed to her feet. Meeting my gaze, she shivered but managed a smile. "You are—"

The demon writhed as if electrocuted, and a green fog lifted away from her skin and flowed to my left.

"Hi, Mr. Shivurr," Maya said, continuing to suck the vapour into a gold bottle held in her outstretched hand. "Who is your friend?"

"Silly girl." Azrileus held her hands palms out toward the jar, and her lips contorted. The emerald mist slowed to a stop before changing direction back toward the body from which it had been torn. "Not even from such a poor vessel as this can you disembody one such as me when I am unwilling to leave it."

"In that case, let me . . ." Stepping closer, I reached back with a fist. "Offer." Punch. "Some." Punch. "Encouragement."

My last blow sent her eyes rolling up in their sockets. Uttering a final snarl, she collapsed, and her sparkling green essence flowed once more into Maya's jar. *Yes!*

"Nice uppercut, Winterboy." Dixon, holding an assault rifle, stood in the swirling snow behind Maya. "Told you, Day. Where there's snow, there's Winterboy."

"That you did, Mr. Dixon." She capped the jar, locking Azrileus inside. "Though I believe I might have figured that out myself."

"Fair enough." Taking in the scene, Dixon aimed his weapon at Azrileus's fallen avatar and came closer. "Everyone all right?"

"Better than ever," I said, telling them about the essence I'd recovered from Sid and the broad strokes of my encounter with Azrileus but leaving out what I'd learned about my ill-fated alliance with the Eurus.

Dixon glanced toward the gurney. "That him?"

I nodded. "I think he's dead."

"Nope," he said. "At least not judging by that monitor."

I gave him a sidelong smile. "Are you a doctor?"

"No," he said with a smirk. "Smartass. But I've seen my share of hospitals." He gestured toward the jar in Maya's hand. "What is that, anyway?"

"An Animavas," she replied, pocketing the container. "Some call it a soul trap. Essential when facing enemy divine."

Dixon's eyes bulged. "Got any more?"

Her chin wagged. "I'm afraid not." She studied the jar. "The gods entrust few mortals with such things. By giving even one to me, Leonidas violated protocol."

"Good thing he did," he replied.

She made a face. "It's strange, though."

"One sec." I stuck my head into the room to which Azrileus had fled from my storm. Another lab, I thought, except this one was in active use, judging by the open bottles, half-filled beakers, and other scattered paraphernalia. "Herr Horst?"

"*Ja?*" Across the room, Horst peered at me from behind a counter, holding his hands by his ears.

"*Bleiben Sie,*" I said, holding a finger to my mouth before closing the door. Stepping back, I waved my hands, burying the door to Horst's lab in a drift of chest-high snow, which I knew from past experience would have swelled to the same height on the portal's far side. If Horst tried to open it again, he'd have to dig his way out first, and without a shovel, it would be cold work with bare hands. Smacking my palms together, I glanced at Maya. "What's strange?"

"Well," she said, "despite her claims, the Animavas worked better than I've seen in the past. There's usually more of a fight, if it works at all, and the mist seemed thin, as if diluted."

Dixon chuckled. "I think you're forgetting Winterboy's encouragement."

I scratched my head. *She started it.* "How did you know I needed you?" I asked, trying to change the subject. "Not that I'm complaining."

"A little birdie told me," she said as Caelus flapped down from above and landed on her shoulder.

"Of course he did." I swallowed, wondering how much she and the raven might have heard of my conversation with Azrileus. If they'd heard anything about my previous involvement with the Eurus, they gave no sign. I looked from Maya to Dixon. "What about Rolf and those guards? You didn't do anything to them, did you?"

Dixon shrugged. "I had to shoot one."

"You're kidding."

Seeing my face, he held up a hand. "He'll live, and the others are fine," he added, as if that made it all better.

"It was truly unavoidable, Mr. Shivurr." Maya motioned to the caged area. "He tried to take Mr. Dixon's weapon when we were locking them into the pen."

My eyes widened. "You put them in with the changelings?"

Her head bobbed. "The truck driver and gate guard too. I had to bring them along on my way in."

I made a face, thinking of the predatory nature of the changelings' Nameless progenitors. "Are they safe in there?"

"They're fine," Dixon said, gesturing to the hall. "Come on. We should move."

I looked down the hall. "Right." If there were other workers in the building, they'd made themselves scarce, but there was no telling when more guards, demons, or even the police might show up. "Let's go."

With Dixon in the lead, holding his rifle at the ready, we retraced our steps.

We met no resistance, but as we neared the exit, moans from my left drew my eye to the chain-link fence. I took a step closer and squinted into the shadows. Beyond the barrier, Rolf, the truck driver, and guards attended to a man who sat leaning against a pillar, holding his arm.

"Hold on." Dashing over to the barbwire-topped fence, I swept off my cap and dug out an Ambrola. "Rolf."

"Yes?" the Stasi guard replied, shooting me a look.

"Give this to him," I said, pointing at the wounded man. I passed the tiny can of Ambrola through the chain-link fence into his waiting hand. "It will help."

Nodding grimly, Rolf opened it. "*Danke.*"

As he kneeled by the injured man, I scanned the holding pen, counting about a dozen changelings milling about the area. *Slaves*, I thought, scowling. "We should take them with us."

Dixon scoffed. "Yeah, sure. They can ride in the trunk."

"Mr. Dixon's right," Maya said. "There's no way to transport so many."

"We've got what we came for, Winterboy," Dixon added. "Let's not blow it now."

I pursed my lips and sighed. "Fine. Let's go."

Outside, we rushed toward Rolf's Trabant, which sat parked next to a dumpster, and an engine rumbled in the distance. Visible past the container's edge, headlights swung into view and stabbed into the darkness, casting tall shadows over the wall behind us.

"Hide," I hissed, ducking into cover as the light swept past. Brakes squealed a short time later and I looked again. Over by the loading dock, a truck reversed and took up position next to the one we'd hijacked earlier.

"We need that truck," I said as the driver cut the engine. "While it's still empty."

The driver stepped down from the cab as the waiting changeling workers came closer with crates.

"What are you thinking?" Maya asked.

Dixon groaned. "He wants to load the infected into that truck."

I thrust a finger at him. "Give the man a cigar."

"Negative." He glared at me. "We've got bigger fish to fry."

I scowled. "It's the right thing to do, Harland. Besides, we might learn something from them. Even if we can't, they'll be proof of what's been happening. We just have to get them to the palace and through the transporter. It'll be a cinch."

Maya frowned. "I'm not sure that's a good idea." She jabbed a thumb in the direction of the building to our rear. "It's only a matter of time before someone calls the police, or lets the guards out, if they haven't already. For all we know, they might already be on their way."

My jaw set. "If they do, I'll take care of it."

If the situation were reversed, I would have wanted someone to do the same for me. Besides, if we could get the infected back to West Berlin, the Bodhi Group could study what had been done to them. And having live victims could only help them pluck the right strings to get Nicht and Nacht pulled from West German grocery store shelves.

She sighed. "I don't suppose I can talk you out of it, can I?"

"Nope," I said, watching the driver light a cigarette and turn away.

"Fine," Dixon said. "We're wasting time arguing." Slapping my shoulder, he stood. "Wait here while I have a word with this guy."

Leaving cover, Dixon raced toward the driver, who turned and recoiled at the sight of the security director's raised weapon. Dixon barked a few words in German, and the driver—middle-aged, dressed in brown pants and light blue button-up shirt with short sleeves—dropped his freshly lit smoke and lifted his hands to his shoulders.

"Come on," I said, and together, Maya, Caelus and I emerged from cover and dashed over to them.

"Search him," Dixon said, keeping his gun trained on his captive.

With a nod, Maya patted the man down. "He's clean," she replied moments later.

"Good," I said, touching her arm. "Then let's get the changelings loaded."

"While you do that"—Dixon grabbed the driver by the shoulder—"I'll put this guy in the cage with the others."

"Good idea," I replied. "Be careful."

He snorted, walking away. "After the week I've had, this is herding kids at the zoo."

"Don't get cocky now," I said, hopping onto the loading dock.

Joining Maya, I grabbed crates from workers before shooing them onto the truck bed. It was surprisingly easy. They all seemed willing to do whatever they were told, no matter who gave the commands—no doubt because of the organisms in-fecting them—and we ordered them all to sit down, ensuring none would fall out or be seen on the drive to the palace.

When most people on the dock were loaded, I strode to the open factory doors. Within, at the far end of a corridor of dark green and orange crates, banks of fluorescent lights high above revealed conveyor belts with stainless-steel guardrails, huge machinery, metal stairs and walkways. About a half dozen people were visible, performing some unknown—at least to me—function in the facility's operation, and two of them regarded me with puzzled expressions for a moment before turning and fleeing deeper into the building.

Uninfected, I thought. Deciding they must be here to manage the workers, I looked back over my shoulder at Maya. "There are more inside."

"Go ahead." She grabbed another changeling's arm. "I'll get the ones out here boarded."

With a nod, I dashed inside and, glancing around for enemies, ordered stragglers toward the truck. I followed the last one back outside and looked toward the lab building.

Come on, Dixon, I thought, seeing no sign of him. Had the Stasi men gotten the jump on him after all? *Screw it.* I hopped down from the loading dock, determined to go looking for him. Maybe we weren't quite friends, but I wasn't leaving him behind.

Before I could take more than a few steps, the lab building door swung open, and I drew up short, my hands lit with frost energy. A half second later, a man stepped through and shambled toward me, and several more unsteady figures came after him. Dixon came last, gun in hand, closing the door after himself. Spotting me, he gave me a nod before rushing to the front of the line and steering his charges in our direction.

"Nice one, Dixon." I smiled and looked at Maya. "Check this out."

"Interesting," Maya said from my side. "Mr. Dixon has a heart after all."

I chuckled. "I wouldn't go that far."

"Onto the dock," Dixon said in German as the procession reached us, and the changelings obediently clomped up the stairs at the loading dock's side.

"What changed your mind?" I asked, helping him hustle the changelings onto the now-crowded truck bed.

He shrugged. "In for a penny, in for a pound. Fortunately, these folks are easy to handle."

I snorted. "Yeah, I noticed that too."

"We should go." Maya closed the truck's tailgate. "Before—"

Blue light strobed from the far side of the factory yard, accompanied by a sudden blaring tone that rose and fell in volume, and two sedans—rooftop lights flashing—slid into view from the right. Bigger than Rolf's Trabant, their top halves were painted white and the lower halves dark green, and the word *Volkspolizei*—People's Police—was stencilled in dark green letters across their white hoods.

"Shit," I muttered as they swung toward us. *Too late.*

Dixon hoisted his rifle. "Looks like we're going to have to shoot our way out."

"Stand down." I pushed the barrel of his weapon to the side. My returning memories had brought back a lot of old griefs I dared not examine, but along with them came old tricks too. One in particular came to mind right now. "I've got this."

Jumping from the dock, I raced to the front of the truck and, stirring the Underfrost with upraised hands, bowled balls of frost in the new arrivals' direction. The frost balls tumbled rapidly, passing inches from the sides of the vehicles, and a swell of frothing snow rose from the pavement in their wake. Car doors banged against snow as the men inside, glancing my way with wild eyes, tried to exit their snowbound vehicles. Over my shoulder, Maya and Dixon held their guns high, aimed at the police car windshields, but held their fire.

"Lower your weapons," I yelled at the police cars, catching what I thought might be a glimpse of a handgun through a windshield, "if you want to live." They might not speak English, but I figured my friends' weaponry and the downward gesture I made with my frost-infused hands were message enough. I stepped closer and traded looks with the occupants, their faces mostly lost in shadow behind the glare of headlights. "Do you know why I stopped you?"

"*Was?*" said a voice, coming from the open driver's-side window to my left.

"That's what I thought." I circled them, filling in gaps and raising the height of the snow drifts until they lifted the cars higher. "For starters, reckless driving." I was careful to leave the top few inches clear. *Don't want anyone suffocating.* "Then there's causing a disturbance. Those sirens are wicked loud. So, for your complete lack of respect for the law, you're going to have to stay in your cars awhile and think about what you did. *Verstehen?*" Without waiting for a reply, I wrung my gloves clear of frost and jogged back to my companions. "That should hold them for a while."

"Nice job," Dixon said, pulling open the driver's-side door. "Come on. Get in the other side."

Rounding the front, I climbed in next to Maya, and before my butt hit the seat, the truck lurched into motion.

"Hold on to your hats," Dixon said, working the gearshift as the truck brushed against a snow drift. "Man, this thing's a beast."

Passing the police cars, their lights still flashing and sirens still blaring, we fled the factory yard.

Chapter 24

Objects in Mirror

The passenger seat was a tight fit for two people. A wide armrest, nearly as high as the dash, divided the driver's seat from the passenger's, forcing Maya and me into a tight squeeze. After a cordial struggle, we sat leaning in opposite directions, with me jammed against the door and her half sitting on my lap.

"We should have burned that place to the ground," I muttered, winching down the window.

"There was no time," Dixon said, adjusting the rear-view mirror. "Be glad we got away with as much as we did."

"Yeah, I suppose so," I said, sinking back in my seat.

"You got one of those Ambrolas?" he asked. "It's been a long day . . . or night." Smirking, he added, "With the time change, I'm not sure which."

Beyond the open windows, the police sirens gradually diminished.

"Sure." Jostling Maya to the side, I managed to wrestle off my hat, lay it on the dash, and reach in to grab one of the potent pops.

Taking the can from me, Maya cracked its seal and handed it to Dixon. "Do you remember the way back?"

"Yeah, I think so." He leaned toward the windshield and looked up. "Let me know if the bird thinks otherwise."

We turned onto another street, and Maya twisted to look out the back window. "Are those sirens getting louder again?"

Conversation stopped, and we all listened. Sure enough, the two-tone tune of police sirens was growing gradually louder, coming from somewhere to our rear.

"Shit." Dixon downed his tiny can of Ambrola and chucked the empty on the dash.

"No way they dug out that fast," I said, leaning out the window.

Several blocks back, flickers of blue light bounced off the walls of buildings, and a police car burst into view from the left and swung toward us. Another two cars, even nearer to us, entered the road from the opposite side, but they lacked the markings, sirens, or rooftop lights of police cars.

Must be Stasi.

"Get ready." Dixon twirled the wheel, turning us onto a new street, walled on each side. "We'll have to take them down. There's no way we can outrun them in this."

I cracked my door. "Slow down a bit."

"What are you doing?" Maya asked as the vehicle slowed.

"You guys keep going," I said over my shoulder. "I'll catch up."

Dixon nodded. "Be careful."

"Can you find your way alone?" Maya asked, concern in her voice.

"I'll figure it out," I said. Whether I could or not, there was no time to worry about it now. "Just get to the palace and don't wait for me. It's better you get these people to safety first." Without another word, I leaped down from the cab and ran a few steps before coming to a stop. *Good luck, guys*, I thought, watching changeling heads rock and bob inches above the truck's railing as it accelerated away. Standing tall, I reached up to adjust my cap. *Shit.* I'd left it sitting on the truck's dash when I'd given Dixon the Ambrola. "Well, that's just great."

I shook my head and pivoted on a heel to await my pursuers. Though the roadway still lay empty, the growing bleat of sirens told me they wouldn't be long.

A few breaths later, two cars swung onto the street and came toward me. Pushing all thought of my hat aside, I stomped a shoe against the roadway and streamed cryogenic energy through my feet. Beneath the frosty deluge, a thin film of ice grew upon the roadway in a widening circle.

Come on. I smiled wickedly, holding my ground as the on-coming cars accelerated, and when they were sixty feet away, I hurled frost balls into the driver's side of each car's windshield. Both frosted over in an instant, even as cracks spiderwebbed upon the glass beneath. A scrunching of metal followed as the cars brushed against each other before veering sharply away. A half second later their tires hit black ice, and they spun sideways. Careening closer, they soon filled my vision.

Shit. With no time to dodge, I sidestepped into the Under-frost, letting the cars slide through me. Even so, I felt myself pushed back a few steps, nudged as if by a fast-moving river of water—even in the Underfrost, solid objects still had slight tangibility for me—and winced at the crunch of metal behind me.

One car sat crushed against the fence lining the sidewalk—its front end curled around a post—and the other car had swung a hundred and eighty degrees and now faced me. The occupants were just dark shapes beyond the blaze of their vehicles' headlights.

Before either driver could accelerate again, I popped back into the warm world and lobbed wads of frost at the nearest car's tires. As they landed, ice shards erupted from them, thrusting through rubber with hisses of escaping air.

The growing blare of a siren from my rear turned me on a heel, and I sighed wearily as a police car—complete with rooftop lights and Volkspolizei markings—barrelled my way.

"*Stirb, Dämon,*" a voice said from my right.

A loud pop and bloom of pain flared in my arm. "Fuck." Clapping a hand to my bicep, I turned in the direction of the noise, spotting a man in Stasi uniform, gun in hand, standing by the wrecked car. "Bastard."

His gun popped again, and I vanished into the safety of the Underfrost, charged him and, resurfacing, laid him out with a frost-laced uppercut. With my arm still burning, I returned my attention to the oncoming police car. I shrouded the area in an abrupt storm of snow and ice, and the police cruiser faded from view in a haze of white, its path marked only by the glow of its blue rooftop lights.

Sidestepping, I moved into the police cruiser's path and cast handfuls of frost, laying down a carpet of ice spikes. Pops of rushing air, scarcely audible above the driving wind, followed, and two floating blue orbs, positioned at the height of a police car, juddered and shot off to my left. A screech of tire rims against concrete and a crash of twisting metal rattled my teeth before falling silent. A long moment later, the wrecked car's siren went silent too, presumably turned off by someone inside, leaving only the wind and my heavy inhalations in their wake.

Still hidden within the maelstrom, I whirled up a hovering frost disc at my feet, hopped aboard, and raced away, moving a half foot above the snowy pavement. I reached the storm's edge, stopped, and held my breath, listening for sounds of pursuit. Hearing only distant sirens, I rotated the frost disc and went after my friends. I smiled as I sailed away. The storm I'd summoned would, I knew, continue for a good while longer and fill the streets with snow for blocks around. *That ought to give them something to talk about over donuts. Or whatever East German cops like to eat.*

Before long, the hulking structures and smokestacks of the industrial district ended. In their place, the prefabricated apartment blocks I'd seen on the drive to the soda pop factory loomed.

Now we're getting somewhere, I thought, listening hard for the sound of a truck. If I could catch up to my friends before the palace, all the better.

As I wound a path through the concrete canyons, my thoughts wandered. *Allying with the Eurus! How could I have been so stupid?* I'd been afraid, I realized, reviewing my reclaimed, yet incomplete, memories. I'd been growing increasingly concerned by humanity's abuse of the planet, and the development of the first atomic bomb had totally freaked me out. I might be a snowman, but a nuclear winter wasn't my idea of a good time. *And being afraid makes you do crazy things.*

I'd talked to Wilhelm about these things first, of course, but he had wanted to wait and see. To intervene only when absolutely necessary to stop total disaster. We'd argued over it several times because it didn't make sense to me. Sure, giving humans a chance to learn how to live in balance with their environment was laudable, but gambling the entire planet on it had seemed nuts then. And it still did now. I loved Earth and all the wondrous creatures on it. That included humans too, but not at the—

I pulled the frost disc up short. *Haven't I seen that building before?* The more I thought about it, the more I thought I had. *Damn. I'm lost.* For the next five minutes, I raced up and down streets lined with buildings that all looked the same, trying to reorient myself. I pulled up short and did a pirouette, clenching my fists.

A fluttering came from above, and a raven settled atop a nearby lamppost. "Are you done sightseeing, Sentinel?"

Oh, thank frost. "Uh, hey, Caelus." I held out an arm. "Did Maya send you?"

"She did indeed." He flew down to land on my upraised forearm. Sidestepping his way to my shoulder, he added, "And a good thing too, it would seem. You are clearly lost."

I shrugged. "Give me a break. It's dark, and all these buildings"—I threw up my hands—"look freaking identical."

"Fair enough, Sentinel," he said into my ear. "I will guide you. As it happens, you are not all that far off. Take a right at the next corner."

We flew over empty streets in silence, except for the bird's occasional word of instruction, and eventually, older buildings, dirtier yet infinitely more interesting, replaced the soulless pre-fab buildings. *Potsdam at last.*

"Let's go through the park," Caelus said in my ear. "It is a more direct route."

"Sure, tell me where to go."

Under Caelus's direction, I navigated down the narrow streets of the old town, passed by a freestanding gate that reminded me vaguely of Septimius's Arch in Caelumburg, and soon entered the gloom of a huge park.

Gliding above footpaths beneath the even deeper darkness of trees, we at last came to the palace, approaching from the side opposite the one from which we'd left. I spotted the transporter shipping crate through a window and drove the frost disc toward it, and the window, doubling as a door, opened at our approach.

"Come on in," Maya said, holding the portal wide and sweeping an arm in invitation.

"Thanks." Zipping inside, I stepped from the frost disc and dismissed it back to the Underfrost with a swipe of a hand. My gaze flicked to the hat on her head. "Oh, good. You grabbed it."

"Of course." Taking off my hat, she handed it to me and fluffed her hair. "Come on. Dixon's taken the changelings across already." Setting Caelus atop her shoulder, she led the way to the shipping container. "We're arranging to have them bused to safety."

Atop the metal stairs, I drew up short, spotting a changeling loitering within the shipping crate. "What's she doing here?"

"She's our way back," she replied. "So neither you nor I have to drink another tainted pop. I know what you're thinking, but I guess the one I drank wore off." She touched her stomach and grimaced. "And I thought it best not to take another one, in case drinking more accelerates the changeling process."

"Maybe," I said with a frown. "We've got to get you looked at soon."

"Agreed," Maya said, grabbing the changeling by the arm. "Anyway, let's get back."

She whispered in the changeling woman's ear. A moment later, the walls changed, and the lights of the Berlin Wall shone through the study room window of the Sebastian Street apartment, looking much as it had earlier in the night.

"I'll be damned," I said.

She smiled. "No magic word required. They only have to wish it."

I narrowed an eye. "But they don't have wishes, do they?"

"They do if we tell them to," she replied. "They seem to obey whatever orders they're given. If we tell them we want them to activate the transporter, then they want that too."

"That's disturbing."

"No argument here." She pulled two crystals from her purse and interlocked them. "This will disable the transporter, so no one else can use it in the future."

"What are those?" I asked.

"A bit of god tech," she replied. "When activated, it disrupts attempts at spatial transpositions within a limited radius. While its power lasts."

"Where did you get that? Leonidas?"

She held the object up to the light. "Tyndareus fetched it for me, when I was back at the hotel. After you and Dixon transported accidentally, I thought it might come in handy."

"Cool." I sighed with relief. "Then the bad guys can't use it to come after us."

"Precisely," she said, setting the crystal device in the corner. As her fingers left it, it faded from view. "They could still try to cross the border and come after us that way, of course." She pushed open the doors to the dining room, revealing a crowd of rescued changelings standing about. "We'll have to keep these people at the hotel until arrangements can be made to help them. Tyndareus is arranging transportation now."

The double doors to our left opened before I could reply, and Dixon entered. Seeing me, he smirked and thrust his chin toward me. "Glad you made it."

I pointed at Caelus atop Maya's shoulder. "A little birdie showed me the way."

"Please," Caelus said. "Might we dispense with the little birdie jokes? I am a raven, not a sparrow."

"The bird's useful." Dixon clapped me on the shoulder and looked at Maya. "I told you he'd be fine." He jabbed a thumb by his ear. "No sign of the CIA agents, or pretty much anyone else, downstairs."

"Great," I said. "Then we should head back to the hotel and regroup."

Maya checked her watch. "Antiphates should be downstairs soon. Why don't you and Mr. Dixon ride back with him? I'll wait here until our people arrive and meet you there later."

"Sounds like a plan." I shot Dixon a look. "You ready?"

Chapter 25

True Confessions

Back in the safety of my hotel room, I deactivated my shapewear, letting my body revert to default form. *Oh yeah.* My snowy flesh tingled, and I almost purred with relief. Freed of my restraints, I twisted my torso back and forth several times.

The drive from the Sebastian Street apartment had been uneventful but long. The driver, Antiphates, had insisted on taking a circuitous route to ensure we weren't followed. After dropping us in front of the hotel, he had driven off to pick up Maya, and Dixon and I had returned to our rooms, our footsteps heavy on the stairs.

I took a few steps, and the room spiralled. My hands shot out reflexively, cushioning my nose's encounter with the floor. *What the frost?* Evidently, hours of maintaining my altered form had taken a toll. I pushed at the carpet, climbed back to my feet, and tried again. After a few trips around the room, my restored limbs didn't feel quite so alien, and my equilibrium returned. I couldn't shake the persistent sensations of longer legs and arms, though.

Deciding to give it time, I flung my cap onto the bed, pulled off my mask and set it down on the side table. After dropping my long coat onto the floor—I'd been trying to drape it over the back of a chair—I wandered over to the window and, for a long moment, looked out. To my left, the sky glowed, but the sun had not yet broken the horizon.

Not long until morning. I lay on the bed and smiled. All in all, the night had gone well. Extracting my stolen essence from the frost changeling, Sid Frigid, had been an unexpected win. Plus,

I'd learned an East German sub-faction of the Eurus were working with demons—Anathema gods—to turn people into catatonics. By infecting them with a plant-fungus symbiont, modelled after Abadom's Nameless. *And using Nicht and Nacht Cola to transmit the infection.* Why exactly, I still didn't know.

Sid Frigid, I could understand. The Eurus's plans to subvert the Allfrost required an Allfrost Sentinel, and without me, they'd been trying to make a substitute. Yet what did the Anathema need with near-catatonic slaves?

Aside from Baduriel, Oborateles, and Azrileus—who must have been freed by the Eurus—the rest of the Anathema were imprisoned or serving in Hades or elsewhere, redeeming themselves. At least, that was where my healing memory told me they should be. Sure, the demon trio now on Earth might want slaves, but there were easier ways to acquire them. Plus, how many thralls did three Anathema need?

I reviewed Azrileus's words to Horst, dismissing the crap about true equality and a better world. That had the air of communist propaganda. No doubt meant to appeal to the Eurus Stasi in order to convince the ideological among them to ally with demons.

What Azrileus had said about preparing the way for her brethren had me most concerned. *Are they bringing more of them?* In the transporter room at Abadom, Baduriel had said, "We will be redeemed." Maybe by striking a deal with the Eurus to free other Anathema, in exchange for his help with the Allfrost.

Classic Anathema. Making a deal with the Eurus yet working their own angle in secret. Not that I could feel much sympathy for the Eurus, who had done much the same to me. Promising to disable all the world's nukes using the Allfrost, all the while intending to affect only the US nuclear arsenal in order to dominate the world.

My jaw tightened. I'd been an idiot, but whatever had happened, whatever I'd agreed to, didn't matter. I had to make things right. I would have to move fast, though. From what I'd overheard, in addition to Sid Frigid, the Eurus had their own frost changeling. With Baduriel's Allfrost know-how, their plan to use the machine could still work, whether they had me or not. Especially if they were close to finding the Allfrost's key chamber, Allfrost Prime.

I thrust down welling panic. *Easy, Shivurr.* Even if they did, they would still need the authentication key, and like Azrileus had said, odds were neither she nor the Eurus had it. And she'd been right about herself. The essence I'd taken from Sid hadn't possessed the key. That meant the Bodhi Group, having the lion's share of remaining vials, were most likely to possess it, followed by me with the next most remaining, and the Eurus a distant last.

Which meant if I didn't have the key already, my best bet was going after the Group's vials next. With Dixon's help, getting them should be a breeze. Then the Eurus's vials, if I still didn't have what I needed. But the chances of it coming to that seemed small. Which was good, since, aside from the Gobi Desert camp, I wasn't sure where else the Eurus Faction's vials might be.

I nodded, feeling better. *Yeah, small chance.* I frowned. *Not zero, though.*

A knock on the door broke my reverie. "Shivurr?" called a voice.

Recognizing it, I strode to the hallway door and pulled it open. "Hey, guys."

Maya, with Caelus on her arm, stood in the hallway with Dixon standing off to the side. "Back to your old self, I see," she said, eyeing me up and down.

"Mostly." I flourished an arm and held the door wide. "I'm glad you're here. We need to talk."

"I thought so too," Maya said, slipping past me, "which is why I asked Mr. Dixon to join us."

"I told you, Day," he said gruffly, following after her. "It's just Dixon."

"How are the changelings?" I asked.

"As well as can be expected," Maya replied. Lifting my coat up from the floor, she tossed it onto the bed and took a seat. "We have people working on helping them."

"What about the soda pop?" I asked, realizing more people were going to be infected as long as it remained on shelves.

Dixon leaned against the desk and crossed his arms. "I've passed it up the chain. Steps are being taken."

"I have done the same," Maya said. "Don't worry, Shivurr. It won't remain in circulation much longer."

"Good," I said distractedly, my mind returning to my involvement with the Eurus. "That's good."

Maya and Dixon shared a glance.

"Is something wrong?" she asked.

"Yeah, kind of." Pushing aside my worries over how Boreas might react, I paced the room and told the gathering everything. All I'd overhead between Azrileus and Horst. Everything I remembered of past conversations with Zelus. It came out in a rush, while I avoided everyone's eyes. When I'd finished, I rubbed my neck and my gaze flicked between Dixon, Maya, and the floor. "Sorry, guys."

"Jesus," Dixon said, drawing in a deep breath.

Maya cleared her throat. "That must be what Azrileus meant about your promise."

"You heard that?" I studied her face, expecting to see anger, but I saw only sympathy. To her side, Dixon's face was now unreadable as he stared at the floor.

Her head tilted toward the bird on her arm. "Through Caelus."

The bird squawked. "I was able to enter the building through an open skylight."

My head bobbed. "Of course." *I should have known.* I looked at Dixon. "I guess you were right not to trust me."

"This changes nothing," he said with a furrowed brow. "Even if you were helping them, you're obviously not anymore."

My eyebrows rose. "You think?"

He nodded. "If you were, why cast suspicion on yourself by volunteering this intel? Why come to the Bodhi Group ten years ago? Why escape with us back here? For that matter, why rescue me from the Gobi Desert?"

"Do not forget," Caelus said, "the Sentinel seeks the vials still in the Bodhi Group's possession, and you are in a position to help him do that."

Thanks, Caelus, I thought, knowing he had a point.

Dixon stroked his chin. "From what this Azrileus woman said about a Eurus mole at the Institute, Winterboy would be just as well off with their help. Maybe more so." He twirled a finger by his temple. "Maybe you were a bad guy before and what the eggheads did—what we did—changed you. I don't know. But helping the Soviets set off nukes and kill people so they can rule the world"—he shook his head—"there's no way you've got it in you now."

I glanced at the floor. "Yeah, maybe." More than ever, I worried about what I might become if I ever succeeded in fully restoring myself. With so much at stake, I'd have to do so. "But will I still be on the right side when I get all of myself back?"

"Don't worry." He smirked and patted his jacket beneath an arm. "If you're not, I'll put you down myself. If I can."

"You can't," I said with a lopsided grin, feeling somewhat better. Even if I turned out to be working with the bad guys, I'd have to hope my experiences and the loyalties I'd built since that time would be enough to keep me from returning to what I was before. "But I appreciate the thought."

Caelus chuckled. "You would make a good demon, mortal." The bird eyed me. "Let us hope Boreas and the other New Olympians are of a like mind. If you truly betrayed them to the Eurus, you may yet find yourself sucked into an Animavas and placed in Caelumburg's castigatorium."

"Bah." Dixon waved a hand. "Sometimes you have to dance with the devil for the greater good. It doesn't make you a traitor to your side. Besides, without Winterboy, we've got no chance of stopping this thing." He shot me a look. "Once we do that, whatever you might have done in the past won't matter."

"Thanks, Harland," I said, glad for his support, unexpected though it was. I cleared my throat. "Anyway, I'm sorry, guys."

"I agree with Mr. Dixon's analysis." Maya stood and placed a hand on my shoulder. "Thank you for telling us, Shivurr. That could not have been easy."

I let out a breath. "It wasn't." But, having gotten things off my chest, I felt a lot better.

"The question is," she began, "what do we do next?"

"Get the vials," Dixon said, "before the Soviets do and keep them from getting this key."

I pointed a finger at him. "Exactly what I was thinking. That and the location of Allfrost Prime. Without both, they're screwed, even if the Eurus have another frost changeling."

"Which means we've got to get to Nevada." Dixon looked at Maya. "Is there a transporter that'll take us there?"

"Manhattan too," I said, reminding him of Azrileus's words.

"Right," Dixon said, aiming a finger my way. "We should head there first."

"Nothing direct." Maya studied the floor. "The closest we can get from Berlin would be Miami, Florida." She grunted. "There are other transporters that would get us closer, but getting to them would mean driving from here through East Germany. Along the one road Westerners are allowed to drive between East and West. It's supposed to be safe, but there are border checkpoints manned by Russian soldiers and East German police along the way. With the Stasi looking for us, taking it might be risky."

I looked at Dixon. "Florida it is, then. If we rent a car, we can drive the rest of the way."

His lip curled. "It'll take a day of non-stop driving just to make it to New York City. Twice that to get to the Institute from there."

She smiled. "The good news is, there is a transporter that goes directly to Los Angeles from Manhattan."

"That settles it," I said. "Manhattan's got to be our first stop."

Caelus spread his wings. "Would not taking an airplane from here to New York be faster than the drive from Miami to New York City?"

I frowned. "Sure, but we'd draw too much attention. I'm still a snowman. You're still a raven."

"No," Dixon said, "the bird's onto something." Taking a few steps, he picked up the bedside phone. "Give me a few minutes."

Maya's eyes flicked to my forehead. "What about the vials you haven't swallowed? Might the key not be in one of them?"

"It might." I removed my hat and looked inside. "I suppose I should drink them now."

Dixon put a hand over the telephone's mouthpiece. "Save them for now. They'll give you something to do on the way to New York."

"Good point," I said, content to wait. I hadn't had another spontaneous freezing episode like I'd had the other day on Smaragnisos, but I was still adjusting to the essence I'd gotten from Sid Frigid. Trying to reintegrate more of myself now might be enough to push me over the edge. Which meant waiting a few more hours before taking more wasn't a bad idea.

He tapped his temple. "That's why I get the big bucks."

Twenty minutes later, Dixon hung up the phone and clapped his hands together. "All right. Change of plans. We're flying from here. I've gotten us seats aboard a military flight leaving Tempelhof for New York in a few hours. And a friend in the Group is throwing some weight around, so there won't be any uncomfortable questions or scrutiny. It'll take a while, but, like the bird said, it'll still be faster than all that driving."

My gaze strayed to the window through which I'd seen an airplane taking off the previous afternoon. "Cool. Thanks for doing that."

"Don't mention it," he said, looking to the door. "I'm going back to my room to shower up and make a few more calls. I want to be sure none of the Group's vials go anywhere before we get to them."

I made a face. "Yeah, that would suck."

He checked his watch. "Our flight leaves shortly after nine. Let's meet downstairs in thirty minutes for breakfast. I doubt we're going to get meal service, and it'll be a long one, so we should fill up now."

"That's a great idea." Maya took Caelus on an arm. "I could definitely use a warm shower and something to eat."

After everyone had left, I sat on the bed and pulled out the paperback Lilith had given me. Twenty minutes later, I retook my altered humanoid form, activated the shapesuit, and went down to join my friends.

New York City, here we come.

Chapter 26

Cabin Fever

After a short drive from the hotel, Antiphates brought the car to a stop at one of the Tempelhof airport entrances reserved for military flights. Dixon got out of the car, strode over to a brown sedan waiting at the roadside and, after a brief conversation, hopped back in.

"Follow them," he said, slamming his door as the brown car moved ahead.

"*Kein Problem*," Antiphates replied.

At the gate, the escort car's driver handed booklets and paperwork to a guard.

"What are those?" I asked, watching the guard flip through the documents.

"Our passports," Dixon replied, "and special authorizations."

My chin dipped. "I've got a passport?"

Maya might have one, but I didn't, and I was pretty sure Dixon, who'd been naked when rescued, couldn't have one either. At least not here.

He put a finger to his lips. "The passports our friends in the CIA had made for us."

"Don't you need photos for that?" I asked.

"The Group's got mine on file." He glanced at me. "For yours, I'm sure they improvised. Not that it matters, no one's looking under your mask today."

After a minute of discussion, the guard went into a nearby security booth, and another guard with a dog approached our car.

I tensed. "They're going to search us."

"Relax," Dixon said. "It's just procedure."

Slowly, the German shepherd and his handler circled our vehicle. When the dog had gotten a good sniff of the doors, tires, and trunk, he rejoined his comrade, who had just emerged from the security booth. After a brief discussion, the guards stepped back, raised the security gate, and waved our escort car through, and we followed.

I let out a breath. "That went well."

Dixon nodded. "I told you."

The roar of jet engines grew louder as we drove in. In the distance, airplanes landed and took off across a massive open circle of concrete and green bordered by trees. To one side, the crescent of the main terminal building stood. Near its middle, white letters read "Berlin-Tempelhof," reminding passengers where they had landed or would soon be leaving. A tall white tower with a ball of white atop it stood to the right, and at the far left of the terminal, the tilted windows of an air traffic control tower could be seen.

"Pretty busy place," I said, twisting in my seat to take it all in.

"It's been busier," Dixon said. "During the Berlin Airlift, cargo planes landed here pretty much every minute for over a year. It was that or let the city go to the Soviets."

"Why's it called Tempelhof?" I asked.

"That I don't know," Dixon replied.

"It used to be Templar land," Caelus said, climbing onto my lap and craning his head to look outside. "Long ago."

"Oh yeah?" Dixon regarded the bird. "How do you know that?"

"Personal experience," Caelus replied. "I wasn't always a raven, nor an ookmir."

No doubt, I thought. As one of the fallen gods, there was no telling how old Caelus truly was. Some gods I'd known were so ancient they'd forgotten their origins entirely.

Our escort vehicle led us to a large gunmetal-grey USAF cargo plane with large props beneath each wing. It stopped at the massive airplane's rear, and a man in his late forties, wearing a suit and dark sunglasses, exited the car's back seat and approached.

"This is Mills," Dixon said as we got out. Putting a hand on my and Maya's shoulders, he added, "These are the VIPs."

"Pleased to meet you folks," Mills replied. "Let's get aboard."

With a wave of his hand, he strode toward the aircraft and up the ramp protruding from the aircraft's rear. Following him, we entered a spacious area about ten feet wide and tall and forty feet or more long, filled with crates of metal, wood, and plastic, with seats lining the walls on both sides.

"Try to keep out of sight, bird," Dixon said after Mills had led us to the middle of the cargo area. "We won't be alone, and I'd rather we not draw any more attention than necessary."

"Very well," Caelus said, hopping from Maya's arm to the floor. He made his way between her legs and eyed us from beneath her seat. "I believe this is the best I can do."

Shrugging off his suit jacket, Dixon tossed it at the bird. "Pull this over yourself if you need to. Just don't crap on it."

"I make no promises, mortal."

Not long after, soldiers with large duffel bags boarded and took seats across the aisle, closer to the aircraft's tail, and the ramp rose, sealing us inside. With well over half the seats still unoccupied, the airplane's propellers came to life with a staccato of burps, vibrating the fuselage. A moment later, my seat lurched to the side.

"Here we go," Dixon said.

The cargo area lacked windows, but by the shifting of my seat beneath me, the pilot manoeuvred through a series of turns. After a short pause, the aircraft's propellers rose in volume, becoming a roar. I leaned right, my stomach lurching as the floor tilted, and grew heavier in my seat.

"How long's the flight?" I asked, practically shouting, when the aircraft had levelled out about fifteen minutes later.

"About twelve hours," Mills replied, also raising his voice above the drone of propellers.

"Why so long?" I asked.

He swirled his finger in a circle. "Props. Much slower than jets."

"Ah, right," I replied. While longer than I had figured, it wasn't all bad. *I can take the rest of the vials.* With plenty of time to adjust to their effects.

I looked around. Mills and the other passengers were a problem, though. I'd have to lift my hood in order to drink, revealing my icy flesh and snow-white complexion. I thought about it for a while before an idea came to mind. Nudging Dixon with an elbow, I spoke directly into his ear while eyeing Mills, who sat just beyond him. "Is there a bathroom on board?"

Dixon's eyebrows wrestled as he regarded me. "Bathroom? I thought—"

Shaking my head, I tapped my cap and glanced upward. "I need privacy."

"Oh, right." He stabbed a finger toward the back of the airplane and grinned. "The honey bucket is at the back, along the wall."

Honey bucket? Following the line of his finger, I narrowed my eyes a moment before spotting a toilet hanging from the wall. *Ugh.* "You've got to be kidding me."

"Nope," he said.

"Right out in the open?" That wouldn't help me. I needed privacy to take the vials.

Dixon grinned. "There's a curtain you can draw around it."

"Uh, okay," I said, starting to unbuckle my seat belt.

He stuck out a hand. "I'm messing with you. You don't want to use that. Take them here."

Meeting his gaze, I motioned to Mills meaningfully. Our escort sat with his eyes closed, facing the cargo crate directly to his front.

Dixon's breath was warm on my ear. "Don't worry about him. He's a special liaison to the Bodhi Group, and he's been briefed on our situation, more or less. He knows enough to keep his mouth shut and not freak out."

"What about the others, though?" I asked.

He held up a finger before leaning over to Mills. After a short conversation, their words lost beneath the drone of the airplane's engines, Mills unbuckled his belt. Standing tall, he stretched his arms and leaned back against the crates, obscuring my view of the passengers sitting on the far side.

Dixon smacked the back of his hand against my arm. "Go on. We'll screen you."

That'll work. Returning Maya's gaze, I removed the last four vials from my cap, leaving the tainted one—the one with the Alterclavis—behind. Placing three in a pocket of my coat, I opened the one still in my hand, hiked up my hood, and drank. Before the vial could take effect, I pocketed the empty and dug out another, repeating the process until all were down.

Hastily, I pulled my mask down.

Dropping the empty vials back into my hat, I reset my disguise and nodded to Dixon, giving him the all-clear. As he and Mills retook their seats, I tugged my cap's brim low. Leaning back against the webbing of my seat, I crossed my arms, waiting for the vials' effects to wash over me.

Maya placed a warm hand on my forearm. "Any problems?"

I flexed my fingers and rotated my head. "Nope, I'm all right."

Four was fewer than I'd taken before the freezing incident, and I seemed to be building up resistance to them, so I wasn't surprised, but it was still a relief to confirm it.

"Good." Dixon smirked. "The last thing we need is you turning into a block of ice."

Slapping a hand to my chest, I said, "I'm touched by your concern." My body tingled, and I felt tired. "Now, if you guys don't mind, I'm going to take a nap."

Hearing no objections, I closed my eyes and the hum of the aircraft soon put me to sleep.

I had a slight headache and a shadow standing over me when I woke. My dreams—an incoherent mingling of people and events from ages past and more recent times—were already fading. As I grasped at them, random memories surfaced, linking with others in my conscious mind, giving context to half-remembered faces and events. Some reminiscences filled me with joy, others sadness, but none were relevant to the current crisis, and I brushed them aside.

"He's coming around," said a woman's voice.

Maya, I realized.

"Are you all right?" she asked, touching my arm.

"Yeah." Blinking away the last vestiges of sleep, I turned my head and nodded.

Dixon loomed over me, holding my hat in his hand.

"What are you doing with that?" I asked.

Glancing down, he pulled his hand from within my cap and handed it back to me. "Looking for an Ambrola."

My eyes narrowed. "Why?" I looked for Mills, but our escort was nowhere in sight.

He shrugged. "I was looking for something to wake you." He glanced to Maya. "You seemed to be in a coma or trance or something."

"Really?" My gaze shifted between the two.

"You've been asleep for hours," Maya replied.

Dixon jabbed a thumb toward the back of the cargo area. "Mills went to use the can. I figured it'd be a good time to talk about what you learned. When you wouldn't wake, I got worried."

I snugged my hat on my head. "You can't access it. It only works for me."

"It was worth a shot." He tilted his torso as if to shield me from view. "The damn thing's glowing again. Can you turn it off?"

"It is?" Touching my hat, I wished the glow away. "How's that?"

"Better," he replied. "How was your sleep? Do you remember the key?"

I thought a moment. "Lots of dreams. Give me a second."

I closed my eyes, letting my mind wander. Trying to direct my recall, I thought about Allfrost Prime. If I could at least remember its location, it would be a win.

After a moment, a cavern of ice, dominated by a massive three-dimensional globe floating at the chamber's centre, came to mind before shifting to a snow-swept plain beneath a starry sky. Lacking identifiable landmarks, I couldn't be sure of its location. Wherever it was, it had obviously been winter at the time, so it couldn't be the tropics or even subtropics. That still left a large portion of the planet to search, though.

Shaking my head, I called up Zelus in my mind, specifically the meeting where he'd been trying to recruit me. It was much clearer now, and I remembered the days leading up to it now too. Unfortunately, none of these new recollections added to what I'd already discovered, either at the palace in Potsdam or at the soda factory complex in East Berlin.

Then all the missing pieces about my involvement with the Eurus fell into place. The agreement. Why I'd changed my mind, and why I'd sought out the Bodhi Group and lost my memories.

Much of it only confirmed what I had already figured out or had guessed, but a few crucial details were added as well. Including memories of when I'd first learned of the Eurus's and their Anathema allies' intention to only affect the US nukes. To extort the West into submitting to Soviet domination. Violating our agreement to disable *all* nuclear weapons worldwide, in order to remove the threat they posed to Earth.

Bastards. Rather than confronting them, I'd kept quiet and, without telling anyone, relocated Allfrost Prime and locked it down. *To ensure they couldn't complete their plan.*

Yet doing so had done nothing to stop Baduriel and the Eurus from continuing to corrupt the Allfrost, damaging its nodes and chambers. I had to stop that too, but without my Sentinel brethren, my options were limited. Sure, going to Boreas and the New Olympians was theoretically an option, but I was ashamed and unsure how they'd react to finding out I'd helped the Eurus.

Before I could go to them, I'd felt I had to fix things. To that end, I'd gone to the Bodhi Group instead, partly to warn them of the Eurus's nuclear plan, but also in the hope they could help me defend and restore the Allfrost. Protecting the Allfrost was my duty, after all, and stopping the corruption provided additional insurance against the Eurus ever achieving their goals. It was a good plan, and at first, the Bodhi Group had gone along with me, or at least had seemed to do so.

At the same time, I'd been increasingly worried about the Eurus figuring out I wasn't on their side anymore. Once they did, I knew they'd be coming after me, and if they ever caught me, it wouldn't be long before they'd get the key and the location of Allfrost Prime from me. One way or the other. The gods are nothing if not inventive.

Lacking a better option, I'd asked the Group to help me remove memories to prevent those secrets from falling into Eurus hands. Of course the Group had agreed, using the opportunity to take away far more, leaving me a ghost of my former self. I snorted to myself, recalling what Dixon had told me about my being seen with high-ranking Soviet Eurus. The Group had had me mistakenly pegged as a Soviet spy from the start.

"Hello?" Dixon snapped his fingers near my face. "You still with us?"

Bobbing my head, I opened my eyes. "Uh-huh."

Maya touched a hand to my shoulder. "What do you remember, Shivurr?"

I glanced at Mills, returning from the back. "I'd rather not say."

Dixon made a face. "Mills, you want to give us a few more minutes?" Shrugging, Mills wandered down the aisle to where soldiers were playing cards. "Let's have it."

Nodding, I told them everything I'd just remembered.

"Jesus." Dixon sighed. "What about the prime chamber's location and key?"

I hung my head. "No luck. And if the bad guys get it first, they'll have no problem using it. Not with Sid or the Eurus's own frost changeling to put it into."

Maya leaned closer. "Any additional insights into the soda and symbionts?"

I considered a moment before answering, "Nope. I don't think it's ever something I knew anything about." I scratched my temple, recalling that Maya had said the colas had only been on the market a few months. "My guess is the soda pop thing started after I went to the Bodhi Group." Recalling Oborateles's and Azrileus's words, I added, "And since it seems like a sub-faction plot, I'm pretty sure the majority of Eurus know nothing about it either."

"Why infect people with symbionts, though?" she asked.

"Control," Dixon said. "With that stuff, you can make anyone do whatever you want, probably think whatever you want. You saw it yourself. Those changelings make handy labourers."

A vision of Maya sucking up Azrileus's essence into a soul trap flashed in my mind. "I think it's more than that." The realization seemed obvious in retrospect. I took a deep breath and let it out slowly. "Divine possession."

Maya's face scrunched. "That's not supposed to be possible."

"They must have figured out a way," I said. "That body you pulled Azrileus out of, it wasn't an avatar." I recalled Azrileus's words when I'd first spotted her through the lab door window. "It was someone infected with a symbiont . . . with Azrileus inside."

Dixon shook his head. "A soda-pop-drinking caffeine fiend."

I smirked. "Or caffiend, for short. And don't forget about the attack at the Charlottenburg apartment."

"You mean Sid?" Maya asked, touching a hand to her collarbone.

"No." I wagged my head. "The other changeling—Cardigan Guy—had powers too. Lightning. The kind of things the gods are known for. I think he might have been possessed then too. By Azrileus or another demon." A demon was an Anathema god, after all. I was talking fast now as things clicked. "I don't know, but think about it. None of the other changelings exhibited those abilities. They didn't even try to resist us."

Her brow furrowed. "But why was Cardigan Guy wandering around West Berlin with Sid?"

"To bring Sid back," I said. "Azrileus and Horst said he liked to wander. My guess is the Stasi Eurus were occupying or controlling Cardigan Guy."

Her eyes widened. "And our people—who were on the lookout for kidnappings and people behaving oddly—happened to intervene."

Dixon pursed his lips. "And the other catatonics?"

"I'm not sure," I said, "but from the sound of things, they were having issues with earlier versions of the organism they're infecting people with." I grabbed at my chest. "Vines and stuff growing out of people are too conspicuous, so I'm guessing they were collecting them before they drew too much attention."

Maya looked thoughtful. "Yet the Eurus already have avatars. Why bother with human ones?"

"The Eurus do, sure," I replied, "but the demons don't."

"You're right," she said. "With only a few Anathema on Earth, the Eurus still hold all the cards. But if anyone can be an avatar, they can level the playing field. They could jump from person to person, making them difficult to pin down."

"It's worse than that." Dixon's eyebrows bunched. "They could control anyone. Be anyone. Cops. Politicians. Even the president. Damn." He blew out a breath. "Lucky we found out before it spread beyond Germany . . . that would have been bad."

Maya folded her arms. "I wonder what Baduriel and Azrileus offered their Stasi allies to betray their Eurus comrades."

I tossed my shoulders. "World domination. Immortality. Godhood. All of the above, maybe."

"Idiots," Dixon said, nostrils flaring. "Trusting traitors."

"Okay," Maya said, "but what's Baduriel's motivation for betraying the Eurus? They've already been promised redemption. Do they not think the Eurus will follow through?"

I turned up my palms. "Maybe they're not betraying them." When I had agreed to help the Eurus, I wasn't betraying Wilhelm. I was simply doing something without him or my other god friends knowing. "Maybe he's just working another angle. As a backup plan."

"That's good thinking," Dixon said. "Whatever the case, the Group is dealing with it now, and our priority is getting the rest of those vials."

I nodded. *One more vial and this might all be over.* After that, I'd have to talk to Wilhelm and get his help disrupting the Eurus's Allfrost endgame. Like Baduriel, Wilhelm was an expert in the Allfrost's technology. With his help, undoing the changes Baduriel had been making should be child's play, though it might take a long time. I wasn't looking forward to coming clean with him, but—

I sat up straight. *The bad vial.*

Chapter 27

Ghost Protocol

My hands flew to the sides of my head. Just because it contained one half of an Alterclavis—the device that had sent Scott and me to the Gobi Desert—didn't mean the substance in which it floated wasn't a stolen part of myself.

I'm an idiot. Sure, the one that had held Dixon's tracker—the one that had led him to me at Dublin Gulch—had been immersed in some fake liquid, but what if the one with the Alterclavis held some of the real me? Doubtful, but I needed to know. The problem was, I couldn't take it out without risking transporting somewhere, switching places with Atriel, who held the other end. *He must have recovered it by now.*

I sat tall in my seat. *I don't need to take it out.* I stood and took off my coat. Folding it carefully, I laid it on my seat.

"Getting too warm?" Dixon asked.

"Give me a sec," I said, sidling past him and Mills. "I need the washroom."

Ignoring the glances of other passengers, I made my way to the toilet at the back of the aircraft, pulled the privacy curtain and, hidden from view, deactivated the suit constricting me, allowing my body to shift freely. Sweeping off my hat, I pulled off my hood and stuffed it beneath an arm.

Let's see. I thrust a hand through my hat's inner crown and felt around inside the null space until my fingers brushed the cloth in which I'd wrapped the tainted vial. *Got it.*

I hesitated, knowing I needed to be careful now. Only storing my half of the Alterclavis in the null space of my cap kept it from activating. As Olivia had explained, things in that space were in limbo, a void without relevant spatial coordinates in the physical plane, giving the Alterclavis nothing to work with. As long as the device remained there. Which meant I couldn't remove the vial without potentially taking another trip.

You can do this, Shivurr. Setting the cap upside down on the lid of the toilet seat, I thrust my free hand in alongside the one still gripping the vial. A moment later, my arms elongated and thinned, flowing through the narrow space, and when I was elbow deep, I unwrapped the vial.

Now the hard part. I took a deep breath and concentrated until my head, arms, and chest shifted. Becoming almost liquid, they thinned into flows of snow and ice, trapped within the form-fitting suit, which shrank to match my altered form.

Ugh. My vision blurred, and I willed away a surge of nausea as my body strove to adapt to the changes. Deciding to go for it, I stood straight, holding the hat above myself, and streamed deeper into the void. When I was chest deep on the far side of the portal, my head and arms partly re-formed, and the nausea diminished. *Thank the Allfrost.*

Holding the vial near my lips, I popped the stopper, sucked up the contents, and swished it around.

There it is, I thought, spitting something solid back into the vial before stoppering it. Still holding the liquid in my mouth, I sloshed the mixture from cheek to cheek. *Huh.* It didn't taste quite like the others. This stuff was more watery, but I swallowed it anyway. Releasing the stoppered vial, I pulled myself free of the hat and restored my head, arms, and torso to their humanoid configurations.

Let's hope this works.

"Shivurr," said a voice by my ear.

I whirled, sweeping an elbow reflexively through the air, but there was no one behind me. *What the hell?* "Dixon?" It had to be him or Mills since the voice was male and no other man on the flight knew my name. Well, Caelus did, but the voice I'd just heard bore no more resemblance to his than Maya's. "I'll be right out." With the incessant roar of the airplane's propellers, I could barely hear myself speak as I added, "Kind of busy."

"Yes," the man said, "but just give me a moment." Unlike my own, his voice came through loud and clear, as if placed inside my head, and I now felt sure it wasn't Dixon or Mills. "I need to get somewhere I can speak freely."

"Uh, okay." I bent to peer through the gap between the curtain and floor. "If you say so." Seeing no shoes, I sat upon the closed toilet. "Who is this?"

"Gary Ashdon," the voice answered. "Do you remember me? I'm a friend."

I thought a moment before answering, "No."

"This will suffice." A man appeared a few feet away, beyond the curtain enclosing me, yet somehow still visible. Even with my eyes shut, he was still there in his white lab coat, smiling. Short of stature and slight of build, he had mid-length wavy brown hair and a clean-shaven unlined face, giving him the appearance of someone in his thirties. "Where are you?" He adjusted his eyeglasses and looked around. "Is this a toilet?"

I snapped my fingers, recognizing him abruptly. "I remember you now. You're one of the Eurus. How are you here?" *And what do you want?* I thought.

Gary shrugged. "You drank the vial I planted. You must have, if we're talking." He grinned. "It was a long shot, but I hoped it might find you."

"Why?" To test a theory, I only thought the question, moving my lips but uttering no sound.

"So we could talk, of course," he replied as if I'd spoken aloud.

"Yeah, right," I mouthed, since thinking my words seemed to be enough for him to hear me. "I might have believed you if you hadn't also put an Alterclavis inside." I kept mouthing the words. It seemed I didn't need to bother, but doing so felt more intuitive, making it easier to be more specific and intentional in what I communicated. "That was you, wasn't it?"

It seemed beyond unlikely to me it had been anyone else.

"Yes," he said, "but we don't have time for this right now." He seemed to be fading. "Your body is already breaking down the liquid you ingested. When it does so fully, our link will terminate. Clearly you don't remember everything yet or you'd know I'm a friend. One who wants to help you foil the Eurus's plans for the Allfrost. To do that, you must return to the Bodhi Institute. The rest of your essence has been returned here, and we must talk. There's much I can tell you about what's been going on."

"Are you nuts? I can't go back there." In truth, I intended to do exactly that, but I wasn't ready to admit it to Gary. Not until I knew I could trust him. "The Group's still hunting for me."

Gary spread his hands. "Once you consume the vials already in your possession, I am sure entering the Institute unseen will present little obstacle for you."

"Okay," I said, drawing out each syllable, "but if you're a friend, why not save me the trouble? You could steal the vials for me and meet me somewhere."

He glanced around. "Even if I could get back into the archival vault, they're safer here. The Eurus are waiting for me to bring them the vials too, and they'll be watching. If I leave, they'll no doubt intercept me, and I'll have to hand them over. I won't be able to resist them, not on my own." He sighed. "Maybe if Atriel were with me."

Atriel? Memories unlocked, and I sat back, stunned. "Atriel's helping you?"

"Of course," Gary replied. "You're the one that recruited us, but we've no time to go over that now. I will catch you up further when you arrive."

"How long can you hold out?"

He stroked his hairless chin. "My last communication should have bought me some time. Until tomorrow at least. After that, the Eurus may come for them in force, whatever I tell them, which is why you must hurry." He looked around again. "At least here, locked in the vault beneath a few hundred feet of earth, they can be defended."

"It didn't stop Baduriel," I said.

"No, I suppose it didn't," he said, "but his attack has raised the defense level here. Soldiers are patrolling the exterior and agents are crawling all over the interior. And, as before, I'll support them to the best of my not-inconsiderable abilities. Between all that, hopefully we can defend them long enough for you to make your way here."

He seemed to be fading from view, and I grabbed at his apparition. "Wait. How did you get into the Institute? Do you work there?"

"Hurry, Shivurr," he replied, all but invisible now. "It's only—"

His final words were lost as he vanished completely.

Resetting my disguise, I plunked my cap on my head, tugged open the curtain, and returned to my companions.

Dixon nudged me as I retook my seat. "What were you doing in there?"

"Taking the last vial," I said.

He leaned in. "I thought you took the last one already."

"There was one more," I said, explaining about the bad vial and what I'd just experienced.

"Gary Ashdon." Dixon's nostrils flared. "Well, that explains a lot." He snorted. "So, he's the mole."

"You know him?" I asked.

"Yep," he replied. "He's a new transfer. A biochemist." He growled. "And the guy that helped me with the tracking vial I used to find you at Dublin Gulch." He wagged a finger. "I should have known something was off when he stood up to Baduriel all by his lonesome."

My eyes popped. "He confronted Baduriel?"

Dixon nodded. "At the time, I figured he'd lost his mind . . . or had a death wish." He shrugged. "I guess he wasn't in danger after all. Not if he's one of these so-called gods."

I shook my head, recalling more of Ashdon. "I don't think he's a full god yet. I think he's a demigod at best. Maybe only an initiate, in the early stages of ascension." I looked at Maya. "Would a demigod be able to defeat Baduriel?"

She made a face. "I don't think so. Not if Baduriel is fully divine. A demigod might be able to slow him down, especially given the element of surprise, but in a straight-on fight I'd expect the demigod to lose. Only a fully ascended could match one for power . . . in which case they're ascended no longer but rather fully divine as well, by definition."

"Well," Dixon said, "it didn't come to a fight. And a good thing too. Ashdon collapsed not long after I got him out of there. I figured it was his condition. That or he'd gotten an electric shock. There was water everywhere after the fire sprinklers went off. Thanks to Baduriel and his fire elementals passing through."

I glanced at Maya and back to Dixon. "What condition?"

"According to his file," he replied, "Ashdon suffers from photosensitive epilepsy."

Maya frowned. "Was there a flash of light before he fell?"

Dixon paused before replying. "Yeah. There was. The lights overhead blew out."

"Hmm," Maya said. "It sounds like he projected his essence."

"What essence?" Dixon asked.

"Crystalline cells," I said. "Remember what Leonidas told us?"

"Oh, right." He looked thoughtful. "Interesting. Then if Ashdon's a demigod, you figure he sent this stuff outside his physical body like some sort of astral projection or ghost."

"Exactly," Maya replied. "And if he's able to do that, he's well into the ascension process."

"But why would he project himself?" I asked.

She lifted her shoulders. "Probably to return to Baduriel and finish their conversation without Dixon around, or at least ensure Baduriel left. With the Anathema acting independently, Baduriel's appearance must have been a surprise, throwing a wrench into Ashdon's plans, so I'm sure he wanted him out of there as soon as possible."

"That makes sense." Dixon shot Maya a look. "As soon as we get the vials from the Manhattan labs, we'll have to use that transporter you mentioned. The Institute is about a six-hour drive from Los Angeles, but I'll see if I can arrange for a helicopter to take us from there."

The corners of Maya's mouth drooped. "Too bad. I was hoping we'd have time to take in a Broadway show."

I let out a breath. "Sorry, Maya. From what Ashdon said, we've not much more than a day before the Eurus attack the Institute and take the vials by force." I leaned back in my seat and crossed my arms. "For now, I'm going to try to catch a few winks."

"Good idea," Dixon said, hopping atop one of the crates and lying back. "In the midst of chaos, there is also opportunity."

"Sun Tzu?" Maya asked, but a snore was Dixon's only reply.

Chapter 28

Take Five

Our airplane had been racing the sun, so despite the twelve-hour flight it was only late afternoon when we landed in New York. After waiting for thirty minutes while Mills smoothed our way through Customs, we disembarked. Handing our fake passports to Dixon, Mills wished us well, and we departed in a white van that had been awaiting our arrival.

An hour's drive later, the van passed through a dark tunnel and entered into the concrete canyons of Manhattan's skyscrapers. Glass towers mixed with brownstone buildings, parks, and playgrounds lined with wrought-iron fences of flaking black paint, littered with garbage. Masses of humanity flowed past us on both sides of the near-gridlocked streets, eyes down, coming close to each other but never touching, and steering wide berths around shady characters leaning by street corners.

"Cool," I said, pressing my nose to my window. "I don't think I've ever seen so many people in one place."

"A first-timer, eh?" the driver said. "You want I should take the scenic route?"

"No," Dixon said, checking his watch. "Take us straight to the hotel. I need to sleep."

Rather than head directly to the Bodhi Group offices, we had decided we'd check into a hotel first. Dixon, unsure of the reception he would receive—having been missing in action until recently—thought it better to wait until after hours, when fewer people would be around.

Plus, it had been a long flight, and gathering our strength now before leaving for the Bodhi Institute made sense.

"Fair enough," the driver said, hitting the turn signal.

Outside, minglings of grimy, graffiti-covered restaurants, retail stores, and apartment buildings gave way to fried chicken joints, porn palaces, and billboards advertising cigarettes. Here and there, filth-covered people, some barefoot and shirtless, sprawled on cardboard with their hands out.

A wretched hive, if ever I saw one, I thought.

Apparently thinking the same thing, Dixon said, "This place has gone downhill."

"Tell me about it," the driver said before telling us of the city's near bankruptcy in the seventies, which had led to the loss of half a million manufacturing jobs, followed by urban decline. "Add crack to the mix, you get all this shit."

"Crack?" I said as we stopped at a red light.

"Cocaine," he replied. "Druggies are ruining the city. Not to mention the dealers, vandals, and muggers. Scumbags." A man wearing a hooded sweatshirt, visible just past Dixon, strode toward the van. "Whoa."

Thunks from left and right drew my eyes to the door locks, which were now in the down position. Dodging right, the dude slipped between the van's bumper and the car to our front and kept moving.

The driver's shoulders lifted. "Sorry, fellas. Can't be too careful. I should've locked those earlier."

"Why?" I asked, watching Sweatshirt Guy make his way to the far side of the street.

Traffic began to move again, and a bus rumbled past my window, its side decorated with a billboard depicting a multi-coloured soda can. "Take 5" was written on the cylinder across an upraised hand, its fingers spread wide.

"You can't be too careful." He glanced at Dixon before meeting my gaze in the rear-view mirror. "Even during the day. Which reminds me, given where you're staying, stay out of Central Park. That is, if you want to keep your wallets . . . or stay alive." He snapped his fingers. "Fucking gang punks will put a knife or bullet in you, just like that. They're animals."

Dixon snorted. "You should work for the tourism bureau."

The driver shrugged. "Don't say I didn't warn you," he said, turning onto a wide street that bordered a park of green grass and trees swaying in the wind.

A block later, we pulled to a stop, and the driver put the van into park and jabbed his chin toward Dixon. "This is the place. Essex House Hotel."

"Thanks," Dixon said, opening his door.

"Forget about it," the driver replied.

On the sidewalk, Dixon turned to Maya and eyed the raven on her arm. "Maybe Feathers should wait in the park. No sense drawing unnecessary attention."

"Good idea," she replied. "Go on, Caelus."

Bobbing his head, the raven took to the air and swept away toward the park.

"Come on," Dixon said. "Let's get inside."

Passing through a stream of pedestrians, we entered the hotel lobby, greeted by red walls, brass, and marble.

After checking us in, Dixon led us to the elevator and handed keys to Maya and me as we ascended. "I got us separate rooms."

I squinted. "Where did you get American money?"

"From Mills," he replied. "Not that I needed it here. The Bodhi Group has a standing agreement with this hotel." The elevator opened, and he checked his watch. "All right. This is your floor, Winterboy. Let's grab dinner in the hotel restaurant in a few hours, then head over to the labs."

"Sounds good," I said, stepping off. "Sleep well." Making my way to my room, I slipped inside and smiled. The room was small, but it had a TV, and I hadn't watched a show in days. Grabbing the television remote from a side table, I plopped onto the bed and began flipping channels. At this hour, there wasn't a lot on, but I found a cop show I hadn't seen before and watched that awhile. Grabbing a menu from a table, I picked up the phone.

"Room service," said a woman's voice.

"Uh, yeah," I said, "I'd like a pepperoni pizza."

"Certainly, sir," the voice replied. "Anything to drink?"

I thought a moment, recalling the billboard I'd seen on the drive over. "Uh, yeah. Do you have any Take 5?"

"One moment, please." The sound of muffled conversation followed. "Yes, we do, sir."

"Great," I said. "I'll take one. Actually . . ." I smiled to myself. *The Bodhi Group's paying.* "I'll take five. With lots of ice."

"Very good, sir," she said.

The door thumped a half hour later, and I leaped from bed, letting in a man wearing a white dress shirt, black slacks, and vest. While the room service guy placed the stuff next to the TV, I signed Dixon's name to the bill, adding a generous tip. Hustling the guy out, I deactivated my disguise. Moaning with relief, I dug into the box and, humming to myself, shovelled a few pieces down, then sat back with a Take 5 in hand.

"Not bad," I said aloud after taking my first sip.

A few sodas and half a pizza later, I reached for the remote again. After I flipped channels awhile, my eyes drifted to the telephone sitting on the desk by the TV.

I should call Olivia.

I rose from bed and took a seat in a plush chair by the window. Doffing my cap, I put my last two Take 5 sodas inside before digging out my Walkman. Slipping in new batteries, I placed the headphones over my ears and pressed out an unlikely sequence on the buttons of the cassette player.

"Hi, Shivurr," Olivia said in my ears. "Are you all right?"

"Uh, just a sec." Thumbing the remote, I turned down the TV volume a few notches. "I'm fine. We're in New York."

"What are you doing there?" she asked.

"There's a vial here." For the next few minutes, I told her about Berlin, the Eurus's plan, the Allfrost's prime chamber and key, the soda, and the Bodhi Group's Manhattan facility. I left out discovering I'd been aiding the Eurus. I knew I'd have to tell her about it eventually, but I didn't want to do it this way, and I wanted to know everything I'd done when I did. "If we're lucky, I'll be drinking it in a couple of hours. I just hope it has Prime's location and key."

"Nicely done," she said, sounding impressed. "But watch

your back with this Dixon character, Shivurr."

I shrugged. "Of course."

"I'm serious, Shivurr. You're far too trusting sometimes. I'm glad you've got Maya to watch your back."

I chuckled softly. "All right." *Mom*, I thought, pleased by her concern. "What about you? Are you guys all okay?"

"We're fine," Olivia replied. "We've had a few close calls, but we're all safe. One second, Shivurr." She paused. "Brad and Lucy are telling me to say hello."

"Cool," I said. "Hi back. Where are you guys?"

"Canada," she replied. "We're trying to make it to Winnipeg now."

"Winnipeg?" I remembered Lucy—a Canadian herself—mentioning the city, and with my cognitive pathways mostly restored, I recalled being there myself, long before the Bodhi Institute. "Why there?"

"There's a transporter there," she said. "One that will take us to Las Vegas, so we can use the one at my house to get back to New Olympus."

"All roads lead to Rome," I said with a smile.

"What do you mean?"

"We're going there too," I replied. "Well, to Nevada at least." I told her our plan to return to the Institute. "Maya says there's a transporter here that'll take us most of the way." An idea came to mind. If we could meet up, we'd be stronger together, and I missed my friends. Besides, I could protect them then. "Hey, is there a transporter that'll take us to Winnipeg from here?"

"I'm afraid not," Olivia said, sounding rushed. "I've got to go now, Shivurr. Call me after you get those vials, all right?"

"Sure." Getting up, I paced the room. "Is everything okay? Has something happened?"

"Nothing you need to worry about," she replied, still speaking rapidly. "You just concentrate on getting those vials, all right?"

"Of course."

"Great," she said, sounding out of breath. "Good luck tonight. I'll talk to you soon."

"You too. Bye, Olivia."

I returned to flipping channels, regretting Olivia and I didn't share an Alterclavis device. If we had, getting to her, wherever she went, would have been easy and immediate. Unlike a regular transporter, the devices were dynamic, allowing spatial transpositions between arbitrary positions while somehow transporting only the holders and things with which they might be in direct contact. All of which made them exceptionally powerful and valuable tech.

Unfortunately, Atriel, not Olivia, held the other piece of the Alterclavis resting in an empty vial in my hat. *Which isn't much help.* Though I now remembered Atriel to be a Eurus friend whom I had recruited to help me, swapping places or contacting him wasn't going to do me any good at the moment. And for all I knew, doing so would send me into the midst of other Eurus who weren't on my side.

Bored, I stood and wandered to the window to look out at the park across the street, curious about what lay beyond the line of trees. Whatever it was, I didn't buy the van driver's claims of roving muggers behind every bush.

Maybe I should take a look. Grabbing the room key from the small table next to the bed, I restored my disguise and made my way downstairs. After being cooped up on the airplane all day, I decided a nature walk was just what I needed. *Why should Caelus be the only one to get a breath of fresh air?*

Chapter 29

Ramble

Out on the street, traffic crawled past the hotel and car horns sounded angrily in the distance as I made my way a block east and crossed to the park. *Still hot out.* A few hundred feet inside, I looked back at the hotel. Its light brown facade rose high above the trees yet was itself dwarfed by the buildings to its rear. I took careful note of its red rooftop sign—ensuring I could find my way back—before making my way deeper into the green space.

Judging by the buildings towering at the park's edges, the place was huge, filled with sprawling meadows of mostly brown grass, quaint graffiti-fouled footbridges, and algae-covered ponds. I walked footpaths bordered by green-painted wooden benches with black lampposts standing sentry nearby, passing old trees, dusty baseball fields and litter-covered basketball courts. More than once my lip curled at the sight of discarded food containers, smashed bottles and soda cans, and old newspapers tumbling in the wind. Though beauty still lay beneath the decay, the park had clearly fallen on hard times.

As I walked, a babble of voices on the path, always just ahead, drew me onward, yet never seemed to get closer. And the few people I did encounter moved to avoid me, keeping their eyes down and mouths shut. Growing increasingly frustrated and curious, I quickened my pace, yet still came across nothing that might explain the incessant hushed, unintelligible voices, and they always remained seemingly over the next bridge or around the next bend.

What's this? I thought, spotting what appeared to be a castle nestled against a backdrop of trees. *America doesn't have castles.*

I padded onto the stone terrace fronting it, taking it all in. By its decoration and layout, it had never been intended for defense. Aside from being tiny—the entire building could have easily fit within the courtyard of Abadom—its defensive formations were purely fanciful, providing no real protection against attack. Still, here among the green, it had a storybook quality that lightened my heart. The word for it arose from long-ago memories. *It's a folly.*

Two men wearing hard hats and carrying lunch pails exited the castle and came toward me. Wary of anyone getting too close, I wandered to the building's left and looked out over a rocky slope and large pond, letting them pass. A few hundred feet away, ducks rippled the water, cutting triangles in the blanket of algae as they swam.

Abruptly, the wind settled and for a moment all was quiet. Even the voices that I'd been following were silent. After a few minutes enjoying the view, I turned and checked the sun's position in the sky. Deciding to head back to the hotel, I took a last look around and made for the pathway by which I'd come.

A few feet from the stone courtyard, the burble of voices rose once more.

That's it. I broke into a sprint, determined to find their source this time, and they soon led me down a dirt path into thick trees where all around me birdsong filled the air, and the day's warmth and humidity eased.

Nice. I inhaled the scents of the forest—wildflowers, warm earth, and leaves—wishing I could relax my disguise and return to my usual self. Shrugging off the impulse, I kept going, determined to enjoy myself anyway.

The path rambled up and down, twisting its way south, past giant boulders and wooden fences huddled in the green. Before long, the trail widened, becoming a clearing, and near its middle, rustic wooden posts held up a peaked roof with benches beneath, presumably there to create a resting spot for weary hikers.

Hey, it's quiet, I thought, no longer hearing the babble of voices that had drawn me here.

Spying a crowd among the underbrush, I ducked behind a tree trunk and peered out at them. Some were on their knees, others bent at the waist, as they scrabbled at the earth, piling soil to the sides of freshly dug holes like children making sandcastles on the beach.

"Welcome, Sentinel." A voice rang in my head, the words deep and sonorous. They seemed more to manifest alongside my own thoughts rather than be heard through my ear canals, reminding me of how I'd conversed with Ashdon on the flight to New York. "Long has it been since last I encountered one of your kind."

"Who is that?" I glanced around, looking for the source. "Show yourself."

"Gulageir," the voice replied. "Eldest Arborati of this grove."

My jaw dropped. The Arborati, sentient trees, were forest shepherds, and I'd met and befriended many over the centuries. I'd most recently seen one fighting fire elementals in Las Vegas, and another had communed with Olivia near her New Olympus cottage, but I hadn't remembered what they were at the time.

"Nice to meet you," I said. "Why did you call me Sentinel?"

"That is what you are, is it not?"

I nodded. "Yeah." There seemed no point denying it. The Arborati weren't fans of the Eurus, and they avoided and hid from mortals. "But I'm in disguise."

"Regardless of your shape," Gulageir replied, "what you truly are has not changed and remains clear to us."

"Okay, but how can I hear you?" I had to assume telepathy was involved, but I wasn't—as Boreas had often reminded me—the best at it. My mind could still be read, of course. If not, Hue wouldn't know my thoughts when I stood in the right spots in an Allfrost chamber, and I wouldn't have been able to converse with Ashdon on the flight to New York. Yet both instances required specific tech to do so. "I'm no telepath."

"Perhaps not, but it matters little while your hands are upon my trunk."

"Oh, right." I looked up at the limbs of the tree. In telepathy, distance matters, and physical contact makes it all the easier. "Of course." A thought came to mind. "Was that you guys I heard?" I asked, describing the indistinct voices that had led me here.

"It was," Gulageir said. "We had hoped to bring you here."

I frowned. "But how did I hear that? I wasn't touching any trees."

"Through the organism within you and the soil beneath your feet."

"Organism?" I studied the ground. *The symbiont.* Having drunk my share of symbiont-infected colas in Berlin, I had little doubt I'd consumed a tainted one—if they weren't all tainted— yet, though I'd felt crappy after each one, I'd seemed to recover fully. I'd figured my body had—as it did with whatever else I consumed—broken it down and destroyed all traces. "Do you mean a symbiont?"

"Indeed," the tree replied. "Or parasite, if you prefer. One with both floral and fungal aspects."

"How can you know that?" I took stock of myself. "I feel fine. More or less." *Actually, come to think of it, I do have a bit of a headache.*

"Through the mycelium," he said, referring to an underground fungal network through which even non-sentient trees communicated. "Fear not, however. Even now, its life fades within you."

I regarded the people, shambling about, noting their hunched shoulders and vacant eyes. *Just like the changelings in Berlin.* "And these people have symbionts too?"

If true, it meant the Anathema's soda plan was more widespread than I'd thought, possibly even global in scope.

"They do," Gulageir said, explaining that he and the other Arborati had sensed the organisms when those infected with them travelled through the park. "Through the mycelium, we called to the symbionts within them, drawing them here."

I smacked my forehead, remembering the pizza and soda pop I'd consumed in the hotel room before coming here. "Take 5."

"I beg your pardon," the Arborati replied.

"It's a soft drink." I told Gulageir about the German sodas, Nicht and Nacht, and the changelings. "I think Take 5's got to be the local equivalent. It's the only thing I've drunk recently." Sure, it tasted different than its German cousins, but I doubted I'd been infected by the pizza, which had been cooked in an oven at who knew what temperature. "And the posters I've seen around town say it's brand new."

"The flow of this foul nectar must be staunched." Gulageir's frustration came through our link. "While we are curing those we can, mortal numbers are vast and too many lie beyond our reach."

"You're curing them?" If true, that would be huge. "How?" I studied the changelings digging in the ground, and the mounds of fresh soil dotting the area, and my eyes bulged. "You're burying them?" *Ugh, and using the other changelings to dig their graves.*

"A necessary step," Gulageir said. "Fear not. They will arise in time, cured of their affliction, and make their way home, likely not even remembering what has happened to them. However, the process takes time and space, and we will soon be overwhelmed."

"I might have a way to help," I said, knowing Gulageir was right. Take 5, and any other tainted sodas, had to be removed from grocery store shelves as soon as possible. Dixon's face popped into my head. "I know a guy."

"Then go now," Gulageir said, "and good fortune, Sentinel. The sooner this soda can be stopped the better."

"Understood," I said, straightening and saying farewell before hurrying down the path and past the gathered throng of changelings. As I walked, I thought of Maya drinking a Nacht Cola in order to activate the Sebastian Street transporter. If she was infected, it was nice to know there might be a cure.

I doubted she'd be too excited about being buried alive, though. Yet, by the time it came to that, if it came to that, she probably wouldn't have enough of her own will left to care.

As I hurried toward the hotel's distant rooftop sign, lost in my thoughts, the trees parted, revealing a lake. Across the water, groups of people milled about a fountain, and behind them, a stone bridge arced across the scene. Unable to go further without getting wet, I took the path to the left, doing my best to follow the shoreline until I reached the lake's far side.

Passing a boathouse, I came to the fountain I'd seen from the other side of the lake and, again spotting the red sign of my hotel above the trees, took a broad, straight walkway south past a group of breakdancing youths.

"Hey, man." A shirtless dude—maybe eighteen or nineteen years old—with close-cropped brown hair, wearing a red track jacket, open in the front, jeans, and white high-top sneakers—chased after me. "You looking to score?"

Glancing at him, I kept walking, making no reply.

"Hey, where are you going?"

A few steps onward, two more punks rose from a park bench fifty feet to my front and came toward me. One wore a blue tank top and shorts, the other a black leather jacket and faded denim pants with rips in the knees.

I shifted direction, giving them space to go around, but the one on the left sidestepped to block my path.

"Are you deaf, mister?" the guy asked. "He's talking to you."

"Hey, what's with the mask?" said the other. "You ugly, man? You been in a fire or something?"

I scowled. "Get lost."

"Nice hat," said a voice behind me.

My cap flew from my head, and I whirled, jaw clenched.

"I think I'll keep it," said the shirtless thug, dancing away a few steps, waving my hat.

"Give it back," I snarled. "Asshole."

He smirked, flipping the cap onto his head. "Nah, it's mine now. Consider it a toll for passing through my park."

My lip curled. "You've got one—"

Something hit me in the back, below the neck, sending me stumbling forward a step.

"Hey." I caught myself, hearing cackles around me. *Screw this*, I thought, standing tall before shifting into the Underfrost. *Never poke the snowman.*

The shirtless thug's mouth fell open. "What the fuck?"

Rushing him, I drew back one of my fists and launched it at his jaw. A foot from his face, I popped from the Underfrost, landing ice-hard knuckles into his nose, which cracked beneath my blow. Lunging, I snatched my cap from his head as he fell, and I vanished again.

Spinning on a heel, I charged the other two, aiming for the gap between them. *Come here.* Their mouths gaped as they looked around, not having moved from where I'd last seen them. Closing the distance, I spread my arms and returned to normal space. Milliseconds later, my forearms hit their throats, and they crashed to the ground, gagging and holding their necks.

"Now you've gone and made me angry." Stooping, I grasped the hand of the guy on the left and twisted his fingers. They made a snicking sound, soon drowned out by his cries of pain, and he cradled his hand. As he blubbered, I pivoted to his buddy and repeated the action, eliciting the same response. "Hurts, does it? Remember that feeling the next time you think about bothering people." I booted one in the rear. "Now get out of here. I don't want to see any of you in this park again. You got it?"

They rolled to their knees, cradling their hands and ran toward the distant fountain, leaving behind the third member of their trio, who lay groaning nearby.

No loyalty among thieves.

Feeling regretful, I walked over to the thug and knelt down. "Are you all right?"

"Fuck you, asshole," he snarled.

A blur of motion came from my left, and I brought up my arm reflexively, feeling a sharp pain below the elbow.

You total . . . dick, I thought as the guy withdrew a switchblade from my arm. Grasping his wrist, I squeezed it hard, sending frost through my hand and into his flesh.

"Fuck!" he shouted, dropping the blade and shrieking as if burned.

"How's that feel?" He tried to pull away, but I only tightened my grip. "Do you feel frosty, punk?"

"Sure, whatever you say, man," he said, tearing up. "Just, please. Let me go."

"I'm going to need an apology first," I said.

"I'm sorry," he shouted, regarding me with bulging eyes. "All right?"

"You'd better mean that." Deactivating my hood, I pulled it high. His eyes bugged wider, and his lips drew back, and the colour left his face. "And don't let me catch you in this park ever again. You're on my naughty list now, and I'll be watching."

He nodded frantically. "Okay, you got it, man. Whatever you say. I'm gone."

"You'd better be." I opened my fingers and pulled down my hood, letting him roll to his feet and stumble after his friends. *Asshole.* I straightened my hat and looked around, but to my surprise, no one seemed to be paying attention.

"Good day, Sentinel," said a voice.

Looking up, I spotted Caelus in the leafy canopy above. "Oh, hey." I bent to grab the switchblade and pocketed it. "You saw that?"

"I did, indeed," the raven replied. "Quite the spectacle. You would have done well in the Bureau."

My brow wrinkled. "The FBI?"

"Retribution," he replied. "You may recall them from the days of fire and brimstone when we still took an active role in the moral development of humanity."

"Oh, right." *Of course.*

For a time, long ago, the gods had tasked a number of the Anathema with finding wrongdoers and meting out punishments. Known as the Retribution Bureau, the department had targeted not only mortals but anyone that the gods deemed deserving.

"Alas, since the schism," Caelus continued, "divine retribution, as a dedicated concern, is limited to only the divine such as me." He chuckled. "Ah, those were wonderful days, though." He looked in the direction of the fleeing muggers. "This is what our permissiveness has wrought. Ah well, perhaps one day the practice will be renewed."

I grimaced, not sure I appreciated being compared to an avenging demon. "They had it coming."

"I don't doubt it," the bird replied. "That is the nature of retribution, is it not? In any case, the woman, Maya, asks that you return to the hotel."

"All right," I said. "I'll be right there."

"Very good," he replied, taking to the air.

"Retribution," I muttered, resuming my walk toward the hotel. As I moved, I felt for the tear in my suit where the switchblade had entered my forearm. Failing to find it, I twisted my arm to look but found no trace of damage to the fabric either. *Nice.*

I had no doubt Caelus had meant his words as a compliment, but had I overstepped? They'd accosted me, stolen my hat, and who knows where it would have led if I'd been a regular person without the strength to take them down? Should I have let them run away without consequence? I didn't think so.

Still, a part of me wondered if I'd have responded to their aggression in the same way even a few days ago. Were the vials changing me back to how I was or into something else entirely? Either way, would I end up liking the person I seemed on my way to becoming?

I shook my head. Of course I would. They had totally had it coming.

Chapter 30

Double Vision

Slipping between cars, I crossed the street to the hotel where Dixon and Maya waited just outside the lobby doors.

"Have a nice walk?" Dixon asked.

I nodded, thinking of Gulageir and my encounter with the thugs. "It was interesting."

"We were worried," Maya said.

I gave her a sidelong look. "Really?"

Her lips quirked up. "Well, not for your safety. Not from anyone normal, but you never know what one might encounter in the big city."

I looked at the hotel doors. "Have you guys eaten yet?"

"Not yet," she replied.

"Good." I looked at Dixon. "We need to talk."

The hotel had its own restaurant, and we asked for a table in a quiet part of the dining room where we could talk without being overheard. Still full of the pizza I'd had in my room, I ordered a Coke with lots of ice.

After the waiter had left with our orders, Dixon nudged my arm. "So, what did you want to talk about?"

"Take 5," I said.

He looked around. "Isn't that what we're doing?"

I chuckled. "It's a soft drink." Keeping my voice low, I told them about the soda, Gulageir, and the changelings in the woods. As I finished my tale, I met Maya's eyes. "Which means there's a cure."

Her lips pulled back. "Buried in the ground? Well, that sounds grand." She shuddered. "I think I'd sooner die."

Dixon snorted. "Either way, you end up in the same place."

"How comforting," she said, rolling her eyes.

"Ah, don't sweat it," he said. "What are the chances it'll affect someone like you?"

Her brow wrinkled. "Like me?"

"Yeah, you know," he said. "Someone that's ascending."

She smiled. "Oh, I'm not an ascendant."

His chin dipped. "You're not?"

"Not at all," she said. "I'm just hired help, an employee."

"How does that even happen?" he asked. "Did you answer a want ad?"

She shrugged. "It's a long story involving Orithyia . . . Olivia as you may better know her. Anyway, I'm not sure I would want to ascend."

"Why not?" I asked.

Maya fiddled with her cutlery. "I'm not sure I want to live forever."

She stopped talking as the waiter appeared, holding plates of food.

"Anyway," Dixon said after the waiter had left, "I'll make a call on our way out. Let the Group know the soda thing is bigger than we thought."

"Thanks," I said. "The sooner the better. People are probably being infected as we speak."

Maya cut into her steak. "What's the plan when we get to the Bodhi Group offices?"

"You two wait across the street," Dixon said, "and I'll go in myself. It'll raise fewer questions that way."

"In that case," she said, "why even accompany you? If we're not going in, I mean."

His shoulders lifted. "So you can watch my back if I need to leave in a hurry. The Group knows about my capture, and they might think I've been compromised. It's possible instead of giving me the vial, they'll try to hold me."

I frowned. "They didn't in Berlin."

"I was careful," he said. "I dealt with them only by telephone and dead drop. Here, I'll be putting myself in their hands. Though my hope is no one here will be expecting me."

"But," I said, "they must know you're coming already, right? Since you told them not to send their vial to the Institute."

"Yeah," he said, "but I told them a Bodhi Group special agent would be by to pick it up, not that I'd be coming myself. So, they should have no reason to think it'll be me. Which is why I had to call in a few favours to keep our flight here under the radar." He raised a forkful of meat to his lips, paused, and lowered it. "Of course, whether they try to detain me will depend a lot on what, if anything, Wallace has passed along to the Group leadership." He looked at Maya. "He's my counterpart at the Institute." Glancing at me, he added, "It's one of the reasons I wanted to wait until tonight. There will be fewer people in the way if I've got to force my way out of there."

My eyes widened. "You want to fight your way out? Someone might get hurt."

"Hopefully it won't be much of a fight," he said. "These labs are secure, but they're not the Institute. I doubt it'll get that ugly anyway. They might fear I've been compromised, but they'd be only guessing." He thrust his fork at me. "Whereas, if they see through your disguise, all bets are off. That's why you've got to wait outside."

Maya took a sip of her wine and swallowed. "So, if they do, you want us to come in guns blazing?"

Dixon's eyes darted to me and back to her. "I think Winterboy here can come up with something better than that." He took a sip of the vodka and Coke he'd ordered. "He broke out of and back into the Institute easily enough and, like I said, this place isn't as secure." He checked his watch. "All right. It's late enough now." He beckoned to the waiter. "Let's finish up and get going."

A short time later, after the security director had called a trusted Bodhi Group colleague about Take 5, we departed the hotel.

"This way," Dixon said, turning down the sidewalk to our right after we exited the hotel's main doors.

"Aren't we driving?" I asked.

"No need," he replied. "The research centre's a short walk

from here." He waved at the cars crowding the street. "And in this traffic, it'll be faster."

I looked at Maya. "What about Caelus?"

Maya jabbed a finger skyward. "He's keeping watch from the air."

"Perfect," Dixon said. "Let's hope there's nothing interesting for him to see."

We walked a block east before turning south, and despite the sidewalks being crowded with people, I didn't so much as bump shoulders with any of them. They came close but always managed to sidestep or shift slightly at the last moment, just before contact, even when I stopped trying to avoid them. *Worried about pickpockets, maybe?*

A dozen or so blocks later, Dixon pulled up short.

"That's the building," he said, pointing to a black-and-white skyscraper of concrete and glass.

"It's big," I said.

"Yeah," he replied, "but there are other tenants. The Bodhi Group occupies only a portion of it." He looked from Maya to me. "All right, I'm heading in. If all goes well, I should be back within a half hour."

"What if you're longer?" I asked.

He looked thoughtful. "Give me an hour, two hours tops."

"And then?"

"Come after me," he said, "if you can and get that vial."

"Good luck, Harland," I replied, slapping his shoulder, "and thanks for doing this."

We loitered by the corner, watching until Dixon entered the building.

"There he goes," I said as a police car cruised by. "I hope this goes well."

"Me too." Maya nudged me. "Why don't we circle the area, Shivurr? We're starting to look conspicuous standing here."

"Sure." The last thing we needed now was a confrontation with the police. I might be able to take down Stasi in the middle of the night in a deserted factory area of East Berlin without making the papers, but not here. The sun was almost down now, but using my powers here, in midsummer, in one of the most crowded cities in the world, would probably put me on front pages worldwide.

Crossing the street, we soon passed by the doors where Dixon had entered. Inside, visible through the ground-floor windows, he stood talking to a guard seated behind a security desk. Nodding, the guard waved Dixon toward the elevators.

I looked at Maya. "He's in."

"So far, so good." Maya grabbed my elbow. "We should keep moving, though."

Together, we strolled along, keeping our eyes and ears open for trouble. At the next intersection, we crossed to the street's far side, turned left, and walked. When we stood across the street from the Bodhi Group's building, we stopped and waited, watching the traffic crawl past.

"He's coming out," Maya said a few minutes later, peering over my shoulder toward the building.

"Already?" Rotating, I looked across the street. Sure enough, Dixon was exiting the building, his face unmistakable as he walked into a pool of street light. "That was quick."

"Did he change his suit?" Maya asked. "I thought it was black."

I squinted. "I don't think so. It looks black to me."

"Maybe you're right." She shielded her eyes with one of her hands. "Must be the changing light."

"Come on." I touched a hand to her back. "Let's meet him at the corner."

Maya grabbed my arm as I turned away. "Wait. He's going the other direction."

I stared, seeing that she was right. "The hell's he doing?"

"Beats me," she said. "Let's find out."

Doing a one-eighty, we hustled along the sidewalk, travelling parallel to Dixon. His height ensured his grey hair remained visible above the majority of surrounding walkers, making him easier to track.

A hundred yards on, I skirted to the edge of a crowd waiting at the street corner for the light to change and looked for Dixon again. I caught sight of him for a moment before a bus passing through the intersection rumbled past, obscuring my view.

When it had cleared, Dixon was gone.

Damn it. Scanning the far sidewalk, I spotted him striding off to the left. Instead of turning toward me, as I'd expected, he'd crossed to the next block and continued to stride down the avenue.

"Is he trying to run away?" I resisted the urge to shout his name, not wanting to draw attention to myself. "Maya?"

"One second, Shivurr," she said with a faraway look in her eyes and a scowl on her face.

"Are you talking to Caelus?" I asked.

Her eyes flicked to me. "Does Dixon have a twin?"

I made a face. "Not that I know of. Why?"

She jabbed a thumb. "Caelus just saw another Dixon exit the Group's building, and he's heading the other way, back to the spot where we left him."

My brow creased. "There are two of them?"

She nodded. "Apparently."

"How's that possible?" Even if Dixon had a twin, what would that twin be doing here today? I supposed for a moment that someone might be wearing a disguise or merely resemble the security director but dismissed the thought. *Caelus wouldn't make that mistake.*

"I don't know," she replied, "but one of them has got to be an imposter."

I grimaced. "Which one's ours, though?" *And is the one we've been hanging out with the original?* A thrill of panic ran through me. Maybe the man I'd rescued from the Gobi Desert was a fake—some guy who'd undergone plastic surgery—planted in my path for me to rescue. The canister could be some sort of post-operative healing chamber. *No, that doesn't make sense.* The Eurus couldn't have known I'd be coming. *Could they?*

Nah, I thought. The Dixon I'd rescued had known things an imposter wouldn't, including that Scott had helped me. That was the real Dixon and the one we'd come to New York with. So, the first Dixon to exit the building, the one now going the wrong way in a dark blue rather than a black suit, was a fake.

"I'm sure you're right," Maya said after I'd told her my reasoning. Her eyes drifted down. "Now that you mention it, the first one to exit walks with even more of a strut than our Dixon."

"Cool," I said as the traffic light changed and we moved again. "Can you ask Caelus to tail Fake Dixon while we meet up with the real one?"

"He's already on his way," she said, jogging by my shoulder through the flood of people spilling toward us from the street's far side.

Chapter 31

Third Rail

Dixon, a boulder in a stream of foot traffic, waved a hand and took a few steps toward us. "There you are." His gaze pinballed between Maya and me. "What's up?"

"Come on," I said, slapping his arm and turning back the way we'd come. "We'll tell you while we move." Dodging pedestrians, I related what Caelus, Maya, and I had seen. "He looks exactly like you. You don't have a twin, do you?"

He shook his head. "I've got a younger brother, but he's not a twin, and he doesn't work for the Bodhi Group either. I'd say you'd mistaken another good-looking guy for me, but a doppelgänger explains a lot."

"What do you mean?" Maya asked.

His lips thinned. "The vials are gone. Supposedly removed by me, not long before I arrived." He blew out a breath. "Still, it raises as many questions as it answers."

I regarded him with a narrowed eye. "You are the real Harland, right?" Though I felt pretty sure of my reasoning, it seemed prudent to check.

He looked down at himself. "Obviously."

"Prove it."

"All right." He proceeded to recount several incidents at the Bodhi Institute, including a few discussions we'd had in private. He finished by repeating details of our conversation at Dublin Gulch when he'd lain injured in a downed helicopter. "Satisfied?"

"I think so." I sidestepped an oncoming pedestrian. "The question is, where did this duplicate come from?"

"If I had to guess," Maya said, "I'd say he's an avatar."

"An avatar that looks like me?" Dixon scowled. "How's that even possible?"

"You were held prisoner by the Eurus," she said. "They may have taken your DNA and used it to create one. It's certainly within their capabilities. They have their own Miraculeum."

"Within a week?" I glanced at Dixon. "But this other Harland looks the same age."

"As I understand it," Maya replied, sounding out of breath, "avatars are often created to match a certain biological age."

My stomach lurched. "If you're right, we'll have to be careful. We can't let him get away—not with the vials—but taking him down won't be easy, and with all these people around, someone's going to get hurt."

Dixon nudged Maya. "What about the jar you used on the old gal Winterboy beat up in Berlin?"

"I didn't beat her up," I protested, giving him a flat stare. "I just helped Maya . . . exorcise her." *The power of the Underfrost compels you.*

Maya laid a hand on my shoulder. "You did what was necessary. However, I'm afraid that jar was the only one I have, and it's still occupied."

Crap. "Does Caelus still have eyes on him?" I asked.

She nodded. "Fake Dixon is only a block ahead now, and . . . uh-oh. He's entering a subway station."

"Oh, man." I stood on tiptoe, looking for a subway sign above the flow of pedestrians. "Can Caelus follow him there?"

She glanced my way. "Not without potentially alerting Fake Dixon."

"Let's run," I said. "If this guy hops a train, we're cooked."

Without another word, we sprinted, zigzagging through the crowd, occasionally nudging and even shoving people aside.

"Don't, Caelus," Maya said, breathing heavily.

"What?" Dixon asked.

She shot him a look. "He's flown down after the target."

"Can't you stop him?" I asked, thinking of the bird's collar.

"It's too late," she said. "If I interfere now, I may make things worse, and there's still a chance he won't be noticed."

Picking out the white block letters of a subway sign in the distance, I raced ahead and flew down a set of stairs into the earth, two at a time. Metal girders and the white tile walls of a mostly empty subway platform waited at the stairway's bottom. As footsteps thundered behind me, the squeal of metal rubbing against metal wailed from the tunnel to my right. I frowned, certain a train had just left with our quarry aboard.

"Any sign of him?" Dixon asked, a few steps from the bottom stair. "Did we lose him?"

"I don't know," I said, noting a faint aroma of urine and garbage upon the air.

Maya held up a hand and touched her ear. "It's okay. He's gone into the tunnel. Caelus is tailing him."

"Really?" I said, hardly daring to hope. "But the train—"

"Is going the other way," she said. "Fake Dixon entered the tunnel as soon as the train cleared the station."

"We're going to need a better name for this guy," Dixon grumbled.

"Come on." I took a step and beckoned them to follow. "Let's catch them."

Moving to the far side, I approached the platform's edge, but before I could jump down, Dixon caught my arm. "Watch out for the third rail. It carries enough juice to kill a horse."

"Which one's that?" I asked.

He pointed. "That one, I think. The one on the outside." He waved a hand. "Actually, I'm not sure. Maybe try not to touch any of them."

"All right," I said, hopping down to the tracks.

Two thumps behind me told me my companions had done the same.

"You can't do that," a woman shouted as we entered the dimness of the tunnel. "That's dangerous."

"Mind your own business," Dixon shouted back.

"She's not wrong," Maya said. "Be ready to get out of the way if we hear a train coming. There should be alcoves now and again in which we can shelter."

Inhaling scents of oil and metallic dust, we walked the tracks. Fluorescent lamps—widely spaced—cast harsh light and wild shadows on the walls, making the tunnel bleak and ominous. An effect occasionally improved by the red, green, and yellow of intermittent signal lights.

"Caelus is just up ahead," Maya shouted into my ear, as a train, its brakes shrieking like banshees, thundered past the narrow nook in which we'd taken shelter. "He's trailed Fake Dixon to a door and is waiting for us there."

"Why didn't he follow him?" I asked after the last railcar had passed us by.

She waggled her thumbs. "He's a raven."

I snorted. A god in a raven's body, stymied by a doorknob.

Following the train's fading howl, we resumed our trek and a short while later found the bird sitting atop a metal railing next to an open space beside the tracks, twenty feet long and perhaps five feet wide.

"He went through there," Caelus said, jabbing his beak toward a dull grey door near the wall's middle.

I gave the door's knob a twist and pushed, jiggling it in its frame. "It's locked."

Stepping back, I rapped a knuckle against the paint, eliciting a metallic ping.

"Break it in," Maya said, kicking the air.

Dixon made a noise in the back of his throat. "Too noisy. If the guy is on the other side, we'll be letting him know we're coming."

"Right." I studied the door a moment. "I've got a better idea. Give me a second." I vanished into the Underfrost and, stepping forward, pressed a hand against the door, which felt spongy beneath my fingers. Pushing harder, my hand sank into the metal up to my wrist. *Here goes.* I lowered my head, leaned forward, and pumped my legs, and my arms sank in to my shoulders. When my nose mashed lightly against the door, I closed my eyes and kept pushing until my face and skull slipped as well. *Come on.* The rest of my body followed with increasing speed, and long seconds later, all resistance abruptly gave way, and I stumbled forward a few steps before catching my balance. I opened my eyes on a poorly lit hallway. *Made it.* Turning about, I popped from the Underfrost, unlocked the door, and allowed my companions inside.

"Nice trick," Dixon said, entering after Maya and closing the door behind himself.

"Come on," I said. "This way."

Dixon pointed in the other direction. "What about down there?"

"Nah." I jabbed a finger at swirls of deep blue that only I could see. "He went this way. There are disturbances in the Underfrost going in this direction."

A screech of metal came from beyond the door through which we'd come, and the floor shook.

"Nice." His lips pursed, and his head bobbed slightly. "I didn't know you could do that."

"Me neither." More accurately, I'd forgotten I could until moments ago. *The vials are working their magic.* From what I now remembered, doing so worked best indoors. The effects were brief to begin with, and wind and other factors tended to wipe out all traces within seconds outdoors. But in an enclosed space with little ventilation, those seconds became minutes. "Come on." Waving a hand by my ear, I walked ahead. "The path's already fading."

We travelled corridors lit with flickering fluorescent light, coming eventually to a staircase with a door at its bottom, set into the middle of a concrete wall. A padlock and chain with thick metal links dangled from a clasp welded to the portal's rusty green surface.

Looking over my shoulder, I held a finger to my lips, then descended the stairs, trailed by the light clang of my companions' footsteps. I crouched by the door, noting faint light in the slight gap between its bottom and frame, before cupping a hand to my ear and pressing it to the metal.

Hearing nothing, I stood and gave the door a gentle nudge, wincing as it swung inward with a rusty squeak, revealing a wide area lit by a few lonely incandescent bulbs. Attached to walls and girders just above eye level, they cast meagre light upon wooden pallets and debris as well as two sets of rusted railway tracks, which ran left and right. Ahead, three short girder-lined passageways ran diagonally between sets of tracks to a graffiti-covered subway car.

"What is this place?" I asked in a low voice. "Another subway station?"

"Abandoned by the looks of it," Dixon said, matching my volume. "Maybe never finished."

"Which way now, Mr. Shivurr?" Maya asked.

"Uh." Movement to the right drew my attention, and I squinted into the darkness. "Wait here a sec."

I padded down the tracks, keeping girders between myself and whatever lay in the distance. As I drew closer, a twelve-foot-tall fence—set across the tracks—resolved into view.

What's this doing here? Something bashed against the chain link, and my hands jerked toward my face. Faded denim and long brown hair shone in the light a moment before sinking back into darkness. *Uh-oh.* I skulked closer, entering into shadow, and took cover behind a metal support. A moment later, my eyes adjusted to the gloom. Beyond the fence, several people meandered, heads hanging, chins against chests. *Changelings.*

Metal squealed and a sliver of light flashed in the murk beyond them, becoming a doorway through which a woman stumbled as if drunk. Two men followed.

"How many does this make?" asked the first man, gripping the woman's bicep and guiding her to the fence lining that side of the tunnel.

The second man dashed ahead of the pair and fiddled with the gate. "At least a dozen today." With a push, he swung the gate inward. "This thing's getting out of hand."

The first dude nudged the woman into the cage. "Don't worry about it. No doubt, the divine have a plan." He fixed his buddy with a stare. "You do not doubt the divine, do you?"

The other guy pulled the gate shut. "I didn't say that."

They turned away and disappeared back through the door through which they'd entered.

Pivoting on a heel, I raced back to my companions and told them what I'd seen.

"What do you figure?" Dixon asked. "More first-generation changelings?"

"Probably." I hadn't seen any symbiont vines growing out of their skin, but in the darkness, details had been hard to see.

He looked thoughtful. "And the guys collecting them? Devil worshippers or more renegade Eurus?"

"The latter, I suppose." I smirked. "It sure isn't the Arborati." *Not down here.* "But if they're renegade Eurus, why don't they know more about what's going on?"

He shrugged. "They're low-ranking if they're on collection duty. In a need-to-know scenario, they'd be the last to know."

I bobbed my head, looking toward the chain-link fence. Being held in a cage seemed better than being buried in the ground, but at least the Arborati were curing those they captured. I wasn't sure what might be done to the people being gathered here. I had to hope they'd be cured too, but I'd sooner trust the Arborati, or Boreas and friends, than leave these poor folks here. Yet, as before, my companions and I had higher priorities.

Maya tugged on my elbow. "Caelus has located Fake Dixon," she whispered.

"Where?" I asked.

She pointed to a subway car sitting at the end of the right-most diagonal tunnel. "There."

"Okay." I sighed and rubbed my face with both hands before lowering them. "First things first. We've got to get that vial. After that, we can figure out what to do about those people."

"Wait." She grabbed my arm. "He's not alone."

"Who's with him?" I asked.

She held up a finger and looked down. "Give me a second." Her brow wrinkled and she gasped. "Shit."

"What is it?" Dixon growled.

"It's Zelus," she said, her voice tremulous. "In the clone body."

"Zelus is Fake Dixon?" I said, eyes wide.

She hugged herself. "That's what the woman he's talking to called him."

Dixon gripped my arm. "The Eurus god you made the deal with?"

I nodded. "I guess he didn't trust anyone else to get the vial."

Something doesn't fit, though. I looked in the direction of the chain-link fence. Zelus wasn't a renegade Eurus. Far from it. He was the establishment. Yet here he was in an abandoned subway station where changelings were being confined.

He must have found out about them, I realized.

How, I didn't know, but he and his minions were either gathering changelings to keep their existence from becoming known to the world at large, or for study. Maybe in an effort to understand what the Anathema and Eurus renegades were doing.

Dixon gave me a stern look. "Can you take him?"

I turned up my palms. "I guess we're going to find out." No matter what, there was no way I could let him escape with the vial. Even if it didn't contain the location or key to Allfrost Prime, I was determined to get every last drop of myself back, if I could. I studied my companions. At least I had them to back me up. *Shame Maya doesn't have another soul trap, though.* "Who's with him, Maya?"

"Her name's Greta," she replied.

"Human?" Dixon asked. "Or another alien ghost in a meat suit?"

Good question, I thought. If the woman in there with Zelus was also a god, even a demigod . . . well, our odds of success were even worse than I'd thought.

"I don't know." Maya's shoulders lifted. "I'm not familiar with her." Her eyes met mine. "How about you?"

I thought a moment before replying. "Doesn't ring a bell."

"Great," Dixon muttered, checking his pistol. "Then we might be up against two of these *gods*."

Maya's lips twisted. "The way Zelus is chewing her out, he's definitely in charge. Maybe that means she's mortal."

"What's he angry with her about?" I asked.

"For failing to catch you," Maya said. "And she's asking for additional help."

"Hmm." I stroked my chin a moment, thinking.

Chapter 32

Oathbreaker

If Zelus wanted me, maybe I could use that, especially if I could convince him I was still a friend. From what Ashdon had said, the majority of the Eurus Faction weren't sure either way. Sure, I'd fought with Atriel when he'd come to rescue me, but that could be chalked up to my memory loss or him not being recognizable.

He had, after all, been wearing a different body at the time. My resistance didn't necessarily mean I was against the Eurus, only that I'd been understandably confused. And Atriel, a true buddy of mine, might also have downplayed our encounter when he got back to the Gobi Desert camp and described what had happened.

At least I hoped he had. If so, maybe pretending to still be an ally could get me close to Zelus and Greta, allowing me to choose the ideal moment to attack.

I shrugged inwardly. It hadn't worked for long when I tried it with Azrileus in Berlin, but it was better than simply yelling "charge" and attacking. Besides, even a short conversation might tell me something. *Like how much time I have.*

I held up a finger. "I've got an idea," I said, laying out what I had in mind.

Dixon eyed me a long moment before nodding. "If it doesn't work, we'll be no worse off."

"Come on," I said, tiptoeing away with my shoulders hunched. "Follow me."

We crept down one of the diagonal passageways connecting rail lines, and at the tunnel's far side, I edged an eye past a metal support and spotted Zelus inside the subway car, fifty feet away, still looking like Dixon's twin. Caelus perched at the roof's edge. Retracting his wings, he ruffled his feathers and dipped his head, cocking it to the side. Doing the same, I heard faint, unintelligible murmurings emanating from the car's open window.

"What's been happening in there?" I whispered to Maya.

"They're about to part ways." Her hands flew to her mouth. "She's going after Orithyia."

Lilith's face flashed in my mind. "That Greta person found us again," the teen had said while relating her and Alan's escape from the Eurus Faction.

My eyes widened. "Zeus's beard." *Of course.* "She's the Eurus that's after Brad and Lucy."

So much had happened since Lilith and Alan had told me about the redhead, I hadn't recognized the name when Maya had first mentioned it. Now that I did, my mind returned to the Schmidts' domus in Caelumburg when Alan and Lilith had recounted their narrow escape from, in Alan's words, "Some red-headed chick from East Germany."

"Great," Dixon said. "Then we can wait and jump this Zelus bastard when he's alone."

I shook my head. "We can't let her leave." *Not to go after my friends.* Olivia could probably take care of herself, being a demigod, but my mortal friends were ... mortal. If I missed this chance to help and they were captured or worse, I'd never forgive myself. "Zelus might have given her the vial already."

It wasn't likely—Zelus was too much of a control freak and it didn't make sense to give it to someone about to go hunting—but we couldn't take the chance. Besides, I figured in Dixon's eyes, ensuring the vial wouldn't slip through our fingers would be more important than saving my friends from Greta.

His jaw tightened. "All right. Then we take them both down."

I smiled beneath my mask. Whatever his faults, Harland Dixon had guts. "Here goes." I slapped his shoulder. "Cover me, guys."

Crossing the fifty feet to the train car, I stepped inside, using an upturned crate as a makeshift step. The interior was dim, lit only by hazy artificial light entering through the subway car's windows, but I could still see Zelus in his Dixon body and the woman, Greta, dressed in jeans, T-shirt and sneakers.

"Who are you?" Zelus asked, eyebrows bunched. "Are you with the cleanup crew?"

I goggled at him. His face and voice were so similar to Dixon's, it was spooky.

"I'm Shivurr." I fiddled with my cowl and raised it from my face, letting my features relax back closer to normal. "I think you've been looking for me."

Zelus's eyes lit. "So you are." He glanced at Greta. "You've been leading us on a merry chase."

"Sorry about that." I extended a hand. "Zelus, right?"

He regarded my hand but didn't take it. "You recognize me in this form?"

I withdrew my hand, noting his voice no longer resembled Dixon's. "I heard you talking."

"And how did you find us here?" he asked, giving Greta another sidelong look.

"I followed you," I said nonchalantly, "from the Bodhi Group offices. Nice disguise, by the way. I almost thought you were the real Dixon when I first saw you."

Zelus looked down at himself. "Yes, this avatar has proven quite useful. It is fortunate our people had the foresight to obtain sufficient samples of his DNA before you spirited him away." He crossed his arms. "I must admit, I am curious as to why you would have done so for your jailer, especially if you are truly still on our side."

"Yeah, about that." I rubbed the back of my neck. "I've been a bit confused. Amnesia, you know?" He kept staring at me stone-faced, making no reply. "I thought I was rescuing an Allfrost Sentinel." I chuckled. "Crazy, right? But I'm better now, mostly."

He pursed his lips. "And you are ready to fulfill your promise?"

An image of austere men and women, sitting about a long wooden table in a marble hall, popped into my mind.

"With your help," Zelus had said long ago, "this world may yet be saved, Shivurr. Do we have your oath?"

I met each of their eyes before replying, "Yes, but only if you all in turn vow to deactivate all nukes. Everywhere on Earth. No matter who they belong to."

One by one, the gathered had inclined their heads and uttered an affirmative.

"Are you well?" Zelus asked, drawing me back to the present.

Damn. I had vowed to help them. *And if they'd kept their end of the bargain, the world might have been a better place.* I pushed the thought aside. *Not that it matters now.* They'd broken their oath first. Likely, they had never intended to honour my all-important stipulation. *Which means the deal is off.*

Coughing, I stood tall. "I'm fine, and yeah, I'm ready. How are things going, anyway?"

"All is in readiness," Zelus replied. "Your absence is all that delays us now."

"Really?" I asked. "Everywhere? Even the Soviet Union and China?"

"Of course," he said. "Worldwide. As agreed. You have my word."

"That's pretty fast," I said, narrowing my eyes. "I thought it would take decades."

He shrugged. "The years you have been absent have been more than sufficient to permit Baduriel, with the help of our people and resources, to prepare a sufficient portion of the Allfrost. After all, it was only those nodes closest to nuclear devices that needed to be modified. All that remains is for you to journey to the prime chamber and issue the command to activate the Allfrost. You are ready to do so, yes?"

"Not quite," I said.

"Ah," he said, "I had a feeling you had had a change of—"

I held up a hand, cutting him off. "No, no. If anything, I'm more convinced than ever the nukes have got to go." I meant what I said about the nukes too, giving my words a ring of truth. "Seriously."

His eyebrows rose. "Then what?"

I turned up my palms. "I don't know where the prime chamber is."

He waved a hand dismissively. "No matter."

"You know where it is?"

"Not yet," he replied, "but we have narrowed the search radius substantially. We believe we are now close enough for someone with your abilities to find it with ease."

Damn. If the Eurus were that close, they'd find it even without me now. With Baduriel's help, maybe they'd find a way around the security measures without me too.

I forced a smile. "That's great."

The corners of his mouth quirked. "Despite your words, you do not seem pleased by the news."

"No, no," I said, raising my hands. "That's awesome. But I've also lost the authorization key. Without it, I can't unlock the chamber to issue the activation command."

He grimaced. "That *is* unfortunate. There is still more of yourself to recover, then?"

"You know there is," I said with a chuckle. "You've got a vial of me in your pocket." Unless he *had* given it to the redhead, Greta, who hadn't moved or spoken since I'd first entered the train car. I held out my hand. "The one I came all the way to New York to get, so if you don't—"

"I am curious." Zelus leaned against the subway car wall. "How did you find the Manhattan lab?"

"Dixon," I said, telling the truth. I'd heard the best lies usually had truth weaved into them.

Zelus looked out the window. "Is he with you?"

"No," I said, possibly a trifle too quickly. "He refused to help me."

"Even after you rescued him?" he asked.

I spread my hands and shook my upturned palms. "Gratitude, right?" I jeered. "He didn't want to violate his oath to the Bodhi Group, so I left him behind."

"Indeed." Zelus scowled. "The security director does hold fast to his ideals." I tensed as he fiddled beneath his suit jacket. "A most stubborn subject." Catching the glint of glass in Zelus's hand, I stepped closer. "It is a pity you do not still have access to him."

I drew back, trying not to seem too eager. "Why's that?"

He held up a vial and studied the swirls of light within. "It is my understanding that the last of your essence—that is, other than what I have in my hand—has been returned to the Bodhi Institute." He sighed. "If the security director had been willing, obtaining it would have been trivial." He grimaced. "I suppose I will have to make the attempt myself instead. Regrettably, we had not yet captured a scan of his brain nor had time to model his normal behaviour for replication."

"So?" I said. "You look just like him."

"Perhaps," Zelus replied, "but Director Dixon is well known to the Institute's denizens. If I fail to recognize his close confidants or do not know things he should know, suspicions may be raised." He bobbed his head as if convincing himself. "Still, with Ashdon's help, I should be able to fool them long enough. If not . . . well, there are too many mortals in the world as it is."

"Maybe you won't need to," I said.

"Oh?" He studied me. "How's that?"

I pointed to the vial. "If that's got what we need." I held out a hand. "Shall we see?"

"Tempting," he replied, slipping the bottle beneath his lapel and fiddling a moment. "Doing so would permit me to quit this body and return to my usual self, which I long to do. However, I sense you are not telling the truth, Shivurr."

My lip curled. "You're reading my mind?"

"Alas, your mind is as hard to read as ever, especially at a distance." He turned to look at the pillar behind which my companions hid. "However, now that I have gone looking for it, I do detect a familiar mind over there. The mind of one Harland Dixon, if I am not mistaken. Given that you lied about the security director being in your company, I think I will hang onto this vial for now."

Shit. "That doesn't work for me," I said, eyeing him. The woman, Greta, sidled to the right as if trying to flank me, and I raised a finger in warning. "Don't move."

Zelus raised a hand, his fingers splayed like the talons of an eagle, and I gasped as an invisible force gripped my chest. A moment later, my feet left the floor, and I flew back, slamming against the wall of the subway car.

Bastard. Fighting to breathe, I slipped into the Underfrost, and the force gripping my torso vanished, dropping me to the spongy floor.

"Wait," Zelus shouted at Greta, whose hands glowed white. "Save your strength." His eyes darted left and right before settling on my new position. "He has fled into the Underfrost." With a wave of his hands, the subway car doors slid closed. "You cannot hide there forever, Shivurr. Not if you mean to return." His hands lit again, this time with fire. "Here, let me help you." Flames shot from his hands as if from a flamethrower but passed through me without doing any harm.

Uh-oh. I could feel myself rising from the Underfrost, pulled by the scorching heat back toward the regular world. To remain submerged, I'd have to go deeper, but I'd be risking a permanent stay if I did so. *Damn.*

I sidled to the side, out of the spray, until, at last, the fire abated. Before Zelus could attack again, I popped from the Underfrost, pushing a protective bubble of energy outward from my core. As it expanded, arcs of lightning shot from Greta's outstretched hands, rippling my shield but failing to penetrate.

My turn. Scowling, I swept my arms high, sending a gale-force wind outward. Zelus and Greta's hair blew back, and ice spread across the walls and windows of the train car.

Collapsing the frost shield, I thrust out my palm and a line of frost energy beamed from it. Along its path of travel, the air rippled and whitened, drawing a line between my extended hand and Greta's shoulder. She screeched, slapped a hand to her wound, and dropped to a knee, and I sent a second ray of frost into Zelus's chest. He gasped as if all the air had been sucked from his lungs and raised his hands defensively. Though his palms absorbed and deflected the worst of my attack, enough cryogenic energy slipped past to keep him on his heels.

Zelus turned his head, grunting as his ear, neck, and hair grew increasingly frosty. His hands, suffused in white, hissed and spat, turning reddish orange, becoming molten as if formed of fresh lava. As they grew brighter, he brought them together, forming a single conflagration. He snarled and shoved his hands toward me, pushing back my frost beam several feet with a growing shaft of fire.

Oh boy. I sidestepped and, dropping my frost beam, conjured a frost ball with my other hand, hissing as Zelus's fire raged past my hip, which broiled even through my clothing. Gritting my teeth, I hurled frost, striking the Eurus god in the knee, and smiled as he dropped to the floor. Giving him no time to recover, I rushed closer, raised a fist, and landed a haymaker in the middle of his imitation face. His eyes rolled in their sockets, but he somehow managed to stay on his feet.

Fall, damn you. Grabbing his lapel, I raised my fist again, but before I could strike, Zelus clapped a hand to my chest. His body lit with electric light, and my teeth gnashed and my vision blurred.

"That's it," Zelus cooed, wrapping me in a bear hug. My consciousness seemed to be slipping away, and I scrabbled for the Underfrost. "Sleep now, Shivurr. You need not fear the darkness. We need you, after all."

I fought for consciousness as stars burst in my vision and glass shattered in my ears. A few loud pops followed, and Zelus released his grip, and the electricity arcing through me subsided. Stumbling back a few steps, I bent over and braced my hands against my knees and tried to clear my head.

Thank frost.

"Stay down, Red," shouted a voice.

Dixon, I thought after a moment. I'd almost thought it was Zelus, but the god lay on the ground before me, a dark and glossy pool spreading beneath him.

"I said stay down," Dixon repeated. "Move again and you'll catch a bullet. You all right, Winterboy?"

Yep, that's Dixon all right. Feeling better already, I turned to face him, hands still on my knees. "Yeah, I'm fine."

"Glad to hear it." He stood in the doorway, knees bent and both hands on his pistol, aiming somewhere off to my left.

Looking in the direction he aimed, I saw Greta kneeling nearby. She had a scowl on her face, and her frostbitten arm tucked close to her side. I felt a pressure encircling my wrist and a shock of electricity, weaker than before, drawing my gaze to Zelus, who regarded me with malevolent eyes.

I pulled away and my hands lit with frost, but before I could do more, Dixon's gun barked again, the sound deafening in the enclosed space, and a hole appeared in the middle of Zelus's forehead.

"Whoa!" I stumbled back as Zelus's grip relaxed and glanced at Dixon. "You shot him."

"Damn right." He shifted his gun back to Greta. "Don't think I won't do the same to you, Red, if you so much as sneeze."

Light flashed at my feet, sending me back a step, and a cloud of amorphous light rose from the prostrate Dixon clone. Within moments, its swirls resolved into a loosely humanoid form with waving ghostly appendages, and the air grew hot.

Oh, shit. Dead as the Dixon avatar might be, the ghost inside wasn't, and that could be bad. Avatars were enhanced, possessing great strength and resilience, but they weren't un- affected by a god's energy manipulations. Which meant that, spectacular as his previous attacks had been, they had almost certainly been restrained because Zelus had been trying to avoid damaging his avatar. With that avatar now dead, he no longer had any reason to hold back.

"Look out." I dashed over to Dixon and caught him in a bear hug.

Holding his arms high, he said, "The hell, Winter—"

He broke off as fire and blistering heat filled the air for an instant before whirling azure and alabaster swelled from my middle, cocooning us in pure cryogenic energy.

That was close, I mused, watching the fiery maelstrom course safely about us, only a foot or so away, colouring my frost shield purple. Licking meltwater from my lips, I released Dixon and touched my nose, which felt shorter than it had been before the fire. *Easily fixed*, I thought, redistributing snow to restore it. When it felt normal again, I redonned my hood, activated its shape-preserving mechanism, and prepared to move.

"How long can he keep this up?" Dixon shouted.

"Not much longer, I hope." The frost shield quivered, and heat and flame licked through it. Recoiling, I buffed the failing shield with more of my dwindling energy reserves. *Come on.* At last, the firestorm collapsed. *Thank the Allfrost.*

"Careful," Dixon said, "it might be a trick."

Heeding his advice, I peered through the frost shield's swirling haze toward Zelus. The god, now a cloud of sheer light, drew into a ball before, with a deep, moaning cry, streaming out one of the subway car's shattered windows. I dropped my shield, relieved, and looked around wearily, wrinkling my nose at the stench of charred flesh, melted plastic, and who knew what else, all of which still sizzled in the aftermath. I spotted Zelus's dead avatar, now several feet from where it had first fallen. *What the hell?* It rose and rolled sideways, revealing Greta beneath. Her face was as red as her singed and dishevelled hair, but she was alive.

I shot Dixon a glance. "Keep an eye on her, will you?"

"Sure thing," he said, levelling his weapon. "All right, sister. Hands up."

Still feeling weak, I dashed over to Dixon's fallen clone and, careful of its smouldering suit, turned it over.

"Don't bother," Dixon said from behind me. "It's dead."

"No duh," I said, wincing at the hole in Dixon's plagiarized face. "I'm looking for the vial, not giving him CPR."

"I'm going to need to talk to Feldman after this," he said, referring to Dr. Emmett Feldman, the Bodhi Institute's resident head shrink. He chuckled without humour. "Though, shooting this bastard is pretty therapeutic."

"Yeah, I bet—" I broke off, recalling that my essence—now in a pocket of the corpse's scorched suit—had a tendency to disappear if not kept cool. Zelus had just released an inferno, and his body still radiated heat.

Chapter 33

Prediction Models

Fearing for the vial's contents, I dug beneath the clone's jacket and pulled out a stainless-steel container, a bit larger than the glass bottles in which my essence was usually contained. *Is this it?* I removed the lid, releasing a whiff of fog and cool air, and found a familiar glass vial nestled inside. *Cool.* Evidently, the folks at the lab or Zelus himself had chosen to package the vial in a specially made insulating container. Touching a finger to the vial itself, I sent a short blast of the Underfrost into it, just in case, and resealed the protective container.

"Jesus, Mary, and Joseph," Maya said from the doorway. "Are you all right?"

"We're cool," I said, holding up the insulated container. "We got what we came for."

"That's grand," she said, climbing aboard. "It's pure roasting in here. Was that a bomb that went off?"

"A most impressive firestorm," Caelus said from her shoulder. "This Zelus has all the skill of a fire demon. He will do well in Hades, if he can be captured."

That he will, I thought, glancing around at the blackened walls, melted plastic, and torched signage. A train squealed faintly in the distance, and I looked back at Greta, who still lay on the subway car floor. "Why were you chasing my friends?"

Sitting up, she smoothed her singed red hair. "To find you, of course."

"The joke's on you," I said, studying her. "They had no idea where I was."

She looked early to mid-twenties, athletic and diminutive with a button nose, full cheeks, and smooth complexion, marred by smears of dirt and a sheen of sweat.

"Even so." She wiped moisture from her forehead, leaving more dirt behind, and raised her chin. "I thought we might use them to draw you out. You have a reputation for loyalty to your friends, and given reports of your amnesia . . . who else might you seek out for help?"

"Why do you sound American?" I asked with sudden realization. "I thought you were from East Germany."

"I am Russian," she said, sounding puzzled. "Where did you—" Her eyes lit, and she smiled. "Ah, yes. I told the surfer boy that. I was just having a little fun practising my accents. They are so very useful when undercover, and after living here so long, my American one is second nature now, requiring little maintenance. You have been in contact with your friends, then. Perhaps pursuing them was less of a mistake than you'd like to admit."

"Search her," Dixon said. "She might be armed."

"Good idea." Staying out of the line of fire of Dixon's gun, I stooped and checked the pockets of her jeans but found no weapons.

"Remove her bracelets," Caelus said. "They may be dangerous. Such things often house our technology."

"Right." I reached for the silver bands on Greta's wrists. *I remember now.* Now that the raven had mentioned it, her lightning attack had seemed to originate from her wrists. I pocketed the bangles, but before I could stand, a glint from her shirt collar drew my attention. Leaning forward, I lifted a small crystal ball pendant attached to a fine silver chain from her chest. "What's this do?"

Greta shrugged. "It's just a necklace."

"Take it," Maya said. "It might be dangerous too."

"Sentinel," Caelus said with urgency in his voice. "I believe there may be trouble coming our way."

Visible through the subway car's broken windows, electricity flashed, originating behind the fence of the changeling holding area.

"What the hell now?" Dixon asked, shielding his eyes from the glare with the palm of one of his hands.

"It's Zelus," Maya replied, squinting into the distance before shooting me a look. "I think he's shopping for a new body."

I winced. "And he's got a lot to choose from."

"Looks like this fight isn't over." Dixon fiddled with his pistol and patted his jacket. "Where's that clip?"

"I believe that's my cue," Greta said, shoving me in the chest. As I fell back, she gripped her pendant in one of her hands, and her lips moved inaudibly. Abruptly, I could see the floor beneath her as she shimmered into and out of view.

"No," I shouted, clambering to my feet. *She must have an Alterclavis.* Having used one a few times before, I recognized the signs. I had thought the one Atriel and I shared was unique, a prototype, given the cutting-edge tech involved, but they must have made more than one set. "Greta's trying to escape."

"Grab her, Winterboy," Dixon snarled. "I'm still reloading here."

"Catch you later, Shivurr," Greta said, lying back.

"Screw that." I lunged toward her and got a flailing sneaker in the face. Seeing stars, I brought my elbows down, trapping her leg before she could retract it. "Grab onto me, you guys." The first time I'd transported via Alterclavis, Scott and the kitchen table I'd been touching had come along for the trip, and I figured chances were good Greta's would behave the same way. "Quick. Before she gets away."

If she escaped, she'd probably return to searching for my friends. Sure, they couldn't help her find me, but she could also try to use them to lure me out or force me to help the Eurus. Either way, I couldn't let her go, but I also couldn't leave my companions behind. I needed every bit of help I could get to stop the Eurus, and Dixon was my best option for getting the remaining vials back.

Greta's unbound knee smacked into my cheek, sparking stars in my vision, but I trapped that leg too.

"Release me," she hissed, wriggling like an eel.

I gripped her ankles tighter. "Not happening."

The air wavered and brightened, and walls of brown leather shimmered into view a foot away. Then the subway car, with its more distant walls, returned. The cycle repeated, oscillating rapidly between here and somewhere else. Neither location solidified, though, as if the Alterclavis were struggling to recalculate parameters for a safe spatial transposition now that I had glommed onto Greta.

"I'm here," Maya said, pressing herself against my back. "Come on, Mr. Dixon."

A flap of wings preceded a sudden weight on my shoulder. "I am with you, as well, Sentinel," Caelus said by my ear.

Visible past the raven's beak, Dixon frowned but did not move. "Are you people nuts? We don't even know where she's trying to go. For all we know, it's right into the middle of an entire mob of these bastards."

"No chance," I said. Greta had apparently come here to report on her progress pursuing Olivia, Brad, and Lucy, and the Alterclavis had to be taking her back to wherever she'd been when her pursuit had been interrupted. Sure, I was far from an expert on the things, but there was no time to debate. "Come on, Harland. Get over here. Trust me." *For once.*

Finally, he growled. "Fine." He reached for Maya's outstretched hand, but he faded to almost nothing even as he did so.

Too late, I thought.

Then her solid hand and his near-invisible one touched, and he and the subway car became abruptly more substantial. I let out a breath, relieved. Upon Dixon touching Maya, the Alterclavis had apparently deemed the security director to be a new passenger, which had reset the transportation process.

The adjustments required to accommodate the change didn't take long, though. Only a half second later, the leather-clad ceiling, semi-translucent, flashed back into view inches below Dixon's neck. Still intangible, it appeared to do him no harm, but his eyes widened, and he dropped into a squat next to Maya and huddled close. An instant later, the subway car vanished again, leaving only solid leather-clad walls behind.

"Is it over?" he asked.

We were now atop a low-slung bed in the back of a van—roomier than Brad's Volkswagen Bus—with walls of button-tufted leather. Nearby, guitar cases nestled against plush high-backed captain's chairs at the far side of the space.

"What the fuck?" said a voice.

A skinny dude with long hair, his mouth wide, regarded us from the front passenger seat. His forehead creased, and his eyes darted frantically, taking in the situation. Over his shoulder, sunlight glared through the front windshield, signalling that, wherever we were, it was earlier here than in the city we'd just left, and the air seemed to have warmed several degrees.

"Cole," Greta shouted, legs wriggling in my grasp. "Shoot them."

"Bad idea," Dixon said as Cole twisted in his seat and fumbled at the dash. Pushing Maya aside, Dixon lunged forward, holding his weapon high. "Stop or die. Your choice."

Cole froze. "Okay, man." He raised his hands as the breeze entering through the open passenger-side window blew his hair sideways. "Be cool."

"Now hand over that weapon." Dixon crouched by the front seats with the muzzle of his pistol pressed against the back of Cole's neck. "By the barrel, unless you've always wanted a third eye."

"Sure thing, man," Cole said as I turned back to Greta.

Laying my weight across her legs to free my arms, I grabbed her necklace. "Unclasp it or I rip it off." For a moment, I thought she'd refuse, but after a pause, she scowled and did as I asked. "Thank you." I lifted my weight from her legs, whipped my hat from my head, and shoved the Alterclavis inside. *No going back now.*

"Where are we?" Dixon asked, handing Cole's gun to Maya.

"Canada," Cole replied, a tremor in his voice.

"Are you trying to be funny?" Dixon cocked his weapon. "What city, dumb-ass?"

Cole cringed. "Winnipeg."

I nodded. "It's where Olivia said she was headed with Brad and Lucy. These guys must be waiting for them here."

"When was this?" Dixon asked, not taking his eyes off Cole.

"Back in the hotel room," I said. "There's a . . ." I hesitated, not wanting to mention the transporter in front of Greta and her minion. "There's something she needs here."

"Grand," Maya said. "Where in the city are they headed? Do you know?"

"No," I said, thinking of the Walkman in my cap, "but I can call her and find out."

"Sentinel," Caelus said, "might I suggest securing these two first?"

"Right," I said. "Let's find something to tie them up."

Under Dixon's direction, Cole climbed between the seats and joined Greta on the bed. While Dixon watched the pair, Maya and I searched the vehicle for something to restrain them until Maya raised two pairs of handcuffs.

"How about these?" she asked, tossing them to me. Returning to the cargo area, she tugged open the van's big sliding door. "Caelus, be a dear and take a look around, will you?"

"Your wish is my command," the raven said wryly. With a few hops and a flap of his wings, he shot out the door and into the air.

"Good call, Maya." I snapped the cuffs—no doubt meant for Brad and Lucy—onto our captives' wrists and pocketed the keys. "We might need Caelus to find our way around too, unless one of you knows the city."

"Not well," Dixon said, "but I've been here a few times. How about you, Day?"

"I'm afraid not, Mr. Dixon," Maya replied, slamming the cargo door.

"Check the visor," I said. "Maybe there's a map."

"An excellent suggestion," she said, slipping into the front again.

While she did so, I studied Greta and Cole, who couldn't have been more different. The petite redhead, having been through fire, face and clothes dirty from the subway car's floor, still smelled mainly of sandalwood and soap, and her fierce, intelligent eyes studied me intently. Whereas the lanky headbanger, stinking of stale sweat, kept his chin down and studied a bandage on one of his hands from behind a curtain of hair.

I checked the cuffs, verifying they weren't pressing too hard against the gauze covering his wound. "What happened here?"

"Dog bit me," he replied without looking up.

My mouth opened. "You mean Bear?"

Greta snorted. "Is that what you call him? How quaint."

What else? My mind fumbled around at the edge of an almost-remembered memory but couldn't quite actualize it. Frustrated, I pushed it aside. There were more important things to deal with right now. "Where are my friends?" For a moment, I worried they had already been caught, but Zelus wouldn't have been chewing Greta out for not having found them yet if they had been. "Tell me, and we might let you go."

"I don't know, exactly," she grumbled. "Prediction models indicated Winnipeg as their probable next destination, so I came here in hopes of finding them. Until you confirmed it, I wasn't even sure it had been the right move."

"So, what was your plan, Red?" Dixon asked. "This city's got a half million people, easy. How were you planning on finding your targets?"

Greta sneered. "The phone book, of course. This is the girl Lucy Heller's hometown after all, and there are few with her surname listed. So few, in fact, that I have men monitoring each address."

I blinked. *Lucy's last name is Heller?* I'd never thought to ask before. Come to think of it, I knew only Alan's surname, and through him his brother Brad's. It just hadn't been important, despite their names being commonplace. I hadn't known anyone outside of the Bodhi Institute when we'd first met, making them celebrities in the small world of my damaged mind, needing only one name. Even now that I had most of my memories back, they were still famous and unique to me. *I wonder what Caleb's last name is.*

Greta tsk-tsked at Dixon. "Surely, you as a former CIA operative would have thought of that."

"And what if she's unlisted?" he asked, ignoring the jibe.

"That's possible," Greta agreed, "which is why I have men watching the roads by which they are most likely to arrive in town."

Dixon frowned. "Then why are you parked here?" He looked out a window. "At a shopping mall."

Greta stared at her subordinate. "That's a good question."

Cole's hair spilled forward, obscuring his pale face and part of the rock band printed on his T-shirt. "We got hungry." He upended his cuffed hands and his fingers glinted with silver rings. "Sorry, Greta."

Who's we? I wondered.

Her eyes hardened. "Idiots." She sighed. "Don't do drugs, Shivurr. It ruins minds. Well, I suppose I must hope my other men have more success."

"What do you care?" I asked. "You don't need to find me anymore. I'm right here."

"Leverage." She held up her hands, displaying the cuffs on her wrists. "Your offer to let me go if I cooperate strikes me as insincere, and I'd rather not do so in any case." Her expression grew serious. "Is there any chance I can convince you to fulfill your oath to the Eurus?"

I scoffed. "Uh, sure. Zero and none."

"Why not?" Greta said. "Nuclear weapons are as much a threat as ever."

I blew a jet of air through pressed lips. "So? Do you think I'm stupid? I know you're not disabling them all, and taking away only the US nukes is going to make things worse. There'll be nothing stopping the Soviet Union or China from invading any country they want and nuking any that resist them."

"Yes," she said, "there will be invasions. That's unavoidable, I'm afraid, if we're to unite the world under our rule."

"You'll have to nuke us, then," Dixon growled. "Better dead than red ain't just a catchy motto."

Her eyelids fluttered. "You can't truly mean that."

"Count on it," he said.

"Even so, you are in the minority, I'm sure." Turning up her palms, she picked sky-blue polish from the nails of one of her hands. "Even in your own country. Most people would rather live, even if it means surrendering freedom, providing they are not otherwise unduly burdened. Bread and circuses, you know? I have seen it the world over."

"Assholes," I said. "Why can't you guys just live and let live?"

"Would that we could," Greta replied, "but if we do nothing, someday the bombs will fall. Launched by one side, then the other, it matters not by whom, until all the world is afire. And only dust and ash will remain."

I threw my hands into the air. "That's why all nukes need to be disabled. On all sides."

She pursed her lips. "Even if nuclear destruction can be avoided—a long shot—humanity must be shepherded from other dangers. Come now, Shivurr. I know you do not remember everything yet, but you know the planet is warming. Why do you think that is? People. Ever-increasing numbers of voracious consumers. And the number increases every day. Yet the West speaks only of consumption and growth. Infinite growth in a finite world. Whatever happened to merely living moderate, sustainable, and happy lives?"

"Capitalism is a cornerstone of democracy, sister," Dixon said. "It ain't perfect, but it's better than the alternative."

She sniffed. "You are an unusual man, Director Dixon. I've read your file, including your mandatory psychiatric evaluations." She studied the air as if reading. "You think most people are idiots, do you not?"

He glared. "What of it?"

Her cuffs jingled as she tried to spread her hands. "Despite your feelings, you support a governmental system where the majority decides how things are done. If most people are idiots . . ." She trailed off, leaving the rest unsaid.

"Whatever," Dixon said, rolling his eyes. "If something affects you, you get a vote. Like I said, our system isn't perfect, but it's the best one around."

Her eyes lit. "Ah, but what if there's a better system? One in which gods rule? The human species—in its current semi-intelligent form—is perhaps a few hundred thousand years old at most. The oldest of the gods have existed eons longer. Why shouldn't humanity be ruled by entities who have memories older than our species? They have the wisdom of experience with which to guide us."

He scoffed. "Thanks. I've got the only god I need."

"I've met mine personally," she replied. "Can you say the same?"

He jeered. "A bunch of alien ghosts. Puppeteers."

"Whatever you believe," she said, "whether nukes ever fall, without the guiding hand of the divine, climate collapse is only a matter of time. After that, humanity's extinction is assured."

Her words struck a chord within me, and I found myself agreeing with some of it despite myself. "Maybe so, but you're liars, and I don't trust you guys . . . not anymore."

She reached for my hand with both of her cuffed ones. "Yes, we lied to get you to help—Zelus and Baduriel knew you'd never agree otherwise—but our intentions were and still are good. Believe me. We have no interest in nuclear war. Far from it. We only want to unite humanity under Eurus rule and be the shepherds they need. Yes, a few may die, but this is about the survival of humanity, the earth, and all life on it."

"How many are you prepared to sacrifice?" I asked softly, taking my hand back. "In the countries that refuse to capitulate, how many are you prepared to kill?"

She looked away. "It won't come to that."

"How many?"

She took a breath and gave me a defiant look. "As many as it takes."

Right, I thought.

The Eurus leadership, being immortal gods, could afford to play a long game. A full-scale nuclear war would devastate the world, but they could always wait for it to recover or even actively rebuild it. Just as Aceso now worked to rehabilitate the planet Antara, beneath the surface of which Scott, Caleb, and I had, days ago, fled from Atriel on our way to Zarechus. It might take thousands of years of terraforming, but they had the time and know-how to do it.

"That's insane," Maya said. "How can you be okay with that?"

"I told you," Greta replied. "It will not come to that. Not if people are smart."

Dixon sneered. "Not if they're sheep, you mean."

"And what's in it for you?" I asked.

Her eyes took on a faraway look. "Eternity."

"You're ascending," Maya said, jabbing a finger at Greta. "Now the truth comes out. You're selling your entire species into slavery for a chance to be a god. You're no hero trying to save us from ourselves. You're an opportunist."

Greta's jaw set. "Is there a rule that says I cannot be both?"

I shook my head. "I can't believe you guys." Ashdon and Atriel, my allies within the Eurus, came to mind. "There must be some of you that are against this."

Her nostrils flared. "As with any group, there's division among those of us who know the true plan. Some think we are going too far, but the majority understand the logic and necessity. They would not have gone to the extreme of involving the Anathema otherwise."

They had no choice, I thought. *They needed Baduriel, as one of the Allfrost's architects.*

"If you're not a full god yet," Dixon said, "how do you know so much?"

She sat taller. "I'm Zelus's protege."

"And how do the changelings fit in?" I asked.

Her brow furrowed. "Changelings?"

"The ones who drank the soda." I smacked my stomach. "The people with the symbionts inside."

"Oh, that," she said. "I am afraid we only recently became aware of these changelings, as you call them." She took a deep breath. "Zelus thinks the Anathema are behind them—scheming devils that they are—most likely in collaboration with disaffected traitors among us. The Anathema must have had help to pull this off." She made a face and shifted her legs beneath herself. "Perhaps, as you suggest, some share your reservations regarding the plan. Others may simply seek a faster route to ascension or a means to rise higher in the Eurus hierarchy." Her eyes flicked to Maya. "People are complicated."

"Whatever," Maya said. "You're—" Her head snapped to the side abruptly. "Caelus has eyes on someone coming this way." She looked at Cole. "Someone like him. Tattoos, long hair, and he's wearing an AC/DC T-shirt."

Chapter 34

Muddy Waters

Duck-walking a few steps sideways, I peered out the front windows at a line of parked cars, stretching left to a busy street and right a few hundred feet to a two-storey wall with big letters written across it.

It's a shopping mall all right, I thought, regarding an abandoned shopping cart in the parking space opposite us. *Just like Dixon figured.*

"Who's coming, Greta?" I asked, shooting her a look.

She paused a moment before answering, "That will be Dennis."

Her headbanger companion wriggled and winced. "Cool. I'm starving." He raised his hands. "Any chance you'd take off these cuffs? My wrist's bleeding."

"Sorry, Cole," I said. "You'll have to live with it for now." I turned to Maya. "How far away is he?"

"About a hundred feet," Maya replied, pointing at the mall. "He's pushing a shopping cart filled with fast-food containers. He doesn't seem to be in a rush, though." She scoffed. "He keeps stopping to take a sip of what looks like a milkshake."

Dixon nudged my shoulder and moved toward the cargo door. "Keep these two covered."

"What are you going to do?" Maya asked.

Sliding the cargo door aside, he stepped to the pavement, letting in a blast of warm, humid air and the hum of traffic from the nearby street. "Circle around and come up behind him. He doesn't know anything's wrong, so I'll jump him when he gets in." He looked at me. "If he gives me any trouble, give me a hand." Before I could reply, he heaved the door shut and was gone.

A short while later, the driver's door cracked open. "Hey, Cole." A man's head popped into view. Greasy and long dark brown hair obscured his face. "Get your lazy—"

"Don't move," Dixon said, pressing the muzzle of his pistol into the back of the guy's head as he leaned over the driver's seat. "There's a gun—" He cut himself off as the guy tried to stand and turn. "For Pete's sake." Hammering the thug—Dennis, I presumed—in the neck, he shoved him forward onto the driver's seat. "Dumb-ass. I've got a gun."

Moaning, Dennis touched a hand to the back of his head. "What the fuck?"

"I said, don't move," Dixon snarled. "*Comprende?*"

Dennis, his head just visible past the back of the driver's seat, regarded me, and his eyes widened before darting to Maya and our two other captives.

"Do as they say, Dennis," Greta said.

Swallowing, he set his jaw and nodded slowly. "All right. If you say so."

"Keep an eye on them," I said, rushing to the front. As Dennis righted himself, I grabbed the front of his T-shirt and held a handful of frost where he could see it. "I've got him, Harland. Don't move, pal, or I'll frost your cornflakes." *Whatever that means.*

"Good man, Winterboy." Dixon stepped back and holstered his gun. After patting the guy down, he raised a pistol into view. "What's this?" He held the weapon by the dude's face. "I bet you didn't declare this at the border, did you?" Without waiting for a reply, he gave the man a nudge. "Get in there."

Dennis sneered. "You ought to be more careful," he said, doing as he had been told. "You push a guy, he might push back harder."

"Uh-huh." Grabbing his bicep, I guided him to the back and set him down alongside Greta and Cole. "Same goes for a snowman." I pulled the Walkman from my cap and put on the headphones, and my fingers danced, pressing out the voice call activation sequence. "Now sit there and be quiet. I've got a call to make."

"Hi, Shivurr." Olivia's voice sounded strained over the headphones. "What's up?"

"Are you guys okay?"

She hesitated before replying. "Yeah, we're fine. We just reached Winnipeg. How's New York? Been to the Statue of Liberty yet?"

I chuckled. "Funny story." Quickly, I told her where I was and how my companions and I had gotten here. "So don't go to Lucy's, if that's where you're headed. Greta's people might be waiting for you."

She sighed. "It looks like they're after us already. Brad noticed a car following us—don't slow down." Her last words had a faraway quality, like she wasn't talking to me. "I know, but keep going anyway." Her voice grew louder again. "They're definitely after us."

"Damn it. How can we help?"

"Where are you?" Olivia asked. "In the city, I mean."

I checked the window. "A shopping mall called Polo Park. There's a sign that says Sears on the wall, if that helps."

"Got it," she said. "Give me a second."

Her voice grew indistinct, but she continued to speak. *Must be talking to Lucy and Brad.*

"Okay," she said eventually. "Lucy says you're pretty close to us. Whoa! Take it easy, Brad. You want to get onto a street called Portage Avenue, Shivurr. Lucy says it's got to be right next to you, if you're seeing the Sears sign. Head west a few kilometres until you reach a park. It'll be on your left. One sec." She paused a moment before speaking again. "It's called Assiniboine Park. We'll meet you there as soon as we can."

"Can you make it there okay?" I asked.

"We're going to try," she replied. "Lucy says she's got an idea about how we can lose them."

"Give me a second." I nudged Dixon's shoulder and—spotting the vehicle's keys dangling from the ignition—relayed Olivia's instructions.

"Understood." He twisted the key and pumped the gas, and the van roared to life. "Hang on."

The van surged forward, and a bang came from the front end as Dixon spun the steering wheel. My hand shot out to grip the front passenger seat to keep myself from rolling into the cargo door. Holding myself upright, I caught sight of Dennis's fast-food-filled shopping cart in the passenger-side rear-view mirror, spinning in a circle.

I sighed with relief. "We're on our way, Olivia." No reply. "Hello?" Still nothing. *Must be the batteries again.* Shaking my head, I stuffed the Walkman into my coat pocket and hung the head-phones around my neck. I couldn't help wishing, not for the first time, that Olivia had chosen to power the modified device using something longer-lasting than conventional batteries. I tapped Maya's shoulder. "Can you send Caelus ahead to make sure we're going the right way?"

"I already have," she said, "but it'll be easier to coordinate from the passenger seat."

"Go ahead. I'll watch these guys."

"Careful." She handed me the gun. "The safety is off."

Taking it from her, I pointed it at the captive trio. "Aren't I always?" I leaned right, steadying myself with a hand as the van changed direction.

A moment later, the engine revved, and I pushed against the floor with my feet to avoid rolling toward the back.

"It's warm here," I said, glancing at Dixon, raising my voice to be heard over the rush of humid air from the open windows. "Is this normal?"

His chin dipped. "For summer? Sure." He shivered. "Be thankful it's not January."

"Why's that?" I asked, giving him another look but keeping the handgun trained on our captives.

"It's colder than a witch's . . ." He trailed off and gave me a wry grin. "Never mind, I forgot who I was talking to. Welcome to Winterpeg, Winterboy."

"Sounds like you've been here before," I said, eyeing our captives.

"The Group's got a presence here," he said. "And I've driven up a few times with friends. Years ago."

"Really? You lived around here?"

"Minneapolis," he said. "It's about seven hours south by car."

"Yellow light," Maya said from the passenger seat.

"I see it," Dixon replied, and the engine pitched higher. "Made it."

"Grand," she said. "Just don't get us killed. We're of no use to anyone dead."

"Yeah, yeah," he said. "What's the bird say? Has he reached the park?"

"He's flying above it now," she said. "It's about four or five streets to go."

Most of the lights were green, fortunately, and when they weren't, Dixon stopped only long enough to confirm the coast was clear before running the intersection. A few traffic lights from the park, automobiles, waiting at another red, blocked our way. With no way around, Dixon lay on the horn and waved his hands, urging drivers to the side, but they only glared at their rear-view mirrors without moving.

"Fuck this," he snarled, drawing my gaze.

"What are you doing?" Maya shouted.

"Going around," he said as the van rocked side to side over the median curb.

Through the front windshield, the occupants of oncoming cars goggled our way. Thankfully, also waiting for the light to change, the vehicles weren't moving, and Dixon managed to steer us back into the proper lane upon reaching the crossroad.

"Nice driving," Maya said as I returned my full attention to Greta and her minions. "The park is on the left at the next set of traffic lights. When we get there, keep going a bit. Caelus says you can make a U-turn and pull over right by the park."

Following her directions, we soon swung around and pulled to a stop in front of a green lawn dotted with oaks, elms, spruce, and pines. A short distance ahead, a paved pathway—populated with pedestrians, dogs, and cyclists—ran off to the right. To one side, a group of youths tossed a baseball while across the walkway, two dudes threw a football back and forth.

"Where are they?" Dixon asked, looking out the back before peering through the bug-spattered windshield.

"They'll be here," I said, doing the same but seeing no sign of any of my friends, nor Brad's VW van. I nudged Maya. "Keep an eye on these guys, will you? I'm getting out." I wanted to be ready, in case they couldn't lose the guys chasing them.

Nodding, she slipped into the back and took the gun from me. Rather than open the cargo door and reveal our captives to park-goers, I slipped into the front passenger seat, still warm from Maya's body. Ensuring my disguise was fully activated, I stepped out onto the sidewalk and, with a quick glance around, walked a short distance up the path.

No sense letting the Eurus see me, I thought, taking cover behind a copse of trees and turning to watch the eight-lane avenue. I snorted, now able to see a red dragon and sword-wielding hero locked in battle decorating the dark blue Chevy van's side. *Scott would love that.*

A few minutes later, a faint but familiar beep rose above the hum of traffic, drawing my gaze away from the flow of cars to the park behind me. Across the grass, the heads and shoulders of pedestrians bobbed just above the stone railing of a bridge spanning a river of brown water that flickered grey in the sunlight. The beeps grew louder and more frantic, coming from the forest of deciduous trees veiling the far bank in deep green. The white roof of a light blue Volkswagen camper van drove into view a moment later. Slowing slightly, it rolled onto the bridge, sending people to the railings.

It's them. The vehicle's horn continued to beep as it crept across the bridge at a hair faster than walking pace. Smiling, I raced toward the sound, dodging two kids on bicycles and a woman walking a dog, and stopped to wait at the bridge's near side, raising a hand in greeting.

Olivia—visible between Brad in the driver's seat and Lucy in the passenger seat—waved back. She looked at Brad, lips moving, and the van soon rolled to a stop in front of me. Tugging on the cargo door handle, I slid it aside.

"Hi, guys," I said, smiling broadly beneath my mask.

Flashing huge white teeth, Olivia extended a hand. A beautiful woman with dark eyebrows, blue eyes, a long, slender nose, and a strong jaw, she looked about thirty, though her real age numbered in the thousands. She wore sneakers, blue jeans, and a navy T-shirt, accentuating her athletic build. "It's lovely to see you, Shivurr."

"You changed your hair," I said, clasping her palm and climbing inside. Her once-mahogany hair was now raven black. No longer braided, it spilled about her shoulders. "It looks good."

"I don't know about that," she replied, sliding the door shut. "You're sweet to say so, though."

"Hey, dude," said a young man of about twenty with short, straight brown hair and feathered bangs from behind the steering wheel.

"Hey, Brad," I replied. "How's it going?"

He snorted. "Surviving." Fit, but not as muscled as his younger brother Alan, he wore jeans, a simple black T-shirt, and dark sunglasses, and his handsome face sported a nascent beard. "Your new look's radical."

Lucy twisted in her seat to face me. "Totally, Shivurr. I'd have never known it was you if Olivia hadn't told us." About the same age as Brad and dressed for summer in shorts and a halter top, she fiddled with her blond ponytail and looked me up and down. "That is you, right?"

"The one and only," I said with a grin, glancing down at myself. "More or less."

Olivia gave me a quick hug. She grabbed my shoulders, leaned back, and gave my disguise the once-over. "You look good."

"So do you." I meant it, but she looked a bit tired, and there was a faint blackening of ivory skin beneath her eyes.

"Where are your companions?" Olivia asked, looking out the front window.

I pointed to the distant van with Dixon at the wheel. "See the dragon?"

"Ah, yes. I've seen it before." Olivia touched Brad's arm. "Bring us up behind them. Drive over the grass, if you have to."

"Sure thing, Olivia." He shot me a look. "Looks like we owe you again, Shivurr."

"Nah," I said as park-goers glared beyond the windshield. "I haven't done anything yet." My eyes flashed. "Oh, did you lose the dudes chasing you?"

Olivia checked the back window. "Apparently." She made a face. "Though, after our less-than-stealthy crossing, that might soon change."

The camper bus rocked side to side as Brad took it slowly over a curb and snugged it behind the Chevy van.

"Yeah," I said. "We need to get to the transporter. Fast."

Olivia pulled the cargo door ajar. "Tell Dixon to follow us, Shivurr."

"Be right back," I said, hopping out and running over to the Chevy.

As I returned to Brad's van, Caelus landed on the side mirror. "Sentinel, Maya has asked that I accompany you to serve as a communication link between vehicles."

"That's a good idea." I raised my forearm. "Hop on."

Once we were aboard, Brad and Lucy gawked at Caelus as I made introductions.

"We've met," Olivia said dryly. "Hello, Caelus. You are looking well."

"You are too kind, Orithyia," he replied, bowing his head. "It is good to fly again."

"I can only imagine." She touched Brad's shoulder. "We should probably go."

"Sure," Brad said, looking at his girlfriend. "Which way, Luce?"

"Just go straight for now," she said. "I'll tell you when to turn."

"Sorry, Lucy," Olivia said. "It seems your visit home is going to be a short one. It's too dangerous to leave you here with the Faction around. I'm afraid you and Brad will have to come back to New Olympus until things settle down."

"Bummer, babe," Brad said, working the gearshift. "I guess you'll have to show me around another time."

I gave Lucy's shoulder a pat. "You'll like New Olympus, though. It's awesome there."

"It's fine." Turning in her seat, she squeezed my forearm. "I wasn't supposed to be back until Christmas anyway, and my parents aren't even home. Anyway, what have you been up to?"

I laughed. "Oh, not much."

For the next while, as trees and two- and three-storey buildings rushed by, I brought my friends up to speed on the broad strokes of everything I could think of that had happened since we had parted ways at Dublin Gulch. Mostly. When I got to the part about the Eurus's nuclear ambitions, I skipped over the deal I'd originally made with Zelus. That was a longer, potentially awkward conversation. One better dealt with later.

"How about you guys?" I asked when I'd finished.

Olivia blew out a breath. "It's been long drives, motels, and gas stations since leaving the LA safe house, trying to get to a transporter."

"I believe it," I said, recalling Alan and Lilith's words. "Lilith mentioned a PI." I struggled to recall his name. "What happened to him?"

The buildings outside were taller now, some thirty storeys high, signalling we'd entered the city's downtown area.

"Carver?" Olivia grimaced. "I'm not sure. We got separated in San Francisco, trying to throw the Eurus off our trail." Her forehead creased. "He's a resourceful man, though. Chances are he's returned to LA by now."

"Turn left at the next light, Brad," Lucy said, pointing at the windshield. "We're almost there."

After the turn, the buildings sailing past became older, varying in height from three to perhaps a dozen storeys tall with ornate facades of brown, red, white, mustard, and sand-coloured stone.

Early twentieth century, I thought. *Hey, I'm remembering more.* "Cool buildings."

"They're Chicago-style," she said. "It's why they call us Chicago of the North. This is the old Exchange District."

"What do they exchange?" I asked.

She shrugged. "Grain, I think. At least, they used to. It's a prairie town. Farming's big around here. Take a right up here, Brad."

"Sure thing," Brad said, doing as she directed. "Lucy says there's a pretty good music scene here too."

"Oh yeah?" I asked. "Like who?"

"Guess Who," Brad said, chuckling.

"Beats me," I said, spreading my hands.

Lucy's eyes twinkled. "He means the band, the Guess Who."

"And there's Neil Young." Brad grinned at me in the rearview mirror. "For what it's worth."

Reaching out, she squeezed his shoulder. "Someone's been listening."

"You know it," he replied.

Several red lights later, we crossed a wide street.

"It's right up here." Olivia leaned into the front and pointed a finger. "Drive into the parking garage up on the right."

"Got it," Brad said.

"Pull over here a moment," she said after we'd entered. She looked at Caelus. "Tell Maya and Dixon to park the van in one of those stalls and join us, okay? Oh, and ask them to make sure the Eurus can't get loose, at least not easily."

"I live to serve, Orithyia," he replied, closing his eyes. "Done."

The Chevy van that had been following us pulled past and its brake lights lit a moment before it swung to the left into an empty parking stall. A few minutes later, Maya and Dixon emerged and came over to us.

"All good?" Olivia asked, looking at Maya as she got in beside us.

"Should be," Maya replied. "We only had two pairs of handcuffs, though, so we had to cuff the men to each other through the steering wheel."

"That's fine," Olivia said. "We just need it to hold them until we're gone." She touched Brad's arm. "Take us up the ramp." Ascending a winding tunnel a few levels, Olivia directed Brad to stop near the middle of a long row of cars. Peering out the windshield, she huffed. "Of all the nerve."

"What?" I asked.

Chapter 35

Split Decision

Olivia scowled. "Can you believe it? Someone's in our spot." She pointed to a sign posted on the wall at the front of the parking space, which read, "Reserved parking for Dr. Smith. Unauthorized vehicles will be towed."

"When's the last time you used it?" I asked, eyeing the fancy-looking Mercedes parked below the sign.

She touched her sternum. "Me? Years ago, but that's hardly the point. It's reserved." She yanked the cargo door open. "Come on, Maya. Give me a hand."

The two women hopped out and walked over to the driver's-side door of the offending car. Gripping the door handle in one hand, Olivia held her other hand by the window. Pressing the tips of her fingers together, she made a plucking gesture, pulled the handle, and opened the door wide. Stepping aside, she walked to the car's front while Maya slipped behind the wheel. With a nod to Maya, Olivia's head lowered, and she pressed her hands to the car's front end. A moment later, the car crept backward.

"Strong woman," Dixon said. "Another god?"

"Demigod," I replied.

Before long, the Mercedes sat in another spot and, laughing, Olivia and Maya waved for Brad to take the newly vacated parking space.

"All right," Olivia said as she and Maya rejoined us. "Let's see how things look on the other side." She stared into the distance. "Okay. Looks good." She smacked her hands together and the cars and walls surrounding us became translucent. A half second later, different walls and automobiles faded into view around us. "And we're here."

"Welcome to Las Vegas," Maya said, echoing her words upon our arrival in Berlin, which seemed like a week ago rather than only a couple of days.

"Amazing," Dixon said, looking around. "I don't think I'll ever get used to that."

The corners of my mouth rose. "It sure beats twelve hours on an airplane."

"Choice," Brad said. "Where to now?"

Olivia waved a hand. "Take us to the exit, and I'll guide you to my place." She turned to Maya as Brad put the van into reverse. "Shivurr told me about the pop you drank. You should come back to New Olympus with us, so we can examine you."

"Good idea," I said. Maya had been invaluable, and I'd miss her, but I didn't want her turning into a changeling. "How do you feel? Any . . . growths?"

She shook her head. "I feel grand. Really."

"Even so," Olivia said, "it's best to be certain. If you have been infected, the sooner we act the better."

"But what about Shivurr?" Maya asked. "He needs my help. This isn't over."

"It's okay," I replied. "You need to take care of yourself first."

"Agreed," Dixon said. "Anyway, Winterboy and I are headed for the Bodhi Institute next, to get the last vials, and you're not authorized to enter. I could sanction it, but I'm not sure what kind of reception I'll receive there, and you might end up in a holding cell next to me if we try."

"Besides," Olivia said, "this tainted soda pop is concerning, and it's best we learn all we can about it. If these drinks are turning human beings into vessels for Anathema, it implies Baduriel has ambitions beyond those of the Eurus. And what the Eurus have planned is bad enough." She looked grim. "If they succeed in subjugating the West, the Eurus will have us on the run in our own backyard, with human agents on their side. Which means the changelings pose nearly as great a threat as the Eurus's nuclear plan."

Rummaging around inside my cap, I located a bottle of Nacht Cola and handed it to Olivia. "Will this help?"

Her eyes lit. "It certainly will," she said, taking the bottle from me. "Good thinking."

"No problem." I groped around more. "I think I've got a Nicht Cola and a couple Take 5s left too." Seeing her grin, I raised a shoulder. "Hey, they taste surprisingly good." Handing Olivia more bottles and cans, I added, "And they don't do me any harm, aside from a bit of a headache."

She hefted a can of Take 5 and tsked. "Yet others who drink it lose themselves—body and, presumably, mind—to the symbiont within."

Dixon touched a hand to his sternum and his lip curled. "To the symbiont and any demon who wants to take a ride."

"Left or right, Olivia?" Brad said as we reached the parking garage exit.

"Turn right," she replied over her shoulder, "then a left at the first street. Maya, can you direct him the rest of the way? You know it, right?"

"Happy to," Maya replied, taking up position behind Brad. "I believe so."

Olivia turned back to me. "Tell me about this Ashdon fellow. Do you trust him?"

I nodded. "Yeah. I remember him now. He's Eurus, but he's on my side. At least he was before I lost my memories."

She frowned. "How do you know him?"

"Well." I rubbed the back of my neck. "That's a long story." One I still wasn't eager to tell.

Her brows lifted. "We've got time."

"Yeah, I suppose we do." *Unfortunately.* "Well, it's like this . . ." For the next while, as I'd done with Dixon, Maya, and Caelus, I confessed to agreeing to help the Eurus disable all the world's nukes, my reasons for doing so, and how I'd tried to fix things. "I would have come to you guys for help, but I wasn't sure how you'd react. I figured if I could fix it myself first, you'd forgive me when I told you."

Olivia looked grim. "I'm glad you remember."

My brow wrinkled. "What do you mean?"

"We've known about it for a while now," she said. "Since shortly after your capture by the Bodhi Group."

My eyelids fluttered. "Why didn't you say anything?"

Olivia shrugged. "You'd forgotten it, and we'd already forgiven you. Why upset you with something you couldn't even remember?" She grimaced. "Now that you do, would you mind telling me how you could trust Zelus? Had we not been clear enough about his duplicity?"

"I know," I said. "It's just, I guess I wanted to believe him. I was scared, Olivia, and now that I've got my memories back, I'm scared all over again. Scared for Earth. All it's going to take is one crazy person getting into power and the world as we know it is done. All the animals, the people, the trees. I couldn't do nothing."

She sighed. "I can't say we weren't disappointed, Shivurr." She gave me a mock slap on the shoulder with the back of her hand. "If you felt that strongly, you should have insisted we listen. Trusted us to see it your way."

"I'm sorry," I said, hanging my head low.

She reached out and raised my chin with her hand. "But your intentions were good, and you were and are trying to make it right. None of us can ask for more than that." She gave me a lopsided smile. "Maybe we've been wrong too. Gambling the world on humanity. I think Wilhelm's love for me may have clouded his judgment. It's given him an affection for humankind, which may not be deserved. Certainly there's little in humanity's past to suggest we won't end up destroying ourselves."

"But he's really forgiven me?"

She paused before answering. "Of course—he loves you too—not that it didn't take some time. You know his temper."

"That's good to know." Ages had passed since Boreas and Baduriel had fallen out, but neither had yet forgiven the other. "That couldn't have been easy for him."

"It wasn't," she said. "Why do you think it took us so long to engineer your escape from the Institute?"

My eyes widened. "You mean—"

"I'm afraid so," she said. "Wilhelm was quite angry, but"—she eyed Dixon with narrowed eyes—"he never imagined you'd suffer so greatly. Can you forgive us as we've forgiven you?"

"Sure," I said with a sigh. "I suppose I had it coming." I glanced at Brad and Lucy, who were hearing this for the first time. "What about you guys? Are you mad at me?"

The couple shared a look before shaking their heads.

"Nukes suck," Brad said. "I get it."

"Right," Lucy said with a nod. "Who hasn't wished they could snap their fingers and get rid of them all?"

I smiled crookedly beneath my mask. "Thanks, guys."

"In any case," Olivia said, "be mindful of Zelus's betrayal in your dealings with this Gary Ashdon. Perhaps he is truly an ally, but he may be working his own game too."

Like Baduriel is doing with Zelus, I thought. "I will." My lips wrinkled. "I sure hope he's an ally. I need another enemy like a hole in the head."

"If all goes well," she said, "use the transporter at my house to return to New Olympus, and we'll give you whatever support we can to get you to Allfrost Prime. Unfortunately, our resources are stretched thin right now. The Eurus have been exceptionally active here on Earth and Zarechus lately, conducting multiple operations. We thought it had to be a prelude to something big, and what you've discovered must be it . . . at least the main part of it."

"That'd be great," I said. "I'll take whatever I can get."

Dixon took a deep breath. "Right now, we need a car to get to the Institute."

Brad glanced over his shoulder. "You're welcome to take Otto."

Dixon squinted an eye. "Otto?"

"He means the van," I said with a smile. "Are you sure?"

"Totally," Brad said. "It's got to be better than leaving him parked at Olivia's place." His eyes met mine in the rear-view mirror. "Just take care of him, okay?"

"Don't worry, kid," Dixon said. "Give me your address, and I'll make sure it gets delivered to your place with a full tank of gas and the keys dropped in your mailbox."

"Won't we need it to get back to Olivia's to use the transporter?" I asked. "Once we've got the vials, I mean."

He shrugged. "I'll have a helicopter take you."

"Just me?" After we were done at the Institute, I'd figured the security director would want to come to consult with the gods and act as a liaison with the Bodhi Group. "You're not coming to New Olympus too?"

"It depends where I'm needed most," he replied. "If you've got these gods helping you already, it may be better that I stay behind at the Institute and keep pushing the Group's leadership in the right directions. Like putting an end to the changeling problem. But we can cross that bridge when we come to it."

"Okay." Thinking it through, I looked at Olivia. "When I get back to your place, how do I activate the transporter?"

She beamed. "I'll set it up to activate automatically for you." Her eyes dropped to my gloved hands. "Do you still have your ring?"

"Of course," I replied, fingering it through the fabric of my glove.

"Good." She put a steadying hand against the ceiling as the van took a turn. "Then the transporter will have no trouble recognizing you, and it'll take you to New Olympus as soon as you enter the basement."

"Nice, that'll be easy." And if it didn't activate for some reason, there was always the transporter in the Allfrost chamber by Dublin Gulch. If it came to that, I'd have to leave Dixon behind, if he was still with me, but it would be better than nothing. I looked at Dixon. "Did you want to call ahead to let the Institute know you're coming?"

"No," he replied. "I'd sooner surprise them."

"What if the Group tries to hold you again?" Lucy asked, looking at me.

I grinned wickedly and summoned a handful of frost. "I'll be a lot more careful this time."

"Even so," Olivia said, "call me on the Walkman to let me know how things are, all right? If I don't hear from you within the next twenty-four hours, we'll launch a rescue mission." She regarded Dixon with narrowed eyes. "One that will make Baduriel's visit seem like an inspection tour by a friendly dignitary. The time for stealth and subtlety has passed, and the Group will hold or harm you at their peril."

"Easy now." Dixon raised his hands in mock surrender. "We're all on the same side." Scanning our faces, he sighed. "You're right, though. The Group may try something, but they'll have to know Winterboy is there first, and I won't be telling them, and with his ability to vanish, staying out of their sight shouldn't be a problem. But you've my word, if something goes wrong I'll do whatever it takes to get him out of there."

Olivia arched an eyebrow. "And violate your duty to the Bodhi Group?"

He looked grim. "To save America from the Soviets? Without hesitation or regret."

She gave him a hard stare. "I'll hold you to it."

"Fair enough," he replied evenly.

After a moment's uncomfortable silence, Brad asked how his brother was doing, and, for the rest of the drive, we spoke further of family, friends, and our respective adventures until the VW van pulled into the Schmidts' driveway. Visible through the windshield, the god couple's Mediterranean-style house still appeared to be the burned-out husk that had been left in the aftermath of a fire elemental attack. To our collective relief, there appeared to be no signs of anyone watching the house. No parked cars, windowless vans, or loitering people.

"What a mess," Olivia said, appraising the ruins of her home as we all stood in the driveway. "Okay, let's say our goodbyes and let Shivurr and Dixon go."

"Maybe we should go with you," Brad said, shaking my hand and slapping my shoulder. "Just in case."

"That won't work," Dixon said. "The Institute's a secure and highly classified facility. I can't be bringing civilians inside with me."

"It wasn't a problem when your agents kidnapped us," Lucy muttered.

"It's better if you guys go back to New Olympus," I said before Dixon could reply. "Alan, Lilith, and Caleb are eager to see you guys, and I can't put you two in danger again."

"What do you mean?" Lucy asked. "You didn't put us in danger."

"Sure I did," I said. "Greta and her goons were chasing you because of me."

"That wasn't your fault," she replied.

I wasn't sure I agreed. By asking for a ride from Lunar Crater, I'd rescued them from one danger and put them into another. "Well, all the same," I said, "I'll feel a lot better knowing you're safe on New Olympus."

"Okay." Darting forward, she gave me a hug. "Just be careful."

"Farewell, Mr. Shivurr." Maya squeezed my shoulder. "Stay safe and see you soon. It has been quite an adventure."

"That it has," Caelus said from her shoulder. "Good fortune, Sentinel."

"Come on, everyone." Olivia swept a hand toward the house. "Let's get inside before the neighbours get curious." As they filed past her, she turned, grabbed my hand, and embraced me. "Good luck, and remember to call me on the Walkman."

"I will." I returned her squeeze. "Bye, Olivia. Say hello to Wilhelm for me."

I stood on the pavement watching her disappear into her fire-damaged home, wishing I could go with them and hoping we'd see each other again soon.

"All right," Dixon said, slapping my shoulder. "Let's move."

Taking a deep breath, I let it out and opened the van's passenger door. "Right."

"So," Dixon said from the driver's seat, after we'd stopped for gas, supplies, and batteries for the Walkman on our way out of town. "I've been thinking about what Schmidt said. Maybe I should go in alone, get the vials, and bring them back out with me."

I shook my head. "Nah. I need to come in with you."

"Why?"

"I want to speak with Ashdon." I looked his way. "Besides, you might need my help to get the vials. You said it yourself, things might have changed while you've been away."

"True enough," he said. "For all I know, the Institute's got a new security director by now. How do you want to play it? Do that invisibility thing?"

"I can't do it for long, safely," I grumbled.

"Right," he said, looking thoughtful. "That leaves either bringing you in openly as an ally or pretending you're a prisoner. I don't like either of those options right now. Not when we may need to head out again right away. Better they don't know you're there at all."

I thought a moment. "I've got another idea."

"Nice," Dixon said after I'd told him what I had in mind. "Are you sure you can do it?"

I nodded. "I practically did it already."

Chapter 36

Hat Trick

We made it to Tonopah three hours later—passing the time by sharing stories from our pasts, which I was happy to do now that I could remember mine. We didn't stay long. Keeping to the edges of the small mining town, we refuelled again, grabbed a bite to eat, and resumed our journey. After another half hour of driving, mostly in darkness, Dixon pulled the van over to the roadside.

"There's the road into Area 52," he said, pointing to a sign lit by the headlights of the van, marking the entrance to Tonopah Test Range. Beyond it, on a remote fringe of the highly classified military installation, the even more secret Bodhi Institute sat, with most of its floors hidden underground.

I rolled down my window, letting in warm, dry air and the chittering of cicadas.

Doing the same, Dixon inhaled deeply. "I love that smell."

"What smell?"

"The desert," he replied. "Mostly sagebrush, I think."

Sniffing the air, I smirked. "I just smell body odour."

"Smartass," he replied with a chuckle, stroking his stubbled cheek. "Not everyone smells icy fresh after two days in the same suit."

"It's a gift." Taking off my hat, I rubbed my skull. "I can't believe I'm coming back here willingly."

"Me neither," he replied with a wry smile. "It'll go better this time, though. Anyway, you'd better hide now. Once we cross the boundary, there's no telling what will happen."

I nodded. "Right." Even under normal circumstances,

security on the military installation was high, but the attack on the Bodhi Institute had raised it still further. By all reports, armed soldiers now actively patrolled the area, looking for trouble. "Here goes." I relaxed my cowl and shapesuit and kicked off my shoes, narrowing my head and torso. My garments' smart fabric expanded and contracted to match my alterations, and my cap fell as I flowed through its inner crown. Once fully inside the interdimensional null space, I tucked and rolled—keeping a hand latched to the exterior—and squeezed my distorted head back through the portal. "Okay, I'm ready."

"Nice trick." Dixon grabbed my cap by the visor and set it on the passenger seat. "You can hang out here until we're close to the Institute."

"Sounds good," I said, not relishing a long stay in the null space. I stretched my neck to see out the side window. "Let me know if you see anyone coming."

"Count on it," he said, putting the van into gear and taking us into Area 52.

We drove southeast until the headlights of a stationary vehicle, its details lost in shadow, flashed on and off ahead of us.

"Looks like a roadblock," Dixon said as a soldier holding an assault rifle walked into the road and held his palm out toward us. "You'd better get all the way inside."

"Good luck." I pulled back into the void and—keeping a hand on the inside of my hat—focused on my surroundings, feeling no tug of wind or gravity.

Above me, a halo of blue identified the portal, casting faint light upon my floating body and possessions. Only darkness lay beyond the cloud of containers and other miscellany surrounding me, providing no clue as to the overall volume of the null space.

Imagining drifting forever into an endless abyss, I tightened my grip on my cap, and a can of soda pop drifted up toward my face. I pushed it down into the black and lit the palm of my free hand to track its path. Sinking rapidly down, it seemed to lose speed with each foot travelled until—ten feet from me—its downward motion reversed, and it inched up toward me again.

Neat. I released my grip on my hat, ready to grab it again if necessary, but remained stationary. Seconds later, far from sinking, I felt myself move gently toward the opening as if tugged by an invisible force and steadied myself with a hand against the perimeter. Apparently, the portal attracted things in the null space, keeping them within easy reach.

I smiled and let out a relieved breath. *Hey, I can breathe.* I inhaled again. *It's breathable all right.* However it got in here, the presence of air meant staying inside indefinitely wasn't going to be a problem. *Unless its supply is finite.* The air seemed to grow staler as the possibility occurred to me, but it might have been my imagination. After a moment, I shrugged. *Doesn't matter.* I didn't need to be down here long.

Five minutes ought to be enough for the soldiers to check Dixon's ID and wave him on. If they took longer than that, chances were they would try to arrest him, and in that case, things were going to get ugly, and I'd have to abandon stealth anyway. One thing was certain, I wasn't leaving without talking to Ashdon and getting the last sample vials.

Nodding to myself, I began counting in my head. When I got to three hundred, I stuck an eye past the portal again, catching sight of ever-changing shadows and light shifting across the VW van's ceiling. Deciding we must be moving again, I pushed my head higher.

"There you are," Dixon said, glancing my way. "We're all clear."

"Any trouble with the soldiers?" I asked.

He shook his head. "It's all good. The patrol leader recognized me." He looked my way again. "We're approaching the building now."

"Already?"

"See for yourself." Dixon lifted my cap from the passenger seat and set it on the dash. "Good?"

"Yeah, thanks," I replied, studying the building. Plywood now replaced the glass windows of the Bodhi Institute's main entrance and scorch marks marred the facade, lit by floodlights arrayed around the perimeter. "Wow."

"Ah, the carpets needed replacing anyway." Spinning the wheel, he took us around the building's side and toward an opening in the wall. "You'd better get low. There are cameras covering the entrance."

"Sure," I said, retreating into the null space until only my face protruded beyond the inner crown. "How's this?"

"Not bad." Grabbing the cap's visor, he set me down on the floor to the front of the passenger seat. "Down there's better." Touching a finger to his lips, he lowered his window and leaned out, waving a hand.

"Dixon?" said a tinny voice, sounding as if transmitted over a walkie-talkie. "Is that really you?"

"Who else?" Dixon asked. "The world's not ready for another me. That you, Lattimer?"

"Holy shit." Lattimer chuckled. "Looks like Mathis owes me twenty bucks. Come on in."

The gate blocking our way rose, and we rolled forward into the parking garage. Inside, perhaps a third of the spots were currently occupied. At this time of night, employees that commuted to the facility were long gone to their homes.

Much drier too, I thought. When I'd last seen it, the sprinkler system had gone off—probably triggered by incoming fire elementals—soaking the cars and floor. I felt a sudden thrill of panic to be returning here, but I pushed it down and focused on my mission. *No going back now.*

"Better duck all the way in." Dixon's hand came toward me, lifting me from the floor. "We've got a welcoming party."

"Okay." I pulled back, leaving one eye beyond the null space, and the van whirled around me, ending in a flash of grey hair before near-total darkness fell. Unable to see anything, I turned my head, pressing an ear beyond the opening.

"Hey, *jefe*," said a voice a short while later, scarcely audible above the rustling of fabric against hair.

"Jimenez," Dixon said as a door banged shut. "Good to see you."

"Where you been, Dixon?"

"No time for that now," Dixon said. "Where's Ashdon?"

"The new guy?" Jimenez replied. "I don't know. Sleeping, I guess."

The sound of a door opening came again.

"Hello, Harland," said a woman's voice. "Welcome back. I'm glad to see you're alive and in one piece."

"More or less, Langford," Dixon said. "Though I could use a shower."

Cynthia Langford, I thought, remembering Executive Director Wallace's assistant.

"I can see that," Cynthia replied dryly. "However, Jeffrey wants to talk to you first."

"Is that so?" Dixon said. "All right. Lead the way."

"Are you armed, Harland?" Cynthia asked.

"What if I am?"

"We got to take it from you, *jefe*," Jimenez said. "At least until you've been debriefed and all that."

"Fine," Dixon said. "Take it."

"Thank you, Harland," Cynthia said. "This way."

The echo of distant footsteps grew louder, followed by what sounded like a door clicking open.

"Director Dixon," said a voice, "it is good to see you back safely."

"Ashdon," the security director responded. "You're up late."

"Not for me, really," Ashdon replied. "I find I do my best work when others sleep. Uh, did you have any luck out there? Finding subject Winterboy, I mean."

Dixon grunted. "Sorry, Ashdon." A breeze caressed my ear. "I'm afraid this cap's all I could find. Hang onto it for me while I talk with Wallace. Maybe check it for clues."

"Very well," Ashdon said hesitantly. "I'm not sure what—" He made a short choking sound. A moment later, something touched the side of my head, warm even through the fabric of my hood. "Uh, yes, good idea. I will run some tests and let you know what I find. I'll see you later, then."

Unsure what was happening, I ducked deeper into the null

space, anchored to the inside of my hat by only the smallest fragment of myself and unable to see or hear anything outside. I lit my free palm and aimed it into the darkness, passing it over full cans, bottles, and other paraphernalia floating in the void. In the spaces between those items, the beam stabbed into darkness but failed to illuminate it. Still, even the light reflecting off my possessions was comforting in the abyss.

Was that Ashdon? I touched a hand to my ear before nodding to myself. He must have looked inside the cap, seen the side of my head, and reached inside to touch it. Either to work out what he was seeing or to cover it with a hand before anyone else could see. *Not that it would've mattered.* Even if Cynthia or Jimenez had gotten a glimpse, chances were high the black fabric of the cowl I wore would have been indistinguishable from my hat's inner lining.

Now I just needed to wait for Dixon to head off with Cynthia and Jimenez, then ask Ashdon to get us somewhere we could talk without being seen. I counted to sixty before pushing an ear past the portal again. Hearing a tap of foot-steps, I took a quick look, squinting slightly at the sudden glare of white walls and floor tiles beyond the opening.

With Ashdon's dark pants and shoes swinging nearby, I narrowed my skull and flowed through the portal, extending my head just beyond the cap's bottom rim. While someone could enter the hallway at any moment from an adjacent room, it was a risk I had to take.

Fortunately, the hallway was empty as I looked up at the man dangling me and my hat at his side. He appeared much as he had in my mind's eye when we'd spoken on the airplane. I smiled, now remembering him from even before his appearance on the cargo plane, when I'd first recruited him to my cause. Before I'd made the mistake of coming to the Bodhi Group.

"Psst," I said, still seeing no one else nearby. His chin dipped and his eyes flared wide as they met mine, and my stomach lurched as the world rotated around me and his face came closer. "Easy. You're going to make me hurl."

His hazel eyes darted in their sockets. "We can't talk here."

"I know," I whispered. "Take me somewhere we can."

"That's what I was doing." His face rose higher, and I pulled back as his chest rushed toward me. "Give me a few minutes," he said in a muffled voice.

"You've got five." I ducked back into the void, where I began counting again.

When I judged enough time had passed, I pushed an eye back through the portal and saw Ashdon's smiling face regarding me from a few feet away.

"There you are," he said. "You can come out now."

"Finally," I said, flowing out of my hat in a stream of snow, ice, and black cloth. "Hey, where are we?"

Chapter 37

Story Time

I resumed humanoid form, reactivated my suit and hood, and rotated on a heel. Taking in filing cabinets, a desk, an office chair, and frames decorating the walls, I turned back to Ashdon, who sat upon a low sofa with a magazine in his lap and my upended hat on the floor by his feet.

"Hello, Shivurr," he said, regarding me above the tops of his eyeglasses.

"Ashdonigarius," I replied, inclining my head.

Glancing to the side, he leaned toward me. "Please, call me Gary, or Ashdon around here." He tossed the magazine onto the sofa. "I'm glad you remember me now, though."

"Is this your office?"

"No," he said. "It's Dixon's."

"It is?" Again, I examined the wall hangings, mainly photographs of Dixon in his earlier years, and furnishings. "Oh, right." I frowned. "It wasn't locked?"

Ashdon smirked. "No, it was."

"Right," I said, returning his grin. *What are locks to a demigod?* "Why meet here, though?"

He stood and handed me my cap. "It's soundproof, and I expect Dixon will return here when he's done with Dr. Wallace."

I made a face. "If they let him."

"Perhaps." Ashdon looked thoughtful. "However, my money is on Dixon taking back his command successfully. The security director has considerable *auctoritas* within the Bodhi Group, and I understand that, while he and Dr. Wallace often clash over matters of jurisdiction, they are both pragmatic and not prone to pettiness."

"Really?" In my experience, Dixon had frequently complained about his executive counterpart, though I supposed that didn't mean he'd been unprofessional in response. "I hope you're right."

"As do I." Ashdon sat once more. "I'm counting on him to get into the archival vault." He patted the sofa next to himself. "Have a seat. Tell me what you have been up to since your escape from here."

I snorted. "How much time have you got?"

He checked his watch. "A half hour at least, I should think, before Dixon gets here."

"All right." I flopped onto the sofa beside him. "Why not?"

For the next while, I brought Ashdon up to speed on my initial escape from the Institute, meeting the gang from California, the showdown at Dublin Gulch, New Olympus, Zarechus, and the Nameless. He listened attentively, making few interruptions. Though when I recounted running from Atriel, he shook his head and gave me a rueful expression. When I finally got to Berlin, Sid Frigid, and the changeling soda pops, Nacht and Nicht Cola, he held up a hand.

"That is most concerning," he said. "Why do you suppose they have been doing this? Infecting people with this flora, I mean."

"To turn people into avatars. That's my guess, at least."

He gave me a sour look. "The Anathema's depravity knows no bounds. As a safeguard, Zelus brought only a handful of them to Earth—most without bodies—to ensure he could control them. It would seem Baduriel has engineered a way around that."

"The infections are not limited to Germany either." I told him about the Take 5 soda I'd found in New York. "And those are just the ones I know about. They could be putting it into other things too, like beer or potato chips."

His brow furrowed. "The question is why bother creating so many vessels? What they are doing would create thousands, perhaps millions worldwide. More than so few Anathema could make use of within the lifetimes of such hosts."

I pursed my lips. "It gives them options. If they need to make a run for it, being able to hop from person to person would make them much harder to catch."

"That's a good theory," Ashdon said. "However, I fear it is more than that."

"Why?"

"Something Baduriel told me," he replied. "I spoke to him briefly, during his attack on the Institute. He intimated the Anathema would soon be redeemed. He did not say how, and I presumed it was bluster or wishful thinking." He blew out a breath. "This changeling business, though—which will create so many potential avatars—suggests a plan to bring more of his kind from Hades to Earth."

"Where is Hades anyway?" With my memory issues, I knew it existed and why but not much more. "In another dimension?"

"It is one of Zarechus's moons," he said, "ruled by a god of the same name. It is beneath its surface that many Anathema toil, supplying energy to Zarechus and its other moons. Consequently, getting to Earth should be problematic for them. Spatial transposition could be used to cross the distance in moments, but all transporters on the moon are locked down and none are direct to Earth. Given that, I wonder how Baduriel intends to manage it."

"I think I know." While on the planet Zarechus with Scott and Caleb, I'd been surprised to come across an Allfrost node in the town below Abadom Castle. When I'd later asked Wilhelm about it, he'd told me about a failed Earth–Zarechus spatial transposition that had been powered by the Underfrost using Allfrost technology. Overly ambitious, that one had damaged Abadom, merging it with multiple Earth-side towns and damaging, if not entirely destroying, all in the process.

"Care to share?" he asked.

"By using the Allfrost to initiate a spatial transposition." I sat back, growing more convinced by the moment. Modifying the Allfrost for Zelus gave Baduriel the perfect opportunity to make other alterations while he was at it. Alterations that would allow him to initiate a spatial transposition. Quickly, I told Ashdon what Wilhelm had told me about the previous failed attempt. "Think about it. Zarechus may be light-years away, but they could be here in moments."

"Light-years?" Ashdon blinked. "Zarechus isn't light-years away." He jabbed a finger at the floor. "It's in this solar system."

"It is?"

He nodded. "On the same orbital path as Earth but hidden from detection by the sun . . . and other measures. Naturally, its gravitational influences must also be . . . well, don't get me started. You don't remember?"

"No," I said as rising memories confirmed his words. "But I do now. How about that? I'd totally forgotten."

"Out of the solar system," he said with wonder in his voice, "I doubt a spatial transposition between planetary systems is even possible. The energy required would be immense." His head tilted. "I'm no expert, though. Even between here and Zarechus, the energy involved is substantial. Which explains the attempt to use Allfrost technology to power one."

"Why's that?"

He spread his hands. "It's clean and limitless, though you'd need some sort of transducer."

A clattering from the hall snapped my eyes toward the door. Dixon entered. Spotting me and Ashdon, he snorted, closed the door and locked it. "I'd have been here sooner," he said, crossing over to his desk, "but I had to chase down a spare key. Lost mine to the Russkies, but clearly locks are no problem for you folks."

"How did things go with Wallace?" I asked.

He shrugged. "It's mostly straightened out, but I'll have to file an official report and submit to an outside debrief. Oh, and the Group wants me to take a medical exam. To make sure I'm fit for duty, and as a final precaution, I suppose. It's only a formality, though."

"That's great." Thinking about New York, I asked, "Did you tell him about the changelings I saw in the subway? Someone needs to help them."

"Of course. I called a friend about that when we stopped for gas in Vegas. Someone should be looking into it as we speak." Fiddling beneath his desk a moment, he raised a bottle of amber liquid and a glass into view. "Anyone else?"

"Please," Ashdon said while I shook my head no.

Plunking another glass down, Dixon poured. "I knew there was something off about you, Ashdon. Winterboy says you were helping him before he came here." Crossing the room, he handed Ashdon a half-filled glass. "That true?"

"It is," Ashdon said, taking the glass.

"But you're also with these commie bastards? The Eurus Faction?"

"We are not commies," Ashdon said. "Just people that believe humanity must be managed for its own and the planet's good."

"A freaking commie infiltrator." Dixon took another sip and scowled. "And this after Green helping Winterboy escape." He downed the remainder of his drink. "If they find out about you, I'll be lucky to keep my job. Two traitors right under my nose. Maybe it's time I retire."

Ashdon frowned. "Don't let my deception bother you, Dixon. It took years for me to make my way here, and I had help doing so."

"All to get to Winterboy?" Dixon asked, walking back to his desk.

"Not entirely."

"Scott isn't a traitor," I said. "He was just helping a friend."

Dixon poured himself a second drink before replying. "Are you kidding me? He helped a Group research subject escape custody. That's treasonous."

"Yeah," I said, "but he wasn't aiding the enemy or handing me over to the Soviets."

The hum of overhead lights momentarily grew in volume before he spoke again. "I suppose."

My head bobbled in agreement. "Exactly. So no one needs to know. Scott was doing the right thing. Like you are by helping me now."

He coughed. "Yeah, well . . . what matters now is stopping this thing. Which means I need to stay in a position to keep helping, so I suppose I can keep Green out of my report for now. At least until it's clear his, and all our actions, were necessary for the good of the country. And the world."

"So you haven't told Wallace about the Eurus plot?" I asked.

"No," he replied. "I've told him only enough to get him off my back. That I was held by Soviet agents, but not where. That I managed to escape, and I've got wind of something big in the works involving the Allfrost. One that may threaten the US nuclear arsenal." He fired Ashdon a look. "And that we may have infiltrators. I'll have to come clean eventually, though."

"You can't do that yet, Dixon," Ashdon said. "If the president comes to believe the US arsenal will soon be compromised, he may order a first strike."

Dixon looked doubtful. "I thought the same at first, but now I'm not so sure. It'll take more than my suggestion of the possibility. The Bodhi Group has great influence, but no president is going to take that step without solid proof. Most likely, he'll order an examination of every nuclear facility. If no evidence of tampering is found and the nukes are still viable, he's more likely to take a wait-and-see attitude."

"And by then it will be too late," I said.

"Yep." He shrugged. "But we've got nuclear subs too. My guess is the Eurus will have a tough time disabling or activating them. Unlike nuclear silos, subs move around."

"I wouldn't count on it," I said. "Baduriel and Zelus must have thought of that."

"The Eurus's intent isn't to activate the nukes," Ashdon said. "Not if they can help it. Zelus's hope is to get the leaders of the Western world to submit to Soviet . . . that is the Eurus's . . . demands."

Dixon sipped his drink and swallowed. "Better we all die before that happens."

Ashdon looked startled. "That's a bit extreme, don't you think? They only mean to control humanity for its own good. At least, that's where they started."

"What about China?" I asked. "Don't they have nukes too?"

"They do," Ashdon said, "but China is already under Eurus influence."

Dixon chuckled mirthlessly. "No doubt they've got their sticky fingers in every communist government in the world. Cuba, North Korea, Vietnam." He shot me a look. "We've got to get those last vials back into Winterboy. Once we've got Prime's location and this authorization key, we can figure out what to do next."

"And what happens to me then?" Ashdon asked.

Dixon's eyes narrowed. "That depends. What's your story? Why shouldn't I have the men waiting down the hall take you into custody as a foreign spy and traitor?"

"Because I'm on your side," Ashdon said. "I have been since Shivurr came to me with what he'd discovered. It's why I came to get him." He looked at me. "When I learned you had already escaped, I had to improvise." He gave Dixon a wry grin. "Your plan to include a tracking device in one of the vials was fortuitous. It gave me the idea to plant my half of the Alterclavis I share with Atriel in another vial. I hoped through it, Atriel might find you, Shivurr, and remind you of our pact." He tapped his temple. "As a surplus measure, I included the mixture that enabled our telepathic link."

"That was you in the archival vault," Dixon said. "When I went down to plant it."

Ashdon inclined his head. "It was."

"You're a fast runner," Dixon growled, staring at the floor. "The Alterclavis device bothers me, though."

Ashdon regarded him expectantly. "How so?"

"If Atriel is also Eurus," Dixon said, "chances are at any given time, he'd be hanging out among them. Which means swapping places with him would be likely to send Winterboy right into their midst, where he'd be captured."

"It almost did," I said with a smirk, reminded of my unplanned trip to the Gobi Desert.

Ashdon shrugged. "That was an unfortunate turn of luck." He sipped his drink, looking thoughtful. "Atriel must have panicked when he discovered where he was, or he'd have waited to speak to you upon your return from the desert or stayed by his own Alterclavis until he returned to the desert himself. If he had done so, things would have been fine."

I cocked an eye. "You think?"

"I do," he said. "After your actions in Berlin, New York, and Winnipeg, things have no doubt changed, but at the time my fellow Eurus still saw you as an ally. Yes, there were doubters when our agents learned the Bodhi Group had you, but Atriel and I suggested you'd been held against your will. An assertion that seemed confirmed by reports of your subsequent memory loss, which showed you weren't being treated as an ally. Given that, even if you arrived among us and resisted, it could easily be explained by your amnesia."

"Right." Dixon pointed a finger at Ashdon. "Once they believed that, you convinced Zelus and crew to send you to rescue him."

"Correct," Ashdon replied. "It took some time to get here, of course. The Group is not easily infiltrated."

Dixon glowered. "Are you actually a biochemist?"

Ashdon glanced down at himself. "Among other things. I have lived a long time. It has given me the opportunity to become knowledgeable in many areas."

"So you're one of these god types," Dixon said.

Ashdon waggled one of his hands. "Not quite. I'm in the process of ascension." He studied his hands. "Though should the Eurus become aware of my actions, I will almost certainly proceed no further. Still, when Shivurr told me of Zelus's true plan, I had little choice but to help him." His shoulders lifted. "I signed up to help guide humanity through this dangerous time, not to make things worse."

"Ascended." Dixon grinned. "That's how you outran me and how you knocked out the security cameras."

"Indeed," Ashdon replied. "An enhanced physiology is one of the benefits of the ascension process."

Dixon stroked his stubbly chin. "What were you doing passed out by the Allfrost dais?"

Ashdon pulled his lab coat away from his chest. "I sent part of myself into the node, in order to inspect it for tampering."

"Right. Your ghost body." He looked at me as if for confirmation. "Like Zelus in the subway."

I pictured Zelus rising from the dead Dixon clone in my mind's eye. "Except Zelus is a full divine." I looked at the biochemist. "Ashdon's still human."

"Which means?"

"It means," Ashdon said, "Zelus is far more powerful, and most of my memory and cognition is still dependent on this body. If it dies, my life is over. Those like him are not so constrained."

Like Atriel, I thought, recalling how he had possessed a nightmarish body when he'd found me in a hallway beneath Caelumburg.

Dixon snapped his fingers. "That's why the demon didn't kill you in the Agora, wasn't it?"

"Indeed," Ashdon replied. "After proving myself to be a Eurus agent, he stayed his hand."

"You took quite a risk," I said. Ashdon was, as he'd said, merely an ascended. If Baduriel killed his human body, it was game over for him, permanently.

He sighed. "Seeing Dixon meant to attack him, I felt I had to intervene. Besides, his arrival was inconvenient to say the least—raising the Institute's security level and disrupting normal operations—and I wanted him gone as soon as possible, without further loss of life."

"I'm surprised you cared," Dixon said, his eyes slits.

"Our goal is to preserve life." Ashdon stared into space with a haunted look. "Not to end it. Others among us may disagree, but that's what I signed up to do at least."

I nodded. It was because he'd displayed that attitude that I'd approached Ashdon in the first place.

"Okay," Dixon said. "Why are you still here?"

Ashdon's brow furrowed. "What do you mean?"

Dixon waved a hand at me. "Shivurr escaped with the planted vials. Why stick around?"

"Well," Ashdon replied, "with the last vials on the way and Shivurr lost again, I thought it best to stay and wait for them to arrive. I hoped to liberate them and return them to Shivurr. If I left them behind, there was a chance my Eurus superiors would abandon all stealth and send a team of gods to take them by force. With Shivurr out of commission, they have been exploring ways to proceed without him, and I feared that these last few vials might be all they needed to do so." He looked at me. "Given that you've not yet recovered the prime chamber's location or the key, it seems I was right."

"Unless the one I got from Zelus has it," I said. "I haven't taken it yet."

"Hopefully," he replied. "In any case, your arrival is timely. My Eurus comrades know the final vials are here now, and they are impatient to have them. If I do not produce them soon, they will come for them in force. If they do, many here will likely die."

I smacked my hands together. "Then there's no time to waste. I need the rest of those vials."

"Agreed." Dixon checked his watch. "No time like the present." He held out a hand as I stood. "Hold up. You're staying here. It's late, but you can't go walking around, not even in that disguise." He got to his feet and looked at Ashdon. "We'll go."

"Fine." I sat once more and took off my hat. "While you're gone, I'll take the vial I got from Zelus."

Ashdon looked confused. "You're not arresting me?"

Dixon regarded the biochemist a moment before replying, "Nope. Not yet at least. You may be here under false pretenses, but I believe you want to help, and we need all the allies we can get. Besides, you saved me from that demon, and I owe you for it."

"That's very good of you, Dixon." A smile bloomed on Ashdon's face. "I don't care what everyone else says, you are all right in my book."

Dixon raised an eyebrow. "Is that a joke?"

"Correct," Ashdon replied. "I have found banter helps people to bond."

"That joke's older than me," Dixon said, unlocking the hallway door.

"Really?" Ashdon scratched his temple. "Perhaps so. That is a downside of long life. One's perspective on time can become somewhat skewed. It is a rather interesting—"

"Tell me on the way," Dixon said, ushering Ashdon through the door. Still holding the doorknob, he turned back to me. "Don't leave this room. We shouldn't be long."

"No problem," I said as he left.

A moment later, the deadbolt's thumb turn rotated, locking the door with a thunk.

Chapter 38

Key Aspect

I stuck my hand into my hat, pawed around inside the null space, and pulled out the Manhattan vial. Opening it, I chugged it without ceremony, capped the container, and returned it to my stash. *Now we wait.*

As the contents took effect, I looked around the office in bemusement. I'd left this building just over two weeks ago, intending never to return. Yet here I sat, in the office of the man who'd been responsible for keeping me here, restoring the last traces of my stolen essence to my body.

Smacking my knees, I lay back, stretching out my legs on the sofa, closed my eyes, and thought of Allfrost Prime and the key to unlock it. As before, I saw the same icy chamber and windswept snow plain, but its location still escaped me.

I frowned, resisting the urge to grind my teeth. *Come on.* For a moment, I considered the possibility that the answers I needed had been lost entirely. Maybe the Group's scientists had spilled a bottle or used it up in their experiments. My stomach roiled and a thrill of panic ran through me. *What do we do then?*

"Try not to panic, Shivurr," said a voice.

I let out a squeal, sat up, and stared. Several feet away stood an image I'd seen in the mirror many times before. A snowman who resembled me enough to be my doppelgänger. "The hell?" My eyes flicked to the door, verifying the deadbolt was still in its locked position. "Who . . . ?" I trailed off, dumbfounded.

The snowman smiled. "Who am I?"

My mind reeled, struggling to make sense of what I was seeing. Had the Bodhi Group captured another of my people or had this guy somehow found me here? Was this a telepathic projection like I'd shared with Ashdon? Swallowing slowly, I nodded. "Are you Borealan?"

"Of course," the snowman replied. "I'm you, after all."

My brow furrowed. "Excuse me?"

"I'm you," he said. "The part you severed from yourself. I'm your memory of Allfrost Prime's key."

I stood and took a few steps toward him, a smile growing on my face. "Whoa." I brushed a gloved hand across his cheek. "You're gorgeous."

The snowman's smile broadened, and he embraced me. "It's great to see you too."

A moment later, he vanished in my arms, leaving me standing there alone, but more myself.

I know the key. My feet tapped, and I hummed a few bars of a tune before stopping myself. Regretting uttering even that much of the secret, I looked around, returned to the sofa, and sat. *It's fine.* I'd recited only the briefest part of the overall performance, and there were no cameras in Dixon's office. Popping from the sofa, I punched the air before thrusting my arms over my head. *Yes!*

I continued to pace excitedly, revelling in my success until, sometime later, Dixon and Ashdon returned. The security director had a pair of shoes trapped under one of his arms, and Ashdon a cup of coffee in each hand.

Coming over to me, Dixon raised his elbow, letting the loafers thump to the floor. "I figured you'd want these."

"Thanks." I had almost forgotten I'd left them in the van when I'd slithered into my hat. Grabbing a shoe, I sat back and pulled it on. "And the vials?"

"Right here." Dixon dug into the pockets of his suit jacket, and a vial glimmered in the artificial light as he pulled it forth. "Here you go."

"Thanks," I said, taking it from him.

"How did the Zelus vial go?" Dixon asked. "Anything?"

My head bobbed. "I've got it. I know the key."

Dixon's eyes widened. "Really?"

"Uh-huh."

He sighed as if relieved. "And the prime chamber's location?"

I grimaced. "Not yet."

"Here are the rest." He handed me more vials. "Fingers crossed it's in one of these. According to Wallace, a couple labs apparently misplaced a few."

"You're kidding?"

"Afraid not," he replied. "Apparently, they're not even sure how long ago they went missing, but they're looking into it. My guess is at least some of it ended up in our frost changeling friend Sid Frigid."

"So that's where Azrileus got her sample," I said, picturing Sid's face inches from mine as I reabsorbed my stolen essence, directly from his open mouth. "And the Soviet Eurus must have the rest. She and Horst sure seemed to think so anyway."

"Agreed," he replied. "That seems most likely."

Ashdon handed a mug to Dixon and gave me a wistful look. "I am glad your essence has been returned to you, but I confess I would have liked the chance to study it."

I squinted at him. "Really?"

"Yes," he replied. "Though I came to rescue you, I am a scientist, and I've long had a genuine curiosity about you and your makeup." He stared into the distance, a beatific smile on his face. "It's why I sought ascension. To have the time necessary to unlock reality's endless mysteries."

"Come on." Dixon pointed to the vial in my hand. "The prime chamber's location is the only mystery that matters right now."

"You've got that right." Throwing back the last few vials, I stood and paced the room, twisting my torso and shaking out my arms to keep my limbs supple. To my relief, despite taking so many vials in rapid succession, I didn't feel as ready to freeze up as I had in the past. Maybe I'd grown used to the process of reintegration, or perhaps, having consumed so many already, I'd grown stronger, making their relative effect less significant. Whatever the reason, the cooling sensation eased after a time, and it felt safe to retake my seat.

"Well?" Dixon said as I did so. "Anything?"

Guided by my thoughts, the same vision of the prime chamber I'd had before appeared in my mind. A vast cavern of ice with a towering ceiling of translucent sky-blue ice, held up by crystal pillars. The huge columns, crackling and sparking with cryogenic energy, sprouted from slopes of sastrugi bordering the chamber's edges.

The vision changed to a crevasse, its depths lost in the curves of ice walls, before the ground shook and the sides of the chasm crashed together. Only a jagged scar of crushed ice—quickly obscured by blowing snow—remained to mark the location of the once-massive tear leading down to the prime chamber.

The view swept left, focusing on a snow-covered mountain, far across a snowy plain. *Mount Erebus*. Memories fell into place, and I knew where the prime chamber was. "Antarctica."

Dixon's eyes narrowed. "What's that?"

"The prime chamber," I said. "It's in Antarctica."

"You're sure?" Dixon asked.

"Absolutely," I said. "Near Mount Erebus. It's a volcano. Do you know it?"

Dixon's head tilted back. "That makes sense."

Ashdon paled. "I feared as much."

"What do you mean?" I asked.

"The Eurus are already there," he said. "Before my arrival at the Institute, expeditions were sent to Antarctica in search of the prime chamber, at Baduriel's behest."

I swore. "Then they already know it's there."

His head tilted left and right. "Antarctica was simply near the top of Baduriel's fairly long list, and at the time, we had no idea where on the continent it might be."

"Which leaves a substantial area to search," Dixon said with a nod.

Memories of Sid Frigid sprang to mind. "Not if they've got another Sid."

He frowned. "The frost changeling?"

"He was visiting Allfrost nodes in Berlin," I said. "As if he knew where to find them." I tapped my temple. "No doubt he got the ability from me."

Dixon's eyes narrowed. "What, you figure he was following some sort of homing instinct?" Seeing my nod, he scowled. "Damn. Then they could just let their guy loose and follow him."

"Possibly," I replied, "but I hid it well, deep under the ice. Even if they're right over it, they'll still have to dig to get to it."

Ashdon grumbled. "That will slow but not stop Baduriel nor the foremost gods of the Eurus pantheon."

"All right." Dixon strode to his desk and picked up the phone. "We need a map of Antarctica."

As he spoke on the telephone, I reviewed my memories of the Allfrost, considering the likelihood of the Eurus finding the prime chamber before we did. Given enough time, even without another Sid, they would find it. That much seemed certain. The question was how long it might take.

From what Ashdon had told me, he'd arrived here at the Institute about ten days ago. Mounting an expedition would surely have taken a few days, so the Eurus had had at best a week to search an entire continent. Even with another frost changeling, they would have an immense area to search.

"Is there any other way they could locate it?" Ashdon asked, as if he knew what I was thinking.

I thought a moment. "I don't think so. Normally, a Sentinel could ask an Allfrost Controller like Hue for the prime chamber's coordinates. Except I cut Prime and all but a minimal number of nearby nodes off from the rest of the Allfrost network. Specifically to prevent that sort of the thing." I stared at the wall without seeing it. Using the Allfrost's Oculi—which allowed remote viewing of areas surrounding nodes—to search for the prime chamber wouldn't work either. Not when the nodes in the area being surveyed were cut off from the larger network. "If the frost changelings can sense nodes—and it sure seemed like Sid could—they would need to get into range of one of the nodes still associated with the prime chamber and follow them from there."

Ashdon winced. "They may not need a frost changeling to do that."

"How do you figure?" I asked.

He shrugged. "I suspect Baduriel has the means to detect Allfrost nodes himself somehow. He's been visiting nodes and chambers. He must have a way to locate them."

"Good point," Dixon said, hanging up the phone. "He went straight for the node we had stored on subfloor fifteen, as if he knew exactly where it was."

"Crap." I held my head in my hands. "If they stumble across the right node, it won't be long before they reach Prime."

He sighed. "What are the chances they'll be able to use it without you?"

I thought about it. "Without the key, they'll have to bypass or break the authentication somehow. If it was anyone else, I wouldn't worry too much, but Baduriel's one of the Allfrost's designers. If anyone can figure out a workaround, it's him."

"Lovely." Dixon thumped his desk. "For all we know, he's got a . . . what did Green call them? . . . backdoor program. If he does, your security measures could be irrelevant."

I nodded. "You're right." Adding such a mechanism during its original construction would have been child's play for Baduriel. In which case, the only thing stopping him would be his inability to find Allfrost Prime. "I've got to get to Antarctica." Once there, I could move Prime again, somewhere far away.

He grunted. "Erebus helps narrow things down, but can you find the chamber from there?"

"Of course." I tapped my temple. "I'm an Allfrost Sentinel. If I can get close enough, I'll find it."

"Antarctica's a hard place to get to, but—" Interrupted by a knock, he waved me behind the hallway door while he pulled it open. Thanking someone, he shut the door, locked it and, carrying a cardboard tube, made his way over to a table by the far wall. "Now we're getting somewhere." Opening the tube, he removed a roll of paper, unwound it, and held the edges flat with his palms. "Come on. Show me where you think this chamber is."

Sidling up beside him, I leaned over the map and pointed to a spot near the coast. "That's Erebus." I tapped the paper inland from the volcano. "Prime is somewhere around here."

"That's a pretty remote location." He aimed a finger at a black dot below and to the right. "McMurdo's closer to Erebus, but the Group has a research station over here, which is nearer Prime. Bodhi Station's smaller than McMurdo, but they should be able to provide us shelter upon arrival and snowmobiles for the trip to the chamber. Plus, we'll encounter only Group personnel there, which enhances operational security. If we can get there."

"Great," I said. "Any chance you can get us on another military flight?"

After the flight over the Atlantic, the prospect of another trip spent in a cargo hold wasn't appealing, but I had to ask.

"I don't see why . . ." He trailed off. "Now that I think about it, it's winter in Antarctica right now."

Isn't it always? I thought before shrugging. "Which means?"

"It's too damn cold," he replied. "The continent is pretty much shut down until November at minimum. That means no flights or ships in or out."

"Surely an exception can be made," Ashdon said. "This is rather important."

"You and I know that," Dixon said, "but the folks we'll be asking to fly us there don't and, as established, we can't tell them why it's important yet. Not without risking starting the thing we're trying to stop." He growled and banged one of his hands against the tabletop. "No one's going to risk a landing in winter without knowing the true stakes. The winds and the cold are simply too harsh. And that's not going to change for months."

I frowned, thinking of the Eurus expedition, and looked at Ashdon. "How did the Eurus get there, then?"

He turned up his palms. "There is a Eurus transporter on the continent." He stabbed a finger at a spot on the other end of the map marked Novolazarevskaja Station. "Near here."

"Figures," Dixon said. "That's a Soviet base." He grabbed a ruler and laid it across the map. "It's close to three thousand miles from there to Erebus. Travelling that far overland in an Antarctica winter would be tantamount to suicide."

"For mortals," Ashdon said. "For Baduriel and other full divine, it will merely present a challenge."

Dixon snorted. "Aren't you a ray of sunshine?"

"Well," Ashdon said, "even if they know exactly where to

find it, it may take even them some time to traverse the distance."

"Let's hope so," I said. "Either way, we can't wait until November. That's months away."

"Could you use the Allfrost to get to Prime?" Ashdon asked. "Using a tholos, I mean."

I wagged my head. "Uh-uh." Using one of the circular buildings to fling a giant snowball with me inside across the world required communication and coordination between the sending and receiving chambers and nodes to ensure I arrived at the right place. "Not while Prime is disconnected from the rest of the Allfrost."

"Even if you could," Dixon said, "you'd be going in without backup." His eyes lit. "Hey, why not ask Schmidt if her people have a transporter that'll take us there?"

"It's worth asking," I said, surveying the map. By Schmidt, he meant Olivia, of course. Dixon often preferred to use people's last names, for some reason. "But even if there is, we'll need to get to it, and it's a big continent. It might take us somewhere as far from Mount Erebus as the Soviet station."

"Wherever it is," he said, "it's got to be better than waiting two months."

"True," I said, still mulling over options. Abruptly, an idea crystallized. "What if the airplane doesn't need to land?"

Dixon gave me a sidelong look. "You're suggesting we skydive?"

"Sure," I said. "I've never done it before, but how hard can it be?"

"It depends on the conditions," he replied, "but it's a solid idea." He stabbed a finger at the map and made a face. "Even from Bodhi Station, the journey to Prime is going to be problematic." He looked at me. "You'll be fine, but that kind of cold is hard on machines, not to mention human beings."

"Not if I make it warmer," I said.

"Excuse me?" he asked, squinting. "Make what warmer?"

"The weather." I spread my hands, turning up my palms. "I've done it before. Not recently, but I could do it before I came here. The vials have given me that back."

"Are you serious?" he asked. "How much warmer?"

"I'm not sure." I thought a moment. "Close to zero, I think."

He eyed me. "Fahrenheit?"

"Celsius," I said happily, knowing zero in Celsius was far warmer than it was in Fahrenheit.

"Now you're talking," he replied with a smile. "When you ask Schmidt about that transporter, see if she can send some help to meet us in Antarctica. If we run into the bad guys, it'd be good to have a few deities on our side."

"Good idea," I said, reaching for my cap. With Wilhelm still on Zarechus and the New Olympians being stretched thin countering the Eurus, I had my doubts anyone could be spared, but it was definitely worth asking. "I'll call her now."

I had to wonder if the attack on New Olympus strongholds and safe houses was a determined effort to wipe them out or just a feint—keeping the Olympians distracted and busy in their own backyard while the Eurus moved ahead with their nuclear ambitions.

"Perfect." Dixon slapped my shoulder. "In case it doesn't work out, I'll get on the horn and see about an airdrop over Bodhi Station."

Chapter 39

Embodied Agent

Flopping down on the sofa, I swapped fresh batteries into the Walkman and pushed the button sequence to connect with Olivia. After first checking that she and my other friends had made it back to New Olympus safely, I brought her up to speed on what I had learned and what I planned to do now, ending with the challenges we faced in getting to Antarctica. "I don't suppose there's a spatial transposer we can use, is there?"

"There is," Olivia said, "but it's unusable."

Adjusting the headphones, I frowned. "Why?"

"Tectonic uplift," she said. "The arrival point is under solid rock nowadays. If you used it, you'd be trapped with no way out. That's if the surrounding rock didn't collapse upon arrival and flatten you like a pancake."

"Crap." I considered whether Frost Walking could get around the problem but dismissed the idea. Pushing through solid objects, even when in the Underfrost, was a slow and difficult process. Passing through a door or wall was feasible, but several feet or more of solid rock wasn't. Even if I didn't get stuck altogether, if it took too long, I'd end up lost in the Underfrost forever. "Can you fix it?"

"Not from this side," she said. "Wilhelm might have some ideas, but he's still not back from Zarechus."

"What's keeping him?" I asked.

"That's a good question," she said. "If he's not back by morning, I intend to find out."

I growled. "I was hoping he'd come with me to Antarctica."

"Sorry, Shivurr," she said. "Do you expect trouble? I could—"

"That's okay," I said, raising a hand she couldn't see. Having divine backup would have been great, but I didn't want to put her at risk or keep her from finding Wilhelm. "It just would have been nice to have company. Anyway, if you find him, tell him what I'm up to, okay?"

"Of course," she said. "Call me again tomorrow, if you can, but don't worry if you can't reach me. If Wilhelm isn't back by then, I may go to Zarechus to find him."

"Sounds good," I said. "Good luck finding him and say hi to everyone for me."

Putting away the Walkman, I sighed. *Speed and stealth are probably best anyway.* I eyed Dixon, stretching the telephone cord as he paced back and forth behind his desk. If he could get us to Antarctica, I'd have to find the chamber fast. If I could do that, we could be in and out without the Eurus even knowing we'd been there. The problem was, the continent was huge.

With that realization, I reached out with my senses, feeling for neighbouring Allfrost nodes, and the location of dozens of them blossomed in my mind. Farther away blazed the nearest Allfrost chamber, which I recognized as the one to which I'd first been drawn after my initial escape from the Bodhi Institute. Despite the damage done to me by the Group, even then I must have retained enough ability to detect that chamber, even if I didn't realize what I was doing at the time.

The knack was a useful and necessary one for folks like me, since nodes drift and are usually invisible unless raised from the Underfrost, either by a Sentinel or extreme winter conditions. Now that I thought about it, the same talent had probably helped me track down the node near Dublin Gulch—the one I'd stimulated to power the nearby Death Valley chamber for my trip back to New Olympus.

Cool. With the ability restored, getting within a hundred miles of Prime should be enough for me to find it. *If we can get to Antarctica.*

Dixon hung up the phone and looked over, bobbing his head. "It's on." His eyes flicked to the clock on the wall. "We're wheels up in a few hours."

"How long will it take to get there?" I asked.

He looked at the ceiling and pursed his lips. "My guess, thirty hours or so."

"Are you serious?" I sat back with wide eyes, once more appreciating the near-instantaneous travel time offered by spatial transposition and the Allfrost transporter. "Sheesh. I guess I'll catch up on my reading."

He smirked. "Be glad we're not going by ship. That would take a week or more, and that's if we could break our way through the ice." Standing, he walked over to the table where the map lay and regarded it. "I've asked Langford to reach out to Bodhi Station to let them know we're coming and ask if they've seen anything that might be Eurus activity." He dragged a finger over the map. "I've also requested one of our satellites be redirected over the Mount Erebus area. If the weather's good, we might at least verify the Eurus haven't reached it yet. It'll take a while, but we should hear something by the time we get to the station."

"Great." I looked away, distracted by a budding realization.

Though I now had the key to unlock the Allfrost's prime chamber, I couldn't use that authorization effectively without an Allfrost Controller. As a Sentinel, I had a user's knowledge of its general operation and capabilities, but not the understanding of how it all worked under the hood. Nor did I have the technical background or ability to directly interface with all its hardware.

For that reason, Allfrost Controllers, as their name suggested, were built to serve as an interface between Sentinels and the machine itself, translating the desires of its operators into tangible real-world results. Only those intelligent holograms—and perhaps the machine's creators, Baduriel and Boreas—knew the intricacies of its operation and the precise and varied calculations necessary to adjust its many chambers and nodes to change weather patterns. While I had no plans to start an ice age, moving Prime to a new location would be just as involved, just as impossible, for me without an Allfrost Controller's assistance.

The last time I had moved Prime, I'd directed Hue, who had been aiding me, to leave the chamber moments before it was cut off from the rest of the machine. By so doing, I had hoped to make it that much harder for anyone to undo what had been done. Which meant Prime lacked an Allfrost Controller to help me when I got there.

I stood and looked down at the floor. "I need to get to the Agora."

Hundreds of feet below, an Allfrost node drifted. Right about where Dixon and Ashdon had told me they'd last seen it.

"Now?" Dixon stared. "Why?"

"I need Hue," I said. "To help me with Prime."

Dixon scoffed. "He's not in the Agora."

"No," I said, "but using a node, I can call for him."

He glanced at Ashdon. "The one in the Agora disappeared."

"It's still there," I said. "In the Underfrost. I can feel it down there."

"Isn't there a Controller on site?" Ashdon asked. "I thought all chambers had one."

"Nope." I retook my seat. "It's a common misconception, but there are more chambers than Controllers, like there are more nodes than chambers."

"Okay," Dixon said, "but how is he going to get here?"

"Through the Underfrost," I replied. "Travelling from node to node."

"Really?" Ashdon scratched his head. "Would he not simply use the Allfrost transporter?"

I shook my head, picturing the tholos launch mechanism. "Controllers use the nodes. It's not as fast or flexible, but it does the job."

"Hmm," Dixon murmured. "We're taking off in a few hours. Can he get here that fast?"

"Absolutely," I said. "It may not be as fast as the tholos, but it's still super fast."

Ashdon pushed his eyeglasses higher up the bridge of his nose. "Even so, why not have Hue meet you at Allfrost Prime?"

I turned up my palms. "Because it won't work. I told you.

Prime and its nodes are cut off from the Allfrost. Bringing him with me is the only way."

His eyes widened. "But can he survive away from a chamber or node?"

I shrugged. "He can with me nearby to sustain him."

Slapping his palms against his desk, Dixon stood. "Fine. Ashdon and I will be your lookouts while you do your thing. Just make sure that disguise stays in place."

Chapter 40

Hue Again

Two men with assault rifles slung over their shoulders turned to face us as we exited the office. They were younger than Dixon, perhaps early thirties, dressed in the uniforms of Institute security: black pants, shirts, and boots. Their black caps looked exactly like my own—mine having been handed to me by Scott after I'd taken down a guard during my escape—but neither one appeared to notice.

"We're heading to the Agora." Dixon pointed down the hall. "You two take the lead and run interference. Keep anyone from getting too close."

Jimenez and Springer, I thought, recognizing them after a few seconds.

Both men, freshly shaven and alert, stood taller as Dixon spoke. Jimenez, the shorter of the pair, a handsome young man of slight build with brown eyes, dark close-cropped hair and a thin face, flashed gleaming white teeth. The other, Springer, of similar age, muscular and fairer-skinned with brown hair and eyes—one of which sported a ghost of a bruise—nodded gravely.

"Elevator or stairs, *jefe*?" Jimenez asked.

"Stairs," Dixon replied.

We descended to subfloor fifteen, passing down a hallway smelling of wet ash, fresh paint, and new drywall before spilling out into a large hall with a high ceiling. Known as the Agora, the space was used as a frequent gathering place for Institute residents. Instead of the usual comfortable couches and chairs, low-slung tables and artificial plants, scaffolding, paint cans, brushes, and rollers now crowded its floor.

Judging by the still-present scorch marks on the walls and pillars, work on repairing the damage caused by Baduriel had only begun.

"Springer." Dixon pointed a finger to the hall's far side. "Make sure no one enters from that direction. Jimenez, keep watch here." As the men took up position, he drew me aside. "Can you do this in the Underfrost? This level's mostly shut down for repairs, but if an egghead walks in and sees you on the dais, chances are it'll get back to Wallace."

"No problem," I murmured, bothered by something. "If Director Wallace doesn't know what's going on, how did you manage to arrange the military flight? Don't you need his approval?"

Dixon puffed out his chest. "Not for that."

"What if he finds out?" Ashdon asked. "Might that not present a problem?"

His throat gave a short rumble. "I'll tell him I'm chasing down a lead on Winterboy. For that, a trip to Antarctica makes perfect sense." He looked at me. "He wants you back, so he'll have no reason to interfere. As long as you're not spotted here."

"Got it," I said. "I'll be discreet."

I walked to the room's centre, where the Allfrost node floated a few feet above the floor. Joining it in the Underfrost, I gave the dais a mental tug and it drifted over, allowing me to step aboard. Making my way to the orb at its centre, I called out for Hue. The node's orb pulsed as its embedded tech routed my unspoken desire through the Allfrost network, establishing a communication link.

"Hello, Sentinel," Hue said in my head. "It is good to hear from you. What do you require?"

"Hey, Hue." I filled him in on the current situation. "I need you to join me at this node right away, but stay in the Underfrost until I give you the signal to cross over and get into my cap."

"Of course, Sentinel," Hue replied. "I feel I should mention that without the Allfrost from which to draw power, I will soon go dormant."

I shook my head. "You'll be okay in my hat. That close to me, I can provide you whatever power you need until we reach Allfrost Prime."

"Very well," Hue said. "I will proceed to your location immediately. I should be there shortly."

"Hurry." I signed off and, after checking that the coast was clear, rose from the Underfrost and let Dixon and Ashdon know what had transpired.

"Good." Dixon looked at Springer and Jimenez and began to walk toward them. "Give me a minute."

Ashdon pointed to a couch set against a nearby wall. "Shall we have a seat?"

"Might as well," I said.

The sofa, still wrapped in the clear covering in which it had been shipped, rustled beneath us as we sat and waited, watching Dixon talk to Jimenez. Only the odd word could be discerned as the younger man cast periodic glances our way.

"I wonder, Shivurr," Ashdon said. "Now that my task here is done, might I have my Alterclavis back?"

I gave him a sidelong look. "Why?"

"To return to the Eurus," he replied. "Primarily to tell them you've come and gone with the vials. By doing so, I hope to forestall an attack on the Institute. Beyond that, I'd like to see what I can do to either delay Zelus's plans or at least get a sense of how far along things are. Who knows, perhaps by sharing what you've told me of Baduriel's soda pop scheme, I may distract them or at least set them to undermining it." He sighed. "And to be frank, I fear that if I stay much longer, Director Dixon will soon attempt to have me incarcerated."

"He wouldn't do that," I said. *Would he?* "Not after you've been helping."

Ashdon looked uncertain. "Perhaps not, but he can't permit me to stay. Not without violating his duty, and I'd prefer not to put him in that position. Already, he's walking a line by leaving me at liberty. Given all that, I believe it better if I excuse myself and go where I'm better positioned to help our cause."

I made a face. "But if I take it out, we're going to end up trading places with Atriel."

"No worries," he replied, tapping his temple. "I can disable auto-activation. Its current settings are just for you. The device is normally meant to be manually invoked, and it allows telepathic communication with the other holder should swapping places be undesirable."

"Huh." I pulled off my cap, trusting my cowl and Dixon's men standing guard to protect my identity. "Pretty neat."

"Quite," Ashdon said. "The one you have is a prototype. Smaller than its progenitors, with reduced energy consumption and capacity. Not enough to transport between planets yet, but sufficient for several terrestrial journeys on a single charge."

"Oh yeah?" I counted on my fingers. "I guess I used up a couple."

"No matter," he said. "There should be ample power left for my journey from here."

"Hmm." I scratched my head, thinking. "All right." I dug into my cap, grabbed vials, and shook them. I'd forgotten to wrap the bottle in cloth again after drinking its contents on the cargo plane over the Atlantic Ocean. "I suppose that'll be okay."

Ashdon might be Eurus, but he'd been an ally in the past, and he'd shown himself to still be one today. Even if he wasn't, there wasn't much he could tell Zelus or Baduriel that they didn't already know.

Well, not entirely. The Eurus only suspected Antarctica as a possible Prime location. Ashdon could confirm that and give near Mount Erebus as a somewhat more precise location.

Still, as an ally, he could do more for our cause among the Eurus than in an Institute holding cell. Besides, if Dixon locked him up, the Eurus would most likely end up attacking the Institute. Sure, they wouldn't get what they wanted, but more people would be needlessly hurt.

Feeling a bottle rattle in my hand, I shot Ashdon a look. "I think I've got it."

I held still as Dixon slapped Jimenez on the shoulder, turned, and strode toward Springer on the room's far side.

When the director's back was to me again, I asked, "Can I just pull it out?"

"Absolutely," Ashdon said, holding out a hand. "Hurry, before Dixon returns."

I inhaled deeply. "Here goes." Pulling the vial free, I looked around. When the walls didn't fade, I exhaled, opened the vial, and dumped the sphere inside it into Ashdon's outstretched palm. "Good luck."

"Thank you," he said, slipping the Alterclavis into a pocket.

As I returned my cap to my head, Dixon rotated on a heel and came toward us.

"What were you saying to them?" I asked.

He glanced over his shoulder. "They're coming with us."

My chin dipped. "They are?"

He nodded. "To watch our backs. In case we run into any Eurus or polar bears."

Ashdon cleared his throat. "Antarctica has no polar bears."

Dixon fired him a look. "Penguins, then."

"Ah, yes," Ashdon said. "I understand they can be quite vicious."

"You'd better believe it," Dixon replied with a smile.

"Do they know who I am now?" I asked, catching Jimenez still eyeing me from across the room.

"They do." He shooed me to the side. "Shove over."

Sidling closer to Ashdon, I asked, "Was that wise?"

"It's fine," Dixon said, squeezing in beside me. "Those boys have been on my team awhile now. They're trustworthy and they know the stakes. Besides, they only need to keep their mouths shut until takeoff. After that, they'll have no one to tell that will care or be able to stop us."

"It's really going to be thirty hours?" I asked, hoping Dixon had been exaggerating.

"Affirmative," he said. "If not more. It's just as well. We'll need the time to go through our equipment and, most importantly, teach you how to skydive."

"Yeah." I searched my restored memories, but I still couldn't recall having ever parachuted in the past. "This should be interesting."

"Don't worry about it," he replied. "It's not that hard." He winked. "Unless your chute fails to open. That hardly ever happens, though."

The Underfrost rippled, drawing my attention to the Allfrost node, and a moment later, Hue appeared above it.

"Hue's here," I said, regaining my feet. "I'll be right back."

I made my way behind a nearby pillar, out of sight of prying eyes. Slipping into the Underfrost, I strode over to the Allfrost node—which was still invisible in the regular world—and, after a brief conversation with Hue, held my cap above him while he flowed inside. With Hue secured, I ducked behind the column again, resurfaced from the Underfrost, and went to rejoin my companions.

"All set?" Dixon asked, meeting me halfway.

I nodded. "I'm ready."

"Good." He checked his watch. "Let's head back to my office. I want to—" He broke off and looked around. "Where's Ashdon?"

I raised my shoulders. "Not sure." *I can guess, though.*

"He went back to his quarters," Jimenez said, coming closer.

Dixon's eyes narrowed. "You let him go?"

"Sure." Jimenez frowned. "You wanted me to stop him?"

Dixon sighed. "Send someone to make sure he gets there. Ashdon is confined to his quarters until we're back from our little trip."

"Don't bother," I said. "He's probably left the building already."

He regarded me with one eye narrowed. "Something you want to tell me?"

"Not really," I said before telling him what I'd done.

"And you didn't—" Dixon's nostrils flared a moment. "Fine." He glanced about at the still-damaged walls. "It's probably for the best." He looked at his two men. "Tell the boys to look for Ashdon anyway and confine him to quarters if they find him. After that, pack any gear you think you'll need and get something to eat. It's a long flight and there's no telling what the food will be like on board. Don't worry about winter gear, though. We'll get that on the plane."

"You got it," Springer said, raising his walkie-talkie to his mouth.

"Come on," Dixon said to me, "I've got a letter to write to Wallace. If our plan goes to shit, he's going to need to know everything."

Chapter 41

Bodhi Station

Over a day later, we approached the coast of Antarctica flying aboard a long-range military transport aircraft. Unlike our flight from Berlin to New York, Dixon, Jimenez, Springer, and I were the only people in the cargo area. Dixon and Springer lay back in their seats, arms crossed, eyes closed, and Jimenez did push-ups, while I eyed the parachutes stacked on the far side of the cargo area, reviewing Dixon's skydiving advice.

Our last stop had been an airfield in New Zealand, where the aircraft's fuel tanks had been topped off. The airplane needed every ounce of fuel it could hold to make the round trip without landing on the frozen continent. Although, as Dixon told me, it had been specially modified to hold more fuel than most cargo planes, even its extended range would be tested by such a long flight.

Abruptly, the pilot's voice blared over the cargo area loudspeakers, informing us we were nearing Bodhi Station.

Dixon got groggily to his feet. "Start getting dressed. I'll be right back."

For the next few minutes, while I returned to humanoid form and reset my disguise, my companions pulled on long underwear, winter jackets, knitted hats, balaclavas, boots, and gloves. Not wanting to risk having my hat blown from my head during the jump, I carefully folded it and tucked it beneath the fabric of my shapesuit. Though I had no reason to fear the cold, I pulled on a thick winter jacket too to better blend in with my companions.

Once dressed, we strapped on our parachutes and checked each other's gear.

"Get those zippers high," Dixon said, returning from the cockpit. "Winter in Antarctica's no joke." Grabbing his own gear, he began hurriedly putting it on. "Listen up. We're about ten minutes out from Bodhi Station now. The pilot's going to lower the cargo door shortly, and he'll bring us over the station at a good jump height and tell us when to bail."

"What do we do when we land?" Springer asked.

Dixon zipped up his jacket before answering, "Personnel on the ground have placed signal flares near the station, marking out a drop zone. This time of year, it's around-the-clock darkness down there, so they should be easy to see. Try to steer yourself as close to them as possible. The weather's unusually good down there right now, but you still don't want to land any farther from the safety of the station than necessary." He reached for his parachute and shouldered into it. "Except for Winterboy here, frostbite and hypothermia are a real possibility, so we want to get down and indoors as fast as possible. The station's got people waiting on the ground. They'll come out to pick us up once we're down."

"Prepare for jump," the pilot said over the loudspeakers. "Cargo door opening in five . . . four . . . three . . . two . . . one." The cargo hold filled with a roar of air and the loading ramp descended, revealing darkness beyond.

"When do we bail?" Jimenez shouted when the hatch had opened fully.

"Soon," Dixon said, pulling goggles over his eyes. "The pilot will give us the go-ahead when we're in the right position. Form a line. Jimenez first, then Springer, then Winterboy. I'll jump last."

"Begin jump," the pilot said a short time later, his crackling voice barely audible above the din.

When Jimenez and Springer were gone, Dixon gave me an encouraging shove. "Your turn, Winterboy."

"Got it." Dashing for the opening, I leaped. "Cannonball!"

Icy air rushed past my face as I fell, and a plain of ice,

illuminated by starlight and the shimmering folds of the aurora australis, rushed up to meet me. Moments later, rectangles blossomed below me, and I knew Jimenez and Springer had deployed their chutes. Nearing my slowly falling companions, I pulled my rip cord, and my canopy's harness tugged hard on my crotch and shoulders. The air flowing past me immediately lessened in intensity.

Spotting points of reddish light blazing far below, I pulled experimentally on the chute's steering lines, and a second set of orange and red danced at the periphery of my vision before sweeping out of view. I dismissed it as a trick of the aurora and guided the chute down to the drop zone. Rolling as I landed, I kept my arms tight to my body as I'd been taught, popped back to my feet and, before the wind could take it, wrestled my chute into a ball before jogging over to my companions.

"Everyone all right?" Dixon asked, glancing around. "No injuries?"

"Not me," I said with a huge smile. "That was awesome."

"All good, *jefe*," Jimenez replied.

Dixon shot a look at Springer. "Good?"

"Yeah." Springer shivered. "But fuck it's cold."

"They should've called this place Coldashellistan." Jimenez whacked Springer's shoulder with the back of his gloved hand. "You know what I mean?"

Oh, right. "Thanks for the reminder." Sucking in a breath, I pushed the Underfrost away, and the air grew warmer. "How's that?"

"How's what?" Springer asked, sounding confused.

"Better," Dixon said with a nod. "Still cold, but a whole lot better. Thanks." He looked to the side, and I turned to follow his gaze. "Here's our ride."

In the distance, the headlights of four snowmobiles bobbed up and down over the ice, coming from a cluster of squat buildings. After brief introductions, we boarded the snowmo- biles driven by station personnel and soon found ourselves, still dressed in our winter gear, ushered into a room in one of the many buildings of the Antarctic research station. Judging by the shelves of books, comfy sofas and chairs, large screen and projector, the room usually served as an entertainment and relaxation area for the station's residents.

"Grab a seat," Dixon said, unzipping his parka. "I'm going to talk to the station head."

Before he could move, the door to the room opened and a woman, wearing blue jeans, a black hooded sweatshirt, and a bright red parka open in the front, entered. By her short grey hair, her slightly stooped shoulders, and the lines on her face, she appeared to be nearing sixty years of age.

Her eyes roved over our group a moment before fixing on Dixon. "Director Dixon, I presume." She extended a hand. "Dr. Rebecca Milton, station head."

He clasped her hand briefly. "Good to meet you, Doctor. Thank you for accommodating our arrival."

"I wish I could say it was no trouble," she said. "However, we are running on a skeleton crew these days, so we are ill equipped to entertain guests."

He spread his hands. "Unavoidable, I'm afraid. If it helps, we won't be staying long today."

Her eyes narrowed. "Oh? How so?"

"We need to head out onto the ice," he replied. "If you can provide us snowmobiles and fuel, we'll be on our way."

"You can't be serious," she said. "For what reason?"

"Can't say," he replied. "I'm sure you understand."

She frowned a moment before glancing toward a map on the wall. "Where do you intend to go?"

Dixon took a step toward the map and tapped a finger to the right of Mount Erebus. "About here."

Dr. Milton's eyebrows rose. "That far?" She waved a hand dismissively. "It's not possible. It's far too cold. Even if you don't freeze, the snowmobiles will."

He shrugged. "They worked fine when your guys picked us up."

She folded her arms. "They were started under shelter and kept running the entire time. The machines can have trouble at minus thirty, never mind minus fifty or worse. You may not realize it, but the weather out there is actually relatively good today."

"I appreciate your concern," Dixon replied. "But we'll be fine."

"Very well." She threw up her hands. "It's your funeral."

He smirked. "Just keep the home fires burning, and we'll be back before you know it."

Her brow creased. "Is this a rescue mission?"

"What makes you think that?" Dixon asked, shooting me a look.

"I thought I saw something outside a few days ago," she said. "Multiple points of light moving across the horizon. Flickering reddish orange, as if from campfires." She made a face. "If campfires moved."

Uh-oh. Could it be the Eurus or Baduriel? The Soviet research station with the Eurus transporter lay on the far side of the continent, which meant a Eurus expedition would have had to journey for days, if not weeks, to make it this far. Then again, for all I knew, they could have been searching for months already.

Dr. Milton rubbed the back of her neck. "I wasn't sure if I'd imagined it. Being isolated for so long does things to one's mind. But now, I'm guessing they were snowmobile headlights. You're either here to rescue whoever I saw or seeking to join them."

"Sorry, Milton," Dixon said. "Don't know anything about that."

"Yes," she said with a sigh. "I expected as much." She turned and made for the door. "Well, come on, then. Let's get you on your way."

Chapter 42

Network Discovery

An hour later, the snowmobile I'd been given bucked beneath me, jolted by ridges in the wind-packed ice and snow of the Antarctic landscape. Dixon rode by my side, and Jimenez and Springer trailed fifty feet behind and farther out. The moon, stars, and southern lights of the aurora australis, shimmering green, provided ample illumination by which to travel, even without the beams of our machine's headlights.

I steered right, taking the machine around a high ridge of ice, and on its far side, the engine buzzed louder as I resumed my former heading, toward distant snow-covered mountains. Guided by my innate awareness of Allfrost chambers and nodes, I didn't need a compass or a map to know which way to go, and at our current speed, Allfrost Prime was about two hours away. By my reckoning—allowing for the time required to enter the chamber and do what needed doing—we'd return to Bodhi Station within six hours.

"You must be loving this weather," Jimenez shouted, his voice muffled by the wind and the visor of his helmet.

"It's a bit cold, actually," I yelled back with a laugh, my voice hollow under my visor.

Again reminded of my companions' vulnerability to the chill, I raised an arm and pushed the Underfrost down, warming the air around us. To me, the change was obvious, but if my companions noticed, they gave no sign. Nonetheless, I felt confident it would be enough to keep them and our machines from freezing up completely.

Now, where's Prime?

After a moment peering into the distance, the shine of an Allfrost node, still hidden in the Underfrost, glimmered about a half mile away. Beyond it, ahead and off to the left and right, other nodes beckoned as well. Noting their position and concentration, I gunned the snowmobile's engine and adjusted my heading. There were many hidden crevasses and snow-covered voids dotting the area, forcing me to use the blues and whites of the Underfrost to navigate a safe route.

As I rode, lost in my thoughts, I considered whether relocating Prime again was the best idea. Doing so would buy more time, but would it be enough? Here in this desolate and hidden place, it had taken only a few decades for the Eurus and Anathema to get within striking distance of finding it. I needed a longer-term solution.

What about disabling it? I nodded to myself. *Breaking it so it can't be misused again.*

Baduriel's changes would need to be undone first, but with Hue's help, a reset command could be sent to every node in the Allfrost network, restoring them to their original programming. Once returned to their original code, they could all be ordered to disconnect from the network, stay in the Underfrost, and shut themselves down. In which case, the Allfrost itself would go dormant. Then it wouldn't matter if Baduriel found Prime or had full access to it. Bringing it back online would require visiting a critical mass of nodes, one at a time, to revive them. In their disabled state, revival would also have to be done by someone capable of stepping into the Underfrost to get to the nodes. Something Baduriel couldn't do. Not without a Sentinel's help.

It was an extreme step. According to Hue and my restored memory, the Allfrost had been holding off rampant global warming. Without it, the melting of the planet's polar ice caps would accelerate, raising sea levels, flooding low-lying coastal cities and towns. Hurricanes, heat waves, floods, and droughts would worsen too. If it wasn't reversed in time, entire ecosystems might eventually collapse.

I shrugged inwardly. Bad as that was, nuclear war was the worse and more immediate danger.

Flickers of orange drew my gaze to the right, where a sunset of orange coloured the air beyond the skyline.

No way. There wouldn't be a sunset in Antarctica for a few months yet. I waved a hand to get Dixon's attention and pointed. "You see that?"

His helmet swung my way, then to the skyline, and a moment later, he waved us to a stop and raised his visor. "What do you think that is?"

I winced. "I was hoping it was the sun coming up."

"Not here," he said. "Not now."

"Yeah, I know." I thought a moment, studying the glow. "If I had to guess, I'd say it's Baduriel, leading a horde of fire elementals." *Probably with some Eurus in tow.*

He nodded. "I didn't want to say in front of Milton, but the satellite imagery came through in New Zealand, and it showed multiple points of light moving across the landscape in this general area. Cloud cover and darkness made it impossible to identify their source, but what else could it be but the enemy searching for Allfrost Prime?"

"Do you suppose this is what Dr. Milton saw a few days ago?"

"Probably." He turned back to the distant light. "It looks like they're still moving, which means they haven't found it yet."

"Let's turn off our headlights," I said. "If they come above the horizon, we don't want them to see us or where we're going."

"Good idea." He looked skyward. "The stars and aurora should be enough to steer by." Turning, he shouted the plan to our companions, who extinguished their headlights without hesitation. "They're a lot closer than I thought they'd be. I guess your old demon pal really can detect Allfrost nodes."

"That or his pet frost changeling," I replied, revving my engine. "Either way, we should get to Prime as soon as we can."

Lowering his face shield, Dixon gunned his own engine and sped ahead, and I raced to catch him before taking the lead once more.

As we rattled over the rough sastrugi, I mulled over the implications. I'd had my doubts about coming here. Doing so risked leading Baduriel to the very thing I was trying to keep from him, but after I'd seen the lights above the horizon, those doubts had vanished. He'd figured out Prime was in Antarctica without my help, and he'd arrived and begun his search even before I had remembered it was here. Now my only choice was to beat him to it and break the Allfrost before he could find it and use it for his nefarious plan.

A few hours later, I slowed and pulled to a stop, knowing we were close to our goal. Leaving the snowmobile running, I got off and stretched, and my arms and legs tingled, still vibrating from the long and bumpy ride.

"Why are you stopping?" Dixon shouted, pulling up beside me. "There's nothing here."

I looked around. Between us and the still-distant mountains lay only a relatively flat plain of featureless snow. *Just like in my visions.*

"It's close," I said. "Give me a second." I walked ten steps to the front of my idling snowmobile. *Time to open the way.*

Raising my arms, I exerted my will, connecting with the snow and ice around me, and a few moments later, the ground rumbled and shook beneath my feet.

Chapter 43

Song and Dance

A crack formed in the ice, and it parted, rising up to the left and right as if pushed aside by massive hands. Snow particles filled the air, obscuring my vision, until at last the noise settled, leaving a deep chasm before us.

Returning to my vehicle, I waved a hand and shouted, "Follow me. Slowly." Driving to the edge of the fissure, I stopped and pointed to a narrow ledge running down the left side of the opening. "We can go down that way."

"Lead the way," Dixon hollered. "It'll be good to get out of this wind."

Nodding, I gave my engine a shot of fuel and, hugging the ice wall, descended, keeping a nervous eye on the abyss.

A few hundred feet down, the trail levelled out, and we entered a tunnel of gleaming sky-blue walls with an uneven ceiling thirty feet above from which six-foot-long stalactites dangled. Wending along its length, our way lit by our snowmobiles' headlights, we exited into an ice cavern, perhaps two hundred feet across. A dormant Allfrost transporter sat near the hall's epicentre, missing the giant snowball that normally oscillated up and down between its stone tholos's floor and ceiling.

"Is this it?" Dixon asked. He'd raised his visor, and with the wind no longer raging, his voice sounded clearer. "Allfrost Prime, I mean."

"This is the place." I cut my snowmobile's engine. Though still chilly, it was warmer here than it had been above, and I judged that restarting the engine wouldn't be a problem. "We made it."

Removing my helmet, I placed it on the seat of my

snowmobile and approached the dormant tholos. Noting several Allfrost node daises positioned among the chamber's many crystal columns, I pulled my cap from beneath my snowsuit and snugged it atop my head. Thick as trees, the columns pulsed with a gentle glow, drawing attention to the runes inscribed upon them.

"What now?" Jimenez asked, still sitting astride his snowmobile.

"Head back up," Dixon said. "Keep an eye out for anyone approaching, and radio if you see anyone coming this way."

"Are you serious, *jefe*?" Jimenez gave Dixon a pleading look. "It's freezing up there."

"You heard me," Dixon said sternly. "You and Springer can alternate every fifteen minutes. Now get going. This is what you get paid the big bucks for."

Jimenez smiled wryly. "If you say so." He looked at Springer. "Don't be late for your shift."

Before Springer could answer, Jimenez gunned his engine and, executing a tight turn, plunged back into the tunnel from which we had come.

I took a few steps and leaped atop the broad circle of stone set next to the tholos, skated across its rink of ice, and pulled to a stop before a marble basin, its outer edge and pediment decorated in carved reliefs.

"What are you doing?" Dixon asked, shutting down his machine and walking closer.

"Unlocking the chamber." With the Eurus nearby, there was no time to waste. I looked at my companions. "Here goes."

I launched into a song and dance, swirling left and right upon the ice. With each careful motion and word, I reenacted the performance I'd given years ago when I'd cut Prime off from the rest of the Allfrost and locked it down. A full minute later, as the song came to its conclusion, crystal pillars all around the chamber, infused with the Underfrost, glowed and buzzed and sparked.

I pulled off my cap and touched a hand to its inner crown. An instant later, a stream of colour flowed from within before coalescing into Hue's vaguely humanoid form.

His featureless head rotated side to side before fixing on me. "Greetings, Sentinel. I see that we have arrived." He looked around a moment. "Ah, and the prime chamber has been unlocked."

"We're in a rush, Hue," I said, describing the light we'd seen on our way to the chamber. "Baduriel's got to be close."

"I see," Hue said. "What do you wish to do?"

"Shut down the Allfrost," I said. "Not permanently. Just until we can be sure it can't be abused again. You can do that, right?"

"Of course." Hue floated toward a nearby dais. "With your authorization, I will first need to bring Prime fully back online."

"You have it."

"Very well," he replied. "Once Prime has been rejoined to the network, I will prepare an update to reset all nodes to their original programming. That will undo any modifications made by Baduriel and prepare the way for a disconnect and shutdown command to be sent to all nodes. When that command is ready, it'll be up to you to authorize its execution." Pivoting, he floated a few feet away, stopped, and turned back to me. "You should know, Sentinel, once you reconnect this chamber, Baduriel may be able to locate it by using Allfrost nodes."

"Yeah, you're probably right," I said with a grimace, "but we'll have to take the chance. Please proceed."

Baduriel was going to find the chamber either way, and with his knowledge of the Allfrost, he might be able to interfere if Hue hadn't completed the shutdown by the time he did. The demon had obviously been subverting other nodes and chambers. Presumably, he'd have found other Controllers like Hue at some of those locations, yet the demon had still managed to do what he had wanted. How exactly, I didn't know. Maybe, as Dixon had suggested, Baduriel had planted a backdoor of some kind during its initial construction.

"Very well." Hue flitted about the room, shifting colour, extending his arms and tapping the air. "This will take some time."

Well, I thought, *if Baduriel gets here before we're done, I'll just have to keep him occupied.* Finishing up and getting out of here before that happened would be better, though. "Hurry, Hue."

Dixon reached for his radio and thumbed the transmit button. "Give me a sitrep, Jimenez."

"Uh, it's freezing," Jimenez replied a few seconds later. "Lots of snow and ice. That's about it."

"All right," Dixon said. "Springer will be up in ten to relieve you."

"Hold on," Jimenez said.

"What?" Dixon looked at me, widening his eyes.

"There's something moving out there," Jimenez replied.

Dixon's expression hardened. "What?"

"Just a sec, *jefe*."

"What is it, Jimenez?" Dixon eyed his radio. "What do you see?"

Hue waved a hand. "Perhaps this will help."

An oblong viewscreen appeared in the air nearby. Within the image, Jimenez, his snowmobile behind him, stood squinting into the distance.

The Allfrost Oculi. I gave my head a shake. In the excitement of our arrival, the Allfrost's node-enabled remote viewing capability had totally slipped my mind. *Thanks, Hue.*

The camera, which I knew would be invisible to the Bodhi Group agent, moved closer, until his face filled the screen.

Jimenez's brow wrinkled and he raised his walkie-talkie. "It's a sail, like on a boat. Over."

"Hue." I waved a hand at the display. "Can you show us what he's looking at?"

The hologram made no reply, but the picture changed until Jimenez's shoulder sat in the lower-left corner of the viewscreen. Beyond him, a dark triangle moved, growing larger by the moment. Swelled on one side, it had the vague appearance of an upraised sabre.

I took a step closer, eyes narrowing. "It's coming this way."

"All right, get back here, Jimenez." Dixon looked at me. "No sense leaving him exposed when we've got a camera feed."

"Right." Stepping forward, I aimed a finger at the triangle. "Hue, can you move the view closer to that?"

Again, the view changed, showing white fabric fluttering and snapping before sliding off the right side of the viewscreen, leaving only the cold Antarctic plain behind.

The camera's not moving with it, I realized.

Before I could ask Hue to fix it, the view changed once more. This time it focused on and kept pace with a parka-clad figure, face hidden by the folds of a fur-lined hood, seated in an iceboat. Little more than a wooden plank attached to steel blades, the vessel swept over the landscape like the slash of a scimitar. As the craft bounced over a rough patch of ice, a furry snout and flash of pink rose from behind the sailor's shoulder and nestled there.

"That's a dog," Dixon said from behind me.

"It's Bear." I stepped closer to the screen, extending a hand as if to pat him. "Olivia and Wilhelm's pooch."

"Who's sailing it?" he asked.

I shrugged. "I'm not sure. My guess is Olivia." I glanced back at him. "She was supposed to head to Zarechus to find Wilhelm, but that was almost two days ago now." *I hope that means she found him.*

I opened my winter jacket and dug into the pocket of the long dark coat I still wore underneath. Pulling the Walkman free, I placed the headphones over my ears and pressed the sequence of buttons that would connect me to my demigod friend.

"Hi, Shivurr," Olivia said above a howl of wind.

"Hey," I said. "Where are you?"

The head of the sailor on the viewscreen swivelled left and right before Olivia answered. "Near the Transantarctic Mountains. I'm almost to your position. Why do you ask?"

"Is that you in the iceboat?" I asked, almost certain the answer was yes.

She paused. "You can see me?"

"Yeah," I said, explaining how.

"Of course," she said. "I should have known."

"I thought you were going to look for Wilhelm."

"No need," she said. "He sent a message to say he's okay and coming home, so I thought I'd come and check on you.

He might even be back at New Olympus as we speak."

"How'd you get here, though?" I asked.

"The spatial transposer," she replied.

I frowned. "I thought it was buried under rock."

"Not anymore," she said. "We fixed it with explosives and golem elbow grease."

"That's awesome." I thought a moment. "But how did you know where to find me?"

"You told me, remember?"

"Yeah," I said, "but how did you know where exactly?"

"The same way we're speaking," she said. "Anyway, let's talk more when I get there. Sailing this thing over this terrain isn't easy."

"Okay." Hearing the low buzz of a snowmobile, I turned toward the tunnel leading to the surface. *Must be Jimenez.* "I'll come up and meet you."

"That would be lovely," she replied. "See you soon."

Securing the Walkman, I raced toward my snowmobile. "You guys stay here," I shouted over my shoulder as Jimenez roared into the chamber. "I'll be back."

Chapter 44

Situational Awareness

A raging wind greeted me as I emerged onto the icy plain and scanned the horizon for Olivia and Bear. Seconds later, my eyes landed on the iceboat as it bounced toward me, only a few hundred feet away now.

As it neared, the gale quelled abruptly, slackening the iceboat's sail, and the craft slid to a stop. Before it had fully settled, Bear leaped from the plank that formed the craft's deck and ran toward me, tail wagging.

"Hey, Bear," I said, giving the dog a hug and getting a wet lick in return. "It's good to see you."

"Same here," Olivia said, furling the iceboat's sail, the lack of breeze making the process easier. "Especially with the Eurus and Baduriel in the area."

"You saw them too?" Releasing Bear, I joined her by the iceboat. "Are they close?"

"Fairly." Her gaze strayed to the chasm. "Prime's down there?"

"Yeah," I said. "Come on. I'll show you."

"Okay." She hefted the iceboat beneath an arm, and the craft's mast wobbled as she took a few steps in my direction. "Lead the way."

"Are you sure you don't want to leave that here?"

She shook her head. "I should hide it first. It may give away our position out here."

"Yeah," I said, "I suppose that makes sense." Getting onto my snowmobile again, I turned to her. "I've got Dixon and two of his men with me, down below."

"Good," she said. "We might soon need all the help we can get."

Throttling my snowmobile lightly, I led the way into the crevasse, and behind us, the wind seemed to accelerate again. Periodically, I stopped to wait for her, since she was slowed by her burden, while Bear ran ahead.

"Hold on," Olivia said a dozen feet into our descent. "Let me stash this boat."

"Sure thing," I said, stopping my machine. "Isn't this still kind of exposed?"

"Maybe." She leaned the iceboat against the wall of the fissure and looked back up the trail. "But they'll have to be right on top of the crevasse to see it now. If they get that close, they'll have found us, and it won't matter anymore."

Crouching, she fiddled with the iceboat's rounded seat a moment before pulling it free of the plank. She turned back to me, holding a sword, still in its scabbard, and shield.

"Is that Caleb's shield?" I asked, recognizing the roundel's eye of black, red, and silver. "The one he took from Abadom Castle?"

"The very same." She mounted the shield on her forearm before strapping the scabbard about her waist. "I thought they might come in handy."

"I hope not." Twisting my torso, I patted the seat behind me. "Hop on. I'll drive us down."

"Thanks." She swung a leg over the back and slid her arms around my waist. "I'm ready."

I glanced at her over my shoulder. "Instead of the sail, why not have Bear tow you?"

Bear, who stood waiting patiently ten feet away, gave a few short yaps.

She chuckled. "Oh, he wouldn't have appreciated that."

"Right," I said with a grin. "I suppose not."

Giving the engine some throttle, I took us down to Allfrost Prime, following Bear, who navigated the icy slope with ease.

Dixon, Springer, and Jimenez turned to regard us as we drove into the ice cavern. Pulling to a stop by the other snowmobiles,

I cut the engine, got off, and met them as they approached. In the distance, Hue continued to flit about, absorbed in his work to restore the Allfrost and prepare the shutdown command.

"Schmidt," Dixon said, giving Olivia a nod. "Good to see you again. Unexpected though it is."

She tossed her shoulders. "I was in the neighbourhood."

Springer kneeled and tousled Bear's fur. "Hey, boy. Who's a good boy?"

Tongue lolling, Bear accepted the rubdown without reply but glanced at Olivia as if redirecting the question to her.

"Oh, he is," she replied, giving the dog a wink. "Most days, he's as cuddly as a bear cub. That's why we call him Bear." She thrust out a hand to Springer. "I'm Olivia."

Standing, Springer clasped her hand. "Don. Good to meet you."

Rotating, she gripped Jimenez's hand and shook it as well. "And you are?"

"Jesus," Jimenez replied. "Good to meet you, *chica.*" His eyes flicked to the shield on her arm and sword on her hip. "You planning to fight a dragon or something?"

Before she could reply, a three-dimensional apparition of the globe, twenty feet in diameter, materialized in the air above a nearby Allfrost node, brightening the chamber with a burst of light.

"Whoa." Dixon stepped closer and pointed a finger at a dot of orange pulsing at the bottom. "What's that?"

"That's us," I said before Hue could answer. Stepping closer, I studied the sphere. "Where are the other chambers, Hue?"

"They will appear momentarily," he replied, "once Prime finishes enumerating the network."

Abruptly, lights showing the current locations of chambers and nodes flickered to life upon the semi-translucent globe. A few moments later, perhaps half of the lights dimmed.

"Why are those dark?" I suspected I knew the answer. At a glance, a higher majority of darkened nodes lay in North America and Europe, though they could be found all over the globe.

"Those nodes are compromised," Hue said. "They are still detectable by the system, but they are operating suboptimally. Of more concern, there are many more that are not detectable at all."

"Which ones has Baduriel altered?"

"Unknown," Hue said. "Determining that will take time. Once I reconfigure the network, I will send out a broadcast, which should restore each node's programming and configuration to their defaults. It will take a while to propagate, but it should return them all to the network and ensure we can trust that any connected are not compromised."

"Good idea," I said. Whatever Baduriel had done to the nodes had to be reversed if we were to enact my plan. "Please proceed."

"Hey, Winterboy." Dixon's voice had a note of urgency. "We've got trouble."

Chapter 45

Comrade Frost

Beyond Dixon's shoulder, the Oculus viewscreen showed a growing orange light. *Fire elementals.* I dashed over to the tholos and leaped onto the departure platform. Standing upon the platform enabled a limited telepathic interface, allowing Hue to intuit my desires and move the Oculus's camera accordingly.

"An excellent idea, Sentinel," Hue said.

Absently, I recalled that I could operate the user interface directly, without Hue, but it wasn't something I typically did. Allfrost Controllers existed to help Sentinels with these tasks, so there had seldom been a reason for me to work the controls directly. Just like Dixon, who could use a computer if he had to, preferred to have others, like my buddy Scott, do the work on his behalf.

As I stepped up to the activation pedestal, a second viewscreen appeared between it and the tholos, and I imagined the view I desired to see. Abruptly, a horde of fire elementals floated over the ice toward the camera. A towering cloud of fog and steam billowed in their wake, raised by the clash between their superheated bodies and the frozen plain.

I turned to face Hue. "Are they headed this way?" The telepathic interface made asking verbally unnecessary, but I felt more comfortable this way, and I wanted to keep my companions in the loop.

"It appears so," Hue replied. "It would seem, as expected, that reconnecting Prime has given away our location."

I moved the camera over the snowmobiles flanking the procession, each one driven by a humanoid figure wearing goggles, a fur-lined hood, and heavy winter gear. Flickering in firelight, the yellow Soviet hammer and sickle on a red background could be seen decorating the riders' shoulders.

"Soviets," Dixon said, stepping up beside me.

"More precisely, Soviet Eurus," Olivia said, "and their mortal Soviet followers."

Between this escort, mingled among the fire elementals, large humanoids wearing heavy furs rode in giant sleds.

Trolls, I thought as the camera closed in on the face of an ookmir driver. The view shifted to one of the massive quadrupeds with great curving tusks pulling the sleds. *Mammoths? Aren't they extinct?*

Dismissing the thought, I squinted, flitting my gaze over the scene. "Where is he?"

"Where's who?" Dixon asked.

"Baduriel." I swept the Oculus's camera over the faces of the incoming foe. "He's not there."

"That's odd." Olivia sidled up beside me. "He's got to be. They can't achieve anything here without him."

I continued to scan the display. "I don't see him."

"They're probably a vanguard force," Dixon said, coming closer. "Sent to secure the location. In chess and war, pawns advance first."

"Either way," I said, "we need to buy time for Hue to finish."

Olivia nodded. "All right. Wait here while he works. Bear and I will go and stall them."

"How?" I said. "There are too many to fight, aren't there?"

"Probably." Olivia hiked her shield and gave Bear a pat. "Then again, we might surprise them."

"We'll back you," Dixon said, hoisting his assault rifle. "I've fought these fire fuckers before, and they're not immune to bullets. I expect the same can be said for the others."

Olivia pursed her lips a moment before replying. "Very well. Just stay back and to my flanks and watch your fire. I don't want a bullet in the back. I'm not bulletproof either."

"Don't worry," he replied. "My boys and I are professionals." He patted the seat behind him. "You can ride up to the surface with me."

Moments later, the snowmobiles rumbled away, leaving me alone with Hue.

"How's it going, Hue?"

"It is proceeding, Sentinel, but I will need more time."

"Okay." Returning my attention to the viewscreen, I commanded the Oculus to follow my companions. "Hurry."

Ascending the chasm, they soon spilled out onto the snow-swept plain and turned left. They drove several hundred feet toward the approaching enemy—who were now less than a mile away—and fanned out before coming to a stop.

Olivia disembarked and, with Bear taking up position at her side, strode a short distance toward the enemy, sword and shield in hand. Glancing left and right, she shouted something. At her words, Dixon and his men kneeled behind their snowmobiles, which they'd all parked broadside to the enemy, and, resting elbows on their seats, took aim with their weapons.

Olivia knelt, patted Bear's head, and her lips moved again. Dipping his head, the dog yapped, licked her hand, and ran over to join the Bodhi Group agents. He snuggled up to Springer, laid his head between his outstretched paws, and appeared to sleep.

At my command, the Oculus's view moved above and behind Olivia and drew back to include the men and snowmobiles with her, leaving the approaching enemy in the background. As the creatures of fire, flesh, and fur drew nearer, Olivia waited patiently, her shield and sword held by her side as if waiting for a bus. When the enemy had closed to only a few hundred feet, she raised her blade high. An instant later, lightning stabbed down from above, striking the ice halfway between her and the nearest enemy, who drew up short.

I need audio. Abruptly, the sound of rushing wind came from the viewscreen.

"Sentinel?"

"Yes, Hue?" I asked, willing the Oculus's audio lower.

"I am afraid there is a problem."

I turned to face him. "What do you mean?"

"I do not wish to alarm you," he replied, "but I have detected an intrusion. Someone is accessing Prime's systems, undoing my work."

My eyes widened. "How?"

"I am trying to determine that now." His hands blurred through the air. Touching controls upon a cognitive interface visible only to himself, my restored memories told me. After a long while, he spoke again. "The intruder is accessing it via an Allfrost node."

"Who?" I was fairly sure I knew the answer. "Can you tell?"

Hue's faceless head rotated to regard me even as his fingers danced in the air. "Baduriel."

"Can you stop him? Lock him out, maybe?"

"I am endeavouring to do so," he replied. "He is quite adept, however, and he seems to possess access even I do not have. This should not be possible."

Clenching my hands, I swore. "He's one of the architects." My fears of Baduriel using a backdoor into the Allfrost were proving to be well founded. Most likely he'd made access even easier for himself in the recent years that he'd been visiting nodes and chambers. "How can he be doing this from a node? I thought he had to get to Prime to do it."

Hue inclined his head. "In order to reconnect Prime to the rest of the machine, yes. However—"

"You've already done that."

"Correct," Hue said. "Now that it is back online, direct access seems no longer to be required."

"I thought even you couldn't—"

"That is also true," he said. "Baduriel has evidently found a way around that."

"Damn it." By unlocking Prime and reconnecting it to the rest of the Allfrost, we'd just given him what he wanted. *Ah, he'd have done it himself, eventually*, I thought, trying to console myself. "He still needs me to authorize commands through Prime, though, right?"

"Correct," Hue replied. "A backdoor might suffice to execute commands local to a particular chamber, but commands received by intact chambers or nodes will not be forwarded along or acted upon if not authorized by an Allfrost Sentinel.

Moreover, authorizations must be verified unanimously by a quorum of other randomly chosen chambers. Thus, whatever commands he sends from here are unlikely to reach the chambers he has compromised. Consequently, I believe the damage Baduriel can do is limited without an Allfrost Sentinel to act on his behalf."

I winced. "He might have that." I told Hue about Sid Frigid, the frost changeling whose stolen essence I'd reabsorbed in Berlin, and how he seemed to be able to interact with the Allfrost. "Could a creature like Sid be used to fake authorization?"

"Perhaps, Sentinel," he replied. "If the creature contains enough of your essence. Given Baduriel's seemingly unrestricted access to Prime, that may well be the case."

"I was afraid you'd say that," I said, eyeing the Oculus viewscreen, where Olivia, Dixon and his men awaited the enemy. "How long until we're ready to execute the shutdown command?"

Hue's ghostly fingers danced in the air. "I cannot say, given Baduriel's interference with my efforts. You must stop him, Sentinel, if I am to complete my work."

I spread my hands. "I'd love to, but I—"

The viewscreen blazed orange, and I pulled the camera back, sweeping it in a wide arc around the scene.

A mass of shadow and flame now stood next to Olivia. Electricity arced over its translucent skin, outlining the shape of a massive dog with three heads, six flaming eyes, and three mouths drooling fire. *Sir Bear?* Panning the camera, I spotted the Alaskan shepherd, Bear, eyes closed, next to Springer, and a wave of memories washed over me. *Sir. Bear. Us.* I recited the words, faster this time, and smiled, recognizing the anglicized pronunciation of the famous pooch's name. "Cerberus."

A rattle of gunfire and a staccato of thrums came from the picture, and I shifted the camera behind my companions to regard them and their approaching foes. A second later, a beam of red shot from Olivia's shield, striking an oncoming soldier. As he fell to the ice, muzzle flashes opened up on both sides, and fire elementals rushed forward, tossing fire.

Ignoring the bullets, Cerberus roared and leaped forward to meet them and, despite his apparent intangibility, knocked the leading two fire elementals flying.

To Olivia's and Bear's side, the Bodhi Group agents' assault rifle muzzles lit up, striking ookmir and men as they tried to move up the flanks of the battlefield.

"He is at a nearby node, Sentinel." Hue aimed a ghostly finger at the viewscreen hanging between me and the tholos. "Shall I show you?"

"Yeah." As much as I would have liked to rush to my companions' aid, I had to stop Baduriel or everything we'd done and were doing would be for nothing. "Please do."

Abruptly, the demon filled the display. He stood upon an Allfrost dais, its edges buried in drifts of snow, somewhere upon the Antarctic plain. His tall frame was lit from beneath by the glowing runes of the stone circle as he danced about, hands moving in a way that mirrored Hue's. Next to him hunched a man with pale bluish skin, wearing a parka and staring vacantly.

Sid Frigid the Second? The camera flicked to the assault rifle and Soviet hammer and sickle on the shoulder of the guy's parka. *Or should I say Comrade Frost?*

"Keep trying to stop Baduriel, Hue." I deactivated my disguise and let my body return to its natural state. The time for hiding was past and, going into battle, I would need to be at my best. Unfettered. *Much better.* "Once I engage him, you should be able to continue what you started. Join me at that dais when things are ready, and I'll return here to give final authorization."

"Do you think this wise, Sentinel? I understand Baduriel is a formidable foe."

"Yeah, but I don't need to beat him." *Though I'm sure going to try.* "I just need to distract him awhile."

"Very well," Hue said. "Good luck, Sentinel Shivurr."

Nodding, I bellied up to the transporter activation pedestal, drew a handful of snow from thin air, and dropped it into the basin. A moment later, snow rose from the stone beneath my feet, and I merged with it—slipping into the interstices between its ice crystals and the Underfrost—until it engulfed me fully.

Chapter 46

Vestigial Minds

The snowball, becoming likewise ethereal, sank back into the stone with me inside before shooting from the floor of the tholos into its ceiling and onward toward Baduriel's position. Short moments later, the frothing snowball, invisible as it travelled through the Underfrost, arced down from the sky. It rematerialized into the normal world, struck the icy Antarctic plain, and collapsed, leaving me standing at the spot I'd chosen, about four hundred feet behind Baduriel.

Taking a moment to orient myself, I bent over, created a frost disc with a swirl of my hands, and climbed aboard. I took a deep breath and blew it out in a rush, and sent myself atop the flying saucer toward my foes.

My plan was simple. Get close and draw my stolen essence from the frost changeling, as I'd done in Berlin. Without my essence, I figured Comrade Frost would be useless, and Baduriel wouldn't be able to execute his plan. Then, rather than risking a fight with the demon, I could get the hell out of Dodge, ride back to Allfrost Prime, help my friends defeat their own foes, and execute the Allfrost shutdown. *Simple.*

Fifty feet from the stone circle's edge, the frost disc juddered, and my arms flailed, drawing my attention to a long and narrow dip in the ice, half-filled with snow. Stepping to the left, I took the disc onto more even ground and edged closer, eyeballing Baduriel and the frost changeling, Comrade Frost.

To hide my approach, I ducked into the Underfrost—the shift almost effortless in the frigid Antarctic air—and steered through a gap between a crescent of snow-topped rock cairns. Before I could get closer, Comrade Frost turned and peered in my direction. As his impassive eyes met my invisible ones, his neck straightened and his lips moved, drawing Baduriel's eyes from the floating orb of light.

Nothing to see here, I thought, still floating closer.

"Chto?" Baduriel said, using a word I recognized as Russian. Standing tall, he turned and looked in the direction of Comrade Frost's extended finger. A finger that—despite my being invisible—moved to follow me, even as I jinked to the side.

What the hell? He can see me.

Abruptly, the demon's hands blazed with fire.

"Are you out there, Shivurr?" he asked, switching from Russian to Latin. With a wave of his arms, flames erupted from the Allfrost node's edges, in seconds rising twenty feet into the air. "Show yourself."

Shit. Waves of heat washed toward me, and the wall of fire flickered, dangerous and impenetrable even in the Underfrost.

"Come now." He spread his hands and peered through the flames. "How long can you stay there safely anyway? Two minutes? Perhaps three?"

I said nothing, looking around for options, beginning to suspect he was right.

Shaking my head, I rose from the Underfrost. "Hello, Baduriel."

Stepping toward the fire wall, he looked me over, and his eyes darted to the frost disc I rode.

"Is that truly you, Shivurrous?" he asked, speaking English, his voice still deep and resonant. "You look different."

Though I was more or less shaped like my usual self now, the form-fitting suit and cowl and the long coat beneath my winter parka were a significant change from the charred winter jacket I'd worn when he'd last seen me in the Abadom transporter room.

"Don't call me that," I hissed. "That's only for my friends."

"No?" He frowned. "Still not entirely yourself, then, if you do not recall our friendship."

Flashes of good times long past, laughing, talking, and adventuring with him, hit me like a wave. They rushed in too fast and jumbled for me to fully process, but they were enough to remind me that Baduriel and I had once been close for a time.

"I remember," I said at last.

"Good," he said with a smile. "Then, now that you are here, help me to redeem myself."

I blew out a breath, shaking my head. "By nuking people? Forcing the world to live under totalitarian rule?"

He scoffed. "You speak of Zelus's plan, not mine."

"Then what?" I thought I knew, but I wanted to confirm it. Besides, as long as he was talking, he wasn't interfering with Hue's efforts. "What's your endgame?"

"Fixing humanity."

His words evoked sadness, bloody images, and remembrances of Baduriel's fall from grace.

The experiments for which he had been condemned weren't meant to hurt mortals. They were meant to help them. He'd been trying to improve humanity, raising them closer to the divine. But those he had chosen to elevate, foolish and vainglorious, had turned on him and led a rebellion against the gods. Many had died, but eventually the upstarts had paid for their hubris, and, despite expressing regret for his involvement, Baduriel had been anathematized.

I narrowed an eye. "Fixing them how?" Before he could answer, my jaw dropped with sudden realization. "The tainted soda pop?"

"Correct," he replied.

I scoffed. "Are you crazy? You're not fixing them. You're infecting them."

He nodded. "To remove their worst instincts. I made a mistake last time. Elevating them without first removing their baser urges. Think of it, an end to violence, slavery, murder, and oppression."

The slogan I'd heard uttered in the East Berlin soda pop factory came to mind, and I sneered. "No freedom. No discord. No pain."

His eyebrows quirked up. "Precisely."

"Bullshit," I said, knowing the truth. "You're turning them into zombies to serve as your own ready-made avatars." I described my encounter with the demon Azrileus, wearing a changeling's body, and Sid Frigid, ending by stabbing a finger at Comrade Frost, who stood watching dispassionately. "You call that an improvement?"

"The ability to inhabit them is a necessary expedient," he said matter-of-factly. "The Eurus will soon know of my plan, if they do not already. When they do, they will oppose me, as Boreas and his faction do. I cannot have them undoing my good works, and I will need allies to hold them in check. Such is the price of my limited resources."

"And the Nameless?" I asked. "How are they necessary?"

His brow furrowed. "Nameless?"

"The guys on Zarechus." I clutched at my chest. "With all the vines and stuff growing out of them," I said, describing how my friends and I had fled the electrified creatures on Zarechus.

"Ah," he said, tilting his head back. "They are an early failed experiment. Regrettable, but unavoidable and, knowing those risks, the reason we chose convicted criminals for the initial trials."

"Regrettable?" I snarled. "You turned people into monsters."

"They were already monsters," Baduriel replied. "That is why they were chosen."

"What about the catatonics in Berlin?" The changelings I'd seen in Germany weren't as monstrous as the Nameless, but what had been done to them still appalled me. "Some of those people had vines growing out of them too, and they weren't criminals."

He waved a hand dismissively. "Merely more failed iterations of the symbiont life form. Less violent but still imperfect. The latest symbiont is much improved and blends discreetly with the host. It will only intervene when strictly necessary, steering thoughts in the right directions, suppressing aggression and so on. In so doing, we shall put an end to mortal wickedness."

My lip curled. "You're infecting innocent people, though. The only thing most of them are guilty of is having a sweet tooth."

Baduriel spread his upturned palms. "To fix an entire species requires more than correcting deviance at the individual level. The worst crimes are perpetrated by groups, often following primitive cultural practices." He tapped one of his temples. "Customs formed out of old brain fears, mingled with a biological imperative to propagate genes. To create a utopia, we must eliminate those barbarisms at their source, across the entire population, criminal or otherwise."

"It's not right."

"Of course it is right," he replied. "Left to their own devices, they will eventually destroy themselves and this world. Is it right to allow that?"

I snorted. "It won't work."

His eyes narrowed. "Why not?"

"Not everyone drinks soda pop."

"Perhaps not," he said, smiling wryly. "But those we do infect will, by operating as a group, wield great political power and influence, and through them, there is nothing we cannot make the rest do or believe."

"Why not guide them instead?" I asked.

He threw up his hands. "Even if that could work, mortals reproduce far too quickly, and the planet cannot sustain them much longer."

"So you plan to cull them too?"

"Unnecessary," he said. "We will simply direct the infected not to reproduce, and the population will naturally decline over time to sustainable levels. Once there, we can keep it there, humanely. And it does not stop there. We can force them to love and respect one another."

My brow furrowed. "How?"

He tapped his temple. "Through the symbionts' influence on their minds."

"Mind control?"

"When necessary, yes," he said. "The latest organism leaves

the host's mind intact, allowing independence, but it monitors and influences the host's thoughts and actions. Not dictatorially, but through subtle influence, suggesting and reinforcing moral, ethical, and altruistic behaviour. Do you not see this means an end to war and conflict? Everyone will have no choice but to love thy neighbour."

I scoffed. "Whether their neighbour deserves it or not?"

He spread his arms. "Think of it. No more opinions. No preferences. No disagreements or hate. Only universal love. No one ever need regret their failings ever again. For there will be no more unkind words, no scorn, or disregard. Earth can become a utopia of acceptance." He extended a hand toward me. "And when enough mortals have been infected, you will not need that disguise to live among them. You will not have to be alone."

I regarded him with one eye narrowed. "Yeah, right . . . and then you woke up." His words described the impossible. The friends I'd made recently, who had accepted me so readily, were the exception, not the rule. "Most regular folks would lose their minds if they knew I existed."

"Ah, yes." He held up a finger. "But with a symbiont inside, we will control the infected's perceptions. Making it trivial to program a host to regard you as whatever you like, no matter what their eyes tell them."

I snorted. "And what about those without symbionts?"

Flames blazed from his horns. "Have you not been listening? Mortals go along with the majority. If enough of them call you human, others will be obliged to pretend or be made to suffer."

The nail that sticks out gets hammered down, I thought, struggling to recall where I'd first heard the phrase. I shrugged. "I don't care if they see me as human. I want them to know and like me for what I actually am. Not force them to pretend." What would be the point of that, anyway? They wouldn't really believe it. It would be imposed from outside themselves. Meaningless. I stabbed a finger at him. "You've no right."

"We have every right," he snarled. "In fact, as their gods, we have a responsibility to guide them to enlightenment. If not for their sake, then for this planet." He turned up his palms. "You have suffered at their hands. Surely you see the need."

"It's wrong, though." For life to mean anything, free will was a must. "You're turning them into mindless puppets."

"Bah," he replied, rolling his eyes. "What does that matter? From what I have seen since returning to Earth, the mortal mind remains largely vestigial. Many primitive practices have fallen out of fashion, perhaps, but still rare are those who think for themselves. Their primal natures still dictate their actions and beliefs."

"I don't know about that," I said, picturing Dixon in my mind. The security director sure struck me as a freethinker. Then again, if he'd grown up in the Soviet Union, would he instead be as assiduous a defender of communism as he was of liberty? Maybe, I had to admit.

Baduriel sneered. "Mortals do not wish to be bothered thinking for themselves. Not for the larger things. They simply think as those around them do, or as their governments tell them to think. Why should we—their ancient and wiser superiors—not do as much for them?"

"All right," I replied. "If what you say is true, what are you doing here? Setting off nuclear weapons isn't going to win you redemption, whatever Zelus might have told you."

He scoffed. "I am not here to do the bidding of Zelus." He waved a hand at the darkness to his side. "Which is why I sent the others of my party ahead."

"Explain," I said, having a strong feeling he wanted to do so.

"I am here to raise an army," he replied.

"Aha." During our conversation in Dixon's office at the Bodhi Institute, Ashdon had suggested Baduriel might have a plan for the Allfrost that went beyond his agreement with the Eurus. It seemed he'd been right. "You are trying to free the Anathema."

"And why not?" Baduriel hissed. "They have toiled long enough beneath that moon. It is time they were given their own chance at redemption—by helping me lead humanity to an evolved and prosperous future."

"It's too dangerous." As I'd told Ashdon, trying to use the Underfrost to power a spatial transposition between Zarechus and Earth had failed before. Leaving the towns involved in ruins. I shuddered to think what must have happened to the townsfolk that had been caught up in it. If another attempt was made, I wasn't too worried about the Anathema, but if people or buildings were in the Earth-side area of effect, it could be disastrous. "Using Allfrost tech to power a spatial transposition practically destroyed Abadom."

Baduriel folded his arms. "Yet much was learned in the process. As with the so-called Nameless, getting things right takes time. But fear not, I have chosen uninhabited areas for their arrival."

"Zeus's beard." I pressed my palms against the sides of my head. "You really are crazy."

Even if Baduriel had chosen unpopulated places on Earth for the Anathema to arrive, there was no telling what a horde of psychopathic demons might do when they reached popu-lated areas. Baduriel might believe he could control them or that they sought redemption, but he had to be insane for thinking so. Especially with who knew how many ready-made hosts—changelings who had consumed symbiont tainted soda pop—awaiting their arrival.

The weird thing was, though selfish goals underlay the Eurus's and Baduriel's ambitions, they were also, in their own deluded ways, trying to help humanity by ending mortal con-flict. One by tactical use of overwhelming force, the other by changing people's biology and nature. In both cases, it meant peace would be achieved by dictating how people lived and thought.

Introducing a utopia at the cost of everything that made life worth living.

Turning, Baduriel held a hand to the floating orb. "If the disastrous Abadom transposition concerns you, help me rather than hinder me." He grimaced. "Without your authorization, I am forced to take shortcuts, bypassing safety measures."

"And then?"

"Then all is forgiven," he said, "and our friendship renewed. Together, we can save both humanity and Earth. Was that not what drove you to bargain with Zelus in the first place?"

I sneered. "He lied."

Baduriel nodded. "Zelus and his fellows seek to rule over mortals and gods both, not just Anathema. They prefer to exploit mortals' fear of death and tendencies toward collective thinking."

I scoffed. "And you don't?"

His chin rose. "I do not seek to rule. Only to end mortal-caused suffering, to elevate them beyond their savage origins."

"Yeah, right," I said. "You need bodies. Fodder for your crusade against the gods."

He huffed. "Is it not right that they, the beneficiaries of my help, help me in turn? They will be vessels for gods. Noble sacrifices in a war for liberty. Is that not better than being made to toil under the Eurus's yolk, or destroying themselves in a nuclear war, as Boreas and his New Olympian ilk are determined to allow?"

"Except you're forcing them to volunteer."

"A necessary step," he said. "They are not yet equipped to make the right choice for themselves. However, once they are elevated, they will understand and be only too happy to assist." He held out a hand. "Join me, so that this wall between us might at last fall. Do that, and I will fulfill Zelus's broken promise to you."

"Yeah, right." Even if I did believe Baduriel would follow through, I couldn't join him. Robbing people of their will, changing their biology, went too far. Not to mention, the Anathema included those the gods considered to be the worst among their number. Sadists and psychopaths, who delighted in death and torture. Maybe some Anathema didn't deserve their fate, but most definitely did, and I didn't trust Baduriel to have vetted them properly. "Even if I believed you, the Anathema don't belong here. There's got to be another way."

Baduriel sighed. "I had hoped you would see reason." Pivoting on a heel, he took a few steps, thrust a hand into the light of the floating orb and looked back at me. "If not for the sake of our friendship, then for your friends."

I stared him in the eyes, my head tilted back. "What does that mean?"

An Oculus viewscreen appeared in the air above Baduriel, growing to the size of a drive-in theatre movie screen. On its surface, a blizzard raged, and Dixon, Jimenez, and Springer lay face down, spreadeagled, watched over by armed soldiers.

Chapter 47

Cooler Heads

A demon stepped into view, touched a finger to the horn curling up from his left temple, and snarled. Much shorter than its twin, the projection had a sharp-angled edge that suggested much of its original length had been lopped off.

Behind him, a second fiend lay in a growing pool of ichor, still-smouldering scarlet flesh steaming the snow and ice on which he lay, and a scattering of fallen soldiers, ookmir, and fire elementals dotted the periphery.

Stooping, the horn-challenged Anathema lifted a jar from the snow and studied it, and his frown became a smile. He turned to face the camera and raised the bottle like a TV game show host displaying a prize.

"The hound has been brought to bay," Baduriel said with satisfaction. "Your companions fought well, but they were out-numbered and outclassed."

I scowled. "Where's Orithyia?" I demanded, using Olivia's older name.

Baduriel waved a hand, rewinding the feed. "She has fled." The view rolled forward, showing her bury her sword into an ookmir's neck before escaping into the growing storm. Abruptly, the view returned to the captured Bodhi Group agents. "But these three were not so lucky."

I swallowed. *Damn it.* "So, what?"

"Agree to assist me, or I order Kakak to end their lives." He winced theatrically. "My compatriot is not known for making such things quick or painless."

"What do I care?" I pointed a finger. "Those are Bodhi Group agents. My captors, not my friends."

"Perhaps," he replied. "Yet I know you. You get attached too easily. Despite what they have done, your conscience will not allow you to let them die. And even Orithyia will perish in this cold, eventually." He wagged a finger. "Think carefully before you answer. They still live only as a means to gain your assistance."

"I . . . can't." From what I knew of Dixon, he'd die to stop what either Baduriel or Zelus had planned, and he'd be right to do so. "Not if it means letting you and your buddies enslave the world."

Baduriel's horns blazed higher. "I feared as much."

The air behind me warmed, and I rotated my frost disc in the direction of the heat. *Oh, shit.*

Fire elementals stood in a semicircle around me—where snow-covered rock piles had sat on my way to the dais's edge—penning me against the wall of fire. Obscured by fog steaming up from their molten bottoms, they watched me with malevolent eyes but did not attack.

Swallowing, I turned back to Baduriel and glanced about, looking for a way past the conflagration separating us. Trying to cross the fiery curtain while submerged in the Underfrost came to mind, but I dismissed the idea. The heat would melt my icy flesh and pop me back into the regular world in an instant. A frost shield might protect me until I reached the far side, though. The problem was, when I raised it, Baduriel would know I'd chosen to fight, and he'd give the command for my companions' executions. Unless I could stop him before he did so.

But how are they communicating? Judging by how the demon, Kakak, had stared at the camera and raised the jar for display at precisely the right moment, they had the means to do so. They had to, really, if Baduriel was going to issue the kill order. *Telepathy?*

It seemed a reasonable guess. If so, keeping Baduriel from concentrating might be enough to disrupt their link. Telepathic communication, I'd learned long ago, required concentration to maintain. It got more difficult with distance, too, and couldn't be easy for the two when miles away from each other, as they were now.

"Last chance, Shivurrous," Baduriel said. "Help me or your friends die, and I compel you to help me anyway."

I thought frantically, casting about for a way to hurt Baduriel and buy myself time to raise a frost shield, storm the fire wall, and take him down.

"Screw you, demon dick," I hissed.

"Very well," he replied. "Then watch the first of your companions die."

On screen, Kakak's lips moved, and he jabbed a finger at a nearby ookmir. With a nod, the troll took a few lumbering steps toward Jimenez and, gripping the agent by an arm, lifted him from the snow.

"Wait," I said, throwing up my hands. "I changed—" Light from the Oculus viewscreen, blinding in intensity, interrupted me. Shielding my eyes with a hand, I peered between my fingers. *What the hell?*

On screen, bolts of lightning stabbed down from dark and roiling clouds, growing in size as they neared the unfolding tableau. One bolt, thick as a utility pole, struck the ice thirty feet from Kakak, where it arced against the plain for a long moment before fading away.

When my dazzled vision cleared, a giant of a man, eight feet tall, a ghostly aurora of translucent green, stood upon the scorched and steaming snow. His insubstantial clothes and armour—formed of divine essence tailored to display an image of power and implacability—were unmistakable.

Boreas. Even to me, his friend, the name by which the ancient Greeks had known their God of Winter seemed a better fit in this form than his mortal alias, Wilhelm Schmidt. *He made it.*

I wasn't sure, but I had to presume the god had returned to New Olympus, heard where Olivia had gone, and followed her here. Whether through the same transporter she had used or by riding here on a storm, I could only guess. The thought fled in a moment as muzzle flashes bloomed in the darkness.

Struck by the fusillade, Boreas sparked, like the night sky beneath a meteor shower, as bullets struck the dust of his ghostly form. Expressionless, he turned to face his attackers and, raising a hand, sent thunderbolts in reply. Each bolt sent a soldier crashing to the ice, twitching.

"Kill them all," Baduriel said as if to himself.

Kakak shouted something and, nodding, the ookmir holding Jimenez dropped the agent to the ice and raised a foot. Before it could be lowered, Springer dashed in from the side, combat knife in hand, and thrust it into the creature's sole. The troll bellowed and hopped in a circle, sprinkling hot blood upon the ice. Rolling out of the injured hulk's path, Dixon scurried over to a fallen soldier and fumbled through the guy's pockets.

Baduriel glared my way. "A pointless and temporary victory." He waved to his fire elementals, and they came toward me, trailing fire that seared the ice, raising clouds of steam.

I staggered the first two with frost balls, ducked into the Underfrost, and rushed toward a third fire elemental. Popping back to the regular world, I gripped its fiery arm. My glove burned and my palm steamed, but I gritted my teeth and vanished into the Underfrost again, taking the elemental along for the ride. When I was as deep as I dared go, I released my grip and rematerialized, leaving the creature behind.

I winced, sent frost to my palms, and rubbed them together, soothing my burns until the elemental automaton reappeared. It took a step, tilted, and fell to the ice—its fires extinguished and body no longer molten—sending chunks of crystal and rock tumbling.

Safe for the moment, I regarded the viewscreen where the battle by the crevasse silently raged, then Baduriel and the frost changeling. Their backs were to me as they huddled by the control orb. No doubt working to activate the demon's changes to the Allfrost to bring his allies here, to Earth.

No, you don't, I thought. A fireball warmed my cheek as it streaked past, and I shrieked as another struck my shoulder, setting my parka alight. *Holy shit.* Patting out the spreading flames, I raised a frost shield. *Damn it. This thing's new.*

My shield shimmered and thrummed, struck by a growing barrage of fireballs as the remaining fire elementals moved closer. Bolstering my defenses, I conjured a ball of frost and dismissed it with a shake of my head. Throwing it meant dropping my shield, and I was currently outgunned. *Better to wait it out.*

I glanced at the destroyed elemental and shook my head. The half-remembered technique from my past was effective but dangerous. Dipping so deep into the Underfrost had its risks, and doing it repeatedly in rapid succession increased those risks exponentially. Not to mention grabbing them one by one would take time, giving Baduriel more time to finish messing with the Allfrost.

It hurts too, I thought, inspecting my burned gloves, my palms still mushy beneath. I rifled through my memories for a solution as the rain of fireballs continued to hammer my shield, sapping my energy reserves. A vision of Volkspolizei car tires punctured by spikes of ice flashed through my mind, and I smiled, grimly. *That's it.*

Spinning about, I rushed the mob, clenching the Underfrost in both hands, and yanked upward. All around me, stalagmites of razor-sharp ice erupted, rising three feet into the air. The upthrusts of ice radiated outward in a wave, covering forty feet in the space of a few heartbeats, impaling my enemies. All around me, transfixed by ice, fire elementals cried out in rage, their shrieks mingling with the hiss of steam that filled the air, obscuring their dying light. Before I could move, flashes from the Allfrost viewscreen lit the Antarctica plain with strobes of orange light.

On screen, fire streamed from Kakak's outstretched hands, immolating Boreas, who raised an arm in defense and roared his defiance. My friend's translucent green arm shifted form, becoming a large kite shield, and his other hand sparkled. Snarling, he hurled lightning, striking Kakak, who twitched beneath the assault.

As the demon fell, a Soviet soldier raced into view, firing a handgun with one hand and holding an open jar high with the other. Almost casually, Boreas swept a hand through the air, still ten feet from the soldier, and the man flew back across the ice like he'd been struck by an invisible car, and the view changed back to the demon, Kakak, climbing back to his feet and staring daggers at Boreas.

Before either could move, Olivia, visible over the demon's shoulder, blurred from the shadows, blasting energy from her upraised shield. Struck between the shoulder blades by the barrage, he fell again to his knees. Giving the demon no respite, mouth open in a soundless snarl, she leaped into the air, bringing her sword down, driving it into and through Kakak's neck, sending the demon's head flying across the snow, leaving a trail of warm red ichor in its wake.

"Yes," I shouted, punching the air.

Kicking the head aside, Dixon, blood staining his parka, staggered closer. As he neared, the demon's headless body rotated and swung a muscled arm, thick as a post, toward Olivia, and her shield thrummed with the impact, and her boots slid back several feet across the ice. Apparently spent, Kakak's body crashed to the ground, red mist wafting from its neck stump like smoke from a chimney.

I scowled, convinced the demon was about to escape, but with a burst of speed, Dixon rushed forward, holding out an open jar, his lips moving. Halting its ascent, Kakak's scarlet cloud hung in the air a moment before streaming toward the security director's outstretched hands, and I grinned. *An Animavas.*

When the last of the red mist had vanished into the open bottle, Dixon used his other hand to cap the god-trapping device shut.

Chapter 48

Endless Time

A rage-filled shout drew my eyes from the scene to Baduriel, who stared up at the viewscreen, his hands still enmeshed with the orb. Glaring over his shoulder at me, he pulled his hands from the sphere and the viewscreen vanished.

"Hell yeah." Buffing my frost shield, I toed the frost disc's edge, sending it racing toward the curtain of flames. *Time to end this.* "It's just you and me now."

"So it is," Baduriel replied grimly.

He raised his hands skyward, and fire surged from his palms. Rising eighty feet into the air, it morphed into a swirling disc of orange, red, and yellow, wider than the dais over which it hung. A moment later, a rain of fire pounded down upon my shield. Its kinetic energy spent, molten material bled through the energy barrier as it washed along the bubble's curve, and I dodged back a step as a hot dollop fell toward me. It struck the frost platform inches from my feet, where it hissed and steamed. Feeling a tap and surge of heat on my shoulder, I shrieked and brushed droplets of fire from my smouldering winter coat.

Yikes. I've got to get out of here. Reversing course, I sailed the frost disc at breakneck speed away from the firestorm, hoping to shed the molten precipitate before any more could seep its way through. The tactic seemed to work, and when I cleared the storm's edge, I turned back to the dais and regarded Baduriel through a haze of fire and fog. *Two can play that game.*

I pulled the Underfrost close, spun in place atop the floating ice platter, and sent cryogenic energy outward into the regular world. With each spin, I drew more power, spinning it about in a wider and wider circle. In the Underfrost, it manifested as ribbons of blinding alabaster—their shades varying by their intensity—forming a maelstrom of snow, with me at the eye of the storm.

My frost disc, buoyed by snow accumulating beneath it, rose higher, and the rain of fire diminished, subsumed by frost, leaving a thickening fog in its aftermath.

Where are you? I sagged beneath a wave of fatigue and peered toward the dais. Near the centre of the storm, a spot of darkness marred the Underfrost's azure shine. *There.*

Heaving in a deep gulp of air, I stood taller, sent more energy to my shield, and sailed toward the black. Roiling fog, thick as soup, soon engulfed me, leaving only Baduriel's dark smudge to guide my way.

Luckily, the wall of fire that had held me at bay had vanished, and I urged the frost disc onto the Allfrost node dais unhindered. Sailing over glowing runes, I made my way to the dais's nucleus, where a column of fire, positioned next to the floating orb, greeted me. Neither Baduriel nor Comrade Frost were anywhere to be seen.

I frowned at the pillar of flame. *Why the—*

A wedge of scarlet flashed in the air and something hot and hard smacked into my throat. My torso's forward motion ceased, but my feet kept moving with the frost disc, and I fell back. My shoulders crunched against the dais's stone a half second later, and I expelled a blast of air as Baduriel, his skin aflame, looked down upon me.

Shit. I rolled away from his grasping hands and, springing to my feet, I smacked at my chest, smothering the flames his touch had ignited. *Nice decoy.*

Ten feet from me, Baduriel flickered like a flashbulb and reappeared next to me, locking his fingers, hot and unyielding, onto my snowy bicep.

"Let me go." Wincing, I swung a fist, landing a frost-charged blow against his cheek, and his fingers loosened on my arm. I struck him again, this time in the nose, and managed to pull my trapped arm free. Scurrying back a few steps, I hunched low and raised half-clenched hands defensively. "Come on."

One of my legs, struck behind the knee, buckled, leaning me back. Before I could right myself, cold fingers gripped my face and pulled me to the ground.

Comrade Frost, I realized, grabbing the Soviet soldier's wrists.

Before I could do more than pry the changeling's hands from my face, Baduriel was above me once more. He appeared in an instant, still covered in a blaze of fire and, shouldering Comrade Frost aside, grabbed my bicep again.

"Regrettably, Shivurr"—his free hand, bright like molten lava, bloomed fire, and he punched down, hammering me in the face—"I cannot let you interfere further."

"Up yours," I snarled, swiping the flames from my cheek.

"I have him now," Baduriel said, looking at Comrade Frost. "Finish it."

"Stop," I shouted. Between my upraised forearms, the frost changeling moved toward the floating orb. "I'm warning you." I ghosted over to the Underfrost and tried to roll away, but Baduriel's fiery hold on my bicep—painful even through the fabric of my clothing—somehow remained firm. *What the hell?*

He chuckled. "No more scurrying back to the Underfrost, Shivurrous."

I tried and failed to yank my arm free. *Damn.* He was right. The heat and flame of his grip kept my upper arm from transitioning to the Underfrost, even though the rest of my body now resided there. At the same time, I couldn't seem to pull him over there with me, as I'd done with the fire elementals. Maybe it was the flames blazing over his skin, the pain in my arm, or something else entirely, but he had me trapped like a rabbit in a snare.

Baduriel extended a hand through my now-intangible forearms and fire shot from his palm as if from a blowtorch. The superheated air popped the rest of me back from the Underfrost to the regular world, melting away my mask and the snow and ice beneath.

"Try to relax now, Shivurr," he said, continuing to hold the blaze to my face. "It will all be over soon enough."

Screaming, I grabbed his wrist and tried to move his hand away. "Screw you."

The razor-sharp fingertips of my other hand elongated with a thought, piercing my gloves, and I shoved them up into his gut. As hot ichor washed down my arm, I sent the Underfrost through my embedded fingers and into Baduriel. Bellowing, he reeled back, letting go of my arm, and I ghosted to safety at last.

Bastard, I thought, stumbling away blind and fingering my face, feeling bare eyeballs where icy lids should be. Several steps later, I tripped, and the ground, spongy in the Underfrost, rose up to meet me. I lay there a moment before climbing to my feet, blinking newly formed eyelids. When a haze of light emerged in my dark vision, I looked toward the blurry light of the dais.

The Soviet soldier, Comrade Frost, stood huddled by the orb with his hands lost in its intensifying glow. Under him, the dais glowed brighter in the thinning fog and snow, emitting a chest-tickling thrum that signalled the associated Allfrost chamber was charging itself.

"Flee or hide, Shivurr." Off to the side, Baduriel held a hand to his wounded gut, and his head turned left and right. "Just do not interfere."

As the dais hummed louder, Hue materialized a few feet from the orb. "Ah, there you are, Sentinel." Firing looks at Baduriel and the frost changeling, he floated directly toward me.

He's with me in the Underfrost, I realized when Baduriel failed to react to his presence. "What are you doing here, Hue?"

"I have completed shutdown preparations, Sentinel," Hue said over the growing noise. "However, a directive issued from this node is preventing code transmission."

I scowled. "Can't you override it?"

"Not without a Sentinel's authorization." He shot a look toward the orb. "As we feared, somehow that creature is masquerading as you, and while he remains joined to the node, none can countermand him."

My fingers clenched as I watched Baduriel pace back and forth near the frost changeling, waiting for me to show myself. Was it already too late? Had the spatial transposition been activated? I had no choice but to hope time still remained. It would have to take time for whatever Baduriel had done to propagate across the entire machine, not to mention execute the calculations and processes needed to transpose volumes of space across such distances.

Yeah. When Scott, Caleb, and I had taken our trip to Zarechus from Antara, the procedure had seemed to take a few minutes at least. There was no reason to think this would be any different, so I probably still had time to interrupt it. I just had to take down Baduriel first. *And fast.* I swallowed. If I failed, countless Anathema would be freed, and humanity subjugated. Under Baduriel's banner, the Anathema might be unstoppable, even by the gods united.

I can't let that happen. I pressed my lips together. *Time to play dirty.*

Spreading my arms, I resurfaced, holding the Underfrost in both hands.

"Ah." Baduriel's hands ignited, and he sidestepped, blocking my view of Comrade Frost. "You have chosen to fight, then."

Taking a deep breath, I took a step toward him. "I'm sorry."

He snorted. "For what?"

"This." Turning up my palms, I wrenched my hands skyward, shaping and directing the Underfrost in my mind. Shafts of ice lanced upward all across the pulsing dais. My onetime friend snarled, stuck through the thigh, shoulder, and chest by six-foot-long spears of ice. He sagged back and slid down the largest shaft, leaving a bloody trail. Grim-faced, I strode toward Baduriel. "It didn't have to end this way."

"This is not the end," Baduriel replied, his fires fading. Behind him, Comrade Frost, himself transfixed through chest and armpits, drew his hands from the Allfrost node orb, convulsed, and fell still. "You must know that." He tried to grin but coughed blood instead. Spitting onto the stone, he continued, "I've got all the time in the world, Shivurr."

My lip curled. "Find a better way to spend it." Lifting my hands, I drew snow from thin air and piled it about him. *Either way, it's the end of you corrupting the Allfrost.*

As it reached his neck, Baduriel looked skyward, and a red mist flowed from his open mouth into the air. I stepped back and let it stream high into the night sky a moment before returning to burying his ruined avatar. With his essence having fled, it was unnecessary but, angry over what he'd made me do, I no longer wanted to see his face.

Baduriel was still dangerous without his avatar, and I wondered for a moment why he had not continued to fight.

I shrugged. Using so much power fighting me while countering the elements here in the coldest place on Earth had probably taken its toll, or perhaps losing his avatar had taken the fight out of him. I knew such things could be disorienting and enervating to the gods.

Or maybe he couldn't do anything more without Comrade Frost, I thought, eyeing the corpse of the Soviet soldier.

I wiped my palms together and strode to the dais's centre with Hue floating at my side. Thrusting a hand into the orb, I pictured my desires and the lights and thrumming of the dais abated.

"Excellent," Hue said moments later. "I have full access once again. If you have no objections, I will return to the prime chamber and resume code transmission. Please join me there as soon as you are able, as I will need your authorization before executing the final command."

"Wait," I said. "Can't we do all that from here?"

He shook his head. "You forget, Sentinel. Authorization for the shutdown must be given from the prime chamber." He looked toward the pile of snow melting nearby. "Perhaps the architect, Baduriel, would have a workaround, but I know of no other way."

I drooped, feeling thirsty and tired. "Fine. Go ahead. I'll meet you there as soon as I can."

"Thank you, Sentinel."

Hue's ghostly body bled to the side and flowed into the control orb.

When the hologram was gone, I fingered the neck of Comrade Frost but, as expected, felt no pulse. Shaking my head, I touched the guy's forehead, pulling forth a rainbow of dust into my palm. The essence passed through the tatters of my gloves and disappeared, reintegrating with my snowy flesh.

Spotting my frost disc hovering nearby, I trudged over to it, climbed aboard, and sent it flying over the ice toward Allfrost Prime.

Chapter 49

Command Execution

By the time I reached the spot where my friends and companions had fought for their lives, the bitter chill of the driving wind had blown new life into me. I weaved past upturned snowmobiles and tracks in the snow, checking the faces of the fallen, relieved to find no one I recognized. Taking the frost disc outward in a widening spiral, I studied the tracks and gouges in the snow before heading for the entrance to the crevasse and descending to the Allfrost chamber, wondering as I did so whether I had stopped Baduriel and Comrade Frost in time.

Bear, now back in his avatar, met me in the tunnel and ran alongside me as I burst out into the chamber. Within, Dixon and Springer hunched over Jimenez, checking his wounds, while Olivia and Hue looked on.

"Welcome back," Olivia said.

"Thanks." I looked around. "Where's Wilhelm?"

She pointed a finger toward the icy ceiling, high overhead. "Riding the storm back to Caelumtor."

I nodded, regarding the trio of Bodhi Group agents. "How's Jimenez?"

Dixon glanced my way and held out a hand. "Do you have one of those Ambrolas?"

"Of course." Jumping from the frost disc, I pulled cans from my hat and handed them to him. "I've got a few more if you need them."

Cracking the can, Dixon held it to Jimenez's lips. "Open his mouth," he said to Springer.

"Sure," Springer replied, doing as Dixon asked.

Olivia's eyes darted over my scorched and burned clothing. "How did it go with Baduriel?"

"He's gone." Sighing, I told her what had happened.

She narrowed an eye. "He just fled?"

"Yeah. I don't know. Maybe he couldn't do anything more without Comrade Frost." The thrum and throb of the Allfrost node's light flashed in my mind, and I winced. "Or maybe he got what he wanted." I looked at the Allfrost Controller hovering nearby. "Is there a way to tell, Hue?"

"Certainly, Sentinel." Hue moved to the dais and tapped the air. "I am afraid it does appear a spatial transposition was initiated." He paused a moment. "However, it was interrupted a short time later. The moment appears to coincide with your takedown of Baduriel and the frost soldier."

Shooting me a look, Olivia asked, "How long was the transposition active?"

Hue tapped the air before looking back to her. "Ten point two-five seconds."

She grimaced. "That's not ideal, but hopefully not long enough for those transporting to have moved away from the area of effect. In which case, they would have returned to their point of origin upon the transposition field's collapse." She bit her lip. "Some may have made it, though."

"Are you serious?" I asked. Seeing her nod, I clapped my palms to the sides of my head. "Then Baduriel's got at least part of his army." I swore a blue streak. "That's why he didn't bother sticking around."

If he had succeeded in freeing more Anathema, I had to hope he could control them and keep them from running wild. Whatever Baduriel believed, I felt sure his demon allies sought only escape, and most of the Anathema were sadists and psychos who delighted in causing misery for its own sake.

She sighed. "If he's gained more allies, he'll be in a better position to try using the Allfrost again to bring the rest someday."

She was right.

Like all fanatics, Baduriel wouldn't give up, and he wouldn't see reason. Not until he'd turned humankind into a new and docile species. And like so many before, he justified it as being for people's own good. Not that Zelus's plan for communist domination was better. With my memories restored, I knew that all too well now too.

I scowled. For most of its existence the majority of humanity had been subjugated. Countless had lived bleak and meaningless lives as outright slaves, indentured servants, serfs, or vassals. The many serving a few worthless assholes, born into their positions or put there by murder and treachery. The Soviet Union was supposed to change all that, but, somehow, it had made things worse than ever.

I had to wonder if humanity was doomed to oscillate between the crazy extremes of madmen. People deserved better. My friends especially. Dixon's fixation on freedom made a lot more sense to my restored mind, which now recalled how rare the freedoms and human rights of the West were in the history of homo sapiens. I gritted my teeth. I couldn't let the Allfrost be used to destroy something so precious. *Imperfect though it might be.*

Sighing, I turned to Hue. "Is everything ready?"

"Affirmative, Sentinel."

"Okay," I said. "What do I need to do?"

He swept an arm toward the Allfrost node near the room's centre. "Simply stand on the dais, touch the orb, and provide authorization."

Nodding, I walked toward it. "Sounds easy enough."

"Hold on." Dixon came nearer. "Springer and I are going to head for Bodhi Station." He looked over his shoulder. "Jimenez needs medical help." He winced. "We could all use some."

Jimenez smiled weakly, his face pale as snow, and raised a can of Ambrola. "I'm all right, *jefe.* This stuff's great."

I glanced at Olivia. "Will it be enough to save him?"

She looked uncertain. "It depends on how severe his wounds are. Ambrola is not as effective on mortals as it is on us."

Dixon's nostrils flared. "Then we'd better move. Bodhi Station has a doctor and medical facilities."

I looked at Olivia. "Is there someone who can help him on New Olympus?"

"Certainly," she said, "but Aceso is the most capable and she is still on Antara. Not to mention, the transporter I used to get here is a long way off. How far is this Bodhi Station?"

I turned to the hologram. "Hue, please bring up a map of the area on the viewscreen."

"As you command," he said, waving a hand.

A topographical map appeared in the air.

"Thanks," I said. "Please mark our current location, any major landmarks, nearby nodes, or human habitations within, say, a thousand kilometres."

"Understood," Hue replied.

Abruptly, glowing dots appeared on screen, labelled with text, identifying our location, Mount Erebus, the Allfrost node where I'd fought Baduriel and Comrade Frost, Bodhi Station, and the larger Antarctic research centre, McMurdo Station, on the coast.

Olivia studied the map a moment. "Bodhi Station is far closer." She pointed at an unmarked spot. "The transporter is over here, so the station is practically on the way, in fact."

"The station it is," Dixon said. "You can catch up with us there after you're done shutting down the Allfrost."

Olivia's eyebrows rose. "You're shutting down the Allfrost? Why?"

"To ensure it can't be misused," I said, explaining my plan. "The nodes will still be there, of course, but restoring it will require each one to be manually brought back online."

She made a face. "Without it countering the effects, global warming will accelerate."

I winced. "I know, but I'm buying time. If I don't, it'll be abused again, by the demons or Eurus. Until we've got more Sentinels to defend and maintain it, it's a vulnerability." I turned up my palms. "Anyway, who knows, maybe mortals will get their act together."

Her lips wrinkled. "They don't have a good record of long-term thinking."

Neither does a child, I thought. *Not until it grows up.*

If humanity was going to be free and survive, the species needed to evolve beyond its primitive origins on its own terms. Not by coercion or redesign as Zelus and Baduriel believed, but by being permitted, as evolution intended, to either fail or make the leap from child to adulthood.

Just like Wilhelm always said, I thought, recalling forgotten conversations with him.

I hadn't agreed with him then, but I did now. My prejudices against mortals had been stripped from me along with my memories. Reduced almost to a child, I'd sort of grown up among them, and while I'd found many to be unkind, there were good people among them.

Not only Scott and my friends, but Dixon, Jimenez, and Springer too. They had been on the wrong side, of course, keeping me captive, but under it all their intentions had been good. Like mine had been in working with Zelus. Like them, I'd been wrong, but I'd learned from the mistake. Given the chance, maybe humanity could learn too.

History didn't favour a positive outcome, but they deserved better than being slaves to the few, or meat puppets for Anathema gods. Sure, there were a lot of bad people in the world, but it wasn't right to punish the innocent along with the guilty.

I lifted my shoulders. "They'll have to figure it out themselves, at least for now."

"Winterboy is right," Dixon said. "Nuclear war and demons running wild in the streets are the more immediate threat. Who knows, maybe the Group can help him restore it someday."

"I suppose so," Olivia replied.

I nudged Dixon's elbow. "Starting the shutdown won't take long. Get Jimenez ready to travel, and we can all leave together. There may be more Eurus out there." Moving to the dais, I held both hands to the orb and my palms tingled. *Time to end this.* "Okay, punch it, Huey. Shut the Allfrost down." I thought a moment. "Everything except the Smaragnisos chamber and its nodes."

Keeping Smaragnisos—which lay within the bounds of New Olympus—active would give me and Hue a place to live and, if I ever did try to restore the Allfrost, a place to start the process.

"Understood," he said. "Initiating shutdown now."

At his words, the daises and crystal pillars dotting the room thrummed and pulsed with light.

"How long will it take?" I asked, eyeing the giant projection of Earth as Allfrost nodes winked out, one after another, upon its surface.

"A few hours," Hue replied. "This chamber will be the last to shut down."

"Can you get back to Smaragnisos before that happens?"

"Yes, Sentinel," he replied. "I have ensured the shutdown process will leave a node traversal path open as long as feasible. I should, however, depart soon. That is, unless you would rather I return with you."

I scanned the chamber a moment. "No, you might as well go back the easy way." I snapped my fingers, reminded of something. "Oh, before you go, put the node where I fought Baduriel on the viewscreen, please." With a twitch of Hue's ghostly hand, the viewscreen changed from the map of Antarctica to a view of the Antarctic ice. My brow wrinkled. "It's gone."

"The node?" Hue asked. "It has returned to the Underfrost."

I waved a hand dismissively. "No, not that. Baduriel's avatar . . . and the frost soldier's. They should be lying in the snow. It's not like they got up and walked away."

"They might have," Olivia said. "Baduriel at least. If he re-entered his avatar, he may have carried off the soldier's body."

My eyes widened. "You think?" I grabbed at my chest. "He was impaled."

She shrugged. "Avatars of Baduriel's type are exceptionally resilient."

"Do we have a recording?" I asked, looking at Hue.

"I am afraid not," Hue said. "No Oculi were active near that node at the time. Shall I conduct a search?"

"No, that's okay." Wherever Baduriel was, even if he was still trying to achieve his goal, he couldn't use the Allfrost anymore. Plus, there might be more Eurus or Soviet soldiers out there, and I needed to help my companions get to safety, not go off half cocked. No, Baduriel was a problem that could wait. *At least until I've got an Animavas in hand to trap him with.* "Head back to Smaragnisos. I'll meet you there when I can."

"Understood," Hue said. "Safe travels, Sentinel Shivurr."

"Frostspeed, Hue."

Drifting over to the nearest node, the Allfrost Controller hologram lost cohesion. When he was an unrecognizable cloud, he streamed into the dais's glowing orb until nothing of him remained.

A snowmobile engine rumbled as I rotated to face my companions.

"All right, Winterboy," Dixon shouted, revving his engine. "Time to move."

"Ready, Shivurr?" Olivia asked.

"Yeah," I said, taking her arm. "We're done here."

Chapter 50

Second Nature

Hours later, Olivia, Bear, and I sat on sofas, watching a movie in the Bodhi Station entertainment room. After I'd resealed the chasm leading to Allfrost Prime, we'd journeyed uneventfully back here. Olivia had driven Jimenez's snowmobile while Jimenez had ridden with Dixon. Not wanting to leave her iceboat behind, she'd tied it to her borrowed machine with some of its rigging. With Bear riding aboard to weigh it down, the ice craft had made the trip without incident.

"Hey there, pal." I patted Bear's flank and gave his head a rub. "I can't believe I ever forgot about you."

He gave a low woof in reply and pushed his scalp against my fingertips. Checking the glove on my other hand, I found no sign of the punctures I'd made during my fight with Baduriel. *How about that?*

Olivia chuckled. "When did you finally remember him?"

I glanced her way. "When I saw his three heads breathing fire on the Oculus viewscreen." I wagged my head, remembering the normal dog he'd been when we'd first met, long ago. "Why didn't Wilhelm stick around?"

"He had to get back to Zarechus," she replied. "There's still trouble there."

My eyes widened. "And he still made a special trip all the way here to help us?"

She nodded. "He was worried." She hefted an Animavas, this one a dark stone jar topped with the carved head of a jackal, and studied the TV screen but didn't seem to see it. "He does so often fret for my safety."

I jabbed my chin toward her hands. "What are you going to do with it?"

Her eyes met mine. "Put it in the castigatorium until the fate of the one within can be decided. I've a spot picked out right next to Azrileus."

Picturing Caelumburg's prison hall, filled with Animavas-topped pedestals, I shuddered.

"Jimenez is going to be all right," Dixon said, entering the room. "The kid's tough."

"Cool." I breathed a sigh of relief. The agent's normally swarthy skin had been ashen when station personnel had carried him inside to be treated, and I'd feared he'd lost too much blood to survive. "That's great news."

Dixon rubbed his face with both hands. "Agreed."

"Where's Springer?" I asked, glancing at Dixon's shoulder but finding no sign of the other Bodhi Group operator.

"He's being treated for injuries," he replied, "and giving blood. Turns out he and Jimenez have compatible blood types."

I narrowed an eye. "Springer was hurt?" The agent hadn't let on.

Dixon slapped at one of his biceps. "He caught a bullet in the arm. Just a graze really, and some minor burns." He ran a hand over his scalp, once bald but now grey with a few days' stubble. "He got lucky."

"Wonderful." Olivia gave my shoulder a squeeze. "In that case, Shivurr and I should head back to Caelumburg. The others must know what happened here."

"Mind if I tag along?" Dixon asked. "I'd like to use one of those transporters to get back to the Group. They need to know what happened here, too. If Anathema did make it to Earth, we're going to need to be prepared."

I looked toward the door. "What about Springer and Jimenez?"

"They'll stay here," he replied. "Jimenez can't travel right now, and I've asked Springer to remain with him and augment the station security force, just in case."

"They'll have lots of time to recover," I said, knowing flights to the continent wouldn't start again until November.

Dixon's eyes flicked to the TV and VHS tapes, and back to me. "They'll survive."

"Very well," Olivia said. "You're welcome to come. Are you ready to leave now?"

Dixon's eyebrows shot up. "Uh, how about we stay the night and leave in the morning?" He sighed and rubbed the small of his back. "I'm not sure about you god folks, but it's been a hell of a day for us mortals."

Olivia smiled. "Of course. I could use a shower and some sleep myself."

"Excellent," he replied, checking his watch. "I'll ask Milton to provide us quarters."

After a leisurely dinner, where we engaged in mostly idle conversation, I retired to my assigned quarters. To my surprise, I slept a dreamless sleep, for the first time in a long while, and the next morning, rested and well fed, we departed for the transporter. Olivia and Bear, snuggled together on her iceboat, led the way, trailed by Dixon and me, standing atop one of my floating frost discs. Lost in our thoughts, we rode in silence, my gaze alternating between the sails of Olivia's iceboat and the vibrant curtains of the aurora australis waving in the distant sky.

Though the terrain flew past in a blur, the security director hadn't even bothered to pull up his hood, protected as he was by the bubble of swirling energy enclosing us. Its resistance to high-speed kinetic impact ensured virtually no wind passed through, and the faster we went, the better it stopped the breeze. Combined with my efforts to raise the temperature around us, he appeared almost comfortable.

I can hardly believe it, I thought, realizing I'd done what I had meant to do when I'd escaped the Institute—found myself. I looked down at my clothing. Not only many of my memories and lost abilities, but after so long in my shapesuit, my altered configuration had become more comfortable to maintain. *Almost second nature*. I fingered one of the holes burned into my parka during my fight with Baduriel. More importantly, the Allfrost couldn't be misused now. Not to bring about nuclear

Armageddon, at least. *There's still more to do, though.* Without the Allfrost, the planet's climate was going to change, and not for the better. Plus, while I felt pretty much restored now, I still didn't know what had happened to my fellow Sentinels or the rest of my people. *Maybe I never knew.*

My mind returned to Baduriel, and I winced. If more Anathema had made it to Earth, I could only hope their numbers were few and that the New Olympians and I could track them down before they could do much harm. Regardless, the infected soda pops and their victims were going to be a problem. Especially consumers of the early formulations, who suffered from catatonia.

I shook my head. *Victories against chaos are always brief.*

Hopefully the more refined versions of the infection would be less obtrusive, as Baduriel had claimed. It stood to reason that he'd told the truth about that, given that a more stealthy infection, which still allowed the infected to be controlled or possessed when necessary, would be more likely to benefit him.

Dixon bumped against my shoulder as we rode over a crease in the terrain, jolting me from my reverie. "This thing needs seats," he said, his voice easily audible within the frost shield's bubble.

I snickered. "You're getting old, Harland."

He chuckled without much humour. "Don't I know it."

"I was just kidding," I said, regretting the offhand joke.

He shrugged. "Don't worry about it. It's something all of us mortals have to deal with eventually, and I've already lived longer than I expected. Considering the risks I've taken."

Olivia, riding ahead of us, waved a hand above her head, and her iceboat tacked into the wind.

"Cool." I slowed the ice platter with a shift of my feet. "This must be it."

Her craft came to a gentle stop, and I brought us alongside it, dropped my frost shield, and disembarked.

Stepping up beside me, Dixon whistled. "Will you look at that?"

Chapter 51

Folks Like You

We stood at the precipice of a vast depression in the snow. Smaller and shallower than Lunar Crater, this pit—save for its rocky bottom—had a surface that was all ice, smooth and round as a porcelain bowl, blemished here and there by pockmarks and jagged stones.

"Your doing, I take it," Dixon said, thrusting his chin at Olivia.

"Not directly." Her eyes flicked skyward. "We have measures in place to keep the transporter clear of ice and snow." She turned, grabbing at the iceboat's sail. "We hadn't expected an upthrust of rock, however. Then again, this transporter had long gone unused before that happened, there not being much reason to come to Antarctica for some time now."

"Tell me about it," he said, helping her bring down the sail and fold the craft in on itself.

"Follow me." Taking the shield she'd been using as a seat on an arm, Olivia hefted the iceboat and walked toward the depression in the snow with Bear on her heels. "And watch your step." We descended the slope and found shattered rock and ice at its bottom. Making our way past knee-high boulders and blasted rock, we entered a deep crevice and descended still further. "Here we are," she said, standing her burden on its tail.

Dixon scoffed. "Are you sure this thing still works?"

"Perfectly," Olivia said, gesturing to her side. "Just huddle up close and keep your hands by your sides."

He folded his arms. "That's not ominous at all."

I sidled up next to her and Bear. "It'll be fine."

"Famous last words," he said, joining us.

As he did so, the air shimmered, and a room with a stone floor and glowing walls replaced the bowl of snow.

Olivia shooed me toward its single door. "Open it, will you?"

"Sure thing," I said, doing as she asked. Exiting, I looked around at the Caelumburg departure hall. The same one from which Dixon, Maya, Caelus, and I had departed for Berlin just days ago. Turning, I held the door, allowing my companions to exit. "We've come full circle, Harland."

"That we have." Dixon looked around. "Which of these will take me back to the States?"

"One second," Olivia said, placing her iceboat against the wall of the tiny stone building from which we had emerged. Wiping her hands, she came over and pointed a few doors over. "That one will take you to Albuquerque. You'll have to arrange transport from there."

"No problem," he said. "Just show me the way, and I'll get out of your hair."

"It'd be my pleasure." Olivia looked at me. "Why don't you take Bear and head to the domus? I'm sure everyone's eager to see you."

I frowned at Dixon. "You're going now? I thought you'd at least stay for lunch."

He shook his head. "The sooner I get back, the better." He stuck out his hand. "I guess this is it for now."

I clasped his palm and shook it. "Take care, Dixon."

"You too, Shivurr," he said, clapping his other hand against my shoulder.

"Huh," I said with a crooked smile. "Thanks."

He arched an eyebrow. "For what?"

"For not calling me Winterboy." I'd gotten used to hearing the code name from him, but I appreciated the gesture nonetheless.

He shrugged. "You called me Dixon."

I chuckled. "Oh, yeah. I guess I did." In truth, I had always thought of him as Dixon in my mind but, knowing he preferred his last name, I'd usually made a point of calling him by his first name, Harland, instead—since he tended to call me Winterboy instead of Shivurr. We'd apparently healed some wounds during our adventures. "I must be tired."

"All right." He slapped my shoulder and looked at Olivia. "Let's move. Before Shivurr and I start braiding each other's hair."

"Nah." I lifted my cap. "I still don't have any." Not that he could see my smooth snowy scalp beneath my shape-holding hood. "I'm working on it, though."

"Bye, Shivurr," Olivia said. "I'll be along after I see Dixon safely through."

"Okay." Eager to see my friends, I couldn't bring myself to argue. "Sounds good."

"Come on, Dixon." Grabbing his arm, she drew him down the aisle, deeper into the grand hall. "Let's get you home."

Bending at the waist, I tousled Bear's fur. "Come on, boy."

I strode from the building with a light step, stood beneath its portico, and looked out over the town of Caelumburg. Its ivory buildings, lit by sunlight breaking through clouds, shone beneath a light mist, and the humid air smelled of flowers.

I danced down the steps to the road below.

It's good to be back. Among friends, old and new. *Safe.* It couldn't last, of course, but I resolved to enjoy it while it did. I had earned a break. A few days to enjoy life awhile. Mortal life is short, and I wanted to share it with my friends while I could.

With that thought, I ran toward the domus with Bear at my side, knowing the way well. Not only from recent days but from long before the Institute. Dodging the rare pedestrian, I didn't slow until we reached the Schmidts' home.

I placed a hand on Bear's back as we entered the front yard. "Shall we surprise them?" I asked, regarding the domus, and the dog gave a low woof, which I took as agreement. "Good call."

Letting the dog inside, I followed on tiptoe and closed the door behind us. I sniffed the air, smelling fried bacon mingled with incense. While Brad and Lucy had probably told the others about my altered state, I wanted to surprise but not scare them, so I deactivated my disguise, pulled off my mask, and returned to my normal form. *Oh, yeah.* It felt so good to be myself again.

Indistinct voices came from the hallway ahead, and I padded toward them. Within the atrium, Scott and my Californian friends, their backs to me, stood in a semicircle at the far edge of the room's rectangular pool. I stepped softly closer, and my eyes narrowed, catching glimpses of a man seated in a high-backed chair in the gaps between my friends. *Wilhelm?*

The man's brown eyes lit as they met mine. "Shivurr."

Dressed like a woodsman, he was mostly bald, and his beard and remaining hair were shot through with grey.

"Virgil?" Snorting, I crossed the room, and my friends whirled to face me, their mouths ajar. "Hi, guys."

They mobbed me before I could take another step, smiling and slapping my back, peppering me with questions they gave me no time to answer.

"It's so good to see you," Lilith said, squatting to stroke Bear's muzzle. "Both of you."

"Totally," Alan agreed, clasping my hand.

"How did it go?" Lucy asked.

"Come on, dudes," Caleb said. "Let him breathe."

"He's right," Brad said. "Give him room."

Caleb's eyes widened. "I am?"

Giving me a hug, Scott drew back and held my shoulders. "Glad you're back, man," he said after inspecting me for a long moment. His eyes shifted to the side. "Where's Olivia?"

I shot a look over my shoulder. "She'll be here soon."

Coming closer, Virgil extended a hand. "Nice to see you again, fella. Sooner than I expected, though."

Taking in his sweat-stained tunic, the ripped knees of his pants, and his muddy calf-high boots, I nodded and returned his handshake. "Me too." I smiled and squinted an eye. "Why are you here?"

"Your ghost friend, Boreas, brought me." He inhaled, blowing it out in a rush. "He figured we should talk about finding those folks you were looking for."

My chin dipped. "What folks?"

"Folks like you."

Author's Note

Shivurr's adventures will continue in the next novel in the *Phantom Frost* series. Visit alfredwurr.com for details about and links to other books in the series.

While you're there, take a few seconds to subscribe to my free, no-spam monthly author newsletter and get in on news about my upcoming releases, deals, giveaways, and more.

If you enjoyed the book, please consider reviewing it. Either way, thanks for reading and supporting my work. It means more than you know.

Acknowledgements

Special thanks to my beta readers for taking the time to read the book and provide invaluable feedback.

Lorelei Pierce
Christopher Cordray

Book cover by Damonza.com.
Editing by Clio Editing Services.

About the Author

An avid fan of science fiction and fantasy, be it in movies, books, video games, or RPGs, Alfred has also been, and in many cases continues to be, an Olympic freestyle wrestler (winning national and international championships), a computer scientist (M.Sc.), a software developer and consultant, and a video game developer.

He lives with his wife, Lorelei, in Canada, where staying frosty comes easy half the year.

Subscribe to Alfred's mailing list to get news, updates, and more at: alfredwurr.com/subscribe. You may also contact the author at: alfredwurr.com/contact-page.

www.ingramcontent.com/pod-product-compliance
Lightning Source LLC
Chambersburg PA
CBHW031739180726
48283CB00005B/1575